Fury of the Beast

M. Ward Leon

Fury of the Beast

Beacon Publishing Group
ISBN (Paperback): 978-1-961504-26-4

Beacon Publishing Group, New York, NY 10001
www.beaconpublishinggroup.com

Manufactured in the United States of America

The greatness of a nation can be judged by the way it treats its animals.

Cover Art: Vecteezy AI

For my Joanie and Meghan

NOTICE! THE HUNTING OF FERAL SWINE ON MARK TWAIN NATIONAL FOREST LANDS IS PROHIBITED.

Bobby Woods and his hunting partner, Jimmy Steelman, had just shot a one-hundred-and-ten-pound feral pig with a bow and arrow for fun.

The initial arrow didn't kill the pig; it lay squealing in agony, trying to get away. The two hunters slowly walked up to their prize. They stood over it, watching the tormented razorback wriggle and squirm in anguish.

"Damn, nice shot, Bobby!" Jimmy hollered.

"Yup."

"Ain't ya going to finish him off?"

"Naw, let's just see how long it takes till he..."

Bobby Woods never finished his thought; he was interrupted when Fu Hao and Sue B each released a 30-inch PANDARUS carbon arrow equipped with a Maifield 3 fixed broadhead blade arrowhead, fired from their HOYT Carbon Defiant Hunting Bow.

Both arrows hit Bobby from behind, each piercing and puncturing his right and left lung, causing him to collapse to the ground next to his trophy.

Jimmy Steelman stood in shock over his fallen comrade as the two assassins dressed in CamoSystems Jackal ghillie suits approached.

The taller of the two aimed a Glock G19 Gen4 MOS 9mm pistol at Jimmy and said in a calm, calculated voice, "Finish the pig off, asshole."

Jimmy nocked the arrow to his bow, drew back the bowstring, and aimed it at Bobby, who was also writhing in misery.

"Not that pig, stupid! The feral pig," Sue B commanded.

Jimmy fired the arrow straight into the pig's heart, killing it instantly.

"Pick it up, now! Follow me," She shouted.

She led him over to a tall pine tree, where the bright yellow and black warning sign warned potential hunters not to kill feral pigs.

She tossed him a piece of rope.

"Tie him up high, next to the sign," Sue B ordered.

He did as he was told, tying the dead pig five feet off the ground by the left rear leg. All the time, he was whimpering, "Please don't kill me. I didn't do nothing, please."

"Quit your sniveling, asshole. Come on," she said as she led him back to where his friend, Bobby, lay dying.

Fu Hao stood silently, watching Bobby Woods gasp, suffering for air.

"For the love of God, do something. Don't let him suffer," Jimmy pleaded.

"You want him dead; you kill him. He was willing to stand by and watch that pig suffer. He gets no sympathy from me," Fu Hao said coldly.

Jimmy picked up his bow and arrow, but by the time he was prepared to mercy kill his friend, Bobby Woods died.

"Okay, drop the archery set, Geronimo. Grab a leg and drag his sorry piece of shit over to the tree," Fu Hao instructed.

By the time he had dragged the body of his dead friend over to the tree where he had hung the feral pig, Sue B had strung a rope over a tree branch and threw Jimmy the end. "Tie it around his ankle." She ordered.

Once it was done, she had Jimmy take the other end of the rope, hoist the corpse up to the level of the pig, and then tie the rope off. Sue B took the traditional yellow ensign blazoned with the Black skull and crossed monkey wrenches and handed it to Jimmy.

"Here, tie this around his neck."

He did as he was told.

"Have you ever heard of Le Gang de la Clé de Singe?" She asked.

"No, Ma'am."

"Can you read?"

"Of course," He said indignantly.

"Good, then read this out loud," Sue B said as she handed him a piece of paper.

"Let it be known that Le Gang de la Clé de Singe declares a proclamation of war against all Poachers, Big Game Hunters, and all Big Game Safari Outfits, as well as anyone anywhere in the world who targets, kills, profits from, or supports the killing of any endangered animals or animals hunted for sport. Be forewarned, do so at your peril. You will be hunted down and pay with your lives. Whether man or woman, there will be no exceptions and no mercy; we will show no quarter. You have been warned."

Jimmy stood like a deer in the headlights; his eyes were as big as saucers.

"Oh, God. Are you going to kill me?" He whimpered.

Fu Hao grabbed her bow and nocked a red-shafted arrow. She raised it high and released. All three watched where the arrow landed. Fu Hao turned to Jimmy and said, "We will give you a running start; we won't pursue you until you reach the arrow. Now, go!"

Jimmy took off, running as fast as he could for a thirty-year-old, slightly overweight, out-of-shape man. By the time he had reached the red arrow, Fu Hao and Sue B were long gone.

As with all successful actions, Le Gang de la Clé de Singe has a tradition of leaving behind a stick in the eye to law enforcement authorities. A single clear fingerprint from someone totally unrelated to the mission, usually someone famous. Today, Fu Hao and Sue B left the fingerprint of United States President Harry Truman on the handle of Bobby Wood's bow.

☠☠☠☠☠☠☠☠☠☠☠

Le Gang de la Clé de Singe got its name from the American writer Edward Abbey's novel 'The Monkey Wrench Gang.' The story is a fictional account of four environmental activists who fight to free parts of Utah and Arizona from corrupt road-builders, miners, and rednecks. Le Gang de la Clé de Singe was started in Paris by two brothers whose father was the CEO of the French oil company Elf, which was involved in the Great Oil Sniffer Hoax of 1979.

Jean-Paul and Philippe Renault were two spoiled rich kids eager to challenge the establishment and upset their father at the same time. They started with some college friends by organizing protest marches, which became increasingly violent; as the oil scandal grew, so did the movement. Eventually, there were clashes with riot police who responded with tear gas and rubber bullets; then, police began making arrests as the protesters fought back. Some protesters started throwing rocks, bottles, and Molotov Cocktails.

Soon, the police response escalated to the use of live ammunition, resulting in the deaths of dozens of protesters, some as young as fourteen. The Renault brothers never dreamed that what started as a way to piss their father off would evolve into an international movement of outrage. Over time, they extricated themselves from the group as Le Gang de la Clé de Singe became increasingly militant and violent. They unwittingly achieved their goals beyond their wildest dreams.

Recently, the death of one of Le Gang de la Clé de Singe's most notorious eco-warriors, Robert Lester, the

Iceman, left a huge void within the organization and severely impacted morale. His death has become legendary.

The Iceman and his team were on assignment in the Abokouamekro Game Reserve in the African country of Côte d'Ivoire. The team was pursuing a gang of poachers who were killing adult chimpanzees, stealing the babies, and selling them on the black market.

During a skirmish with the poachers, the Iceman was betrayed and captured. He was handed over to corrupt government officials who tortured him for weeks, parading him around as if he were a trophy. Knowing he wouldn't be able to withstand many more enhanced interrogations, he sent word to his team that they should assassinate him during a major news event.

According to a secret diary that he kept, the corrupt police Detective, a man named Kouassi, wanted to show off his prize to the world's media one more time before handing the notorious leader of Le Gang de la Clé de Singe, Robert Lester, aka the Iceman, over to Interpol. There, he would stand trial and most likely be sentenced to life in prison.

Kouassi had the Iceman brought out in handcuffs and shackles, dressed in his prison uniform of day-glow orange. The Iceman's face was drawn and ashen. He had lost at least fifteen pounds, and he looked to be a man who had given up the ghost, yet his eyes were defiant.

Detective Kouassi stood in front of the Iceman, surrounded by armed police in uniform.

There was a scrum of about sixty reporters and TV film crews vying for position. Several members of his team managed to make their way to the front of the crowd, acting as a film crew.

Iceman spotted them in the crowd and smiled. One of the team looked over his left shoulder at the Pentecostal Church steeple behind him, then back to the Iceman; he gave a slight nod of acknowledgment.

He briefly looked up at the sky, took a deep breath, and then glanced toward the steeple. He saw two tiny flashes of light just nanoseconds before the bullets fired by Sue B and Fu Hao struck Detective Kouassi and him in the head, killing both instantly.

That was the message the Iceman had relayed to his team from prison. He preferred death to a life of incarceration.

Months after his death, the leaders of Le Gang de la Clé de Singe decided to shake up the leadership of the frontline troops, promoting those who had shown exceptional bravery in the face of combat.

It was determined that Fu Hao and her partner, Sue B, would be promoted to action leaders, taking charge of the Blue Team. The Red Team, the Iceman's team, would be commanded by the Icelander Odin, who had been the Iceman's second in command for the last three years.

In the past, the Red and Blue teams have always worked together under independent leaders.

The Red Team will include Fu Hao, Sue B, Cowboy, Sassoon, and Hazael, while the Blue Team will include Odin, Lu Wei, Vulcan, Bellator, and Venus.

The military wing of Le Gang de la Clé de Singe was under the command of SEAL Team Commander William T. "Wooch" Brown. Brown is best known for spearheading several successful SEAL kill missions against ISIS that the American public will never hear of, at least not in their lifetimes.

William Brown was born into a military lineage that spans four generations, starting with Captain Robert Archer Brown. He served with the 7th Ohio Cavalry, known as the "River Regiment" because its men came from nine counties along the Ohio River. He distinguished himself in the Battle of Cynthiana and the Battle of Cumberland Gap. He fought alongside General William E. "Grumble" Jones during the Franklin-Nashville Campaign, where he was killed leading a counterattack that helped shift the tide for the Union when all seemed lost.

During the Spanish-American War, his great-great-grandfather, Lieutenant Leonard Archer Brown, fought alongside Teddy Roosevelt's Rough Riders in the Battle of San Juan Hill. He was part of the Gatling Gun Detachment, which Colonel Roosevelt credited with the success of the charge. After the war, he taught cavalry tactics and artillery at West Point.

During the Battle of Belleau Wood in World War One, Wooch's great-grandfather, Captain Julius A. Brown, led the 3rd Battalion, 5th Marines. After taking heavy casualties on Hill 204 east of Vaux, the French repeatedly urged them to retreat; Captain Brown responded, "Retreat? Hell, we don't go backward, only forwards."

Captain Brown, while advancing on the Germans, discovered they had been moving in the wrong direction; instead of admitting failure, he pressed on through the forest's narrow waist, breaking through the enemy's southern defensive lines, who often had to resort to only their bayonets or fists in hand-to-hand combat, ultimately clearing the forest of Germans. It was considered one of the bloodiest and most ferocious battles U.S. troops fought in the war.

In 1941, before the United States entered World War Two, a group of American pilots volunteered to assist the Chinese in fighting the Japanese. They formed a fighter squadron called the Flying Tigers. Under the command of General Chennault, ninety-nine discharged pilots from the Navy, Marines, and Army signed up as mercenaries with a private military contractor, the Central Aircraft Manufacturing Company.

A. William Brown was among six squadron leaders who served in the 3rd Squadron Hell's Angels, Flying Tigers. Their main mission was to defend the Burma Road from Japanese bombing, maintaining this crucial supply route.

They proved so successful that the Japanese stopped their raids on Kunming while the Tigers patrolled the region.

The Curtiss P-40 Warhawk was the aircraft of the Tigers. It was a nimble workhorse that could endure a lot of damage and typically would bring its pilots home safely. Squadron leader Brown flew 26 missions and achieved 12 victories. After the US entered the war, he was assigned to the Eighth Air Force in England, flying P-51 Mustangs as escorts for B-17 bombers over Germany. He was shot down twice; the second time, he was captured and sent to Stalag Luft III, where he participated in the so-called Great Escape. He made it as far as Amsterdam, where he was shot and killed.

William T. Brown joined the Navy SEALs in the fall of 1967. After completing the intense training program, he was first deployed to Da Nang, Vietnam, to train South Vietnamese forces in combat diving, demolitions, and guerrilla as well as counter-guerrilla tactics. In 1968, the North Vietnamese launched the Tet Offensive, aiming to break America's will to continue the war. For Brown and the SEALs, their missions became deeply personal. He and his team were dispatched north to disrupt enemy supply lines and troop movements. Brown served as the team's sniper and earned the nickname "Wooch" when his spotter noted that "Wooch" was the sound victims made every time he claimed a headshot. By the end of his Vietnam tour, William T. "Wooch" Brown had earned a Navy Cross, two Silver Stars, four Bronze Stars, and five Commendation Medals, and he achieved the rank of Captain.

Captain William T. "Wooch" Brown served on the ground during Desert Storm, Operation Gothic Serpent, and Operation Red Wings; after 9/11, he was promoted to Commander and assigned to the Pentagon for planning and operations. He and his team conducted dozens of strikes against al Qaeda, resulting in the deaths of more than eighty-seven top al Qaeda leaders. In 2014, in response to the rapid territorial gains made by ISIL, Wooch and his team developed over twenty Quick Reaction Force operations, helping to stop ISIL's advance.

After 48 years of service, SEAL Team Commander William T. "Wooch" Brown retired quietly and without ceremony, just a quiet dinner at the White House with the President, Vice President, and several of the military's top brass.

His involvement with Le Gang de la Clé de Singe stemmed from witnessing the cruelty and reckless attitude towards animals while in the military. The senseless killing of animals out of boredom or for sport always disgusted him, so after giving a speech at UC Berkeley on the topic of 'War and its Effect on Animals,' he was approached by several members of Le Gang de la Clé de Singe. They persuaded him to work with them covertly, alongside others like himself—former military personnel, corporate leaders, government officials, and private individuals worldwide—all operating behind the scenes.

☠☠☠☠☠☠☠☠☠☠☠

For years, Le Gang de la Clé de Singe has dedicated itself to fighting anti-environmental groups and companies that have, for generations, exploited and damaged the world's resources for their own financial gain, neglecting the environment for future generations. Le Gang has now targeted big game hunting organizations, hunters who kill animals and even endangered species for sport, and those who profit from selling items derived from these creatures. Le Gang de la Clé de Singe is not opposed to hunting for food or culling herds for the greater good and the survival of the species but killing for sport must end.

So, they created a creed that perpetrators will be hunted down and will pay with their lives. Be it man or woman, there will be no exceptions and no mercy; they will show no quarter. Their trademark features a black skull with two crossed monkey wrenches on a bright yellow background. Whenever they take action against a poacher or hunter, they place a flag with their logo around the victim's neck with a note bearing their mantra.

Due to this, they were labeled as an eco-terrorist organization by the United Nations, and their members are considered wanted criminals. Because of this, all field combatants use pseudonyms as a precaution against being captured; no one can reveal anyone's real identity, only their field name. Each person chooses their field name and never discloses their birth name for their safety and that of their comrades.

☠☠☠☠☠☠☠☠☠☠☠

THE RED TEAM

Veronica Ventura and Yum Wu couldn't be more different. Veronica was five-foot-eleven, had long blond hair, green eyes, and weighed one hundred and ten pounds—simply beautiful. She came from Greenwich, Connecticut. Her father was a hedge fund banker, and the Venturas ranked among the ten wealthiest families in America. Her father, Jonathan Ventura, was well acquainted with David Leeway, a notable American real estate mogul who once ran for President; they often played golf together at least once every two or three months at one of Leeway's golf resorts in West Palm Beach, Florida. Veronica and Sasha Leeway attended the same prep school, Greenwich Academy, growing up, but they had very different views of the world. While Sasha loved killing things, Veronica volunteered at animal shelters, rescue centers, and vet clinics.

Years later, Veronica wasn't surprised to see that Sasha was really into big-game hunting, since her family had gone on hunting trips during all their school breaks. They once debated each other on the topic of big game hunting while on the school's debate team. It was an energetic debate, with each side holding their ground. Emotions ran high, and what started as a heated discussion turned into a personal attack, with Sasha storming off stage in anger. That was the last time they ever spoke to each other.

Sasha graduated from The Wharton School of the University of Pennsylvania and then went on to work for her father. Veronica graduated from UCLA and spent three years in the Peace Corps in Nepal, where she joined Le Gang de la Clé de Singe and recruited Yum Wu.

Yum Wu is five feet four inches tall, has pitch-black hair and brown eyes, and weighs 180 pounds. Standing side by side, they look like the perfect odd couple but are actually the ideal even pair. Yum was originally from the small town of Jinchang, in the People's Republic of China. Jinchang is in the center of Gansu province, bordering Inner Mongolia to the north. It's known as China's 'Nickel Capital.'

Yum Wu's father was a miner, and his father's father was a miner too, spanning eight generations. Her mother died during childbirth, and Yum and her father lived just outside town on the west side of Hongshan Crossing, which literally separated the city from the rural community. The land they lived on was all dirt, with no plants or trees growing, making life depressing for Yum. She only found joy in practicing target shooting for the People's Republic of China Olympic Women's 50m Rifle 3 Positions Team. The event involved athletes shooting from fifty meters in kneeling, prone, and standing positions.

At first, when Yum began trying out for the team, many of the officials scoffed and laughed at her because of her physical appearance. After only her first try, they were all silenced when she obtained a near-perfect score.

Yum had been hunting with her grandfather from a young age; she was an excellent shot but didn't enjoy killing animals. However, she enjoyed the challenge of hitting a target with precision and accuracy. She spent hours practicing target shooting for over twelve years. When she heard that the People's Republic of China Olympic trials for the Women's 50m Rifle 3 Positions Team were being held in Beijing, she and her father made the twenty-two-hour bus trip to Beijing for the tryouts, which she successfully completed.

While they were in Beijing, they received news that her grandfather and uncle were both killed in a major shaft collapse at the Mojiang Mine, where there had been numerous recent complaints from miners about unsafe conditions. The mine owners dismissed these complaints as unfounded, and the government supported the owners, taking no action for neglect and blaming the miners for being careless and not following safety protocols. When Yum stood with the miners to protest against the government, she was told to stop, or she would be arrested and removed from the Olympic team.

Yum and her father were arrested and spent seven months in prison. She was sent to the Provincial Women's Prison, where she was forced to work at the Jiuzhou Clothing Factory. During her time there, she was systematically beaten and raped by the prison guards.

Her father, Bohai, along with dozens of other protesters, was sent to Lanzhou Prison. It was a high-security facility that included several workshops where prisoners were forced to do labor. Prisoners were deprived of food and medical care, and those who didn't complete their forced labor were tortured. Bohai died after five months of imprisonment, having succumbed to multiple beatings; his family was never told the full truth about how he died, only that he was dead.

After Yum was released from prison, she decided to leave China. She knew that her life would be hell if she stayed, so she made her way through the twelve-hundred-mile journey, on foot, across Qinghai Province to Tibet. Qinghai was a large, sparsely populated province spread across the high-altitude Tibetan Plateau. She mainly traveled at night to avoid being seen and carried a Chinese Hanyang Arsenal Experimental Semi-Automatic Rifle that was her grandfather's—he had owned it since 1918 and kept it in excellent condition. It was the only thing she had that had any sentimental value to her. She was prepared to use it if she had to, as she had decided that she was not going to be taken alive and face prison again.

On day sixteen, she reached Amne Machin, a peak standing six thousand two hundred eighty-two meters high in the Kunlun Mountains, a sacred site for Buddhist pilgrims. She was close to death from exposure when several Buddhist monks from the Wutong monastery found her and took her there. She received medical care and stayed under their protection for six weeks until she was strong enough to continue her journey to Kathmandu. After another ten days, she finally crossed the well-guarded border under the cover of a severe blizzard. She wasn't unscathed; she suffered severe frostbite—losing three toes on her left foot and two on her right—but she was free.

She eventually found work as a chambermaid at the Hotel Yak and Yeti, a hundred-year-old, five-star hotel on Durbar Marg Street in the heart of Kathmandu, where she learned to speak English. She worked there and, by sheer luck, met Veronica Ventura while visiting the Garden of Dreams, which was created in the 1920s and featured half a dozen pavilions, fountains, and hundreds of urns and birdhouses.

A couple of pre-teen boys were teasing a dog near a small pavilion in the garden's center. Both Veronica and Yum heard the dog's yelping in distress and went to check, each approaching from opposite sides. They arrived almost at the same time, and each took action to chase the boys away. The sight of a tall, white Anglo woman and a short, stocky Chinese woman working together to chase and shout seemed to scare the boys, who soon ran off to cause trouble elsewhere. The two got along quickly and became fast friends after a few days. After Veronica learned about Yum's talents, she recruited her into the Gang. Once the Gang learned of Yum's shooting skills, she and Veronica were paired as a sniper and spotter. Veronica named her Sue B, in honor of her hero, Susan B. Anthony, and Yum decided to go by Fu Hao, an infamous Chinese female warrior from the Shang Dynasty.

☠☠☠☠☠☠☠☠☠☠☠

Manco Capac, also known as Gianfranco, a small man from Peru, was a direct descendant of the Inca tribes that fought against Spanish explorer Francisco Pizarro, who invaded the Incan Empire in 1532.

Gianfranco joined the Gang after his father and four brothers all died in a copper mining accident. It happened because the board chairman decided that rescuing the workers was too costly and would hurt the stock price. He believed the men knew the risks when they chose to become miners, so he put in minimal effort for the media.

Two months after the mining accident, the chairman's car brakes failed while descending the 5N toward Oxapama. His car went off the highway at high speed and crashed into Rio Chontabamba; he was unable to escape and drowned. Foul play was suspected, but no suspects were ever detained; the case remains open as an unsolved crime.

Gianfranco joined Greenpeace and took part in several peaceful protests against Peru's mining industry, which had been responsible for excessive air and water pollution, illegal dumping of toxic waste, and poor safety conditions for miners. As his frustration with peaceful protests grew, he was recruited by Le Gang de la Clé de Singe to adopt a more aggressive style of protesting.

☠☠☠☠☠☠☠☠☠☠☠

Sassoon worked as one of three veterinarians at a private Clinique Vétérinaire in Dakar. He handled everything from domestic animals to farm animals, as well as the occasional wild animal. The Senegal zoo was too poor to have a veterinarian on staff, so, on occasion, he was called upon to tend to the animals since he was the newest member of the team, having just graduated from veterinary school in Paris and wanting to start his career with some adventure rather than just caring for cats and dogs. One day, while reading Le Monde newspaper, he saw a veterinary position in Dakar, Senegal, in the classifieds. Two months later, he applied for it and received an acceptance letter with a two-year contract.

On his first day, he was urgently called to the Parc Forestier et Zoologique de Hann because one of the male lions had been injured. This was his first experience working at the zoo, but when he arrived, I could see that the lion had been badly beaten. The attendant claimed the lion attacked him while he was feeding it and that he feared for his life. Sassoon spoke to several witnesses, who said he was teasing the lion and that the man was the aggressor.

After tending to the lion, he walked around and saw that many animals appeared to have been mistreated. He went to the proper authorities and filed an official complaint. Nothing was done; he got the runaround.

It turned out that the clinic would receive calls to come out to the Zoo once or twice a month for injured animals. His fellow doctors continued to complain to the officials as well, writing and sending letters to the newspaper, but to no avail.

One day, he was visited by a man from Le Gang de la Clé de Singe, known only as the Iceman, who said that he had read some of the letters and articles and suggested that he could help. Sassoon, of course, had heard about the organization and was cautious because of all the wild stories he had read about them. Sassoon told the man that he didn't think he wanted or needed their help. The man asked him to think it over, and he would stop by from time to time to see if he had changed his mind.

Several weeks went by before he received a call from the zoo informing him that one of the chimpanzees had died. Sassoon was preparing for surgery on a farmer's ox, so one of his colleagues went there and brought back the body to perform an autopsy on the poor creature. They discovered that the young chimp had been beaten and strangled to death. Two days later, the Iceman came back again and finally decided to ask for their help.

One week went by without any calls from the Zoo, then two weeks, a month, and six months—nothing. Eventually, Sassoon learned from the Zoo staff that several attendants had quit suddenly and were replaced by more caring and responsible individuals. It appears that the people who left were relatives and friends of the Zoo's officials, which is why they were protected. But months later, the true story of what motivated them to leave was finally revealed.

It happened late at night; the three men responsible for mistreating the animals were abducted at gunpoint and taken to a lion enclosure at the zoo. One of the men, who had been teasing and torturing the lions, was stripped naked, bound, gagged, and restrained to a chair with his legs spread apart, with honey poured onto his genitals. A female lion was released into the cage, and it reportedly went straight to the man, mauling him and nearly castrating him before retreating back into her enclosure. The other two men observed this and were warned that any further abuse of the animals would result in similar punishment. The following day, all three men resigned, and the man who was mauled was taken to the hospital, where he soon died from an infection. The case remains unsolved.

Sassoon was later approached by the Iceman from Le Gang de la Clé de Singe, who asked if he would be interested in joining the group, as they always wanted to have people from the medical field, including doctors and veterinarians, join their cause. At first, Sassoon was unsure, but the more he thought about how best he could help abused, injured, and even endangered animals, the more he decided to join this noble effort.

☠☠☠☠☠☠☠☠☠☠☠

Willie Tyler, who everyone knew as Cowboy, was from Terlingua, Texas. Its name, from nearby Terlingua (three tongues) Creek, was coined by Mexican herders, Comanche, Shawnee, and Apache's who lived on its upper reaches.

Willie grew up on the Bar T cattle ranch working as a ranch hand, herding cattle, breaking horses, fixing fences, and taking part in cattle drives. The only possessions Willie had were the clothes he wore, his saddle, his horse Buck, and a Winchester Model 92 Lever Action Rifle that his father left him on his deathbed.

Like most cowboys in west Texas, Willie didn't put much stock in these liberal, tree-hugging, leftist, commie groups with their "Save the Whales," "Global Warming," "PETA," and "Save Endangered Species" crusades until after one of the old-time cattle drives, where he drove the cattle herd from Terlingua to Fort Stockton, about a 200-mile trek. The drive took eight days, and it ended with a wild west celebration and rodeo; there was also the 10th Annual Texas Coyote Roundup, which aimed to see how many coyotes one could kill over a week for a cash prize of a thousand dollars.

Willie had killed coyotes and even wolves before when they threatened the cattle herd, but never for sport. He always felt a little guilty after killing one, but he figured that was part of being a cowboy, watching over and protecting the herd.

Once the cattle were driven into the stockyards' pens, he put old Buck in the corral and guheaded into town to have a couple of drinks with the boys and maybe find a young lady to spend the night with.

As he and his friends were passing Historic Fort Stockton, they saw the first-day kills lying next to the adobe brick visitor center. Over 200 coyotes were laid out side-by-side, and that was just day one. A large crowd of men, women, and children was standing around laughing and joking. That bothered Willie: he felt there should be some respect shown; after all, coyotes and wolves, unlike humans, don't kill for sport; they kill to survive.

"I've seen enough, fellas; I'm outta here," Willie said.

"What's the matter, Tyler, no stomach for death?" His trail boss, J.T., teased him.

"Not for sport," Willie said as he walked away from the crowd and headed to the Crazy Mule Saloon.

Willie hadn't realized that a man and woman had followed him into the bar. He stood at the bar and ordered a

Lone Star Beer. While waiting, the man who followed him asked, “Are you in the coyote-killing derby?”

“Me? No, I don’t abide by killing for sport. I’m okay with hunting for food, but to kill for fun, no. You?”

Hardly, my friend, Venus here and I are doing a little hunting, but not for sport. Hi, I’m Gianfranco. Did you know that over 400,000 coyotes are killed in the U.S. every year?

“No shit!” Willie said after taking a drink.

Venus asked, “You a real cowboy?”

“Yes, ma’am. A bunch of fellas and I from the Bar T drove a herd of about five hundred heads from Terlingua to here in eight days.”

After a lot of soul searching, Willie Tyler decided to do something meaningful with his life, to make a difference. The sight of all those dead coyotes that died for nothing, but greed made him realize. So, Willie drew his back wages and left the Bar T to join one of those liberal tree-hugging leftist groups, Le Gang de la Clé de Singe.

“Glad to have you on our side, cowboy?”

“Why, thank you, ma’am; I do have one concern.”

“What’s that, cowboy?” She asked.

“What about Buck, my horse? I ain’t going to just leave him or sell him.”

Gianfranco responded, “We wouldn’t think of it. There is a farm ranch in the foothills of East Texas, a sort of rescue ranch where Buck will be well cared for, and you’re more than welcome to visit him at any time.”

“Alrighty then, pardner, count me in.”

“Welcome aboard, Cowboy,” Venus said.

☠☠☠☠☠☠☠☠☠☠☠

Hazael, a Syrian from Aleppo, joined Le Gang de la Clé de Singe shortly after the fall of Aleppo during the Syrian Civil War. He was a Colonel in the Free Syrian Army fighting against the al-Qaeda-affiliated al-Nusra Front and the Russian-backed Syrian government.

After four years of fighting, with tens of thousands of deaths, airstrikes targeting rescue workers, summary executions of civilians and captured soldiers, and the use of chemical weapons, Hazael could see that the end was near. He escaped into Turkey under cover of night, making his way mainly on foot to Istanbul, then into Bulgaria. From there, he connected with some freedom fighters heading to Ukraine to help fight against Russian aggression in Crimea. He joined the Ukrainian Insurgent Army (UPA), was made a battalion commander, and fought and defeated the Red Army in several battles before being medevacked to a hospital in Kyiv, where he recovered for twelve weeks after being wounded by a Sukhoi SU-57 Russian fighter jet during a strafing run. Eleven of his men were killed or wounded, including himself. Hazael sustained a wound to his left leg, shattering the femur and requiring a metal rod to replace it. He considered himself lucky not to have lost the leg.

For his bravery and service, he received the Medal for Military Service to Ukraine, the Order for Courage 1st Class, and Ukraine's equivalent of America's Purple Heart, the Sacrifice of Blood Medal. He was also granted Ukrainian citizenship, but because of his wound that caused him to develop a noticeable limp, he was considered unfit for combat duty.

While Hazael was recovering in the Feofaniya Clinical Hospital, he read an article in Ekspres, the Ukrainian national newspaper, about the slaughter of six European Bison by a group of poachers who illegally assist American big game hunters seeking to add 'unique and endangered' species to their resumes. Not only do they help the hunters find and kill the animals, but they also facilitate forging false documents to help export the trophies back into the United States.

The article listed the name of an organization seeking volunteers to help stop the killing of the 3500 Bison still remaining in the wild. Unbeknownst to Hazael, the listed organization was a front for Le Gang de la Clé de Singe.

Once out of the hospital, he considered joining the organization. Since Le Gang de la Clé de Singe needs to ensure that the recruit isn't a government agent trying to infiltrate the federation, they conduct a background check and assign the applicant a task that involves taking a life as a form of initiation.

Hazael and two other members encountered a poacher/guide and hunter after they had just shot a Bison. Hazael had been indoctrinated into the ritual and reasoning behind taking the lives of those who dare kill an animal for sport and dressing the bodies with the yellow ensign as a warning to other potential eco-criminals.

As Hazael approached the two captives standing beside the dead Bison's body, pointing a Webley Mk VI Revolver in his right hand and the yellow flag with the black skull and crossed monkey wrenches, he asked, "Have you heard of Le Gang de la Clé de Singe?"

The poacher said nothing, while the American hunter arrogantly demanded, "Look here, I'm an American, and I demand to see the American counselor immediately."

"Oh, you do, do you?" Hazael asked as he shot the poacher in the head.

POW

"Oh, God, please no! I didn't know that this was illegal. I swear, I won't do it again." He pleaded.

"I'll ask you again. Have you heard of Le Gang de la Clé de Singe?"

The man looked down and uttered, "Yes."

"So, you know that the penalty is death?"

The man stood with his eyes closed, trembling and whimpering.

"Sorry," Hazael said as he raised his pistol and fired.

POW

He and the two other members placed the bodies next to the Bison, draped the flags around their necks, and tucked the proclamations into their pockets. Later, when they returned to base camp, they called the police and the press to inform them of the bodies' location.

Shortly after that incident, he was issued several new passports and assigned to join the Red Team.

Fu Hao and Sue B were enjoying some well-deserved rest and relaxation in the village of Stjørdal, Norway, which overlooks the Trondheim Fjord. Winter was beginning to settle into Norway, so when the call for an assignment came, even though they enjoyed skiing, they were ready for a warmer climate.

They were supposed to meet with the Red Team in Toulouse, located in southeastern France, in an area called the Dombes, for their first of many assignments.

It appears that a group of illegal poachers is capturing common frogs and toads, severing their hind legs, and selling them as a delicacy.

When frogs and toads gather to breed in pools of water, they become easy targets for this type of harvesting. The poachers simply cut off their legs while the amphibians are still alive and leave them in the pool to die a painful death that is both bloody and full of frogspawn.

Besides being illegal, it's shocking, callous, and a brutal treatment of animals.

When Fu Hao and Sue B arrived at Le Grand Balcon Hotel, which overlooks the Place du Capitole in the city's main square, the members of the Red Team were waiting for them in the lobby.

"*Bonjour, Fu Hao et Sue B., bienvenue à Toulouse*", said Sassoon.

"*Merci mon cher*," Sue B answered as they hugged and kissed on the cheek.

"After we check in, let's meet in the bar for a drink," Fu Hao suggested.

Fu Hao and Sue B went to the reception desk and checked in.

"Bonjour, may I help you?" The receptionist asked.

"Yes, we have a reservation, la. My last name is Chang," Fu Hao said.

"Yes, Madam, we have you staying three nights in our Saint-Exupery Suite. May I please have your passports?"

"Here you are," Fu Hao said as she handed the receptionist their passports.

"How many keys would you like?"

"Two, please."

As the receptionist handed Fu Hao and Sue B each a key, she asked, "Would you like some help with your luggage?"

"Yes, if you could have the porter bring our bags to the room. I'd really appreciate it," Fu Hao said as she handed the porter twenty dollars.

The porter gave a short bow and a big smile and said, "Merci, Mesdames."

Fu Hao and Sue B headed to the hotel bar since the Le Grand Balcon Hotel was the former home of Aéropostale's aviators. Aéropostale was a pioneering aviation company that operated from 1918 to 1933, and its pilots bivouacked in the Le Grand Balcon Hotel.

The ultra-modern bar honors Aéropostale's most famous pilots, like Jean Mermoz and Antoine de Saint-

Exupéry, by displaying large black-and-white portraits on its walls.

They all gathered around a table where the six of them could speak freely. Cowboy took the liberty of ordering six bottles of La Bière des sans Culottes, France's top-rated beer.

"Cheers!" He said as he held up his bottles.

A chorus of "Cheers" was the response.

Gianfranco took a big swig, leaned on the table, and asked, "What the hell are we doing here? To save a bunch of frogs? Frogs!"

Fu Hao shot Gianfranco a cold stare. "So, you think we only focus on species you consider worth our attention. Animals that are what? Larger than a dog, or maybe an elephant?"

"No, I'm just saying…"

"These people don't kill frogs simply to cut off their legs. They cut off the legs while the frogs are still alive and then discard them like trash, causing the frogs hours of pain before they die. Doesn't a frog suffer just as much as any other animal that has been mutilated?"

"No. You're right. I'm sorry," Gianfranco said apologetically.

"Tomorrow morning at 0600, we will head out to Lac du Laragou. We'll scope it out. The poachers usually strike when the frogs emerge at night," Sue B announced.

"I've already contacted Doctor Leblanc," Sassoon said.

"And?" Fu Hao asked.

"He says that he'll help."

"Excellent. This should send a clear message," Fu Hao said.

Henri Moreau and his younger brother Charles were known to the local authorities as small-time criminals. They had been arrested mainly for petty crimes but occasionally committed robbery, muggings, loan sharking, and extortion. Recently, they became involved in a new illegal venture on the black market involving frog's legs.

The brothers Moreau and a few accomplices have found what appears to be an easy way to make money in the lucrative gourmet food market.

They would wait until late in the evening and then head out to a lake armed with powerful flashlights, Frabill Folding Fishing Nets, and a twelve-inch fish fillet knife. They would walk along the lake shore, shining their flashlights on the water's edge where frogs, mesmerized by the light, would be scooped up in the nets. They would grab the frogs, cut off their legs, and toss them aside like trash. Catching hundreds of frogs each night; once they drained the lake of frogs, they would move on to the next one.

Sassoon, originally from Marseille, has many ties in Toulouse. His sources say the Moreau gang has recently been poaching the waters of Lac du Laragou.

Little did Henri Moreau know that he and his gang would become a part of local folklore.

Fu Hao, Sue B, and the Red Team took shelter in a small grove of Ash trees on the lake's edge. As the sun set, they put on their Shinobi Shozoku uniforms. Shinobi Shozoku is the traditional attire worn for ninjutsu combat.

The all-black Shinobi Shozoku uniform includes the fukumen – a scarf headband, Uwagi – a jacket, Tekko – hand coverings, Dodzime – a wide belt, Igabakama – narrow leg trousers, and Kyahan – leg wraps. The Shinobi Shozoku uniform had proven effective in many night missions. Since there would be no moon, the team would wear the AGM Global Vision NVG-50 Night Vision Goggles.

Each member carried the Sig Sauer AS50 sniper rifle and the P226 sidearm. Both are equipped with QDL Silencer Suppressors.

Once the sun set, they didn't have to wait long before Moreau and the gang arrived. The four poachers were together, collecting dozens of frogs.

Fu Hao and Sue B were the team's top marksmen. They were tasked with lightly wounding the Moreau brothers, while Gianfranco and Cowboy took out the other two accomplices.

"On my mark. Three. Two. One. Fire."

PHIFF PHIFF PHIFF PHIFF

Four shots simultaneously. All four men fell to the ground. Two dead, two wounded. The Red Team surrounded the fallen, guns at the ready. Gianfranco and Cowboy helped the Moreau brothers to their feet.

Sassoon spoke in French and asked, "Monsieur Moreau, have you ever heard of Le Gang de la Clé de Singe?"

"Yes," He responded

"And you know the penalty for what you are doing?"

"You cannot mean that applies to these meaningless frogs!"

"Even the lowly frog shall not be abused and mutilated," Sassoon said.

Fu Hao told Sassoon, "Ask him who should die, Him or his brother."

"*Qui devrait mourir, toi ou ton frère*?" Sassoon asked.

"What do you mean?" He asked.

"Only one of you shall live."

"You cannot be serious?"

"Deadly," Sassoon said as he removed his pistol from its holster, cocked the gun, and pointed it at Henri Moreau's head.

The older Moreau lowered his head and muttered, "Mon frère."

PHIFF

A red mist covered Henri's face with the blood of his brother Charles. Sue B had fired one shot into the back of Charles Moreau's head. At the same time, Hazael plunged a needle into the neck of the elder Moreau, injecting him with a cocktail of propofol and benzodiazepine, putting Henri into a deep unconscious state.

The team placed the traditional yellow ensigns with the black skull and crossed monkey wrenches around the necks of the dead, with a typewritten proclamation in each of their pockets that read:

"*Let it be known that Le Gang de la Clé de Singe declares a declaration of war against all poachers, big game hunters, and all big game safari outfits, as well as anyone anywhere in the world who targets, kills, profits from, or supports the killing of any endangered animals or animals hunted for sport. Be warned, do so at your own risk. You will be hunted down and pay with your lives. Whether man or woman, there will be no exceptions and no mercy; we will show no quarter. You have been warned.*"

The Red Team then transported the unconscious Henri Moreau to Dr. Leblanc's office, who had been a longtime friend and supporter of the eco-terrorist group Le Gang de la Clé de Singe from its early days. He was actually one of the founding members back in the late sixties.

"Bring him here, into the operating room," Leblanc said to the ninja-dressed warriors carrying the unconscious man.

Fu Hao was about to remove her hood when Leblanc said, “Don’t! I do not want to see your faces. It would be better if I couldn’t identify you. Now, put him on this table and wait outside. I will come get you when I’m done.”

☠☠☠☠☠☠☠☠☠☠☠

Henri Moreau woke up in his apartment, lying under the covers in his bed, feeling like he had a terrible hangover. He doesn’t remember going out drinking. What an unbelievable nightmare he had. It was awful; all his friends and even his younger brother had been murdered.

He glanced at his bedside alarm clock; it was nine-thirty. He couldn’t remember when he had slept so late, so he flipped off the covers to jump out of bed.

YEEEOWWWWWW!!!!!!!

He began screaming for help, “Acidemia! Aidez-moi!”

His neighbors told police that when they finally forced open the door, they found Moreau in his bed; both of his legs had been amputated. His severed legs were lying next to him in bed. He kept screaming until the ambulance arrived and sedated him.

The bodies of his younger brother and two accomplices were found shot dead at Lac du Laragou; aside from the Le Gang de la Clé de Singe yellow flags and declarations found on the bodies, a pair of frog’s legs were found stuffed in each of their mouths.

Henri Moreau was discharged from the hospital, given a wheelchair, and spent the rest of his life wandering the streets of Toulouse begging for spare change. The children would tease and taunt him, calling him “*l’homme grenouille*,” the frogman.

The incident at Lac du Laragou became forever known as *Le massacre des tueurs de grenouilles* – the slaughter of the frog killers.

The Red Team was sitting in the Air France lounge at Aéroport Marseille Provence, waiting to board KLM flight 2002 to Amsterdam, Schiphol. From there, they fly to Jomo Kenyatta International Airport, their final destination: Nairobi, Kenya. —a grueling total of twenty-three hours of flight time. Thankfully, Odin and the Blue Team will be there to greet them. They will have two days to acclimate before heading to their next mission. Eliminate a rogue gang of big game poachers targeting Kenya's Ishaqbini Hirola Conservancy, reportedly gunning for a pair of rare giraffes.

There have been unsubstantiated reports of two white giraffes, a mother and her calf. The giraffes are not albino but have a unique white hide due to a condition called leucism. Unlike albinism, animals with leucism continue to produce dark pigment in their soft tissue, which is why their eyes are dark colored.

Because the giraffes are such a high target, both the Red and Blue Teams have been assigned to try and protect these miracles of nature.

Odin was waiting curbside, standing beside a 2013 black Ford Expedition four-wheel drive, which seats eight. It featured a roof rack for storing all their gear.

Once everyone was on board and accounted for, Odin got on the A104 and parked at the Nairobi Hilton in under twenty minutes.

"So, how did it go?" Odin asked.

"Let's just say I think the wild frog population will be safe for the foreseeable future," Fu Hao quipped.

Once everyone was settled into their rooms, it was decided that the teams would meet for lunch at the Garden Pool Restaurant.

The restaurant was surrounded by lush green plants on a tiled patio overlooking the pool. Baskets of flowers hung from poles with bright-colored canvas covers with built-in misters that shaded and cooled the customers from the scorching African sun.

The team leaders sat in the middle of the table with their team members sitting mingled among each other. The philosophy was that the teams never competed against each other; on the contrary, they should feel camaraderie and kinship with each other.

Sue B asked Odin, "Have we contacted our people in the African Wildlife Federation?"

"I have. They're sending someone to act as our guide. Mr. Godfrey Nderitu has worked in the field, tracking and hunting down poachers, as well as working undercover. He's very experienced and supposedly knows all the right and wrong people. He should be arriving here soon. I've asked the folks at the front desk to send him up here as soon as he arrives," Odin stated.

"Do we have a plan yet?" Asked Gianfranco.

"I can only give you all a big-sky overview at the moment. As you all know, any combat plan, no matter how well planned and thought out, goes right out the window once you're in the field. The moment you engage the enemy, it's all about how well you can adapt to changing situations.

Currently, our plan is for everyone to travel deep into Ishaqbini Hirola Conservancy in the morning, establish a base camp where Lu Wei and Hazael will send up and monitor a fleet of drones to locate the white giraffes and determine if we can get a fix on the poachers.

Once we determine the locations of both, we will send out the two teams. One team will stay with the giraffes, while the other will pursue the poachers. From there, it's all improvisation," Odin explained.

The waitress came by the table to ask for orders.

Fu Hao asked the group, "Shall we have her bring us some local dishes, and we can all share?"

Everyone appeared agreeable, so the waitress brought out several local specialties: a couple of orders of Kachumbari, a salad of fresh tomato, onion, and spicy peppers; Nyama Choma, barbequed beef and goat; Mandazi, fried bread; and an order of Bobotie, a dish made of spiced minced meat baked with an egg-based topping.

Halfway through their meal, a Black man dressed in khaki with white hair approached the table and announced he was looking for Odin. He seemed to be in his late sixties.

"I am Odin," Odin said.

"Godfrey Nderitu," The man said.

"Please, won't you join us?" Odin asked.

"Thank you. Don't mind if I do."

Odin took a few minutes to introduce the members of the Red and Blue teams to their guide.

Godfrey looked at Fu Hao and Sue B, smiled, and asked, "I remember working with you ladies a couple of years ago with a couple of fellas I don't see here. Whatever happened to Rodin and the Iceman?"

"The Icemen was killed last year on assignment, and Rodin has fallen off the face of the earth," Sue B said.

"Rodin has retired to who knows where," Fu Hao added.

"I understand that. Sometimes, it feels like we're losing the battle. If nothing changes, at this rate, we will lose every elephant in Africa in 10 years, no matter what we do.

Can you imagine an Africa without elephants, lions, or rhinos? It is a heartbreaking concept. So, I really understand why Rodin would need to step back. I'm also sorry to hear about Iceman; he was a true warrior. He will be missed," Godfrey said with tears in his eyes.

"That's why we're here, to see that won't happen," Fu Hao said.

"The fight continues," Odin added.

☠☠☠☠☠☠☠☠☠☠☠

Early the next day, before the sun rose, the teams began the five-and-a-half-hour trip to Garissa—a sizable town in the middle of nowhere on the banks of the Tana River. The land is flat, red-dirt desert, and barren, except for a narrow strip of about half a mile of green fields on either side of the Tana River.

Most of the buildings are one-story cinderblock shanties with tin roofs, placed directly next to each other to form a long, continuous row of multicolored homes. Blue, green, lavender, senna, ochre, lavender, senna, green, blue, and then a mix of all those colors again.

The two-lane paved roads are crowded day and night, bumper to bumper, with a mix of cars, pickups, big rig trucks, motorcycles, and three-wheeled motorized cab-like vehicles called tuk-tuks for as far as the eye can see. Most days, all the streets are lined with men sitting on their motorcycles, watching and waiting for something, anything to happen.

On the roadside, crowds of pedestrians line the streets. Hundreds of people cannot afford a car or a tuk-tuk. Old men, children, and women, most dressed in traditional hijabs, walk to and from the open-air bazaars that set up along the sides of the roads. Women sell fruit, vegetables, clothing, and assorted cuts of unknown meats, both domestic and wild, under multicolored beach umbrellas.

As they drive along the main drag, Garissa-Dadaab Road, between their hotel and the open markets, they encounter an open patch of dirt where a small herd of half-starved cattle lies about.

The three-vehicle caravan, led by their guide, Godfrey Nderitu, pulled into the gated and guarded parking compound of the Tana Garden Hotels. The hotel is a three-story ochre-colored building with white trim around all the windows. Three large arches are in front of the hotel and Tana Café's entrance.

They found the hotel to be clean and, above all, safe. They looked forward to getting a good night's sleep in a comfortable bed; starting tomorrow, they would be living in the bush for the foreseeable future.

The teams gathered around the pool to enjoy a day of rest and relaxation; they ordered six pizzas and several dishes of Shawarma (gyros), Kuku Choma (grilled chicken), fries, and Mushkaki. The gathering lasted late into the night until Godfrey Nderitu reminded them they were leaving at 6:30.

As they were leaving and heading up to their rooms, Cowboy uttered under his breath, "Party pooper."

Nderitu took exception to that remark, grabbed the Cowboy, and threw him into the pool, where a Red Team vs. Blue Team pool fight erupted, delaying lights out for another hour and a half.

Both team leaders knew that it's good to have some lightheartedness and joy, especially when your business is death.

Garissa-Dadaab Road was starting to come alive as they headed west out of town. They crossed the Tana River on the A3 until they reached the B8, which headed south for the four-hour trip to the small village of Witu. Witu lies just inland from the Indian Ocean settlement of Kipini, located at the mouth of the Tana River.

When the caravan stopped at the village of Minjila for fuel, Odin, Sue B, and Fu Hao received a call on their satellite phones warning them that a terrorist attack was happening nearby in the villages of Lamu.

Al-Shabaab, a Somalia-based ragtag militia linked to the Al-Qaeda terror network, has started attacking villages and ambushing travelers. It has been reported that they have beheaded three people and set fire to several houses in dawn attacks on the villages of Maleli and Witu.

"You are not obligated to continue your mission under these circumstances. Everyone here at command central will understand." Commander Wooch said.

Odin said, "We understand, Commander. Give us a minute to confer."

The team leaders felt that this had to be a group decision. The three of them went to the teams and explained the situation.

"We all signed up for a cause. Unfortunately, that cause didn't include battling radical extremist terrorists. So, we leave it to you to decide: do we stay and try to finish our mission, or do we go? There will be no repercussions of disgrace," Fu Hao said.

"How many of you want to continue?" Odin asked.

Of the eleven team members and their guide, Godfrey Nderitu, everyone voted to continue with the mission. Odin called Wooch back, "Wooch, we decided we're going forward."

"Okay, keep me posted. Don't hesitate to contact me if you run into trouble. And remember to try to steer clear of these maniacs."

"Will do."

"Good hunting."

"Thanks, Commander."

With the vehicles all gassed up, the teams headed into the Ishaqbini Hirola Conservancy in search of two white giraffes. They took the C112 east, and within twelve miles, the three SUVs switched to four-wheel drive and went north off-road toward the Ishaqbini Hirola Conservancy.

They drove for another five hours, then stopped to set up camp. While the rest of the Red and Blue Team members started preparing the camp, Lu Wei and Hazael launched a fleet of drones. At first, they only needed two members to look for the giraffes and the poachers. However, now that a terrorist group was loose, a third member was required to monitor some drones and watch for Al-Shabaab. It was decided that Venus would operate the third drone.

Three Raytheon Killer Bee reconnaissance drones were launched for observation. If and when they required an offensive attack drone, they had two Kratos XQ-58 Valkyrie unmanned combat aerial vehicles. The Valkyrie is equipped with two weapon bays loaded with four Joint Direct Attack Munition (JDAM) laser-guided bombs.

They pitched camp on the banks of the Tana River under a grove of Umbrella Trees surrounded by hundreds of Sodom Apple shrubs, so thick that if one were looking for them, they would be found.

As night fell, the team leaders had the team members check their equipment and weapons for potential encounters with poachers. After the equipment check, they settled down for a meal of pork and beans, collard greens, and Chapati Za Ngozi bread. Before lights out, the team leaders issued the sentry orders.

No matter how many missions they had had in Africa, it always took several nights to get used to the sounds of the night: the lion's roars, the hyena's "laughter," the grunts of a pod of hippopotami, and all the other nocturnal creatures roaming the night.

☠☠☠☠☠☠☠☠☠☠☠

Edwin Mutia, Adesh Abdikarim, and Kevin Mwimbi have been poaching animals from the Ishaqbini Hirola Conservancy for over ten years without ever getting caught. They've killed almost every type of animal that has entered the conservancy at one time or another. Elephants, zebras, lions, water buffaloes, giraffes, baboons, rhinoceroses, hyenas, jackals, warthogs, and hippopotami.

They have a man who pays them well for their skins, tusks, meat, and animal organs for native and voodoo medicine men. But killing the white giraffes would be legendary; they would have powerful ju-ju within the Kikuyu Tribe.

Edwin Mutia is the oldest of the three. He is forty-three, married, and has six children. Adesh Abdikarim and Kevin Mwimbi are both in their mid-thirties, married, and have three kids each. They all live in the small town of Garsen on the west side of the Tana River. When going south on the B8, you would turn left onto Garsen Road. It's the only paved road leading into the town center. Edwin Mutia, Adesh Abdikarim, and Kevin Mwimbi live in two-bedroom cinderblock houses next to each other, close to the river and away from town.

The man they work for is Robert Lewis, a white South African living in Mombasa, four hours south, in an exclusive condo complex called the Palms, across from the Indian Ocean. The Palms is a gated and guarded complex with three buildings, two pools, six tennis courts, and an eight-hole golf course. Mr. Lewis has a nice ocean view from his top-floor penthouse, which has three bedrooms and two bathrooms.

He hired his team of poachers to kill the two white giraffes and bring back their heads and skin. They can sell the meat and keep whatever they can get. He already has a buyer for the head and skin. One Russian oligarch, Sergey Chernyshevsky, made billions from privatizing oil companies and his close ties with Vladimir Putin. He has prepaid Robert Lewis a sum of 15,500,000 Kenyan Shillings, about one hundred and fifty thousand US Dollars, for two mounted white giraffe heads and white giraffe-tanned skins.

☠☠☠☠☠☠☠☠☠☠☠

"Odin, I've spotted the giraffes. I estimate that they're approximately seven kilometers north by northeast," Lu Wei shouted out.

"And I have what looks like a Toyota pickup heading in that direction," Hazael alerted.

"Saddle up," Sue B ordered.

The teams unpacked their ghillie suits and picked up their weapons.

A ghillie suit is a type of camouflage clothing designed to blend into the background environment, such as foliage, snow, or sand. Usually, it is a net or cloth outfit covered in loose strips of burlap (hessian), cloth, or twine, sometimes made to resemble leaves and twigs, and can be augmented with scraps of foliage from the area.

The team started slipping into their ghillie suits and wrapping their rifles in tactical sniper veils.

"Did you all remember to put on the Rid-A-Tick patches? Those little bastards' bites can kill you if left untreated," Odin said.

They all nodded their heads affirmatively. "Okay, and are everyone's radio headsets working?"

Each member carried the Sig Sauer AS50 sniper rifle and the P226 sidearm. Both are equipped with QDL Silencer Suppressors.

The U.S. Army developed the rifle to increase range and assist snipers in rugged terrains like Afghanistan's mountains and deserts. It features a computerized scope that can mark a chosen target and a special trigger that doesn't fire until it's certain the bullet will hit its mark. The effective range exceeds 1,250 yards.

Once ready, the Red Team headed toward the giraffes while the Blue Team drove to see if they could intercept the poachers. Lu Wei, Hazael, and Venus would be the team's eyes in the sky and stay in constant communication.

Lu Wei and Hazael could see that the teams couldn't stop the poachers from arriving too late. When the mother giraffe saw the men coming toward her calf, she charged to defend her young. They watched in horror as the poachers slaughtered the adult giraffe. With her mother fallen, the calf instinctively ran to her, seeming to cry out that the poachers had shot and killed her.

The three killers wasted no time; Edwin Mutia pulled out a chainsaw and began to cut off both of their heads, while Adesh Abdikarim and Kevin Mwimbi started skinning the majestic beasts.

"They're down! We're too late!" Lu Wei shouted.

"Where are they?" Fu Hao asked.

"Red and Blue, you're about one click from them. You have them boxed in between you," Hazael said.

The teams parked their vehicles and approached from opposite directions. Their eye in the sky directed them so they wouldn't shoot at each other. Since Odin was the senior officer, giving the ultimate command was up to him.

"Red Team leader, how is your advantage?" Odin asked.

"We have a clear shot," Fu Hao stated.

"Take out two; we need the third alive for questioning."

"Roger that. Red Team, Sue B, and I will take out the man wearing the blue striped shirt and the man in the wife-beater. Cowboy, wing the man in the red tee shirt."

"Arm or leg?" Cowboy asked.

"Leg. We don't want to chase him."

"Roger. Red Leader," Cowboy affirmed.

"On my count. Three, two, one. Fire!"

PHIFF PHIFF PHIFF

Fu Hao and Sue B's targets both dropped like a sack of bricks—two clean headshots. The skins of the white giraffes were permanently stained with their killers' blood and brains. The third man, Edwin Mutia, was struck in the lower left leg, just below the kneecap. He was hit with such force that one minute, he was standing upright, and the next, he was lying flat on his back, looking up at the sky.

He saw what appeared to be alien creatures approaching; they looked like forest animals covered in branches and shrubs, carrying rifles. He was about to faint when Sassoon quickly gave him an injection of adrenaline to keep him awake and tended to his wounded leg. Sassoon determined that the bullet had hit and shattered his tibia. He mainly cared for his leg to stop the immediate bleeding.

Odin lifted his balaclava, knelt beside the wounded man, and asked, "What's your name?"

"Edwin Mutia."

"Edwin, who sent you?"

"I cannot say."

Odin looked up at Vulcan and nodded. Vulcan placed his boot on the wounded man's legs and began to apply pressure.

ARRRGGGGHHHH!

"Edwin, who sent you?"

"I cannot say. He will kill me!" He screamed.

"What do you think we'll do?"

Odin nodded again to Vulcan.

ARRRGGGGHHHH!

"Okay! Okay!" Edwin screeched.

"Edwin, who sent you?"

"Robert Lewis."

"Where can we find him?"

"Mombasa," He muttered.

"Edwin, have you ever heard of Le Gang de la Clé de Singe?" Odin asked, holding up the yellow ensign.

"Yes," Edwin said as he began to weep.

Odin stood up, drew his revolver from its holster, and shot Edwin Mutia in the head. He hung the skull and crossed monkey wrenches flag around Edwin's neck, along with a copy of the manifesto in his pocket.

They placed the poacher's bodies beside the two decapitated giraffes; then they called the park police at Ishaqbini Hirola Conservancy to report the location of the giraffes and their killers before returning to camp.

By the time they got back to camp, Lu Wei and the others had packed up and dismantled their campsite. They were prepared to leave. Odin, Sue B, and Fu Hao estimated they had less than six hours before the news about the giraffes and poachers spread across Kenya. They wanted to reach Robert Lewis before that happened.

☠☠☠☠☠☠☠☠☠☠☠

THE BLUE TEAM

Mikkael Einarsson was an Icelander who called himself Odin after the God of war and death; he was from Reykjavík, Iceland.

Odin became involved in environmental causes in high school by protesting the Japanese whaling ships being allowed refueling privileges. He opposed the building of the Kárahnjúkastífla Dam because it caused irreversible environmental damage to the surrounding area. It also devastated the habitat of the pink-footed Goose and reindeer.

He then joined more activist groups, such as Saving Iceland, where he made underground protest videos for Anarchy Media. Afterwards, he joined Greenpeace International and spent three years as a Rainbow Warrior defending the Amazon reef against the world's oil companies, a fight they eventually won.

He signed on with Sea Shepherd, where he was on the front lines of Operation Jairo off the coast of Nicaragua at the Estero Padre Natural Reserve in the battle to save the Eastern Pacific Hawksbill sea turtle population from poachers.

The poachers not only capture and kill the adults for meat and shells but also dig up and steal the eggs.

Odin decided that a more aggressive approach was necessary than just warning shots and damaging vessels. He and about a dozen like-minded eco-warriors chose to take matters into their own hands. They waited patiently on the nesting beaches for the sea turtles to come and lay their eggs. On average, sea turtles deposit around 100 eggs in a nest, and it takes two to three hours for them to dig the nest and lay the eggs before the mother turtle slowly drags herself back into the ocean.

Once the turtles had left, half a dozen poachers rushed to the nests and started digging up the eggs. Odin and his team hurried out from the dunes, where they had been hiding, shined hand-held spotlights on the poachers, and stopped their attempt to steal the eggs.

Odin shouted, “Halt! Put your hands in the air. Don’t move.”

Pedro Rodrigues, a fellow crew member, shouted in Spanish, “¡Detener! Pon tu mano en el aire. No se mueva.”

One of the poachers turned around and fired a gun at Odin and his team. Odin grabbed his Smith & Wesson Model 410 .40mm matte black semi-automatic pistol and fired back, hitting the man who shot at them in the upper thigh.

Once the gunfire started, the other five men all scattered. After a long chase, all five poachers were caught and brought back to the wounded man, who was moaning.

“¿Alguno de ustedes habla inglés?” Pedro asked.

No one acknowledged that they spoke English.

Cindy, one of the Sea Shepherd crew members, asked, “What are we going to do with them?”

“We could kill them all as an example to others,” Odin suggested.

Pedro said, “Let’s tie them up and turn them over to the police.”

“What? So, they get a slap on the wrist. They’ll be back out here next week. I say we kill them all,” Odin pleaded.

But Pedro and the rest finally persuaded Odin to change their way of thinking. They called the police. The six poachers were arrested, spent two weeks in jail, and paid a small fine.

Three weeks later, news spread quickly through the small village of Punta Venecia about the murder of four men who were found shot dead at the turtle nesting beach of Estero Padre Natural Reserve.

No charges were ever filed, but four days after the killings, Odin left the Sea Shepherds and joined the more aggressive action-oriented organization, Le Gang de la Clé de Singe.

Since joining, Odin has risen in the ranks and is now the leader of the Blue Team.

☠☠☠☠☠☠☠☠☠☠☠

Lu Wei grew up in Yulin, a prefecture-level city in the Shanbei region of Shaanxi province. His father was a famous porcelain craftsman, highly respected and honored until the Cultural Revolution led by Mao Zedong. His father was denounced and sent to a "reeducation" camp where he was tortured, beaten, and eventually died from malnutrition. His mother committed suicide when she heard of her husband's death.

In 1966, Xing Bao was drafted into the Red Guard, which was initially viewed as counter-revolutionaries and radicals. Soon, Chairman Mao himself legitimized them.

To survive, Xing Bao endured the chaos for ten years until 1976. After Mao's death and the arrest of the Gang of Four, a gradual undoing of the Maoist policies from the Cultural Revolution started.

Xing Bao returned to his hometown, Yulin, to see if he could reconnect with any surviving family members. But unfortunately, all his family had scattered across the county, and there were no records left; he was alone.

Xing Bao became involved in animal rights in June during the annual dog meat festival. Over 10,000 dogs are killed for human consumption. He and a small group of activists raided the dog compounds and released thousands of dogs; he was promptly arrested, beaten, and sentenced to one year in Guizhong prison. After his release, he was met by members of Le Gang de la Clé de Singe to see if they would be interested in continuing the fight, not just for animal rights but also worldwide.

Xing Bao adopted the name Lu Wei, a corrupt politician from his own province, to constantly remind himself that absolute power corrupts absolutely.

☠☠☠☠☠☠☠☠☠☠☠

Ivanna Shevchenko came from a small town outside Odesa, Ukraine, called Yuzhne, a port city on the Black Sea. Her grandfather owned a small fleet of fishing boats; his grandfather had handed it down to him. About eight years ago, the government announced that private fishing fleets would become part of a state-owned commercial enterprise. They had no choice. Those who refused were harassed, and equipment was damaged. So-called 'accidents' happened to crew members, and a few were killed—her grandfather was one of them.

To fight back, a small group of resisters began publicly protesting by marching in the streets and clashes with police. They tried to draw global attention to their cause, but there was not enough outcry worldwide.

It seemed their cause was so minor compared to all the other injustices in the world that theirs was a lost cause. Some of them began to fight back using tactics the State had previously employed against them: they sabotaged their equipment and harassed their crew members. They were labeled thugs and terrorists and had to go underground. One day, a man named Mars, like the Roman God of War, approached them and offered assistance from Le Gang de la Clé de Singe in their struggle against the State.

They formed hit squads against opposition leaders, sabotaged equipment, sank many State-sponsored ships, and generally caused chaos. They took revenge in kind; if one private fishing vessel was sunk, then two of the State's fishing vessels were sunk. If one of the local fishermen was killed, two of the State's fishermen were killed.

For several months, they wreaked holy Hell against the state-run fleet, but soon the Ukrainian government sought help from the Russians. The odds were just too great. They finally had to disband, so she and several others from Yuzhne left and joined Le Gang de la Clé de Singe.

Ivanna chose the name Venus Victrix (Venus the Victorious), a goddess who would bring victory to her cause.

João Pesqueria was often bullied as a child in the small town of Estremoz, Portugal, because he was born with a severe case of facial asymmetry. It was a condition where one side of his face was not the same as the other. In João's case, the right side of his face was two inches lower than the left. The condition could have been somewhat corrected, but his family couldn't afford the surgery.

He was taunted and mocked throughout his youth. Then, at the age of fourteen, João took his first karate class at the youth center. By the time he was nineteen, he had earned his Advanced Brown belt, his first Kyu rank. From then on, no one called him names or teased him after he broke the nose of Vinicius Carneiro, the town bully. This was a great relief to all of his victims.

He left Estremoz for Lisbon at twenty-two and took a job with Greenpeace International aboard the Rainbow Warrior ship. His first stop was the Philippines to join a coal blockade. Their goal was to stop coal shipments to the Pagbilao coal-fired power plant.

The Philippines ranks among the countries most vulnerable to rising sea levels, more frequent cyclones, and other devastating effects of climate change. The coal plant's planned expansion would mean an additional 5 million tons of climate-wrecking carbon dioxide released into the atmosphere each year—double the plant's current output. Moreover, the expansion isn't the only concern. The government is planning to build eight new coal-fired power stations, which would pose an even greater risk of climate challenges if they were allowed to be completed.

The Rainbow Warrior anchored beside the docked coal ship Medi Firenze for three days, preventing larger coal-carrying vessels from unloading. An enormous banner reading "Quit Coal" was hung between the Rainbow Warrior's masts to send a clear message to the Philippine government that they should stop building and expanding coal-fired power plants.

On the fourth day, a Senator sent a message of support to the Rainbow Warrior crew, stating that he had just introduced a resolution in the Senate calling for a halt to the construction of new coal-fired power plants—a peaceful way to address the issue.

João spent over eleven years working with Greenpeace, helping Iceland reduce the killing of Minke, Sei, and Fin Whales from 500 to just 25, persuading Xerox to stop purchasing timber pulp from StoraEnso, the Finnish national logging company, which was cutting down one of Europe's last remaining ancient forests, and contributing to the end of deep-sea bottom trawling, a practice that severely damages vulnerable marine ecosystems.

These are all noble causes, but it took too long for João to see results. He was searching for an organization that could deliver immediate outcomes. That's when he decided to join Le Gang de la Clé de Singe. He adopted the name Bellator, the Latin word for warrior, and everyone who has met him believes that to be true.

☠☠☠☠☠☠☠☠☠☠☠

Emmett Washington grew up in a small one-story house on 503 4th Court W, across the street from the Titusville AOH Church of God in the Graymont section of town.

The front of the house was yellow brick with a faded sky-blue roof, bordered by maroon trim around the roof line and all the windows. The rest of the house was painted sky blue, matching the fading of the front roof.

In summer, all the windows stayed open day and night because they had no air conditioner, and during winter, the family slept in front of two wood-burning fireplaces for warmth, as they had no heat. Emmett's father, Luther Washington, was serving ten to fifteen years for armed robbery at Fountain Correctional Facility in Atmore, Alabama. His mother, Sarah, worked as a maid at Bob's Motel and Café during the day. At night, she took in people's laundry and made potholders from scraps of cloth, which Emmett and his six brothers and sisters would go house to house trying to sell for a dollar each.

Emmett was the oldest and a member of the Titusville Posse, a notorious Birmingham street gang, for many years. Once, after a drug deal went south, a rival gang drove by and shot at his house, killing two of his siblings and his mother.

Emmett and three other members of the 'Posse' were arrested on a weapons charge while they were on their way to carry out a revenge killing. At seventeen, he faced five years in prison until the DA made him an offer that changed his life. Instead of jail time, he was given the chance to join the Marines.

He was sent to Camp Pendleton for boot camp, 12.5 weeks of the toughest training in the military. The Marines' DIs (drill instructors) quickly turned the street-smart gang-banger into a Marine through intense physical drills, mental training, and instruction.

Emmett started as a wisecracking, tough-as-nails guy, thinking he could defy the system. But this wasn't his Marine drill instructor, Sgt. Roger Loughran's first rodeo; he had dealt with street tuffs before and quickly set Emmett straight. After graduating from boot camp, Emmett became a corporal, applied, and was accepted into the Marines' most elite unit, the Marine Raider Regiment.

The Marine Raiders are elite units that conduct special amphibious light infantry warfare. They are the equivalents of the Navy SEALs. He was told that if he were accepted, due to the extensive training program he would have to go through, he would need to extend his enlistment by an additional six years. He was accepted and did so.

During a 16-hour firefight with the Taliban in the Garmsir District, Helmand Province, Afghanistan, Corporal Emmett Washington, serving with B Company, Battalion Landing Team, 3rd Battalion, 8th Marine Regiment, 14th Marine Expeditionary Unit, II Marine Expeditionary Force, received a Silver Star and a Purple Heart for his actions.

As gunfire rained down on their position, Corporal Washington immediately provided cover fire in hopes that his squad could find shelter. Washington leapt from the driver's seat of his Humvee to man an M240G machine gun and sprayed rounds into the mountainside. At the same time, his platoon sergeant fired a barrage of Mark 47 Striker 40 automatic grenade launcher rounds.

He noticed his corpsman was wounded as they were advancing on the enemy. Washington jumped out of the vehicle and sprinted a hundred meters through enemy lines to retrieve and tend to the corpsman's wounds. He then carried the wounded man back to the safety of the Humvee.

The enemy's position became more difficult to locate, and their sniper fire was extremely accurate. Once back at the vehicle, the squad managed injuries and constant fire, but they were reassured that reinforcements were on the way.

A sniper's shot hit Washington, damaging his night vision goggles and Kevlar helmet, causing the bullet to fragment and enter the right side of his skull. Despite being wounded, Corporal Washington kept firing more than two hundred grenade rounds from an M293 grenade launcher mounted beneath his service rifle at the enemy.

Two hours later, three UH-60 Black Hawk helicopters landed in the danger zone, evacuating the severely wounded. Under cover of the Black Hawks, the Raiders managed to retreat to a safe location where the other wounded Marines were evacuated.

During his three completed tours in Afghanistan, Sergeant Emmett Washington received one Navy Cross, two Silver Star Medals, and two Bronze Star Medals.

Emmett was sent to Baghdad to start the process of leaving the Marines before returning to the States. While in Baghdad, he and a couple of Marine friends came across a strange situation where tourists paid a fee to punch a drugged tiger in the head and then took pictures with the tiger. He was appalled. He couldn't believe that such a thing was permitted.

A large crowd stood around, watching and laughing. Corporal Washington stepped forward and shouted, "Stop this! What the Hell is going on here!"

The four men, who appeared to be the tiger's owners, started shouting and yelling at the Marines to leave.

Standing beside Emmett, a man in the crowd said, "This sort of thing should not be allowed."

"I agree. I'm going to see about getting the police."

"Won't do any good. They'll do nothing," The man said.

Emmett asked, "Are you stationed here?"

"Me? No, I'm with Le Gang de la Clé de Singe. Ever hear of us?"

"The animal rights organization?"

"That's putting it mildly. My name is Odin."

"Sergeant Emmett Washington."

"A pleasure. How long are you here for?"

"I'm actually on my way out. My tour is almost over."

"Well, we are also always looking for a few good men, as they say. Here, take my card. Once you're out and if you're interested, give a call, and someone will get back to you."

Washington took the card and looked at it. Just a phone number. 888.634.5789, nothing else. And he placed it in his pocket.

"So, what can we do to stop this?" Emmett asked Odin.

"This," Odin said as he pulled a Glock 9mm pistol from behind his back and fired four rounds, striking each of the four men surrounding the tiger.

People, including Emmett and his three friends, hit the ground as an old red Toyota pickup pulled up. Four individuals wearing black Ninja outfits jumped out, placing the drugged tiger in the bed of the pickup. They then tied a yellow banner around each of the dead men's necks, stuffed a piece of paper into their pockets, and drove away.

Once the truck had gone, people continued with their day as if nothing had happened, walking past the bodies of the four dead men lying in the street.

After three tours of duty and all the senseless killings, this incident was relatively mild in comparison.

Emmett eventually returned home to Birmingham but struggled to find a good job. He received many 'Thank you for your service' messages but few job offers. He ultimately took a job as a security guard with Alabama

Power Company, the electric company serving more than 1.4 million customers in southern Alabama. After just three months, he was bored out of his mind.

At the Birmingham Zoo on Tiger Day, he was with his brothers and sisters and their families one day. The zoo was celebrating Kumar the Tiger's birthday; the Malayan tiger was turning seventeen. There were stories, games, exhibits, and seminars to raise awareness of the plight of the world's tiger population.

While listening to a man discuss the challenges of tiger research, poaching, and the impact of big game hunting on the tiger's future at the Safari Café, Emmett opened his wallet. He took out the card Odin gave him in Baghdad.

"Hello," A monotone voice said.

"I'm calling to speak to Odin," Emmett said.

"Odin isn't here at the moment. Can I help you?"

"Odin suggested that I call this number."

"What is this in reference to? If you don't mind my asking."

"He said I should call if interested in joining Le Gang de la Clé de Singe."

"Did he? When was this?"

"Baghdad. A little over a year ago."

"And who might you be?"

"Emmet Washington, from Birmingham, Alabama."

"And what do you do, Emmett Washington, from Birmingham, Alabama?"

"Currently, I'm a security guard with Alabama Power. And prior to that, I was a sergeant in the Marine Raiders for eight years."

"Could you hold on for a moment, Emmett?"

"Sure."

Several minutes of silence passed. When, finally, a different voice answered.

"Hello, Emmett. My name is Samson. I wonder if you'd be interested in meeting with me tomorrow evening—

say around eight o'clock—to discuss potential employment."

"Tomorrow night? Sure. Where?"

"Vulcan Park."

"Where? It's a big park."

"Outside the Vulcan Center, wear a plain red baseball cap—no logos, just plain red."

"How will I recognize you?"

"You won't. Oh, and come alone."

CLICK

The next night at exactly 8 pm, standing at the base of the 56-foot Vulcan statue that overlooks the city atop Red Mountain in Vulcan Park, wearing a plain red baseball cap, Emmett Washington waited for someone he didn't know to approach him.

"Are you Emmett Washington?" A woman's voice said from behind.

He turned around and saw a tall, beautiful blonde woman wearing blue jeans, a plaid long-sleeve flannel shirt, cowboy boots, and a plain red baseball cap.

"Yes, I'm Emmett Washington. And you are?"

"My name is Venus."

"Venus? Venus, what?"

"Just Venus. Let's go sit and talk on that bench over there."

As they approached the bench, Emmett noticed a couple of men standing next to a pay-per-view binoculars, taking turns pretending to look at the stunning views from high on the red mountain. He figured they were there to protect Venus if things got rough.

"So, Venus, what part of the Ukraine are you from?" Emmett asked.

"Mmmm, very good. I'm from Yuzhne, just outside of Odessa. And you?" She asked, smiling.

"Born and raised right here in Birmingham."

"So, Emmett Washington, why are you interested in joining Le Gang de la Clé de Singe?"

Well, I suppose I need another cause to fight for—something meaningful. I looked into Le Gang de la Clé de Singe, and after sorting through all the political biases, I basically agree with the principles you stand for.

"We ask this of everyone. We are all willing to do whatever it takes and die for our beliefs. Are you?"

"I am," He said without hesitation.

"Prove it," Venus said as she handed Emmett a pair of rubber gloves and a Smith & Wesson Model 10 .38 Special revolver. The serial number had been filed down so the gun would be untraceable.

"See that man wearing the blue and white striped rugby jersey?"

"Yeah."

"That's Roland Jameson, owner of Jamie's Deli Barn and an international big game hunter. Have you heard of him?"

"Sure."

"On his last trip to Africa, he posted on Twitter that he shot and killed three male lions in a single day."

"You want me to kill him in cold blood?"

"The man has killed more wildlife than he's sold corned beef sandwiches. Yes, I want you to kill him. That's what we do, Emmett. If his death prevents others from needlessly killing, then his dying won't be in vain."

Emmett stood looking at Jameson, trying to decide whether or not to take that step. Once he crosses that line, there's no turning back.

"You can give me back the gun and walk away, no hard feelings. We know that not everyone has what it takes for this kind of life. You can return to your nine-to-five security guard job, Emmett. That's fine. "

He slipped on the rubber gloves and said, "Let's go."

They approached Roland Jameson, who appeared to be waiting for someone. As they moved closer, Venus whispered, "Once you shoot him, drop the gun and walk away slowly. You'll see a white and red Ford Bronco in the parking lot. A man with a bushy beard will be behind the wheel. His name is Tolstoy. Get into the front passenger seat and wait; I'll be along shortly."

Jameson turned as he heard footsteps approaching him from behind. He smiled.

Venus smiled back and asked, "Excuse me, are you Roland Jameson?"

"Yes, have we met?"

"No, we haven't. Mr. Jameson, have you ever heard of Le Gang de la Clé de Singe?"

The look of realization spread across his face as he saw the gun in Emmett's hand. Before he could say a word, a flash came from the gun's muzzle, and a roaring noise erupted.

BOOM

Emmett dropped the gun and did as he was told; he slowly walked away. He glanced over his shoulder and saw Venus placing a yellow object around the man's neck. He made it to the Bronco and sat in the passenger's seat. The driver, Tolstoy, said nothing. He sat watching with a Glock 9mm on his lap. The man was on high alert.

Minutes later, Venus walked to the Bronco and got into the passenger's rear seat. The three of them pulled away. As they exited the park, several Birmingham police cars passed by.

Tolstoy finally spoke, "How'd it go?" He asked.

"Went very well. I think we have a promising new member. Tolstoy, this is Emmett; Emmett, this is Tolstoy."

"Nice to meet you," Tolstoy said.

"You too," Emmett replied.

He half turned towards Venus and asked, "What's with the names Odin, Venus, and Tolstoy? What gives?"

"Everyone chooses a name—an alias to go by. That is why if you or someone else gets captured, you can only tell them people's aliases. It's for everyone's protection."

"Got it. Makes sense."

"So, who will you be?" She asked.

"Vulcan, the Roman god of fire and forge," Emmett said proudly.

"I like it. Whad'ya think Tolstoy?"

"Excellent. Welcome to the cause, Vulcan."

☠☠☠☠☠☠☠☠☠☠☠

When Bellator broke into Robert Lewis' apartment, he found him alone and fast asleep. He only woke up briefly after Bellator injected him with a dose of propofol, which sent him back into a deep sleep.

Lewis was unaware that the Blue Team had begun administering large doses of melanin and exposure to UV rays.

Melanin is a dark brown to black pigment found in people's and animals' hair, skin, and the iris of the eye. It is responsible for tanning skin exposed to sunlight. When produced in excess and combined with overexposure to UV rays, it can permanently darken the skin.

After twelve hours of an IV drip with saline solution and large amounts of Melanin and constantly turning him like a rotisserie chicken every half hour, Robert Lewis, who was once a proud member of the South African white supremacist group the Afrikaner Weerstandsbeweging, was now as black as the ace of spades.

When Lewis was finally revived, he discovered himself tied up and gagged with restraints securing him to a chair in his living room. He was completely naked, sitting in front of a full-length mirror.

From behind the gag came a muffled scream.

EEEYYYAAAHHH!!

Robert Lewis looked into the mirror and couldn't understand what he saw. It was him, but not him. He was now Black; they had shaved his long blonde hair. Robert Lewis was staring at a bald Black man where a long-haired blonde white had once sat.

Sue B, wearing her Shinobi Shozoku ninja uniform, walked in from the kitchen after hearing his suppressed scream.

"So, Mr. Lewis, Whad'ya think?" She asked.

MMMPPPHHH!!

"I hear ya. I mean, you're expecting to get the heads and skins of a couple of endangered white giraffes, and then POW, here you sit, black as tar. Weird."

MMMPPPHHH!!

"I know, and on top of that, you took a whole lot of money from a Russian oligarch. Who, from what I hear, isn't all that understanding when he doesn't get what he's paid for."

MMMPPPHHH!!

Sue B took her revolver from behind her back, pointed it at Lewis, and said, "If I remove your gag and you start to scream, I'll have to kill you. You understand?" She said as she screwed the silencer onto the gun's barrel.

He nodded, and she ungagged him.

"What have you done?" He asked, panicked.

"We turned a South African bigot into, what is the derogatory term your racists call black people? Oh, yeah, Kaffir. You, Mr. Lewis, are now a Kaffir."

"Why?"

"Oh, for the same reason that you kill and mutilate endangered species. Because we don't care." She said coldly as she stuffed the gag back into his mouth.

"Now I'm going to give you an injection that will knock you out for an hour or so. We'll lay you back in your bed, and by the time you wake up, we'll be long gone."

MMMPPPHHH!!

As she was preparing to give him a small dose of propofol, she looked down at his crotch and giggled in his ear, "Mmmm, it's too bad that we couldn't make you black all over. Sleep tight, sunshine."

The knocking on the door woke Lewis from a deep sleep. At first, he thought it was just a weird dream until he looked at his hand. As the knocking grew louder, he jumped out of bed and hurried to put on khaki Docker shorts.

He stealthily looked through the peephole in the door. There stood Sergey Chernyshevsky, with two goons standing behind him, looking ominous. He could see that Chernyshevsky was angry. The Russian turned to one of his goons and said something in Russian, who nodded in acknowledgment. They all left.

Lewis tiptoed to the window overlooking the parking lot. He watched as the three of them climbed into Chernyshevsky's steel gray 2018 GLS 580 Mercedes SUV and waited there in the parking lot.

Lewis stood in front of the full-length mirror in horror. He was black from the top of his shaved head to the tips of his toes. His life, as he knew it, would be forever changed. The first scary thought that popped into his head was how he would get money from the bank; all his IDs were useless.

First things first, he had to get out of town without Chernyshevsky seeing him. Chernyshevsky wasn't a forgiving man; Lewis had heard stories of what he had done to those who crossed him. Those people were never seen or heard from again. He did have one big advantage: Chernyshevsky wouldn't be looking for a black man.

Lewis packed a change of clothes in a backpack along with some personal items. He dressed in worn-out blue jeans, an old sweatshirt, Converse sneakers, sunglasses, and a blue baseball cap. Then, he walked out of the building right in front of Chernyshevsky and his henchmen. He left his Land Rover Discovery in the garage and headed into town to the Bank of Africa. The Changamwe branch is located in the Mombasa Cage Inn Hotel building. He inserted his debit card into the ATM and withdrew the maximum amount of 5500 Kenyan shillings, about five hundred US dollars.

He took a cab to the Mombasa SGR train station to catch the A3 to Nairobi, which departs Mombasa in 45 minutes. While waiting for the train, he noticed two thug-like men inspecting every white man.

He boarded the train to Nairobi and connected to the train going to South Africa. He couldn't use his original passport, so while in Nairobi, he purchased a false passport under the name of Kevin Mwimbi, one of the poachers who was recently killed in the white giraffe debacle.

After weeks of traveling, he finally settled in Wolmaransstad, a maize-farming town located between Johannesburg and Kimberley. Lewis understood he needed to stay under the radar, so he reserved a room at the Kenalemang S Shack, a mainly black guest house near the Caltex service station where he worked as a pump jockey and mechanic.

One day, a steel gray GLS 580 Mercedes SUV, the passenger side tinted window rolled down slightly, and a Banish 45 9mm handgun silencer peeked out.

PHIFF

Robert Lewis died instantly from a gunshot to the forehead as the Mercedes sped away. It was never confirmed, but rumors suggest that Chernyshevsky discovered him hiding in the small town of Leeu-Gamka in the Western Cape province of South Africa. He was working, pumping gas at a Shell station off the R353 highway.

Rumor has it that Chernyshevsky received an anonymous package in the mail. The envelope included photographs of Robert Lewis disguised as a black man with a postmark from Wolmaransstad, South Africa. Also in the package was a yellow banner with a black skull and crossed monkey wrenches.

Four weeks after Robert Lewis was shot to death, the Blue Team visited Chernyshevsky's private mansion on the island of Montserrat. They found him sunning himself by his pool. He was in the company of two beautiful young women in string bikinis lying on either side of him. His two goons stood nearby behind him; they were supposed to be acting as bodyguards but were too busy ogling the two nymphs sunning topless.

Had they paid attention and done their jobs, they might have had a chance to survive. But alas, no. Odin fired two bullets at once, and Lu Wei silently took down the two thugs where they once stood.

Venus, Bellator, and Vulcan approached the three sun worshipers dressed in their Shinobi Shozoku ninja uniforms. Venus and Bellator each carried a Sig Sauer P226 pistol with QDL Silencer Suppressors. Vulcan held a Barebones Living Japanese Nata tool, a 24-inch chisel-tipped blade machete. Vulcan spent hours honing and sharpening the blade until he claimed it could slice a piece of meat so thin that it had only one side.

"On your feet!" Shouted Venus, pointing her pistol at the three sunbathers.

The two girls screeched and tried to cover themselves; Chernyshevsky defiantly took his time standing. He glanced behind him to see that his two guards were lying dead behind him.

"What is it you want?" He demanded.

Vulcan stood before Chernyshevsky, "Have you heard of Le Gang de la Clé de Singe, Mr. Chernyshevsky?"

"*Da*," He answered.

"Any last words?" Vulcan asked.

"*Poshel na khuy*!" He snarled.

"Fuck me? No, fuck you," Vulcan said as he started to lift his machete. In a flash, he swung it and then lowered it back to his side.

Chernyshevsky stood looking at Vulcan and laughed, "You missed!"

Looking Chernyshevsky in the eye, Vulcan softly said, "Shake your head."

As Chernyshevsky did, his head fell off his shoulders and bounced into the pool. The two young escorts fainted and collapsed; they were placed back onto the pool lounges unconscious.

By the time they awoke, the three bodies were laid next to each other with yellow ensigns of Le Gang de la Clé de Singe draped around their necks.

The severed head was still floating in the pool. It remained there until the police, who had received an anonymous phone call, arrived at the scene of the heinous crime at the private residence of Sergey Chernyshevsky.

Aside from the dead bodies and two hysterical bikini-clad women running around the scene, rambling incoherently about a group of Japanese ninjas attacking and killing Sergey Chernyshevsky, the police discovered a 24-inch chisel-tipped blade machete with a single fingerprint. After analyzing the print through COCIS (Combined DNA Index System), they identified a match. However, the authorities were quite puzzled when the results indicated that the print belonged to the former Premier of the Soviet Union, Nikita Khrushchev.

The authorities also found a Russian flag flying on the flagpole in his front yard and the yellow ensign of Le Gang de la Clé de Singe beneath it.

While the Blue Team was handling Sergey Chernyshevsky, the Red Team was sent to Hamburg, Germany. There has been a lot of chatter about the torture of animals for so-called medical experiments at Das Reinhart Laboratorium von Pharmakologie und Toxikologie.

There have been numerous reports from animal rights groups, along with smuggled out photographs and videos revealing the horrific and hellish living conditions of monkeys, cats, dogs, and rabbits that are tortured daily.

One of the most distressing and disturbing videos showed monkeys chained to the wall with metal neck braces, screaming in agony during tests. Another video depicts cats and dogs left bleeding and abandoned to die in their own filth after toxicity testing. The video that provoked widespread outrage was of animals being intentionally poisoned to see how much of the chemical they could endure before dying. It looked like a scene straight out of Nazi concentration camp experiments.

Several animal rights groups tried taking legal action to shut down the laboratory, but it was unsuccessful. The leadership of Le Gang de la Clé de Singe decided that the time for playing nice is over, so they're sending in the Red Team.

The Red Team arrived at Flughafen Hamburg on KLM flight 598 from Cape Town, South Africa. As they deplaned in Terminal 1, they were directed to go through the arduous task of clearing customs. The process took over two hours until the whole team made it through customs.

When they finally stepped outside, a middle-aged man in a black chauffeur's uniform held a sign that said, Ms. Lóng. Fu Hao was quite amused when she saw it; Lóng means dragon in Chinese.

"That's us," She announced to the group.

"Ms. Lóng?" The man asked.

"That's me," She said.

"Very good. Do you need any help with your baggage?" He asked.

"No. We're good. As you can see, we travel light."

"Please follow me. The car is right outside."

The six of them did as they were asked. Sitting at the curb, a midnight blue BMW Alpina XB7 SUV was parked.

"My name is Vermeer." The chauffeur said as they were all secure inside the vehicle and driving away from the airport.

Fu Hao made the introductions for everyone to their contact, Vermeer.

"Have you been with the organization long?" Fu Hao asked.

"About six years. How about you?"

"Close to ten. Me and Sue B joined together."

"Yeah, I've heard of you two. Super snipers, they say."

"Nay, don't go believing everything you hear." Fu Hao said.

A voice from the back seat said, "She's just being modest. Both of them can knock out a gnat's eye at a hundred yards," Cowboy said.

"How about you, Vermeer?" Sue B asked.

"Oh, me? I'm a bit of a handyman," He said.

"Now, who's being modest?" Fu Hao stated.

"Don't let this mild manner fool you. Mr. Vermeer here is also known as the "Der Todesengel," the Angel of

Death, or "Das Gespenst," the Ghost. I've heard that once the man placed crumpled newspapers and bubble wrap around his bed to detect whether someone approached. They were dead!" Sue B said.

"So, you're *Der Todesengel*," Cowboy said with reverence. "It's an honor, sir."

"Enough!" Vermeer insisted.

They drove in silence for a few moments before Vermeer announced, "I have booked us all rooms at the Hotel Hafen Hamburg. It's quite a historic hotel located overlooking the Norderelbe River. I got us all rooms overlooking the river. I thought that once we checked in, we could all meet in the Tower Bar for drinks."

"Good idea," Fu Hao said as they pulled into the entrance drive, where three bellmen rushed to assist.

"I've already checked in, so I'll see you all upstairs in an hour. Is that all right?"

"Perfect," Sue B said.

The following day, after breakfast, Vermeer had the BMW Alpina XB7 SUV waiting in front of the hotel. Once everyone was aboard, Vermeer pulled out of the driveway and made a left onto Bernhard-Nocht-Straße until he came to a roundabout, then onto St. Pauli Fischmarkt, which ran parallel to the river.

St. Pauli Fischmarkt eventually became Klopstockstraße, which led to the Elbtunnel, which ran under the Elbe River to the south side of Hamburg, the more industrial warehouse area.

Before reaching the lab, Vermeer stopped at an all-brick house set back from the street, hidden behind a six-foot hedge. The driveway was gated and guarded by two German Shepherds.

Vermeer pulled up to the gate, got out, walked up to the dogs, and commanded, "Sitzen! Bleibe!"

After they sat down and remained there, Vermeer opened the gate and drove in; the dogs never moved. He turned to the Red Team and said, "It's okay; they won't bother you. Come on inside."

Inside, it seemed more like a warehouse than a home. There were various weapons, explosives, ammunition, clothing for different combat scenarios, foodstuffs, and electronic gear—everything one would need for war. Since the teams rarely traveled with their gear and weapons from one assignment to another, they were continually reoutfitted wherever they went. Most of the time, they traveled with only the clothes on their backs.

After everyone was suited up, they reviewed the plan once more. They all gathered around a large conference table in the living area. Vermeer had a schematic of the laboratory. The plan was for Hazael to enter the laboratory dressed as a Securitas troubleshooter, claiming he detected an issue in their security system that he needed to check on.

Once inside, he cuts the phone lines, the security system, and internet access. After that, he radios the team, and they enter the building dressed in all-black Secret Service paramilitary uniforms, wearing black balaclavas and brandishing assault weapons.

At the same time, several animal rights advocates will capture and relocate all the animals to animal sanctuaries.

☠☠☠☠☠☠☠☠☠☠☠

Hazael wearing a Securitas uniform strolled up to the receptionist and said, "*Guten Morgen, ich bin hier, um Ihr Sicherheitssystem zu überprüfen.*"

The receptionist looked perplexed until Hazael presented her with a work order stating that Securitas had detected an issue that needed immediate attention.

She smiled and said, "*Einen moment bitte.*" As she called someone. Hazael stood waiting for a few minutes until a man in a lab coat came out and asked him skeptically, "Ich bin Herr Schmidt. *Was ist los mit dir*?"

Hazael explained that he was there to investigate an issue the company had discovered while monitoring the system. But if Herr Schmidt was satisfied that everything was okay and willing to take responsibility if something should fail, all he had to do was initial this form, and Hazael would be on his way.

Usually, when someone has to take responsibility for making a decision that could come back to bite them in the ass, they will always take the less controversial choice so they can blame someone else.

Hazael shrugged and started to walk out when the man hollered, "*Warten! Geh weiter*."

Hazael smiled and asked where the security control panel was located.

"*Keller*," The receptionist said as she pointed to a door leading to the basement off to the left of the receptionist's desk.

The basement was filled with lab and office equipment along with animal cages. The security control panel was on the opposite wall from the stairs, hidden behind numerous stacked cages. Hazael quickly opened the panel door and disabled the security system, all communications, phone lines, and internet service. He also sent a signal to his Securitas company van, which was equipped with an industrial cell phone jamming dish aimed directly at the Das

Reinhart Laboratorium von Pharmakologie und Toxikologie building. Now, all cell phones were disabled.

"All systems down. Go! Go! Go!" Hazel radioed.

☠☠☠☠☠☠☠☠☠☠☠

Within minutes, a group of imposing figures wearing paramilitary uniforms, brandishing assault weapons, entered the building, shouting that this was a raid and that everyone was to get on the ground.

"Dies ist ein Überfall. Jeder am Boden!"

The Red Team quickly moved through the building, rounding up and separating the clerical workers from management and those who did the experiments.

The clerical staff were placed in a large conference room, with their hands and feet zip-tied. Mouths gagged. The researchers and lab workers were taken into a room where more than a dozen monkeys were being forced to stand by having their necks clamped in a metal neck brace.

The workers' hands were zip-tied, and they were told to stand together against the wall while animal rescuers removed all the animals. Every animal, from monkeys to tiny mice, was taken and transported to animal sanctuaries all around the country.

The company's President, Helmut Werner, was caught trying to disguise himself as a janitorial worker; unfortunately for him, Le Gang de la Clé de Singe had several inside informants who could identify everyone responsible.

"Herr Werner, sprichst du Englisch?" Odin asked.

Werner nodded and replied, "Yes."

Fu Hao held up the yellow banner and asked, "Have you ever heard of Le Gang de la Clé de Singe?"

"Of course. But we are not hunters; we are doing vital medical research. These are not endangered species. These are just ordinary monkeys, cats, and dogs." Werner said dispassionately.

"Would you say that you treat these ordinary animals humanely and with dignity?" Sue B asked.

"Humanely? They are just… animals. You're upset that we use them for medical experiments, so if they die, they die. They are here to help save human lives. If they die in the search for a cure for cancer, would you still care about them?" Werner said smugly.

Odin asked, "Is that what these experiments are for, a cure for cancer?"

Werner's attitude changed from smug to one of contrition. "Not exactly."

"What exactly?" Odin asked.

"We're doing experiments for a cosmetic manufacturer."

"Cosmetics!" Fu Hao sneered as she and Sue B escorted Werner over to the metal neck braces attached to the wall and placed the metal harness snugly around his neck. They did the same with five others, securing them in the metal stanchions, men and women.

Hazael joined Odin, Fu Hao, and Sue B, where those responsible for the torture were gathered. He pulled out a piece of paper and began to read, "*Let it be known that Le Gang de la Clé de Singe declares a proclamation of war against all Poachers, Big Game Hunters, and all Big Game Safari Outfits, as well as anyone anywhere in the world that targets, kills, profits from, or supports the killing of any animals that are endangered or hunted for sport. Be forewarned, do so at your peril. You will be hunted down and pay with your lives. Whether man or woman, there will be no exceptions and no mercy; we will show no quarter. You have been warned.*"

He then read it in German: *"Lassen Sie uns wissen, dass Das Massaker an der Schraubenschlüsselb ande Kriegserklärung gegen alle Wilderer, Großwildjäger und alle Großwildsafari-Outfits sowie gegen jeden auf der Welt erklärt, der das Töten anvisiert, tötet, profitiert und / oder unterstützt von gefährdeten Tieren oder von Tieren, die für den Sport gejagt werden. Seien Sie gewarnt, tun Sie dies auf eigene Gefahr. Sie werden gejagt und zahlen mit Ihrem Leben. Sei es, Mann oder Frau, es wird keine Ausnahmen und keine Gnade geben; Wir werden kein Viertel zeigen. Du wurdest gewarnt."*

The Hamburg police arrived at Das Reinhart Laboratorium von Pharmakologie und Toxikologie after receiving an anonymous phone call reporting that Le Gang de la Clé de Singe had carried out a raid. The caller said they should be sure to bring a lot of body bags when they come.

By the time Detective Hans Müller arrived on the scene, hundreds of reporters and camera crews were crawling everywhere. Police had placed barriers surrounding the entire building and patrolled with guard dogs to keep reporters out.

"How bad is it?" Müller asked Officer Schäfer, one of the first responders.

"Thirty-six dead."

"Where?"

"Follow me," Schäfer said, leading the detective up to the third floor. Inside, thirty men and women lay neatly in five rows of six, all shot in the head. Each had a yellow insignia with a black skull and crossed monkey wrenches around their necks and had photographs of tortured animals placed on their chests. The remaining six, including

President Werner, were still attached to the wall in their neck braces, standing. Scattered among the human bodies were animals that had died from the lab's experiments.

Müller muttered, "*Jesus Christus*."

The following day, the headline in Germany's largest newspaper, the Süddeutsche Zeitung, read: "***DAS MASSAKER AN DER SCHRAUBENSCHLÜSSELB ANDE***." (The Monkey Wrench Gang Massacre)

Thirty-six researchers and staff were found shot to death at Das Reinhart Laboratorium von Pharmakologie und Toxikologie by the notorious murderous eco-terrorist group known as Le Gang de la Clé de Singe.

Sources inside the police tell this reporter that the human dead were mixed with the carcasses of animals, including monkeys, dogs, and cats, which were reportedly tortured at the lab.

An anonymous caller, claiming to represent Le Gang de la Clé de Singe, stated that the raid was in response to numerous complaints and lawsuits that were never resolved or dismissed. Meanwhile, hundreds of animals were being tortured, experimented on, and killed for trivial reasons such as testing cosmetics and hair dyes.

"Animals giving their lives to help the advance of medical research is one thing, but for such triviality is another, and in such a torturous way is unforgivable!

This aggression will not be tolerated. Take heed! Be it man or woman, there will be no exceptions and no mercy; we will show no quarter. You have been warned," the representative of Le Gang de la Clé de Singe declared.

The Hamburg Police Forensic Unit spent three weeks thoroughly searching the crime scene for any DNA samples, fingerprints, or physical evidence. They found nothing, nada, zip, except for a single fingerprint belonging to Mahatma Gandhi of India. That fact was never made public.

☠☠☠☠☠☠☠☠☠☠☠

Afterward, the Red Team disbanded and began traveling in pairs to different parts of Europe. They would all reconvene in one week at the entrance to the Basilica *Sagrada Família* in Barcelona, Spain.

The Sagrada Família Basilica, designed by the genius architect Antoni Gaudí, is known throughout the world as Barcelona's most famous monument. A project that started over 135 years ago and is scheduled to be completed in the year 2026.

Once everyone was in Barcelona, they would start on their next mission. It was decided that Vermeer would join them as a temporary team member for this mission.

Rolf Pflüger, also known as Vermeer, grew up in Stuttgart, Germany. The son of a political activist, his father was part of the *Hitlerjugend* (the Hitler Youth) during World War II, and his grandfather was a foot soldier in Hitler's Wehrmacht who was killed at the Battle of Stalingrad. Rolf's father, Willi, was twelve years old at the end of the war. In 1945, the *Volkssturm* (the People's Storm)—a national militia mainly made up of elderly men and boys in their pre- and early teens—was drafted to fight the advancing Russian and American troops closing in on Berlin. Willi and sixteen other boys were tasked with placing land mines in the streets to slow the Russian troops. Willi's war ended in less than four hours. Of the sixteen boys in his unit, only two survived. Willi and his friend Hans removed their uniforms and escaped with a group of elderly civilian women and other children, running into and hiding in an open field.

The Russians captured them, raped all of the women and girls regardless of their ages, and the boys were subjected to beatings.

Late one night, Willi and Hans managed to escape but were recaptured by the Americans, who treated them kindly.

Rolf's father spent the rest of his life trying to make up for the evils that Germany had perpetrated on the world. He was killed in 1999 by a group of neo-Nazi skinheads during a political rally.

Having seen what destruction and evil lies can reap, Rolf's father, Willi, dedicated his life to fighting for causes to improve the world. Rolf grew up in a family that believed in doing the right thing, not the easy thing, which was mainly going along with everyone else and not thinking for yourself. As a result, Rolf was considered an outsider, a loner.

While in college in West Berlin, Rolf took risks to help people in East Berlin escape to freedom. He also participated in demonstrations and protests against anti-nuclear weapons, a moratorium on dumping radioactive waste into the oceans, a ban on mineral extraction in Antarctica, and organized and helped establish the most successful orphaned elephant rescue and rehabilitation program.

Once, at a rally to save the golden eagle, Germany's official emblem, he was approached by a member of the local chapter of Le Gang de la Clé de Singe. A Russian man who called himself Rasputin. After explaining what Le Gang de la Clé de Singe was all about and that they had been watching him because of his military background, passion, and dedication to justice for the underdogs and down-trodden.

Rolf Pflüger, who speaks eight languages—German, English, French, Italian, Portuguese, Japanese, Russian, and Spanish—joined the movement three days later and chose the name Vermeer after Johannes Vermeer, the Dutch painter known for depicting domestic interior scenes of middle-class life during the Dutch Golden Age.

By three o'clock, all members of the Red Team had arrived at the designated meeting point, the entrance to the Sagrada Família Basilica. The last to arrive were Fu Hao and Sue B. They had been in contact with headquarters and received the mission details.

Their mission is to stop the systematic hunting and killing of the world's most endangered wild cat species, the Iberian Lynx. Currently, only 400 are known to live in the wild. Besides hunting the cats and habitat destruction, their main food source comes from local people snaring rabbits, which severely reduces the Lynx's prey population.

Tomorrow, they are heading off to Doñana National Park–a reserve in Andalusia, southern Spain, to put the fear of God into hunters and poachers.

Their local contact was Santiago Guzman. Guzman owns a large, family-owned bee farm called El Abejar, which has been passed down in the Guzman family for over three hundred years. He will meet the team in the lobby of the Hotel Colonial Barcelona, a charming hotel just a short distance from the Barcelona Port Vell in the historic Gothic Quarter, with La Rambla's street-food stalls, artisan leather shops, and Catalan restaurants.

The Red Team arrived at the hotel in three taxi cabs. As they entered, they were surprised by the magnificent and spacious lobby, since the exterior gave no hint of how modern the inside would be—polished dark mahogany floors with alternating brown and cream-colored overstuffed Chesterfield sofas. Over the reception desk hung a giant pair of stylized stained glass butterfly wings. The rooms were just as impressive. Compared to some hotels and hostels, not to mention the bivouacs they've endured, this was like staying at the Four Seasons.

They spent the evening wandering through La Rambla's street food stalls and shops. Ultimately, they all ended up at La Flor del Norte, where they sat and enjoyed tapas and drinks on Passeig de Colom, a wide avenue lined with palm trees that overlooks the harbor to the Balearic Sea.

By eleven, everyone had begun to return to the hotel around the corner. Five o'clock comes around quickly.

☠☠☠☠☠☠☠☠☠☠☠

Rolf Pflüger's first assignment for Le Gang de la Clé de Singe as Vermeer was to assassinate the kingpins of South Africa's most prolific wildlife trafficking gang, the Zhāng-Xu syndicate.

It was an unusual criminal operation since Quinhua Xu and Ju-long Zhāng, both Chinese nationals, were husband and wife. They ran their activities from their home in the affluent, gated community of Bishopscourt, Cape Town, South Africa.

Six Winchester Ave was a modest four-bedroom, four-bathroom house purchased for just over one million six hundred thousand dollars, paid for in cash. Their property bordered the Kirstenbosch National Botanical Gardens, offering a stunning view of Table Mountain from their backyard.

Due to crime in wealthy neighborhoods, most homes are surrounded by 10-foot-high walls topped with CCTV, metal spikes, electric fences, window burglar bars, and at least one panic button wired directly to an armed response team licensed to shoot to kill. Statistically, South Africa is one of the world's most dangerous places to live. For

Quinhua Xu and Ju-long Zhāng, it was about to get even worse.

Rolf Pflüger was traveling on a United States passport under the alias Jerry Mathis. When he went through customs in Cape Town, he told the agent he was there on business. He mentioned he planned to stay in Cape Town for a couple of weeks and that he would be staying at the Silo Hotel. The customs agent's reaction showed he was impressed.

"The Silo Hotel is very nice," The agent said.

"Yes, it looks very nice. I've never stayed there before, but I've heard nice things about it." Vermeer answered.

"And what do you do for a living?" The agent asked.

"I'm a writer."

"Books?"

"I wish. No, I'm a freelance writer. For business magazines. I'm doing an article about Sasol Limited."

"Well, have a good stay in Cape Town, and be careful."

"Yes, I've heard Cape Town can be dangerous."

☠☠☠☠☠☠☠☠☠☠☠

The Silo Hotel has been renovated from a 1924 grain-silo complex located on the Victoria & Albert Waterfront. It was once considered sub-Saharan Africa's tallest building, standing nearly 200 feet tall. The hotel has only 28 rooms, with rates starting at $1,400 and going up to $10,000 for the penthouse suite.

Once he exited Cape Town International Airport customs, Vermeer grabbed a taxi. The 30-minute ride to the hotel was smooth. Inside, he took the elevator up to the sixth-floor reception area. The concierge stood behind a blood-red reception desk, proudly wearing his Cles d'Or lapel pin on his Armani suit jacket next to his name tag, Henri.

"Good afternoon, sir, and welcome to the Silo. How may I assist you today?" He asked.

"I believe that you have a reservation for a Jerry Mathis."

After several clicks of the keypad, Henri smiled and said, "Yes sir, Mr. Mathis, we have you staying with us for three weeks. Is that correct?"

"That is correct, Henri."

"I see that you've requested a Superior Suite."

"Correct."

"Very good. We have you in 9A. It has a fabulous view of the waterfront."

"Excellent, Henri."

"Do you need any help with your luggage, sir?"

"Actually, no. As you can see, I travel pretty light." Vermeer said, holding up a medium-sized soft bag.

"Very good. And how many keys would you like?"

"Just one."

Henri handed Vermeer his key card, pointed to the elevator bay, and said, "If there is anything you need to make staying with us more enjoyable, please don't hesitate to ask me or any of our staff. I hope you enjoy your stay with us, Mr. Mathis."

"Thank you, Henri, you've been most kind."

Once Vermeer settled into the room, he called the front desk.

"Yes, Mr. Mathis, how may I help you?"

"Hello, Henri. I was hoping you might arrange a rental car for me?"

"Certainly, Mr. Mathis. What do you have in mind?"

"A Mercedes would be nice."

"I know that Hertz has the C-Class available. Would that be all right?"

"That would be fine, Henri."

"How soon do you need it, sir?"

"Whenever it's available."

"I call you when it arrives."

"Thank you, Henri."

"My pleasure, sir."

CLICK

Vermeer hung up the phone and put on his assassin 'uniform': black cargo pants, a lightweight black cashmere pullover, and a plain black ball cap. When the phone rang, he had just finished lacing up his Corcoran Combat Boots.

"Hello?"

"Mr. Mathis, there's a Ms. Imka here to see you. Shall I send her up?"

"Yes, thank you, Henri."

CLICK

Moments later, there was a knock on the door.

"It's open," Vermeer shouted.

The door opened slowly, revealing a beautiful woman in her 30s, about five-foot-eight, with dark skin. Her hair was styled in short box braids that fell to her shoulders, ending in colorful wooden beads. She wore a vibrant African-inspired V-neck jumpsuit decorated with patterns in oranges, blues, reds, and yellows. Her skin tone resembled a perfectly mixed White Russian.

She shut the door, smiled, and asked, "Mr. Mathis?"

Vermeer just nodded, as he was speechless by her beauty.

"Hello, I'm Imka, and I have something here for you," She said as she held up an aluminum Zero Halliburton travel case.

Vermeer took the case, placed it on the bed, and opened it. Inside was a special Mk13 'takedown' sniper rifle with a silencer that fit inside the 13x18-inch case and a Beretta 92FS 9mm fitted with an AL-GI-MEC suppressor.

Vermeer looked at Imka, grinned, and said, "Very impressive. Ammo?"

She held out a small backpack. "I'm sorry, but we couldn't fit everything into the case," she said with a touch of regret.

"No worries."

Imka said, "I have a diagram of the Zhāng- Xu's home for you as well."

"Great."

The hotel phone rang.

"Hello?"

"Mr. Mathis, your car has arrived."

"Thank you, Henri. Would you tell them I'll be right down?"

"Certainly, Mr. Mathis."

"Thank you, Henri."

CLICK

"Want to go for a drive?" Vermeer asked.

"Where?"

"Zhāng-Xu's place. And if you don't mind, you can drive while I study the house plans."

The Red Team reached Doñana National Park from Barcelona at 8 pm after stopping at a safe house in Seville to gear up with their weapons, gear, and ghillie suits. Once they arrived at the park, Hazael dropped them off and went on to Playa Mata del Difunto to set up the drone launch site.

The Red Team traveled on foot to Madre de las Marisma (Mother of the Marshes) and the Guadalquivir River, which runs through the park. At dawn, they would pack up and move to a known spot of the Iberian Lynx called Lucio del Lobo, the Wolf's Pike. There, they would wait as long as it takes to engage the hunters in battle.

Santiago Guzman took the point and led the Red Team to *Lucio del Lobo*. The terrain was ideal for their needs: initially flat grassland quickly sloping up into a hilltop covered with trees and shrubs, perfect for covering the A-team below.

Both teams were settled into position well before the sun rose over the marshlands and scrub woodlands. Sue B and her team were spread out a hundred yards apart, well hidden among the tall grasses.

"A-team leader to A team, come in," Sue B said.

"A1, check," Sassoon answered.

"A2, check," Gianfranco said.

Above them, Fu Hao's B-team was in position as well, hidden in the rocky tree-lined hill overlooking the A-team. They were also spread out, giving their teammates maximum coverage.

Because they anticipated a large group of hunters, the Red Team chose to use semi-automatic sniper rifles instead of the Sig Sauer bolt-action rifle. Sue B and Sassoon carried Savage Axis II XP semi-automatic sniper rifles equipped with QDL Silencer Suppressors. Gianfranco had an M1918 BAR Browning Automatic Rifle.

Up above, the B-team's Fu Hao and Cowboy were using Savage Axis II XP semi-automatic sniper rifles with QDL Silencer Suppressors. At the same time, Vermeer and Guzman were also issued BARs. Between the seven of them, they packed some significant firepower.

The teams spotted several Iberian lynxes at dawn around the edges of the meadows. They tend to stay stationary during the day and become active at dusk.

Hazael remained in close contact as the Hermes 900 UAV, an Israeli drone, circled overhead. It has a 36-hour flight time, powered by the Rotax 914 turbocharged, four-stroke, four-cylinder, horizontally opposed aircraft engine.

The seven of them lay in position until five-thirty that evening when they heard from Hazael.

"Red Drone to Red Leaders, over."

"Red Leader one, over," Sue B answered.

"Red Leader two, over," Fu Hao said.

"Red Leaders, this is Red Drone; I have what looks like twelve bogeys heading your way with an approximate ETA of twenty minutes. Over."

"Copy that," Fu Hao said.

"Copy," Sue B replied.

The twelve hunters would normally have hunted in pairs, but word had spread that Le Gang de la Clé de Singe was concentrating its efforts on protecting endangered species worldwide. They felt that there would be safety in numbers. They were all carrying brand new Savage Axis XP 6.5 Creedmoor Bolt Action Rifles. They were given the rifles free for joining the Worldwide Affiliates of Safari Partners, aka W.A.S.P., as part of a promotion to gain members and bolster their numbers.

Red Team observed that five of the hunters were carrying rabbit carcasses that they had snared to be used as bait for the lynx.

When the hunters reached the river's edge, a pair of female Lynxes and their cubs were approaching from the opposite side of the Guadalquivir.

"As soon as any of them takes aggressive action, open fire," Sue B whispered into her headset.

One of the hunters, a man who looked to be in his sixties, spotted the lynx; he raised his rifle and took aim through his scope as the others stood and watched.

Sue B whispered, "I got this." She aimed and fired one shot.

PHIFF

The hunters standing nearest to him were all sprayed with a fine red mist of blood and brains as his head exploded from the .308 that Sue B fired.

They stood frozen in complete disbelief and shock until a hail of bullets came raining down upon them.

PHIFF PHIFF PHIFF BAM BAM BLAM BLAM PHIFF PHIFF PHIFF BLAM BLAM BAM BAM BAM BAM BLAM BLAM BAM BAM BLAM BLAM PHIFF PHIFF PHIFF PHIFF PHIFF PHIFF BLAM BLAM BAM BLAM

As one of the hunters dived for cover, he shouted for the others to do the same, "*¡Ponerse a cubierto!*"

In the blink of an eye, seven hunters lay dead; the remaining five took cover and started to return fire.

POW POW POW POW POW POW POW POW

As skilled hunters as they were, they were no match for the battle-hardened Red Team. The fight ended nearly as quickly as it began. The air was thick with gun smoke, fear, and death. An eerie quiet settles over the battlefield, just like it always does after a deadly encounter.

With cover from Fu Hao's B-team, the A-team advanced across the river to assess the damage and check for survivors. There were none.

Sassoon radioed the B-team and gave the all-clear signal. By the time the B-team arrived, the bodies of the hunters and rabbits were all lined up next to each other in a single row. They then began placing the yellow ensigns around each hunter's necks, along with a copy of the proclamation in each of their pockets explaining why they were killed.

Hazael arrived to pick up the team after dismantling and stowing the drone in its trailer. He also brought several large wooden crates filled with hundreds of wild hares, which he released as the Red Team boarded the black Chevrolet Suburban.

The team made sure they left no evidence behind except for their trademark fingerprint, then piled into the vehicle dirty, smelly, and exhausted.

As Santiago Guzman got into the driver's seat, he quipped, "If we're lucky, within a year, this place will be up our eyeballs in wild hares."

Guzman drove the Red Team on the hour's journey to the port of Cádiz Bay, where they would catch the '*Marta Perez*', a Spanish cargo ship heading south to Walvis Bay, Namibia, Africa.

The Red Team said goodbye to Santiago Guzman, their local contact. Guzman will continue to monitor the Iberian Lynx to see if people have learned anything or if another encounter is necessary.

☠☠☠☠☠☠☠☠☠☠☠

Imka took the wheel of the silver Mercedes C 350 Sport. She headed down Nelson Mandela Blvd until it merged into the M3. They drove past the University of Cape Town, Newlands Forest, and the Kirstenbosch National Botanical Garden to the Bishopscourt section of Newlands.

Six Winchester Avenue sat back off the road by a good three hundred feet down a long, straight driveway. The red brick driveway was lined on either side with Olinia ventosa trees, also known as the hard-pear tree, which can grow over 20 meters tall. These trees were a mere 10 meters tall.

A ten-foot stucco-covered concrete fence with electrified metal spikes and a double row of razor wire surrounded the property. Vermeer observed several CCTV cameras spaced at twenty-foot intervals and at least six German Shepherd guard dogs patrolling the yard freely.

"What do you think?" Imka asked.

Vermeer smiled and said coyly, “Piece of cake.”

He had her drive past the house two more times, once around 10 pm and again at 4 am. He surveyed the back of the house from a spot in the Kirstenbosch National Botanical Gardens and the front from the Liesbeek River Park across the street.

Vermeer spent the better part of two weeks scouting and observing the comings and goings of the Quinhua Xu and Ju-long Zhāng. He ascertained that at any given time, there would be at least six to eight additional members of the gang staying at the house.

He decided to attack in broad daylight when they would least expect it. During his two-week observation of the house, he noticed a blind spot in the CCTV. A small shed behind the house was used for monitoring and controlling the electric fence, the CCTV cameras, and the alarm system. The shed was surrounded by eight-foot chain-link fences that kept the dogs away, preventing them from being attacked if a repairman needed to work.

Vermeer had Imka drop him off inside Kirstenbosch National Botanical Gardens as soon as they opened. He wore his ‘uniform’ and carried a backpack over his shoulder.

Making his way to the back of Quinhua Xu and Ju-long Zhāng’s house, Vermeer took several hours to assemble, load his weapons, and prepare for battle.

He took an R29X Crossbow and fired an arrow into the telephone pole next to the electronics shed. A thin but extremely strong metal cable was attached to the arrow shaft, and he secured the other end of the cable to a Jackal berry tree.

As he was preparing to cross over to the house, he noticed an armed man who appeared to be on sentry duty noticing the wire. Vermeer quickly grabbed the Mk13 sniper rifle with a silencer, aimed, and fired, hitting the man in the back of the head as he was transfixed on the arrow with the cable attached. A fine red mist painted the left side of the electronic shed as the man collapsed to the ground.

Vermeer transversed across the cable over the electrified fence until he stood atop the electronic shed. He remained still for several minutes, waiting to see if he had been noticed.

He then dropped to the ground, opened the shed door, and disconnected all the CCTV and security alarm systems. When he finished, he climbed onto the main house's roof and entered the attic through a dormer window. The attic was immaculately clean; it appeared never to have been used.

He slowly walked on the strutting beams, carefully avoiding making any noise towards the attic access door where an attic ladder would have been attached. But there was no ladder, which was good news for the assassin. Attic ladders tend to make a lot of noise, impeding the stealth needed when assassinating a large group of potentially heavily armed men.

Vermeer cracked the access door to see or hear if he could ascertain if anyone was nearby.

SILENCE

He was about to open the access door when he heard somebody approaching. It was an armed Asian man carrying an Israeli open-bolt, blowback-operated Uzi submachine gun. Vermeer reached into his boot and grabbed a six-foot-long piece of piano wire. He quickly fashioned a noose, quietly opened the access door, snagged the man around the neck, and hoisted him three feet off the ground while swiftly attaching the other end of the wire to an attic rafter until the man died. He then pulled the body into the ceiling through the attic access door.

He shut the attic door while he completed the flag ritual. Once that was completed, he dropped down from the attic and walked through the upstairs, looking for Xu and Zhāng. All the bedrooms were empty.

Downstairs, he could hear panicked Asian voices. He guessed they realized the CCTV and security system were down. The sound of several men running up the stairs reminded Vermeer of a cattle stampede. Vermeer entered the master bedroom, shut the door, and waited.

He didn't have to wait long. The door gradually creaked open, and three men armed with various firearms cautiously stepped into the room. They searched the area for the intruder, but unfortunately, they failed to look up. Sitting on the built-in shelf above the bedroom door was Vermeer, clutching the strangled man's Uzi.

TTRATT RATT TRATT TARAT TTRATTT TRATT RATT TRATT TARAT TTRATTT TRATT RATT TRATT TARAT TTRATTT

Vermeer heard the front door fling open and footsteps running away from the house as he walked down the stairs to the lower floor.

When he got to the front door, he saw a small Asian man and woman, Quinhua Xu and Ju-long Zhāng, ru-engine-wards a fire engine red Mercedes-Benz SLS AMG.

Ju-long Zhāng was shouting, "Where are the dogs? Where are the dogs?"

Vermeer pointed to the six sleeping German Shepherds sleeping off the drug induced steaks that he fed them before jumping the fence.

"They're over there!" He hollered.

Vermeer stood in the doorway and watched as the red Mercedes-Benz SLS AMG blew up into a gigantic fireball when Ju-long Zhāng hit the ignition switch.

BARROOOMM

"Ah, now that's a waste of a $206,000 piece of machinery," Vermeer said to himself.

He went back into the house, went upstairs to 'flag' his victims, and placed a note in each of their pockets, declaring that they were all killed for animal trafficking and poaching. As he was leaving, he could hear the sirens of the police and fire departments approaching.

He then retraced his steps back into the Kirstenbosch National Botanical Gardens, walked back the same way he came, and met Imka waiting for him in the parking lot.

"How did it go?" Imka asked.

"Smooth as Chinese silk," He said with a wolfish grin.

"Good evening. I'm Nigel Williams, and this is the BBC World Headline News. Our top story this hour comes from Cape Town, South Africa, where there are reports that seven members of the Zhāng–Xu Syndicate were brutally murdered by the international eco-terrorist group known as Le Gang de la Clé de Singe.

A spokesperson from the South African Police Service told the BBC that four gang members were found shot; one appeared to be garroted, while Quinhua Xu and Ju-long Zhāng were burned to death when their Mercedes SLS exploded from a car bomb.

The Zhāng-Xu Syndicate was under investigation for wildlife trafficking involving pangolin scales, rhino horns, ivory, and hippo teeth. A government official stated they exploited South Africa's natural resources, harmed the economy, fueled corruption, and threatened national security.

Although the government of South Africa does not condone Le Gang de la Clé de Singe's actions, it is not sorry that the Zhāng-Xu Syndicate is out of business.

Meanwhile, in other news……"

☠☠☠☠☠☠☠☠☠☠☠

The South African Police Service forensic unit discovered incriminating evidence and multiple fingerprints belonging to other Chinese nationals with criminal records at Zhāng-Xu's residence. The fingerprint seemed oddly out of place — it was found on a rafter in the attic. That fingerprint belonged to the late Hong Kong/American actor Bruce Lee.

This fact was never released to the public.

☠☠☠☠☠☠☠☠☠☠☠

When Vermeer and Imka returned to the Silo Hotel, everyone was talking about the attack by the Zhāng – Xu syndicate. As Vermeer passed the front desk, Henri asked, "Have you heard about the massacre of the Chinese illegal wildlife traffickers, Mr. Mathis?"

"Yes, I did, Henri. I heard it on the car radio. I'm curious, what are your thoughts on the subject?" Vermeer asked.

"Well, personally, while I don't normally approve of violence, I find the poaching, mutilating, and killing of animals to be unconscionable. So, I think they got what they deserved. I hope I didn't offend you, Mr. Mathis."

"Not at all, Henri. I appreciate your honesty."

"Thank you, sir. I hope you have a pleasant evening."

"You as well."

Vermeer and Imka made their way to the bank of elevators.

"Care for some dinner?" He asked.

"Hmmm, that would be nice," She said.

"Great. What do you recommend?"

"Feeling adventurous?"

"Always," He said with a grin.

"Belly of the Beast."

"Sounds intriguing."

"There are no menu options or set number of courses. We show up and trust them to satisfy us with seasonal fairness."

"Perfect."

That evening, they started with fresh mussels as an appetizer. Then came several small plates: venison medallions with creme fraiche, locally caught hake with gruner veltliner, Greenfield's beef tongue with spider pig grenache, pap & vleis (cornmeal with meat) with doolhof pinotage, and finally, they finished off the meal with deconstructed baked Alaska.

Driving back to the hotel, Imka asked, "So, what did you think?"

"Wow. That was almost as good as sex," Vermeer said with a look of contentment.

"Mmmm, we'll see," She purred.

☠☠☠☠☠☠☠☠☠☠☠

Vermeer was sitting in the British Airways Galleries Lounge, waiting to board his flight to London's Heathrow, when his cell phone rang.

"Hello."

"Can you talk?" The voice on the other end asked.

It was SEAL Commander Wooch on the phone.

"Yes, sir," Vermeer replied.

"Is it too late to change your flight?"

"To where?"

"Madrid, Spain."

Vermeer looked at the large board showing all the British Airways flights' arrivals and departures. He found that a flight to Madrid was set to depart two hours after his original flight to London.

"Looks possible, sir. Let me see what I can do."

"Good. Call me back if you have any problems," Wooch said.

"Will do, sir. Can you tell me anything?"

"Olé."

CLICK

Several years ago, the Worldwide Affiliates of Safari Partners, also known as W.A.S.P., launched a challenge against the eco-terrorist group Le Gang de la Clé de Singe in a real combat campaign on the desert island of Kanacea in the Pacific Ocean, not far from Fiji. It was scheduled to be televised as a pay-per-view event on cable TV. The title was "Winner Take All."

If Le Gang de la Clé de Singe wins, the Worldwide Affiliates of Safari Partners would agree to stop all big game and sport hunting. However, if the Worldwide Affiliates of Safari Partners win, then they would agree to stop killing big game hunters and only focus on poachers. Each team would be limited to five participants; the team that loses all five members would be the loser. It was a 21st-century version of the Roman Gladiator fight-to-the-death battle royale.

In the end, Le Gang de la Clé de Singe won, with a final score of 5-0. However, shortly after they lost, Worldwide Affiliates of Safari Partners, also known as W.A.S.P., claimed that the combat was somehow rigged and that Le Gang de la Clé de Singe cheated. They therefore refused to honor their agreement, and the big game hunting resumed, and, as a result, so did the hunting and killing of big game hunters.

Recently, W.A.S.P. has been trying to lure Le Gang de la Clé de Singe warriors into ambushes by announcing big-game hunts and sending a small secondary team to follow, hoping to catch the eco-warriors unaware and trap them in crossfire. So far, they have not been successful.

Rumors were flying that W.A.S.P. might be setting a trap over the hunting rights of the Iberian Lynx. HQ had contacted Fu Hao and Sue B to be on alert. If attacked, headquarters were prepared to send a backup team within hours. The leaders of the Red Team felt confident that they were well prepared to handle any contingency.

They all agreed on the plan to sneak into Doñana National Park under cover of night. Since the terrain was hilly to mountainous, they would split into two teams. The first team of three, led by Sue B, would operate on the ground, while the second team of three, led by Fu Hao, would take the high ground.

Sue B's A-team would consist of herself, Sassoon, and Gianfranco. They would take the open grasslands mixed with shrubs, perfect for a team wearing Ghillie suits to blend into the environment and remain undetected.

Fu Hao's B-team, made up of Cowboy and Santiago Guzman, would be up on the high ground, giving cover. Hazael would operate the sole drone and relay vital information about the enemy's position to the team leaders some twenty miles away on the deserted beaches of Playa Mata del Difunto.

☠☠☠☠☠☠☠☠☠☠☠

That night, as the Red Team was sailing to Walvis Bay, Namibia, the Seville police and Spain's most popular newspaper, El País, received an anonymous tip to the location of the bodies of twelve Iberian Lynx poachers could be found.

The police and several reporters from different news outlets arrived almost simultaneously. The twelve deceased men were known poachers, most with multiple arrests and convictions. All the weapons owned by the twelve had been wiped clean, except for one fingerprint belonging to the fascist General Francisco Franco.

The headline in the morning edition of El País read:
"12 cazadores furtivos cazados hasta la extinción,"
(12 poachers killed to extinction.) *Last night, police were alerted to the deaths of twelve known poachers who were killed by the notorious eco-terrorist group called Le Gang de la Clé de Singe. The group claims to have taken revenge on the twelve men for hunting Iberian Lynx and illegally snaring six wild hares, the Iberian Lynx's primary food source.*

The Iberian Lynx is an endangered species; only 400 are known to exist in the wild. They're on the brink of extinction due to hunting, habitat loss, and the declining rabbit populations. In a call to this newspaper, Le Gang de la Clé de Singe announced that they released several hundred native wild rabbits into the area. Our reporter found evidence of this when he arrived at the scene. He claimed that he was surrounded by what looked to be hundreds of bunny eyes staring at him.

The names of the dead are being withheld until all families have been notified.

Mr. Thurston Bentley Hart the Third was appointed as the new president of Worldwide Affiliates of Safari

Partners, also known as W.A.S.P. Once he gained full control of the organization, he decided that after the humiliating beatdown W.A.S.P. suffered at the hands of Le Gang de la Clé de Singe during the "Winner Take All" debacle, this would be WAR! No more Mister Nice Guy. They would do whatever it takes and spend whatever it takes to eliminate Le Gang de la Clé de Singe completely.

He was planning to infiltrate their organization to identify their members, disrupt and sabotage their plans, and lower morale. He thought like a businessman and not like a general. Still, he felt he had an ace in the hole, SEAL Team Commander William T. "Wooch" Brown, who was not only a lifetime member of W.A.S.P. but had been a tactical and strategic consultant with the organization for the past five years.

Bentley Hart the Third thought that he knew all about Wooch, but he knew only what Wooch wanted him to know.

But what Bentley Hart the Third doesn't know is Wooch's involvement with Le Gang de la Clé de Singe. It stemmed from witnessing the cruelty and cavalier attitude towards animals while serving in the military. The mindless killing of animals out of boredom or for sport always disgusted him, so after giving a speech at UC Berkeley on 'War and its Effect on Animals,' he was approached by several members of Le Gang de la Clé de Singe who convinced him to work with them behind the scenes. They collaborated with others like himself—ex-military, corporate leaders, government officials, and private individuals—operating covertly worldwide. So, while Bentley Hart the Third attempts to infiltrate the enemy, the enemy has a double agent sitting at the right hand of the "King."

☠☠☠☠☠☠☠☠☠☠☠

During a torrential rainstorm, British Airways flight BA0456 landed at Adolfo Suárez Madrid-Barajas International Airport at 09:50 a.m. The final approach was so bumpy and turbulent that even many seasoned travelers tossed their cookies upon landing.

Vermeer's plane was parked at the last gate in Terminal T4S, designated for all international flights within the Schengen area. *(The Schengen Area is an area consisting of 26 European countries that have officially eliminated passport and border controls at their mutual borders.)*

He and his fellow travelers, all bleary-eyed and nauseous from the roller-coaster landing, made their way through Spain's customs and out into the passenger pick-up area. Holding a placard with the name Mr. Harrington was a young man smartly dressed in a chauffeur's uniform. Vermeer walked towards the man and said, "That's me."

"Mr. Harrington?" The young man queried.

"That I am, son," Vermeer replied.

"*Bienvenido a España.*"

"*Gracias.*"

Outside at the pick-up and drop-off area sat a midnight blue Maserati Levante 4x4.

"Nice car!" Vermeer exclaimed.

"Si, señor. The engine was built at the Ferrari factory in Maranello."

"Sweet. V8?"

"Oh, si, si, señor. She can go from zero to sixty in under four seconds."

"Beautiful."

"*Si, hermoso.*"

"And you are?" Vermeer asked of the chauffer.

"Excuse me, Mr. Harrington. I am Banderas. At your service."

"Well, Banderas, where are we off to?"

"Señor Wooch suggested the Hotel Gran Meliá Palacio Los Duques."

"It sounds luxurious."

"As the brochure says, "The Palacio de los Duques Gran Meliá is located in the heart of Madrid. Behind its Elizabethan-style façade, it boasts incomparable architectural splendor, combining timeless luxury with an avant-garde flair," Banderas boasted.

"Very impressive."

"It is."

"No, I meant you."

"Well, I had worked in an ad agency when I was younger for a short time."

"Copywriter?"

"Si."

"I knew it."

"First time in Madrid?"

"Madrid, yes. Spain. No. Beautiful country. Oops, I mean *hermoso país.*"

"Very good, señor."

"So, Banderas, are you a native of Madrid?"

"All my life."

"Are you a fan of the bullfights?"

"When I was younger, but now that I know how mistreated the animals are, no way. I think it should be outlawed, as do many young people today. It is a very cruel sport."

"Not much a sport when you cripple your opponent before the game begins."

"I agree, señor."

"Well, I'm here to help even up the score."

"*Muy Bueno*." Banderas said with a smile.

☠☠☠☠☠☠☠☠☠☠☠

PETA (People for the Ethical Treatment of Animals) wrote about the inhuman torture of bullfighting in an article placed on their website titled "Torture Before the Fight Begins." The article reads as follows:

'The odds are stacked against bulls many days before the fight begins. Selected for their "athletic" appearance, they endure physical and mental torment for at least two days before a fight.

Their nostrils and ears are blocked, petroleum jelly is rubbed into their eyes, needles are stuck into their genitals, and a strong caustic is rubbed on their legs to throw them off balance and prevent them from lying down. They're drugged with sedatives and stimulants and then laxatives to weaken and incapacitate them.

An Unfair Fight to the Death

A bull begins his fight to the death from a dark box in which he has been kept for two days. He runs, desperate and confused, toward the light of the arena – seeking freedom – but instead meets his gruesome fate. Many bulls have collapsed at this stage, only to be propped up and forced to endure further torment.

First, come the picadors *on horseback, thrusting and twisting spear-like weapons into the bull's neck in a gruesome attempt to weaken his muscles. This results in gaping wounds to him as well as unnecessary injury and suffering to the horses involved.*

Next come the banderilleros , brandishing colored sticks with sharp harpoon ends. They plunge them into the bull's back to incapacitate him further, resulting in so much blood loss that he becomes even weaker. The torment continues as the banderilleros make him dizzy and disoriented by running in circles around him.

Last is the matador, who provokes a few charges from the maimed and incapacitated animal. He attempts to kill the bull by aiming his sword at an artery near the heart , but usually misses, puncturing the lungs and heart in the process. If the matador fails to kill the bull, an executioner is called in to sever the animal's spinal cord, which paralyzes but doesn't always kill him.

Often, the bull is still alive and conscious during his final moments, in which his ears and tail are cut off as a trophy for the matador before he's dragged from the arena as the crowd boos him.'

Ever since the humiliating defeat in the Battle of Kanacea Island during the televised live cable show "Winner Take All," which millions of people from around the world watched, Thurston Bentley Hart and the executive board of W.A.S.P. are seeking revenge. Their millions of members are demanding some form of retribution. They want blood; nothing less will suffice.

Worldwide Affiliates of Safari Partners called for a special emergency convention at Caesars Palace in Las Vegas. They have reserved the 51,000-square-foot, pillarless Octavius and Forum Ballrooms, plus an additional 25 breakout rooms, for special operation planning.

In attendance would be a literal who's who of the hunting world. The elite hunters were coming from all around the world: a right-wing superstar musician bowhunter hailing from the Wolverine state of Michigan, two sons of a president, dozens of TV hunting personalities, bow-hunters, women hunters, trophy hunters, and big game hunters, hunters from just about every country in the world.

All came to Las Vegas with one purpose: to eradicate the menace known as Le Gang de la Clé de Singe. The deadly thorn in the side of hunters around the world.

"This aggression must stop!" Bentley Hart the Third shouted on the opening night of the convention in front of twelve thousand screaming W.A.S.P. members.

"This time, it's WAR!" He bellowed.

CHEERS HOOTS WHISTLES HOWLS SHRIEKS

"We are going on the offense. We're tired of being victims. From now on, they're the ones who are going to be wearing the ensign around their necks. This ensign!" Hart shouted as he held up a black flag with the capital initials of W.A.S.P. in bright yellow.

The crowd went nuts. There were nonstop cheers, hoots, whistles, howls, and shrieks from the crowd for six minutes. There were even a couple of overly enthusiastic members from the great state of Texas who actually fired their guns into the ceiling.

Unfortunately, the city of Las Vegas, the folks at Caesars Palace, and the LVPD frown upon firing weapons in a crowded ballroom ever since Stephen Craig Paddock, the perpetrator of the 2017 mass murder, killed 58 people and wounded more than 850. The five hombres from Texas were arrested and thrown into the pokey overnight and fined $5000 each. All but one paid the fine, Mr. Roger Denton couldn't, so he spent the next 90 days in the Las Vegas Detention Center.

On day nineteen, an inmate, who went by the name Tay Tay, decided that he wanted Mr. Denton's blanket and pillow. Roger Denton told Tay Tay to fuck off. A minor scuffle broke out that was quickly tamped down by the corrections officers. Threats were made, inmates took sides, and an uneasiness fell over cell block 3F.

At approximately three-thirty that night, Tay Tay and two other unnamed inmates entered Denton's room, assaulted, stabbed, and raped him, and then took his blanket and pillow. Afterward, Denton was placed in protective custody for the remainder of his time to be served. When he got home to Midland, Texas, the story had somehow gotten there before he did. People were not kind to poor Roger; even his friends would make snide remarks like:

"Poor Roger, when he was in Vegas, he really took it up the ass."

"Poor Roger, he's always the butt of jokes."

"Poor Roger got it ass backwards."

"Poor Roger got fucked over in Vegas. Literally."

It got to the point where everyone started calling him "Poor Roger." Six weeks after he returned from Vegas, Roger Denton ate the end of a .357 magnum revolver while sitting in his Dodge Ram dually pickup parked outside his apartment. The bullet not only went through his head but also through the roof of the truck cab and shattered a window of an upstairs apartment half a block away.

At the funeral, all his friends said the same thing, "Poor Roger."

☠☠☠☠☠☠☠☠☠☠☠

The Palacio de los Duques Gran Meliá is a 19th-century palace five minutes from Madrid's Royal Palace, the Royal Theater, and Almudena Cathedral.

The hotel incorporates a slick modern interior that starkly contrasts the hotel's Elizabethan exterior. The rooms and suites are all influenced by the 16th-century artist Velázquez's masterpiece 'Las Meninas.'

Banderas pulled up to the hotel entrance, handed Vermeer a card, and said, "Call me at this number day or night. If you need anything, just let me know."

Vermeer took the card, memorized the number, handed the card back to Banderas, and said, "Thanks. How about we meet here for breakfast at nine?"

"I'll see you then."

Vermeer grabbed his bag and entered the hotel lobby.

A tall blonde statuesque women in her twenties greeted Vermeer, "*Bienvenido señor, ¿registrándose?*"

"Yes, I have a reservation. Last name Harrington. Greg Harrington." Vermeer said as he handed the beautiful receptionist his Canadian passport.

"Si, Mr. Harrington. We have you staying for eight nights. Is that correct?" She asked.

"Correct." He answered, not being able to take his eyes off of her.

"First time in Spain, Señor Harrington?'

"First time in Madrid."

"Business or pleasure?"

"Pleasure," He said with a smile.

"Well, if there is anything that I can do to make your stay here at Palacio de los Duques Gran Meliá more pleasurable, please do not hesitate to ask. My name is Alejandra," She said with a slight twinkle in her emerald green eyes.

"Gracias, Alejandra. I will."

"We have you in room 333. Do you need assistance with your luggage?" She said, handing him his key.

"No, thank you. I travel pretty light," He said as he held up his leather duffel bag.

"Enjoy your stay, Señor Harrington."

After the initial keynote speech from President Hart, several notable world-class hunters from the U.S. and Africa talked about their experiences and encounters with the eco-terrorist group, how they survived, and what they think should be done to put an end to Le Gang de la Clé de Singe for once and for all, getting the attendees all up. To keep the excitement going, the crowd was provided with a heavy metal musical interlude by none other than the "Minnesota Madman" himself, Billy Jackson. Billy was a real redneck at heart; he just loved killing anything that had a parent with a bow and arrow.

Billy had killed or wanted to kill anything that swam, walked, or flew, anything on two or four legs that had scales, feathers, or fur. His mountain cabin on Lima Mountain, just south of the Canadian border, was filled with mounted animal heads, stuffed birds, and fish. All the floors, chairs, and sofas were covered with animal skins. It was a taxidermist's wet dream.

The "Madman" played for almost an hour, but by the time he'd finished his gig, the ballroom had pretty much cleared out, with many complaining of headaches.

The next speaker was the right-wing's golden boy, SEAL Team Commander William T. "Wooch" Brown. When he was introduced, a unanimous thunderous chat arose from the ten thousand plus members of W.A.S.P. "Wooch."

Wooch Wooch Wooch Wooch Wooch Wooch Wooch Wooch Wooch Wooch Wooch Wooch Wooch Wooch Wooch Wooch Wooch Wooch Wooch

It went on for over ten minutes straight, non-stop. Every time he tried to speak, the chats grew louder. Finally, the chats started to fade away.

"Thank you all for that most kind reception. First, I'd like to thank President Hart and all the members of the Worldwide Affiliates of Safari Partners and the NRA for the fine work they're doing in protecting our rights as hunters and gun owners.

There's a menace out there, an evil that is trying to take away our rights. Not only our constitutional rights, but also our God-given rights to hunt. As it says in Genesis 27:3, *Now then, take your weapons, your quiver and your bow, and go out to the field and hunt game for me.*

In Genesis 1:26, *God said, Let us make man in our image, according to our likeness; and let them have dominion over the fish of the sea, and over the birds of the air, and over all the wild animals of the earth, and over every creeping thing that creeps upon the earth.*"

A deafening roar erupted throughout the ballroom, shaking the walls and chandeliers overhead.

Wooch raised his hands to call for quiet before speaking again. When silence came over the room, he spoke again.

"Ladies and gentlemen, we are facing an army of Godless anarchists who will not rest until every one of us is either dead, surrendered, or bent to their will.

I don't know about you, but I will never yield. I would rather die with my gun in my hand than have some whining little liberal tree-hugging snot-nosed punk who's never experienced the thrill of slaughtering a defenseless creature forcing me to give up my rights to kill, eradicate, and even annihilate an entire species if I want to.

Because we're Americans by God, there isn't anybody who can tell us what we can and can't do, especially some God Damn Frenchie pussy organization. Am I right? Are you with me?"

CHEERS

"I can't hear you! I said, are you with me!"

Wooch Wooch Wooch Wooch Wooch Wooch Wooch Wooch Wooch Wooch Wooch Wooch Wooch Wooch Wooch Wooch Wooch Wooch Wooch Wooch

Of course, Wooch didn't mean a thing he just said. The majority of the W.A.S.P. members were a bunch of redneck good ole boys who couldn't hunt their way out of a paper bag.

They get all dressed up in camo, spread deer piss around a deer feeder, and sit their asses up in a tree and wait for the deer to come to them. And nine times out of ten, by the time a deer would go around, they would be shitfaced from drinking a six-pack of Budweiser, and they would muff the shot, causing the poor animal to suffer while the "hunter" would get off another shot or two.

Wooch figured that maybe 2% of W.A.S.P. were serious, legitimate hunters who would actually hunt their prey; the rest were posers and wannabes.

His main goal that day was to urge the membership into a shooting war with Le Gang de la Clé de Singe, a war, even though the eco-terrorist group is wholly outnumbered, that would be able to win. Unlike the W.A.S.P. members, the eco-warriors of Le Gang de la Clé de Singe are dedicated defenders of wildlife and are ready to lay down their lives for the cause, whereas the W.A.S.P. members, by and large, are not willing to die just so they can hunt.

☠☠☠☠☠☠☠☠☠☠☠

José María Ordóñez is currently Spain's most famous matador. He is better known as *"El Gallo Pinto"* (The spotted rooster).

To date, Ordóez has killed 1,849 bulls and is on track to become the matador with the most kills ever. Every Sunday, the standard bullfight consists of six kills: each ritual killing lasts twenty minutes. Three matadors alternate in the massacre, which usually lasts two and a half hours.

El Gallo Pinto lives in the wealthiest neighborhood of the Spanish capital, El Viso. On the corner of Calle del Sil and Calle de Ega, number 48, sits an ochre two-story stucco, red-tiled mansion hidden behind a ten-foot ivy-covered fence.

Numerous video cameras, security alarms, motion sensors, and secret devices kept intruders, aficionados, and fanáticos out. Ordóñez also hired two bodyguards after a failed kidnapping attempt.

At age 35, the matador José María Ordóñez resembled the Italian actor Giancarlo Giannini. He had a slight build and wild, unkept pitch-black hair in contrast to a well-manicured mustache, and all the women loved his piercing blue eyes. At any time, day or night, a flock of women would gather outside number 48 Calle del Sil, waiting just to get a glimpse of *El Gallo Pinto*.

Vermeer knew he would have his work cut out for him to complete his mission. He disagreed with Ernest Hemingway when he wrote, "Bullfighting is the only art in which the artist is in danger of death and in which the degree of brilliance in the performance is left to the fighter's honor."

"Not so, Mr. Hemingway. I, too, am an artist of death. We shall see if El Gallo Pinto dies with as much honor as El Toro," Vermeer said to himself as he stood outside number 48, devising his plan.

"Wooch," The gruff voice answered.

"Wooch, it's Vermeer. Is this a good time?"

"What can I do for you?"

"I need some help."

"Name it."

Vermeer laid out his plan to the ex-SEAL Commander for the assistance he needed to complete his mission.

"It shouldn't be a problem, son. Give me a day or two, and I'll get back to you," Wooch said.

CLICK

☠☠☠☠☠☠☠☠☠☠☠

Two cold, steely eyes appeared from behind the slit in the iron gate, then a gravel voice asked, "*¿Qué deseas?*"

Vermeer held up his ID card and said, "Good morning. Greg Harrington, Connoisseur Magazine. I have an appointment with Señor Ordóñez."

The slit slammed shut.

Vermeer heard muffled voices as if people were communicating on a walkie-talkie. There was the sound of several metal bolts sliding back and the metal door slowly opening just enough to let Vermeer pass through. After he entered the courtyard, the door was quickly shut behind him.

The man who peered through the slit in the door was a short, stocky, bald man. He looked to be as solid as a brick wall. He was dressed all in black and showed no expression. As he gestured for Vermeer to follow him, the man said, "*Sígueme.*"

Vermeer did as he was told. He followed the man into the house, where he was greeted by a silver-haired man wearing a formal butler's suit who appeared to be in his seventies.

"Good morning, Mr. Harrington. Señor Ordóñez will receive you in the den. Right this way," The butler said in perfect English.

As they walked through the house, he said, "If you don't mind my asking, where did you learn to speak English? You have no trace of an accent."

"Thank you, sir. As a young boy, I spent many years in America," the butler said.

As they approached the doorway to the den, a clone of the man at the gate appeared. The man was also dressed in all black, had a bald head, and was built like a fireplug. As Vermeer entered the den, the bodyguard gave Vermeer a patronizing once-over and then left the room.

Seated on a leather sofa was the great *El Gallo Pinto,* reading a copy of Connoisseur Magazine. He placed the magazine down on the coffee table in front of him. The coffee table had a wooden top that sat upon legs made of bull's horns. Horns from some of the bulls *El Gallo Pinto* had killed in the ring. On all the walls were hundreds of photos of him in the bullring, posters from his many "*Corrida de Toros,*" and numerous framed bull's ears. On his desk were a couple of the bull's tails used as paperweights.

Ordóñez stayed seated as he greeted his soon-to-be assassin. He smiled that million-dollar smile that had melted the hearts of many young girls and women and said, "Welcome, Señor Harrington. Please be seated."

"Gracias. Thank you, Señor Ordóñez. I appreciate you taking the time to meet with me on such short notice," Vermeer said as he took a seat across from the matador.

"The pleasure is all mine. I am an avid reader of Connoisseur Magazine and am honored to be featured in such a prestigious periodical."

"If you don't mind, I'd like to wait until my photographer arrives for the interview. I like to have him photograph my subjects as we talk. I think it's more intimate. He phoned me and said he had a bit of car trouble, but he assured me that he would be here any minute," Vermeer said.

"Not a problem. Can I offer you something to drink, Señor Harrington? Coffee? Tea?"

"A cup of tea would be nice. Thank you."

"Diego, some tea for Señor Harrington," Ordóñez said to the old man standing by the door.

Diego, the butler, gave a slight bow and answered, “Sí señor,” as he left the room.

“Señor Ordóñez, please call me Greg,” Vermeer said.

The great *El Gallo Pinto* smiled and said, “*Bueno*,” not returning the gesture.

Afterward, there was a moment of awkwardness, then a bodyguard entered the room and announced that someone claiming to be a photographer with Connoisseur Magazine was requesting entry.

“*Señor, alguien que decía ser fotógrafo de la revista Connoisseur solicitaba la entrada.*” The guard said.

“It appears that your man is here.”

“*Esta bien. Déjalo entar,*” Ordóñez said to his guardian to allow the photographer to enter.

A few moments later, carrying several bags, Banderas entered the den. Vermeer stood up and went to help Banderas set up the equipment.

“Señor Ordóñez, this is Lorenzo Ramírez, my photographer.”

“*Hola, Señor Ramírez.*”

“*Hola, Señor Ordóñez, es un honor*,” Banderas said.

Vermeer asked, “Señor Ordóñez, may I use the bathroom?”

“Of course, it is straight down the hallway to your left.”

“Gracias. Lorenzo, I’ll be right back,” Vermeer said as he left the room.

Vermeer walked down the hall, past the bathroom, toward the front door; once outside, he gave a short whistle to the guard to get his attention. As the man turned around, Vermeer drew a Beretta 92FS 9mm with a silencer from his shoulder holster and fired two shots. He struck and killed bodyguard number one.

PHIFF PHIFF

Vermeer walked back into the house and headed to the den, where bodyguard number two stood outside the door, peering in and watching Banderas set up the lights. He was so engrossed in observing Banderas's performance pretending to be a photographer that he didn't notice Vermeer approaching, nor did he see or hear the two shots that Vermeer fired, which took a rather large chunk of his head off.

PHIFF PHIFF

When Vermeer walked into the library, Diego was setting the tea service down on the coffee table. Vermeer pointed his weapon at Diego and calmly said, "Diego, I need you to follow Señor Ramírez and do not try anything foolish. Do you understand?"

"Sí, señor."

Banderas took the old man to the living room on the other side of the house. He then gingerly proceeded to bind, gag, and blindfold Diego to the chair.

"Just remain calm. No harm will come to you."

"*¡Qué diablos está pasando!*" Ordóñez shouted.

"Señor, have you ever heard of Le Gang de la Clé de Singe?"

"Yes, but I am not a poacher or a big game hunter." He proclaimed.

"That is true. However, you do kill for sport. You, señor, are responsible for the torture and death of thousands of animals, and for that, you must pay."

"This is ludicrous. I am but one man. What about all the others?" Ordóñez demanded.

"Oh, they will be dealt with, too. But your death, señor, will open the world's eyes to the price one must pay for playing such a sport," Vermeer replied.

"You're mad!"

"Possibly. I'll tell you what we're going to do, *El Gallo Pinto*. We are going to have our own '*la fiesta brava*.' Just you and me.

You will play the part of the bull, my amigo, and I'll be the matador. Instead of horns, you'll have two *puntillas* (daggers that run into the base of the bull's cranium).

But before we get started, we have to prep you like the bulls are prepped before they are sent into the ring. First, we will inject you with a cocktail of sedatives and stimulants," Vermeer said as Banderas gave Ordóñez an injection in the base of his neck.

Once the drugs took effect, the great matador was stripped naked, needles were stuck into his genitals, his nostrils and ears were stuffed with cotton, and his eyes were rubbed with Vaseline petroleum jelly. As Banderas helped him to his feet, Vermeer handed him the two daggers.

They stood approximately ten feet apart. Vermeer held up El Gallo Pinto's capote (red cape) and shouted, "*Toro!*"

Struggling to stand and in agony, Ordóñez blindly lunged towards Vermeer, swinging the puntillas wildly. Vermeer stood completely still and waved the red cape as Ordóñez passed by. The more Ordóñez tried to rub the Vaseline from his eyes to see, the more it irritated them and the more he couldn't focus. He was having difficulty breathing from the cotton stuffed up his nose. The pain from the needles jammed into his testicles was excruciating. Every time he took a step, a sharp white pain would shoot up into his brain. Again and again, Ordóñez lunged, charged, lurched, and ran, flailing his daggers. Vermeer stoically performed a *molinete* (a right-handed pass in which the matador and the cape spin as the bull passes).

"How does it feel to be treated as the bull, Señor Ordóñez?" Vermeer asked.

El Gallo Pinto stood, sweating profusely, his breathing labored, his body aching.

"*Vete al infierno, bastardo!*" He growled.

After fifteen minutes, Vermeer saw that Ordóñez was nearly exhausted. He had one more charge in him before he would just collapse to the ground. As Ordóñez summoned the strength for another charge, Banderas handed Vermeer the *espada* (the matador's sword).

Ordóñez bellowed out, "*RAAAAAAAAH!*" as he charged toward the blurred red shape, wildly swinging the two daggers. Vermeer stood poised at the ready with the sword. As Ordóñez approached, Vermeer leaped up and thrust the blade into Ordóñez's upper right shoulder, forcing the cutlass deep into his torso at such an angle that it pierced the heart, killing him instantly.

As Vermeer placed the yellow ensign around *El Gallo Pinto's* neck, Banderas found the security camera's recording system and deleted and disarmed it, leaving no trace of their presence.

Vermeer removed the gag and untied Diego, leaving the blindfold on.

"Diego, I want you not to go into the den. Señor Ordóñez is dead, as well as his bodyguards. I suggest you stay here. I will call the police as soon as I leave. Do you understand?" Vermeer asked.

Diego nodded.

Before leaving, Vermeer left a single fingerprint of the Spanish surrealist artist Salvador Dalí.

☠☠☠☠☠☠☠☠☠☠☠

Following the advice of SEAL Team Commander William T. "Wooch" Brown, one of the top leaders in command, they called in the two leading hit squad teams from Le Gang de la Clé de Singe to be deployed to the African nation of Botswana to engage in the undeclared war between W.A.S.P. and Le Gang de la Clé de Singe over the slaughter of Botswana's annual quota of 300 elephants. Usually, Botswana sold their quotas to multiple foreign hunters. However, this year, the total quotas were purchased at a premium price of two hundred thousand dollars per elephant, totaling sixty million U.S. dollars, all bought by Worldwide Affiliates of Safari Partners.

The 300 fortunate hunters who will receive a license to hunt and kill an elephant will be selected through a lottery. Each interested participant will pay ten thousand dollars. Only one ticket per person will be available, and a total of three thousand tickets will be sold. The event will be called "The Great Elephant Hunt."

The odds of winning one of the elephant expedition packages were 10 to 1. What they didn't announce was that the odds of someone surviving the expedition were over 1000 to 1.

Worldwide Affiliates of Safari Partners wanted and got worldwide publicity by announcing they would send three hundred hunters in one group to Botswana to conduct one massive elephant hunt. And they defied anyone to try and stop them.

Le Gang de la Clé de Singe sent out a communique the same day stating that this hunt was in direct violation of the "Winner Take All" agreement, which stated that W.A.S.P. had agreed to cease all big game and sporting hunting activities. But if they were fool hearty enough to proceed with such a ridiculous venture, they did so at their peril. They signed the letter with, "Of course, you know this means war!"

Over the course of two weeks, to avoid any suspicion, the members of the two teams separately made their way to Gaborone, the capital city of Botswana. Each team was stationed in separate villages surrounding the capital.

The Red Team stayed in Mmopane, a village in the Kweneng District about 15 km from Gaborone. There are only red dirt roads, most of which have no street names or signs, and most houses have no numbers.

A large number of homes are built more like compounds, with tall concrete walls enclosing each property. Each compound contains several buildings, some of which include additional dwellings, garages, or tool sheds. The safe home they stayed at was at 5836 Moshoeshoe Road.

They arrived at night in a panel van. For security purposes, the outside lights were not on. As they piled out of the van, their contact, Dineo Kabelo, greeted them.

Dineo was a small black man in his mid-forties. He was balding, thin but wiry, and always wore thick, black-rimmed glasses with blue lenses. He had an infectious smile and always smiled. Dineo spoke excellent English with a British accent. He was a member of the Botswana antipoaching unit specializing in fighting the illegal ivory trade. The unit is called the Giants Club and has branches in four other African nations in an effort to protect the elephant population.

As Dineo showed the team to their lodgings, he made it clear that they should remain as quiet as possible when outside, as they didn't want to attract undue attention. He said an armed guard was stationed at the entrance gate, which was locked at all times, and several armed sentries were patrolling inside the compound as well.

The dwelling they were assigned was a cinderblock building with a 3x4 window on either side of the metal front door, the only door. There was a small air conditioner in one of the windows. It is way too small and inefficient for the room's size. Inside were six bunk beds and one bathroom with a shower. Opposite the back wall were metal containers containing all the equipment they would need for their mission: weapons, ammunition, clothing, dried foodstuffs, and miscellaneous gear.

Dineo apologized, "I am sorry for the meager accommodations. We are a poor country; anything more extravagant would draw undue attention."

"No need to apologize, Dineo. This will suit us fine," Fu Hao said.

The Blue Team was bivouacking fourteen miles to the east in the village of Metsimotlhaba. Their assigned compound was even more fortified than the Red Teams'. In addition to a six-foot concrete wall surrounding the property, there were three feet of electrified wire.

The Blue Team's local contact was Gorata Tsheko, a woman in her twenties who resembled a young Oprah Winfrey. She works as a game ranger at S, the third-largest park in Botswana. She is part of a select group of female rangers known as the Wonder Women of Botswana. They are recognized for their relentless efforts in protecting wildlife and pursuing poachers. Many poachers would prefer to face a male ranger rather than one of the '*Chobe Angels.'*

The Blue Team's accommodations were sparse and monk-like, similar to the Red's. Odin and his team were as appreciative of the assistance and shelter as Fu Hao and Sue B.

"Good evening. I'm Nigel Williams, and this is the BBC World Headline News. Our top story this hour comes from Madrid, Spain. There are confirmed reports that the world-renowned matador, José María Ordóñez, better known as El Gallo Pinto to his millions of adoring fans, was found brutally murdered in his home yesterday.

A spokesperson for the Madrid Police Department told the BBC that Señor Ordóñez was tortured, mutilated, and then killed with his own sword. Police believe that his murder was carried out by the international eco-terrorist group known as Le Gang de la Clé de Singe.

A worldwide manhunt is in progress. Sources say that Ordóñez's butler was able to give the police a detailed description of the two men responsible for Ordóñez's death.

Recently, there has been a public outcry to ban bullfighting, especially from young Spaniards. 58% of adults in Spain oppose bullfighting, claiming that the sport is cruel and barbaric.

A spokesperson for the Fundación Toro de Lidia, an NGO that promotes bullfighting in Spain, told the BBC that bullfighting is an integral part of Spanish culture. It is a tradition that forms part of the nation's cultural heritage and legacy and has been immortalized in numerous works of art. And this tradition will not be defeated by a group of terrorist thugs.

Meanwhile, in other news……"

Madrid Homicide Police Detective Santiago Velazquez, an eighteen-year veteran, had thought that he'd seen just about every horrific thing one human could do to another; he was wrong.

When he arrived at the murder scene of José María Ordóñez, what he saw brought horror to a new level. The medical examiner looked as white as a ghost, and this from a man who had seen a lot.

"What do we have, doctor?" Velazquez asked.

"This man has endured the ghastliest agony imaginable. His nose and ears were stuffed with cotton, petroleum jelly was rubbed into his eyes, he had needles inserted into his testicles, and I believe he must have been drugged.

It looks to me as if he was forced into a macabre game of bullfighting, with him as the bull. The cause of death was the stabbing with the *espada* into his torso. And look here, both his ears have been cut off and stuck on the wall above his desk.

What kind of sick person would do such a thing?" The ME asked.

"I don't know, doctor," Velazquez answered.

"That's what we do to the bulls before they enter the ring," Officer Lopez quipped.

Lopez was a rookie officer who, although he thought the murder of Ordóñez to be abhorrent, understood the irony.

"What did you say?" Velazquez snapped.

"I said that everything done to Señor Ordóñez is what happens to the bulls. The drugging, the cotton in the nose and ears, Vaseline in the eyes, even the needles in the testicles. Believe me, I do not condone what he endured. I'm just pointing out why what was done was done."

"Thank you for your expert opinion, rookie." Velazquez said sarcastically. "How about you interview the butler to describe these two killers unless you have an opinion on who they are?"

Lopez spent an hour getting a detailed description of the killers from Diego, the butler. Diego gave an excellent of both assassins. Unfortunately, Vermeer and Banderas wore disguises to alter their appearance: fake beards, colored contact lenses, body suits, colored hair, and even shoe lifts. The police would be wasting their time looking for ghosts while Vermeer, aka the "*Der Todesengel.*" The Angel of Death slipped silently away.

☠☠☠☠☠☠☠☠☠☠☠

Off in the horizon, the sun's golden rays stretched upward into the crisp, misty blue of the morning sky. Odin sat watching as he cradled a weathered old tin cup filled with steaming coffee, which warmed his whole being. Odin was perched atop the roof of their shack, slipping into a meditative state, when Lu Wei, holding up the satellite phone, called out, "Odin, a call."

The moment was lost, and Odin was snapped back into reality.

"Who is it?" He asked.

"Wooch."

"I'll be right down," Odin said as he climbed down from the roof, trying not to spill any mocha java.

"Hey, Wooch, Odin here."

"I've just spoken to the leaders of the Red Team; the W.A.S.P. elephant hunt is beginning in a couple of days. The hunters and their guides will be staying at two hunting lodges. Half will stay at The Tlou Lodge and the other half at Camp Letlotse. Both are located in Chobe National Park. The Tlou Lodge is located on the park's western border in the Chobe Forest Reserve. I'm sending the Red Team there. The Blue Team will be assigned to the hunters at Camp Letlotse on the Chobe River."

"Very good. When should we head out, sir?" Odin asked.

"Hmmm, probably in three days. But first, I'm assigning a special agent to your team."

"A special agent?"

"Yes. A fellow named Devol. An expert in the field of microbots. Ever hear of them?"

"No, sir."

"Microbots are robots smaller than a grain of sand that move through the body. They are currently being used for minimally invasive surgery to open up clogged arteries, treat hyperthermia, and even cut and drill biomaterials to remove them."

"Well, that sounds like a marvelous medical breakthrough, sir, but what did it have to do with us?"

"Odin, as you know, almost everything invented to benefit humankind can be weaponized against humankind. You and the Red Team are going to infect the W.A.S.P. hunters with microbots that have been programmed to kill them from the inside. Thereby, hopefully avoiding bloodshed."

"How are we going to infect them, sir?" Odin inquired.

"You'll be briefed by Agent Dovol. Any other questions?" Wooch said.

"No, sir."

"Good, Devol should be arriving sometime this morning."

"Aye, aye, sir."

CLICK

"Hello, I'm Châtelet," said the tall, pale, lanky woman.

"Welcome. I am Fu Hao, and this is my co-leader, Sue B. Commander Wooch told us that you would be joining us. Come, and I'll introduce you to the other members of the team." Fu Hao said as she walked over to where the team checked their weapons and equipment for the umpteenth time.

"Team. I'd like you all to meet Châtelet. She's the microbot specialist," Sue B announced.

"Hello," Châtelet said.

"This is Cowboy, that's Sassoon, Gianfranco, and Hazael," Sue B said.

They all smiled and mumbled their greetings.

"Châtelet, Wooch gave us the elevator pitch on microbots, but we were still not 100 percent clear on what we're dealing with. Would you mind?" Fu Hao asked.

Châtelet smiled, "Yes, of course. A microbot is a robot about the size of a grain of salt; it is an untethered machine with partly or wholly self-contained functional capabilities for locomotion.

Originally designed to help perform functions like cleaning out arteries that are blocked with plaque, performing highly targeted tissue biopsies, or even treating cancerous tumors. But they can also be programmed to damage tissue, destroy arteries by boring through them, causing strokes and heart attacks, among other things."

"How are they introduced into the body?" Cowboy asked.

"By injection," Châtelet said.

"And just how are we going to inject them? I don't think they're going to be volunteering up to get lethal injections, do you?" Fu Hao asked.

"We think we have that issue solved."

☠☠☠☠☠☠☠☠☠☠☠

After all the introductions had been made, Devol began his presentation. He explained the science of the microbots to the Blue Team as Châtelet had done for the Red Team. And was asked the same question. "How are we going to inject them?"

"Insect nano drones," Devol said.

"Insect nano drones?" Odin queried.

"That's right. A drone that looks identical to and is the same size as a mosquito. It can be remotely controlled and is equipped with a camera and a microphone. It can land on you, leave an RFID (Radio-frequency Identification) tracking device on your skin, and inject the victim with deadly programmed microbots.

It can fly through an open window or attach itself to clothing until the environment is more conducive to attack. Like a real mosquito, it is attracted to carbon dioxide emissions. We can control the timing of their attacks for when the victim is sleeping," Devol explained.

"That's incredible," Venus said.

"We will emit small swarms of mosquitoes to each hunter to be assured that they will be infected."

"What about detection?" Vulcan asked.

"Not a problem to the authorities; it appears to be a mosquito bite. To the medical examiner, the cause of death will appear to be either a stroke, heart attack, or any number of common diseases and viruses. Such as Ebola, Marburg Fever, Hemorrhagic Fever, or the Reston Virus."

"Won't the cops question everyone dying at once?" Odin asked.

"Let them question all they want. I'm sure there will be a few that will survive, and that's where you guys come in. Not to be condescending, but you will clean up the old-fashioned way whatever we miss."

"Will people know that we're behind the deaths?" Asked Odin.

"Commander Wooch said that a communique will be sent out afterward, alerting people that Le Gang de la Clé de Singe is responsible."

"Amazing," Venus said.

"Commander Wooch's orders say we are to leave for Camp Letlotse tomorrow morning," Devol said as he handed Odin his cell phone with the order.

Odin read it and immediately deleted it.

"All right. We're on the move tomorrow at 04:30. Make sure you've checked all your gear and are ready to move out at first light. Fall out," Odin ordered.

Odin and Devol went to discuss their mission with their guide, Gorata Tsheko.

Fu Hao and Sue B had gotten the same briefing from Agent Châtelet. They, too, had pretty much the same reaction as the Blue Team: one of amazement.

Dineo Kabelo, the Red Team's guide, had been coordinating the transportation for their morning journey to Tlou Lodge, located on the western border of Chobe Park.

The Red and Blue Teams were packed and ready to go by noon. The leaders of both teams were now re-evaluating their missions with the new additions to their teams and the special agents assigned to them. This new kind of warfare would take some getting used to.

Vermeer's cell phone vibrated as Air France flight 1401 from Madrid touched down at Charles De Gaulle Airport and taxied to the gate. The text message simply said, "Message. Mobile phone vending machine, Terminal 2. Phone # 8."

Vermeer made his way to Terminal 2, found the Mobile phone vending machines, and stood waiting by phone number 8. He didn't have to wait long when the phone rang.

"Hello?" Vermeer answered.

"Wooch, here. Nice flight?"

"Very nice. Thanks for the first-class ticket."

"Well, I heard such good things about the Spanish Inquisition," Wooch said with a chuckle.

"I just hope certain people got the message."

"Oh, I believe the message was received loud and clear."

"I'm glad."

"Outside, in passenger receiving, there is a young woman holding a placard with your name on it. You'll have a couple of days of downtime while your next assignment is being finalized."

"Very good, sir."

"*Laissez le bon temps rouler.*" (Let the good times roll)

CLICK

☠☠☠☠☠☠☠☠☠☠☠

"I'm going where ?" Vermeer asked.

"Ulaanbaatar." The anonymous woman's voice on the other end of the phone replied.

"Just where the Hell is Ulaanbaatar?"

"Mongolia."

"And what, pray tell, is in Mongolia?"

"Not what, but who."

"Okay, who, pray tell, is in Mongolia?" Vermeer asked.

"Mohammad Khan."

"And I would know him from?"

Mohammad Khan is one of the world's top ivory and endangered species smugglers in Asia. He was recently arrested along with five others in Botswana, but he vanished, first to Nairobi, Kenya, and then to neighboring Tanzania. Interpol issued an arrest warrant for environmental crimes, one of the first of its kind. He was re-arrested in Egypt, but before they could extradite him, he escaped again—this time to Ulaanbaatar, the capital of Mongolia.

He has been found guilty in absentia and sentenced to eighty years in prison, plus a fine of eleven million US Dollars. However, Mongolia has been dragging its feet in extraditing him back to Botswana. Meanwhile, he successfully operates his smuggling ring while in exile. That's where you come in."

"You want me to capture this Mohammad Khan and bring him back to Botswana?"

"No. We want you to terminate Mr. Khan with extreme prejudice. Do you understand?"

"Yeah. You want me to whack him."

"Poetically put, sir."

"Resources and local contacts?" Vermeer asked.

"Your contact is Gurragchaa. He will be waiting for you at the station."

"Station? You mean airport."

"Sorry, no. Train station. You're booked on the Moscow-to-Ulaanbaatar Trans-Mongolian Express. It leaves Moscow tomorrow night at 11:55. We've managed to book you a first-class compartment, but unfortunately, there weren't any compartments with private toilets. But there are two WCs per carriage."

"Oh, goodie," Vermeer said sarcastically.

"At least we have you on a nonstop Aeroflot leaving Paris tomorrow at 9 a.m. and arriving in Moscow at 2 p.m. local time."

"Oh, by the way, just how long of a train ride is it from Moscow to beautiful downtown Ulaanbaatar?"

"Er, 99 hours."

"Excuse me!"

"99 hours."

"That's more than four days! What the Hell am I going to do for four days?"

"I understand that the train runs along Lake Baikal, and there are a lot of other beautiful sights." The unidentified voice said sympathetically.

"You're kidding, right?"

"Well, at least the train is unique because it's usually filled with Russian and Mongolian traders."

"Great. I bet they're a group that really knows how to party."

"Oh, and one more thing."

"Yeah?" Vermeer asked with some trepidation.

"The local police make several cabin inspections along the way."

"Just how many stops does the Magical Mystery Tour make?"

"Twenty-eight stops."

"Perfect. This just gets better and better."

Vermeer took a taxi from Moscow's Sheremetyevo International Airport directly to the Moscow Yaroslavsky Railway Station. He arrived shortly before four in the afternoon. He checked his watch. There were only eight hours until the 'midnight special' departed. One thing he had to admit was that this was prime people-watching. Unlike in Europe or America, these people came from every imaginable indigenous ethnicity and race. He wandered around for a couple of hours, observing both the wealthy and the poor, the haves and the have-nots.

He stumbled upon a small diner tucked away on the station's upper floor. A large sign outside the restaurant read *Кафе и кулинария.* Translation: Café and cooking. They had images of pizzas, pasta, burgers, wraps, salads, and Chinese noodle dishes in the window.

Behind the counter were large color photos of the dishes. Vermeer pointed to the photograph of a pizza and said, “Pizza.”

The girl behind the counter, taking orders, looked at him, smiled, nodded, and said, “Pitsta. A pit?” as she made a gesture of drinking something.

“Coca-Cola,” Vermeer said, grinning and pointing to the refrigerated case with glass bottles.

Sitting at a table near the counter, he asked the young girl, “*Ty govorish' po-angliyski?*” (Do you speak English?) A phrase that he knew how to ask in twelve different languages.

She smiled sadly and said, “*Net.*”

He sat there slowly, eating his pizza and nursing his Coca Cola for close to an hour. Then he handed the counter girl a ten-dollar bill and said, “*Proshchay.*” (Goodbye.)

Vermeer wandered around the station for a couple of hours, then crossed the street to a grocery store to stock up on essential supplies for his journey. First and foremost, toilet paper. Then, ear plugs, a cup, fork, knife, and spoon. He bought four large bottles of water, fruit, several bags of junk food, cookies, and crackers. And finally, two books, English copies of Boris Pasternak’s *Doctor Zhivago* and Aleksandr Solzhenitsyn’s *One Day in the Life of Ivan Denisovich.*

By the time Vermeer finished shopping, it was nine o’clock. The train was finally available for boarding. He found his cabin and dropped off his luggage, then walked down to the club car to have a couple of drinks. He sampled a couple of Russian beers.

The first one was a pale lager, *Klinskoye Svetloe*. A crisp, hoppy beer that is specially brewed with rice to remove the beer's natural bitter taste. The second was a pilsner, *Zhigulevskoye.* Apparently, it was the only beer available during the Stalin years; since then, it's been revamped to be a cheap drinkable pilsner with a twist-off plastic cap. Always the mark of a quality brew. Saving the best for last was AF Brew Lobotomy Frontal Triple-Bourbon Imperial Stout. The beer has been barrel-aged in three types of bourbon barrels and welded together.

After two of those, Vermeer was three sheets to the wind. He made his way back to his compartment just as the *Provodnik* (conductor) came by to check his tickets and passport.

"*Bilety i pasporta.*" The *Provodnik* demanded.

Vermeer handing him his passport and ticket was the last thing he remembered before he passed out until 10 am the following day, when he woke up, head throbbing. It was as if a herd of buffalo was dancing the flamenco on his cerebellum, and his tongue felt like it had been fitted wall to wall with a cheap, deep-piled shag carpet.

The first stop that Vermeer was conscious of was Nizhny Novgorod, Russia's fifth-largest city, which sits at the confluence of the Oka and Volga rivers. But like most cities, there is little to see from the train station. He did get off the train during the stop to stretch his legs and get some fresh air.

As the train continued, Vermeer became aware of the gentle sway from side to side of the car and the hypnotic rhythm of the train as it rolled over the rails.

CLICK-CLACK CLICK-CLACK CLICK-CLACK CLICK-CLACK CLICK-CLACK CLICK-CLACK

The next large city, Kirov, located on the Vyatka River in "European Russia," is a major transport and railway hub. Vermeer observed that the further west he traveled, the more provincial and less modern they appeared.

The days began to meld into one another. Traveling over such vast and expansive open plains, the landscapes weren't all that different. The monotony was only broken up whenever they pulled into a small village or the occasional "city."

CLICK-CLACK CLICK-CLACK

On the third day, late in the afternoon, the train pulled into Krasnoyarsk, a city known for its natural landscapes. The author, Anton Chekhov, judged Krasnoyarsk to be the most beautiful city in Siberia. As it was getting dark and the city was all lit up, Vermeer had to agree with Chekhov. Visually, Krasnoyarsk rivaled many European cities.

CLICK-CLACK CLICK-CLACK

That night, at the end of day three, the train turned south and headed towards Mongolia. When Vermeer woke up, they were just crossing the Mongolian border. Stopping at Tarbagatay, Gusinoozyorsk, the cosmopolitan town of Selenduma, population 2,574 and only 64 streets, Ozhida, Selenge, was a pleasant change of scenery. From Siberia's flat, arid countryside, this small, quaint town sits in the beautiful, lush basin of the Orkhon and Selenge Rivers. Finally, something interesting to look at.

As the train pulled out of Selenge station, Vermeer glanced at the route and checked off another stop. There were only three more stops and eight hours until Ulaanbaatar.

CLICK-CLACK CLICK-CLACK

"Darkhan!" the conductor announced as the train slowed, creeping into the station. Because the Buddhist monastery of Kharagiin is located just outside of town, there looked to be a convention of Buddhist monks on the train platform surrounding any passenger who looked to be a tourist departing the train and asking for donations.

Vermeer considered going outside but decided against it. He'd wait until they reached Zuunkharaa, a town known for its excellent vodka production. He weighed the options, but vodka won after four days on the Trans-Mongolian Express.

CLICK-CLACK CLICK-CLACK

At 6:50 am, the train pulled into Ulaanbaatar. The rail station was enormous, and Ulaanbaatar was the rail center for the trans-Siberian Railway and the Chinese railway system.

As he exited the train, Vermeer handed the conductor a US twenty-dollar bill. He left the train, walked through the gigantic station, a mélange of people from China, Mongolia, Russia, Asia, and Europe, and headed to the street where the taxi and limo stand was.

A young man held a sign that read, “Tony Sharpe.” Vermeer approached the man, held up his arm, smiled, and said, “I’m Tony Sharpe. You must be Gurragchaa?”

“Yes, sir. Gurragchaa. At your service.”

☠☠☠☠☠☠☠☠☠☠☠

Camp Letlotse is located in the Savuti region within the heart of the Chobe National Park. The campgrounds are positioned on the banks of the dry Savuti Channel and next to the famous Savuti Marsh. The area is renowned for its large population of bull elephants and boasts one of the highest concentrations of wildlife on the African continent.

Camp Letlotse is a relatively small camp compared to some of the larger, more touristy camps. It consists of 25 Meru-style tents, each accommodating two guests. Although the camp is small, the accommodations are nonetheless first-class.

By the time the Blue Team pitched their campsite six miles away, the first fifty W.A.S.P. guests had arrived at Camp Letlotse and were getting ready for a sumptuous meal of local delicacies in the dining tent. They provided everything from Botswana’s national dish of Seswaa, a beef stew, to the more adventurous snack of Mopane worms, which is described as tasting like burnt steak, crunchy and salty. None of the hunters went for the Mopane worms.

☠☠☠☠☠☠☠☠☠☠☠

Five hours to the east, Fu Hao and Sue B's Red Team set up camp on the Namibian side of the Chobe River, just a mile from Tlou Lodge. Tlou Lodge is a more upscale safari camp. It has 50 thatched cottages, each with wooden decks and individual hot tubs, and they all have private views of the Chobe River, which runs yards away from the camp.

The Red Team could clearly see the Tlou Lodge from their camp's position in the thick scrub brush across the Chobe River. The river wasn't deep in case they needed to get across quickly. However, Sue B had noticed several large crocodiles sunning themselves on the riverbanks—something to be mindful of. Anticipating such an eventuality, they brought along an F470 Combat Rubber Raiding Craft—the exact same model that is standard issue that the Navy SEALS use.

While Cowboy, Sassoon, and Dineo Kabelo, the Red Team's scout, reconnoitered the area, the rest of the team set up camp. The first tent they set up was for Châtelet, their special techno agent, so she could begin test runs with several drones of various sizes.

The first drone she sent up was a surveillance drone, a Puma AE (All Environment), to observe what was going on at Tlou Lodge.

She surveyed a large gathering of all the hunters, organizers, and staff meeting outside the outdoor fire pit. Over sixty people appeared to be gathered, drinking, eating, and enjoying themselves. It was a social gathering rather than an official meeting, which would come the next day before the hunt started. She also observed over a dozen heavily armed men patrolling the area.

"Whad'ya seeing?" Fu Hao asked, looking over Châtelet's shoulder at the monitor.

"See there. The main group is attending a meet-and-greet. But I noticed a dozen armed men patrolling the grounds," Châtelet said as she pointed to the guards.

Fu Hao stared at the screen and asked, "Can you get closer or enlarge the images?"

"Sure," Châtelet replied as she zoomed in on the men.

"Hmmm, they don't look like military, more like a private security outfit. They shouldn't be a problem to take out."

"I can take them out without firing a shot," Châtelet said.

"Kill them?" Fu Hao asked.

"I could, but I could also just knock them out for several hours."

"With what?"

"Propofol. The stuff they use in medical procedures."

"Would you be able to knock them out with the tiny dosage administered by those tiny mosquitoes?"

"Oh, yeah. This is an extremely highly concentrated mixture of Propofol. In fact, any larger dose would be lethal." Châtelet said as she held up a small vial containing the medication.

"Cool. Let's get ready to rumble."

"Great. I'll prepare all my insect nano drones."

"Right. Knockouts for the guards and staff and elimination for everyone else."

"You do realize that the others won't die right away. For some of these diseases, it will take several days. But they will start to show symptoms immediately."

"Will they be able to hunt?"

"I will give them a separate injection of Ipecac. It causes vomiting. They use it for the treatment of poisoning."

"Mmmm, I like your thinking, girl."

"Well, I better get started preparing the swarm."
"If you need any help, just holler."

☠☠☠☠☠☠☠☠☠☠☠

The Blue Team was doing the same sort of preparation a hundred miles to the west. Gorata Tsheko, the local scout, along with Vulcan and Bellator, ventured out to scout the enemy's camp and get a lay of the land.

Meanwhile, while flying the AeroVironment RQ-ll Raven drone, a small hand-launched remote-controlled unmanned aerial vehicle (SUAV), George Devol and Venus discovered that Camp Letlotse was also guarded by a dozen armed private security guards patrolling the perimeter. Once they realized what they were up against, they began preparing their swarms of insect nano-drones for takeoff.

It was decided that the Blue Team would attack Camp Letlotse with their army of microbots on day two of the hunters' arrival. They had received information from an inside source that several high-ranking dignitaries would attend Tlou Lodge festivities on the first evening of the inaugural kick-off of "The Great Elephant Hunt." These same dignitaries would then participate in a similar gala at Camp Letlotse the following night.

The brass at Le Gang de la Clé de Singe wants it to appear as if the dignitaries from W.A.S.P. were the carriers of the outbreak. In the meantime, if any hunters did make their way out to hunt big game, the teams would turn to pursue them to protect the wildlife by any means necessary.

☠☠☠☠☠☠☠☠☠☠☠

"Ladies and Gentlemen, I want to warmly welcome and congratulate all the first winners of "The Great Elephant Hunt."" Thurston Bentley Hart the Third, President of Worldwide Affiliates of Safari Partners (W.A.S.P.), said with a big toothy smile.

"I have spoken with the Minister of Environment, Natural Resources Conservation and Tourism, Boipelo Mooketsi, who said that this season has an excellent crop of bull elephants."

This comment brought massive applause from the hunters, guides, and staff.

Hart continued, "Minister Mooketsi will join us for our evening banquet. This is just a small mixer so everyone can meet, get to know each other, and have a chance to become better acquainted with your guide.

Please check in with our club secretary, Ms. Kiest, at some point this afternoon, who is seated at the welcome table next to the bar. She will match you up with your guides.

Dinner is at eight o'clock, so until then, drink up, ladies and gentlemen, and enjoy yourselves.

Châtelet was recording Thurston Bentley Hart the Third's welcome speech from the mosquitoe microbot, which had a built-in microphone on the left shoulder of his $1200 khaki Paul Stuart safari jacket.

Châtelet and George Devol had coordinated their preferred drugs to use for numerous possible scenarios before joining up with their respective teams. Each had an arsenal of over three thousand pre-prepared mosquitoes and was cataloged for their particular disease category. They all contained a mixture of venom and preprogrammed murderous microbots that would aid in advancing the specific disease the mosquitoes would be injecting into the victim.

The majority of the mosquitoes would be carrying Ebola. However, to confuse the treating doctors, they would infect some others with Marburg Fever, Hemorrhagic Fever, and the Reston Virus.

The ideal objective was for world health authorities to believe that there had been a major viral outbreak in Botswana and to shut down all hunting within Chobe Park.

☠☠☠☠☠☠☠☠☠☠☠

While out scouting, Gorata Tsheko, Vulcan, and Bellator came across three native men who had just killed a female Elephant. They were in the process of butchering her. Vulcan and Bellator aimed and dropped two of the poachers simultaneously. The third man took off running.

"Bellator, you go check on those two. Gorata, let's go get this asshole." Vulcan shouted as he began the pursuit.

Gorata joined in and took the lead. He began to diverge from where the third man had started running.

"Follow me. We'll head him off!" Gorata whispered.

They ran through thick brush and eye-level grass until they came to a clearing.

"Wait! Back up into the brush."

Vulcan, wearing his ghillie suit, blended so well into the brush and grass that he was invisible to the naked eye. Gorata knelt behind the assassin as they waited. It wasn't but minutes before they heard someone running hard. When the man reached the clearing, he stopped. He was out of breath, and his breathing was labored.

The movement of Vulcan standing up, pointing his Sig Sauer AS50 sniper rifle, caught the man's attention. He threw up his hands, dropped to his knees, and pleaded, "Please do not kill me."

Vulcan handed Gorata his rifle and drew his P226 pistol from his holster. With his left hand, he reached inside his suit coat pocket and produced the yellow ensign with skull and cross monkey wrenches.

"You know who I am?" Vulcan asked the man, groveling before him.

"I do. You are the monkey man."

"Do you know the penalty for poaching?"

"I do. But I have to feed my family, sir. I have a wife at home, sir."

"No, my friend, you have a widow at home."

PHIFF

Vulcan dressed the poacher with the yellow flag around his neck, placed a copy of the manifesto in his pocket, and hoisted his lifeless body over his shoulder. They then made their way back to where Bellator was waiting. He had placed the signature flags on the two dead bodies and Laying them side by side next to the elephant they murdered. Vulcan dropped the man he killed next to his accomplices.

"When we return to camp, we'll call the rangers and give them the GPS coordinates," Vulcan said as they headed back to camp.

☠☠☠☠☠☠☠☠☠☠☠

Vermeer followed his driver to a fairly beat-up white Russian UAZ minivan that had been converted into a camper.

Vermeer looked at the van and back to Gurragchaa, noting, "Interesting choice of vehicle."

"I thought it best to try and be inconspicuous," Gurragchaa said with a hint of a smirk.

"Okay, sure, but is this really your van?" Vermeer said.

"Right," Gurragchaa said sheepishly.

"Hey. No worries."

Gurragchaa got into the driver's seat and turned the key.

Grrrrrrrrrrrr Grrrrrrrrrr Grrrrrrr VaRoom

A sense of panic and embarrassment rushed over Gurragchaa, but once the engine kicked over, he gave a big smile as he dropped the lever into first gear and drove off.

"How was your journey?" Gurragchaa asked as he turned out of the train station and headed to the hotel.

"Honestly, not too bad. I did get a lot of reading done. Wouldn't want to do it again."

"I'd like to travel someday."

"Is this your first assignment?"

"It is. You?"

"Oh, no. I've had dozens all around the world."

"Really!"

"Are you originally from Ulaanbaatar?" Vermeer asked.

"Yes. For the last two years, I have been working as a park ranger at Khukh Serkhiin Nuruu National Park, located on the border of Hovd and Bayan-Olgii, near the town of Deluun.

Khukh Serkhiin Nuruu means 'Blue Goat'. It has the largest concentration of endangered argali sheep in the world. The park is a refuge for many endangered species, including the snow leopard, Altai deer, and the ibex.

I was there when the son of an American President shot and killed one of our endangered argali sheep. It had the largest ram's horn ever recorded at six feet two inches. Of course, he got special dispensation because of who his father was.

That was the day I decided to join Le Gang de la Clé de Singe. I am so tired of these wealthy self-serving people who think just because they have the money, they can do whatever they want and get away with it." Gurragchaa said.

"You realize that this could get messy and people will die?" Vermeer asked.

"I do. And I do believe that I am ready."

"Have you ever killed anyone before?"

"No," Gurragchaa said sheepishly.

"Gurragchaa, I need to know that if things get hairy, I'll be able to count on you. It's better I know now. Be honest."

"You can count on me," Gurragchaa said as he pulled into the Blue Sky Hotel's driveway.

The Blue Sky Hotel looked like a gigantic blue shark fin towering twenty-two stories up into the sky, dwarfing everything in the surrounding area for miles. The ultra-modern luxury hotel is in the bustling Sukhbaatar District, in the heart of Ulaanbaatar's leading shopping and business area. Everywhere Vermeer looked, there were sky cranes all around from an influx of Chinese and Russian investments: corporate headquarters, hotels, condos, and apartment buildings springing up all over the downtown area. There seemed to be no rhyme or reason to which building was next to another. The Blue Sky Hotel was tucked between the Hewlett-Packard Corporate headquarters and a farm implements showroom featuring tractors, plows, and combines.

As a bellhop came to open Vermeer's door, Vermeer said to Gurragchaa, "Swing by for some dinner. Is six good for you?"

"That would be very nice. Thank you."

"Good, I'll see you then," Vermeer said as he stepped out of the car.

He walked into the hotel lobby with the bellhop close behind, carrying his small leather duffel bag.

"Good afternoon. Do you have a reservation?" Asked the young man standing behind the marble reservation desk as he gave a slight courteous bow. He was nattily dressed in his Calvin Klein navy blue pin-striped suit, powder blue button-down oxford shirt, and yellow and blue club tie. His name tag was pinned above his upper coat pocket, "Qadan."

Vermeer smiled and answered, "Yes. Reservation for Sharpe. Tony Sharpe."

"Ah. Here we are, Mr. Sharpe. I see we have you staying with us for seven days. Is that correct?"

"That is correct."

"And I see that you've prepaid for your stay. I'll need to see your passport and a credit card for any incidentals," Qadan said.

Vermeer handed the young man his "fake" passport and platinum American Express card, "Here you go."

"Mr. Sharpe, I see that you are requesting an Executive Corner Room. I have you in room 22G. It has a magnificent view of the Chinggis Khaan Garden, Sukhbaatar Square, and the State History Museum of Mongolia.

Here is your key. The bellman will show you to your room. If there is anything we can do to make your stay more enjoyable, please just let us know.

"Thank you, Qadan; I appreciate it," Vermeer said as he took his key and handed Qadan a US twenty-dollar bill.

"Oh. Thank you, Mr. Sharpe. Enjoy your stay."

☠☠☠☠☠☠☠☠☠☠☠

"So, what do you feel like eating? You have a choice of Korean, Japanese, or European here at the hotel," Vermeer asked.

Gurragchaa didn't hesitate, "Korean!"

"Korean it is. Off to Le Seoul."

They rode the elevator down to the second floor and were greeted by a man and woman dressed in traditional Korean garb, who welcomed them to the restaurant with a gentle bow.

"Two for dinner?" The young woman asked.

"Yes, please," Vermeer replied.

"Follow me, please."

"May we have a seat by a window?" Vermeer asked.

"Yes, of course," she said, walking them to a window table overlooking the Choijin Lama Museum.

"How's this?" She asked.

"Perfect," Vermeer said.

"Your waitress will be with you in a moment, gentlemen." She said as she handed them some menus and then walked away.

Vermeer studied the menu and appeared to be totally confused, asking, "Gurragchaa, what do you recommend?"

"You've never had Korean?"

"Never," Vermeer admitted.

"Well, you're in for a treat," Gurragchaa said, grinning.

"So, Girragchaa, is this *olgoi khorkhoi* I've read so much about real or just a load of crap like Sasquatch, Yeti, and the Loch Ness Monster?" Vermeer asked.

"Oh, no, Mr. Sharpe, I can assure you that the creature is real. One has never been captured because touching any part of it causes an instant, painful death. I have been told that it preys on camels and will lay its eggs in its intestines."

"Have you ever seen one?"

"I have not, but my 85-year-old Uncle Dzhambul saw one once when he was a boy. It frightened him so much that he has never gone back to the Gobi Desert again."

Vermeer stared past Gurragchaa, sitting across from him, and tried to visualize this mythical creature. His concentration was broken as the waitress stopped by the table and asked, “May I get you gentlemen something to drink?”

“Two Airags, please,” Gurragchaa said.

“Yes, sir,” She said with a bow.

“Airag?” Vermeer queried.

“Yeah, it’s made with fermented mare’s milk and salt. It’s often called horse milk vodka.”

“Horse milk vodka?” Vermeer said.

“Welcome to Mongolia.”

Happy hour was over when Thurston Bentley Hart the Third announced that the Minister of Environment, Natural Resources Conservation, and Tourism, Boipelo Mooketsi, had arrived.

“Please, ladies and gentlemen, may I have your attention? Our honored guest, Minister Mooketsi, has just arrived. Can I ask you all to please proceed to the dining room? Thank you.”

The hundred or so drunken hunters, guests, and W.A.S.P. representatives staggered their way to the dining room. The round tables, which seat six, were draped with white tablecloths. In the middle of each table was a flowered centerpiece with a stuffed Steiff elephant lying on its back with its legs in the air.

At one end of the dining room was one long table where the honchos sat. Bentley Hart the Third could see that everyone was heavily inebriated and had difficulty finding their assigned seats, so he made an executive decision. He stood up and began tapping his wine glass with his dinner knife, trying to get everyone’s attention.

“May I have your attention, please!” Bentley Hart the Third shouted.

People stopped, some swaying from drunkenness, and looked at their fearless leader in anticipation.

"Since we're all anxious to have our dinner. Might I suggest that you take the first available seat you find. I think that it will be a good thing. So, if you would just take the first seat that you find, we can start the dinner service. Thank you."

It seemed to work overall. Although there were a couple of minor skirmishes, they were easily sorted out, usually when the drunker of the two forgot what the tiff was about.

As dinner continued, no one noticed the swarm of mosquito drones hovering just outside the main window of the dining room. With all the windows open, Châtelet easily targeted each individual hunter while they sat and ate. Unaware of her presence, she placed at least three mosquito drones on each person. She planned to wait until they returned to their rooms before attacking and infecting them.

After the main course and while dessert was being served, Bentley Hart the Third stood again and got everyone's attention.

"Ladies and gentlemen, may I have your attention, please? First, I'd like to thank the good folks here at Tlou Lodge for their gracious hospitality and sumptuous meal. Let's give them a round of applause, shall we?" Bentley Hart the Third said.

applause applause applause

"Next, I would like you all to give a big W.A.S.P. welcome to the man who helped make the Great Elephant Hunt possible. Let's give it up for Minister Mooketsi." Bentley Hart the Third said, invitingly, encouraging the crowd.

applause applause applause

Mooketsi, who was half in the bag, stood up, bowed, and, with a toothy smile, said, "Thank you. Thank you. It is my privilege to welcome you all to participate in the first-ever Great Elephant Hunt of Botswana. And as we say in Tswana, "*Masego kea o O nne le masego*." Which means good luck."

applause applause applause

By the time dinner and all the speeches were over, it was close to midnight. Almost everyone started making their way to their rooms. There was a small group of intrepid souls who wandered back to the firepit for more drinking and debauchery.

Châtelet started with people in their rooms. Using the cameras on the mosquito drones, she waited until the hunters were asleep in their beds before maneuvering them into striking position. The best place to inject the victim was on the side of the neck. For each person, she would try to inject them at least twice, and if she could, three times, just to be sure.

After Châtelet had infected everyone in the rooms, she released the microbots and had them form a swarm that hovered above the campsite until she was ready to bring them home.

She then attacked the people sitting outside around the firepit. They were a bit trickier because they were still awake. But because they were totally shit-faced, their reactions were way too slow to swat the drones. Ultimately, Châtelet infected all the hunters, guides, and most of the staff. It was decided not to infect the leaders until they were at Camp Letlotse.

At three in the morning, Châtelet attacked the security guards, rendering them unconscious so that the Red Team could cross the Chobe River and recon the camp.

While they were investigating, they proceeded to sabotage the hunter's gear. They fouled some of the firing pins on rifles, replaced live ammunition with duds, and placed ground glass into all of their boots so as to irritate their feet, causing much discomfort. They also sabotaged the hunter's vehicles, tampering with the fuel and brake lines.

They poured a couple of liters of Coca-Cola into their Land Rover's gas tanks, which will turn the whole mess into a caustic sludge. Finally, they disabled all their cell phones so they couldn't communicate with anyone or call for help if needed while out on the hunt.

By sunrise, the mission was accomplished. All intended victims had been infected, and all microbots, minus six, were all present and accounted for. As the last of the mosquito drones were placed back into their case, Fu Hao and Sue B stopped by to check on Châtelet, their techno-wizard.

"Success?" Fu Hao asked.

"All good," Châtelet reported.

"You look all done in, girl. Why don't you go and get some rest now?" Sue B said.

"Think I will," Châtelet said as she started to leave the command tent.

"Nice job," Fu Hao said.

"You've helped save hundreds of elephants," Sue B added.

"Thanks, guys. That means a lot."

Châtelet was fast asleep by the time her head hit the pillow.

That morning in the mess tent, only four people weren't feeling nauseous and just plain crappy. The four were the three executive officers of W.A.S.P. and Minister Boipelo Mooketsi, Minister of Environment, Natural Resources Conservation and Tourism.

There was lots of moaning and groaning; nobody seemed to be able to keep anything down, especially the Mara. A traditional African breakfast platter of scrambled eggs, pap (a cornmeal polenta), spicy vegetable relish, grilled tomatoes, and sausage. It tastes fabulous. Unfortunately, it looks greasy and slimy to someone who feels seasick and hungover.

As the wait staff placed the dishes in front of the ailing guests, more than half began retching. They leaped up out of their chairs and ran out of the mess tent, trying not to throw up before getting outside. Some made it. Some didn't.

"This is very odd," Bentley Hart the Third said to Ms. Kiest, the W.A.S.P. club secretary, as they sat at a corner table, thankful not to be in the thick of things.

"Have you ever seen anything like this before?" she asked.

"No. Never."

"Think it had to do with last night's dinner?"

"Couldn't be. We all ate the same thing, and we're not sick. I'm guessing it's just too much drinking. We should never had an open bar."

By the time Minister Mooketsi walked into the mess tent, the majority of hunters and guides had left. There was a slight odor of regurgitation lingering in the air.

"Good morning, Minister Mooketsi," Bentley Hart the Third said.

"And a good morning to you and Ms. Kiest."

"Good morning, Minister. You look rather chipper," She said.

"I feel chipper," He proclaimed.

"As do I," Bentley Hart the Third said.

"I assume that everyone is preparing for the hunt," The Minister said.

"Most of them are. A few seemed to have gotten shitfaced."

"Shitfaced?" the Minister queried.

"You know, schnockered, blotto, loaded, hammered, fried, ripped, stinko, tanked, wasted, sloshed, plowed."

"Drunk," Ms. Kiest interjected.

"Ah, drunk. *Gesuip*. I see," The Mooketsi said.

A waiter approached the table and asked Mooketsi, "Can I get you some breakfast, Minister?"

"Yes, please, and coffee, black."

"Yes, sir."

After breakfast, Bentley Hart the Third, Ms. Kiest, and Minister Mooketsi saw the two hunting teams off and wished them good hunting.

The three then took Minister Mooketsi's private helicopter to Camp Letlotse for their Great Elephant Hunt party that evening.

Shortly after takeoff, Bentley Hart the Third happened to see a black ATV with four people dressed in what looked like camo speeding southeast. He was going to say something, but lost his train of thought when Ms. Kiest pointed out a rather large herd of elephants.

☠☠☠☠☠☠☠☠☠☠☠

A fraction of the hunters and their guides felt strong enough to try hunting. All told, six teams headed out into the bush. All of the guides were native-born Africans: John Kingwood, Robert Ackley, Jon Scott, Roger Williams, David Hendricks, and Richard Verson. The guides were a mixture of Afrikaners and British ex-pats.

The hunters were from all across America. Billy Ray Sawgrass, Baton Rouge; Jeremy Allman, Aspen; Andrew Webber, Detroit; Arthur Lennox, Boise; Bert Sommer, Sacramento; and Bob Smithers, Birmingham.

While Châtelet was getting some well-deserved shuteye, the Red Team saddled up their gear. It proceeded to follow and intercept any hunters who ventured out to kill elephants, or anything else, for that matter. Since one team member had to stay at base camp to monitor the hunters via the Puma AE surveillance drone, only five members could go out on patrol. It was decided to play zone defense. Red Team One was made up of Sue B, Fu Hao, and Dineo Kabelo, their scout. They would patrol everything north of the Chobe River, while Red Team Two, with Cowboy, Sassoon, and Gianfranco, would cover everything south of the Chobe. It was, therefore, up to Hazael to be the eyes in the sky and report to the teams the location of the hunters and their guides.

The hunters and guides thought it better to travel in two separate packs. Half would cross the Chobe River and head north, while the other half would stay on the southern side of the river.

Guides Kingwood, Ackley, and Scott would team up with hunters Billy Ray Sawgrass, Jeremy Allman, and Andrew Webber. They would cross the Chobe and go north towards the Sioma Ngwezi National Park. Guides Williams, Hendricks, and Verson will have Andrew Lennox, Bert Sommer, and Bob Smithers with them as they head south into the Kasane Forest Reserve.

Both hunting packs would travel in a Land Rover Defender modified to accommodate six passengers, one driver, and one scout seat attached up front next to the left front headlight. The vehicle was open with an overhead canopy.

The two Red Teams would use modified Can-Am Maverick X3 X RC Turbo RRs. They're quick, nibble, heavy-duty, rugged, and small. They can handle sand, mud, rocks, and rivers. They're built for any terrain and can handle any weather. And best of all, they're fast, like a bat out of Hell.

The Mavericks were painted matte black. The seats, shocks, tires, and even the wheels were black. The only color was a small yellow skull and cross monkey wrenches on either side. Mounted on the roll bars on each side were black rifle scabbards that held the Sig Sauer AS50 sniper rifles.

The Red Team was all dressed in their ghillie suits, armed and ready to go. They each headed out to their destinations. It wasn't too long before Hazael alerted Red Team One.

"Red One, I have eyes on a Land Rover traveling north on the B8 into Namibia."

"Roger that," Fu Hao said as she stepped on the accelerator, driving parallel through open fields. Within ten minutes, the hunter's and guides' vehicle was spotted. She stayed just far enough back to keep them in sight and not be seen by them.

"Red Two, I see your target heading southeast in the bush. There are no roads once you leave camp; I will guide you."

"Roger. Where off," Cowboy answered.

They crossed the Chobe River far south of their camp so as not to leave any tracks that might lead back to base camp. Once they were on the other side of the river, it only took twenty minutes for Red Two to spot their quarry.

"Red One. I have spotted a herd of elephants off to the left, about half a click, and heading your way."

"Roger. Any indication that bogeys have detected them?" Fu Ho asked.

"No. No, wait, they're veering towards the herd. ETA about five minutes."

"Roger. Over," Fu Hao said as she slammed her foot down on the accelerator. The force of the turbo kicked the Maverick into hyperdrive, pushing everyone back deep into their seats. They beat the Land Rover to the herd, giving them enough time to set up an ambush. Fu Hao dropped Sue B off to the herd's right while she and Dineo swung over to the elephant herd's left. They parked the Maverick behind a small grove of Sycamore fig trees.

Having worn their ghillie suits, Fu Hao, Dineo, and Sue B blended into the fields of the tall Wool and Blady grasses. As they waited hidden, they could hear the Land Rover approach. It stopped less than fifty feet away, not because they had planned to, but because the tampering of the vehicles had paid off.

Sue B had brought a twelve-foot metal rod with Le Gang de la Clé de Singe yellow flag, black skull, and cross monkey wrenches attached to a small black box. When activated via radio signal, the box would raise the flag above the six-foot-tall grasses and bushes.

"God damnit! I told them back at camp to be sure and check to see if these bloody things were working properly," John Kingwood, who had chosen to be the driver, shouted.

"Ah, fuck it. Let's get out and walk a bit. We know there are elephants around here. Come on, we'll worry about the truck later," Richard Verson, the senior guide, said.

Fu Hao whispered into her microphone, "Sue, Dineo, let's start at the front of the truck. Sue, you take the fat one in the first seat. Dineo, you pop the one wearing the backward baseball cap, and I take out the driver. After that, take your shots."

"Roger," Sue B acknowledged.

"Copy," Dineo said.

"On my mark. One. Two. Three. Fire!"

PHIFF

PHIFF

PHIFF

In the blink of an eye, John Kingwood and Billy Ray Sawgrass were slumped over in their seats with large chunks of their heads and brains splattered all over the other members of their hunting party.

It took several seconds for everyone to comprehend what had happened. At that moment, when confusion engulfed them, Sue B tripped the contraption and raised the yellow ensign. When Ackley spotted the flag, panic ensued.

"Motherfucker! Look!" He said as he pointed to the flag.

He and Scott instinctively grabbed their rifles and took cover, as did Jeremy Allman. Unfortunately, Andrew Webber freaked out, jumped out of the vehicle, and began running unarmed straight towards their assailants.

"Let them pass. Concentrate on the others," Fu Hao said as the frightened man ran past them within inches.

The guides and hunters formed a defense line behind the Land Rover. Fu Hao and Sue B left Dineo in place while they maneuvered to outflank their prey.

Dineo fired a shot, striking the front-left tire to accentuate the hopelessness of their situation.

PHIFF

The tire exploded. *BAAROOM!*

Fu Hao and Sue B swung a wide arc around the hunters and guides, positioning themselves right behind them. They were easy pickings. Sue B shot and killed Jon Scott. Jeremy Allman threw his rifle down, held his arms up above his head, and shouted, "Don't shoot! I surrender!"

As he began to walk away from the Land Rover towards Dineo, Allman felt a pain in his chest. It was as if someone had hit him as hard as they could with a 20-pound sledgehammer. He fell to his knees. As hard as he tried, he couldn't seem to catch his breath. The more he tried, the more blood filled his mouth. He fell backward, lying on his back, looking up at the sky. As Jeremy lay on the ground dying, he saw what he thought were angels soaring high above him; they were, in fact, several Griffon vultures circling above, having detected the sweet smell of death.

Knowing there was no way out, Ackley decided that he wouldn't just wait to be picked off. He checked his AR-15 and said to himself, "Fuck it. At least, I'll go out fighting."

He stood up and began running towards where they thought their attackers were—screaming and firing his automatic weapon in every direction, hoping to kill someone at least.

POW POW POW POW POW POW POW POW POW POW POW POW POW POW POW POW POW POW

Sue B and Fu Hao were 45 degrees off to his right. As Ackley passed their position, the two women assassins stood and fired two shots in unison, dropping the guide no more than twenty feet from the Land Rover.

PHIFF PHIFF

The whole encounter lasted less than fifteen minutes, from the first shot to the last. As they began laying the bodies out, Sue B said, "Dineo, would you mind continuing while Fu Hao and I bring back those other two?"

"Not at all. Take your time," Dineo replied.

It wasn't more than five minutes when Dineo heard a gunshot in the distance. He smiled to himself and said, "Girl's rule."

☠☠☠☠☠☠☠☠☠☠☠

Gurragchaa dropped Vermeer off in front of the LUX—5 Residence Apartments, a sixteen-story Mongolian luxury apartment building complex in the affluent Chrystal Town area of town.

"Leave the car running," Vermeer said as he got out of the car.

He walked into the lobby and headed straight to the bank of elevators, stepped into one of the waiting cars, and pressed the penthouse button. Vermeer wore a black crew-neck T-shirt under a black suit jacket. He had on a pair of Vuarnet Glacier 1315 sunglasses with orange lenses and side shields.

When the elevator reached the fifteenth floor, he pulled his Beretta 92FS 9mm fitted with an AL-GI-MEC suppressor out of his shoulder holster, cocked the pistol, and held it behind his back.

As he exited the elevator car, he knew that Mohammad Khan lived in penthouse number 4 to the right. Waiting in front of the door was an imposing figure. It was one of Khan's bodyguards, standing nonchalantly with arms crossed and leaning against the door.

Vermeer was thirty feet away when he fired the first of three shots.

PHIFF PHIFF PHIFF

By the time he reached the door, the big man was no more than a bulbous welcome mat. Vermeer stood to the right of the doorknob, out of view of the peephole, and knocked on the door. He heard the peephole lid being raised, then muffled voices.

"Batu? Batu!" The voice was calling out to Batu, the dead man.

There was no answer. Then, there were more muffled voices before the voice shouted, "*Tend khen baina?*" (Who's there?)

Finally, the door slightly cracked open, maybe half an inch for the man to peer out. Vermeer placed his Beretta 92FS against the door and fired one shot, striking the person behind the door in the side of the head.

PHIFF

His death was followed by a hail of gunfire through the front door, tearing it into shreds.

POW POW POW POW POW POW POW POW POW POW POW POW POW POW

While the gunmen were destroying the door, making a hole big enough to drive a truck through, Vermeer took the time to pull the pins on two stun grenades, then lobbed them into the apartment.

BARROOM BARROOM

Vermeer waited a few seconds to let the smoke dissipate, then walked in with his Beretta 92FS held at shoulder height. Inside, he found three men unconscious, lying on the floor, moaning. He eliminated each one with a single shot to the head as he passed each one. He continued to the bedroom, where he found Mohammad Khan franticly trying to load a banana clip into an AK-47. When he saw the assassin, he dropped the rifle, raised his arms, and pleaded for his life.

"Please don't kill me. I am a wealthy man. I will pay you anything you want. Please."

Vermeer waved his Beretta 92FS in a gesture that said, "Get moving." The two of them walked out of the battle-racked apartment and towards the elevators.

"Try anything funny, and I'll blow your brains out. Understand?" Vermeer asked.

Khan nodded.

People from the other apartments started to wander into the hall, looking to see what had happened.

"It's just a small gas leak, folks. Nothing to worry about," Vermeer said in a reassuring tone.

As the elevator doors opened and the two stepped into the car, Vermeer stuck his head out and announced, "We're just going down to speak with the manager."

They began to hear the muffled screams of shock when the tenants found the bodies of the dead bodyguards in Khan's apartment as they were descending.

"You go ahead of me when we get out. Walk slowly. There's a white UAZ van right outside; get in the back."

They walked through the lobby and straight into the waiting van when the doors opened. Khan did as he was told, stepping into the side door with Vermeer right behind him.

Grrrrrrrrrrrr Grrrrrrrrrr Grrrrrr Grrrrrrrrrrr Grrrrrrrrrr Grrrrrr

"I told you to leave the car running!" Vermeer said.

Grrrrrrr Grrrrrrrr Grrrrrr VaRoom VaRooooom

The van lurched forward, and then they were off. Heading west on Ikh Khuree Street, weaving their way through mostly small streets to the major two-lane highway skirting the southern edge of town, the Naadamchdyn Zam.

As Gurragchaa was driving, Vermeer zip-tied Mohammad Khan's legs together and his hands behind his back. He then duct-taped his mouth and placed a black bag over his head.

"Just sit back and enjoy the ride, my friend," Vermeer whispered.

They drove well into the night, going due west but eventually swinging towards the south. By sunrise, they had entered the Gobi Gurvan Saikhan National Park, the largest national park in Mongolia. It stretches some 27,000 square kilometers on the northern border of the Gobi Desert, its destination.

"Thank God for GPS," Vermeer said as they stopped literally in the middle of nowhere. They were surrounded by nothing but miles and miles of dunes.

Vermeer removed the hood from Mohammad Khan's head, allowing him to see the vast and endless sea of sand.

Vermeer cut the zip-ties from Khan's hands and legs, as well as removing the tape from his mouth. Vermeer opened the van's side door, pointed his Beretta 92FS at the prisoner, and said, "Out."

"What is it that you want with me? I demand to know!"

Vermeer held up the yellow ensign and asked, "Do you know what this is?"

Mohammad Khan lied, "No."

"I suppose you never heard of Le Gang de la Clé de Singe," Vermeer asked as he tied the flag around Khan's neck.

Khan lied again, "No."

"Well, that's too bad. Now, get out of the van, or I'll shoot you where you sit," Vermeer ordered.

Mohammad Khan slowly began to move towards the door. He ran some scenarios through his mind about trying to wrestle the gun away from his assailant. But every scenario ended with him being shot.

"Does anyone ever come out here?" Vermeer asked Gurragchaa.

"Maybe an occasional camel train. Otherwise, there is no reason for anyone to venture this far into the desert. Besides, there have been sightings of the worms out here," Gurragchaa said.

Khan stepped out of the UAZ van, looking terrified. He moved towards Gurragchaa, his eyes as big as saucers, beads of sweat on his forehead and upper lip, and beseechingly asked, "Worms? What worms?"

"*Olgoi-Khorkhoi,*" Gurragchaa said coldly.

"The Mongolian Death Worm," Vermeer smirked.

"Please, kind sirs, I beg you, please, no!" Mohammad Khan begged, falling to his knees.

"Sorry, friend. I would love to stay and chat, but as they say in Mongolia, it's the early Death Worm that catches the Khan," Vermeer said as he and Gurragchaa got into the van and began to drive away.

Mohammad Khan began to run after the van. But, being in terrible shape, he had to stop and catch his breath. He could feel something deep beneath the sand as he stood bent over, with his hands on his knees, wheezing. There seemed to be undulation, a tremor ebbing upwards. He started moving again; he hadn't sensed any movement while walking. By this time, the van was far away.

"Have you ever seen the Death Worm?" Vermeer asked Gurragchaa.

"Once. As a child, it was blood red and shaped like a sausage, about two feet long. It had no head or legs, and it was so poisonous that merely touching it meant instant death. But it can also kill you from a distance; it has the capability of spraying its victim with venom or by means of an electric discharge like the electric eel."

Looking into the rearview mirror as they were driving away, Gurragchaa saw Mohammad Khan standing with his hands on his hips, having difficulty breathing. All of a sudden, he began wiping something off his feet and legs, then collapsed to the ground.

"Look! Look quickly into the review mirror!" Gurragchaa shouted.

By the time Vermeer had spotted Mohammad Khan, he was rolling around, flailing, and being engulfed by what looked to be dozens of blood-red alien tentacles dragging him down below the sand.

EEEYYYYAAAAAHHHHH

Within minutes, he was gone, and the sand was smooth as glass, as if nothing happened. Seconds later, a small yellow piece of fabric emerged from underneath the sand.

Vermeer thought for a moment that it had come to the surface almost as if it were to mark Mohammad Khan's final resting place, but then a strong sirocco came and blew the saffron banderole high into the sky.

"Whatever you do, Gurragchaa, don't stop the van. If we get stuck, you'll be the one getting out and walking for help," Vermeer said with a devilish grin.

☠☠☠☠☠☠☠☠☠☠☠

Red Team Two crossed the Chobe River three miles west of the camp, where the water was only knee-deep. They then drove at a 45-degree angle to intercept their prey at the entrance of Kasane Forest Reserve.

They had arrived about five minutes before the hunting party did. They parked their black Maverick facing the oncoming Land Rover and blocking the road. Gianfranco stood in front of their vehicle, holding his Sig Sauer AS50 sniper rifles at the ready. Cowboy and Sassoon had wandered off into a small grove of camel thorn trees by the left side of the road, while Sassoon found several thick velvet raisin bushes to take cover behind.

As the Land Rover approached, it slowed down to a crawl and eventually stopped. The driver, Rich Verson, turned to Roger Williams, who was sitting next to him, and said, "Who the fuck is this guy?"

Williams stood up in the Rover, leaned on the front windscreen, and shouted, "Oy, mate, get out of the road!"

Gianfranco didn't budge.

"Don't make me come over there and kick your ass!"

Gianfranco stood perfectly still, with the exception of his right thumb imperceptibly releasing the safety on his Sig Sauer.

Roger Williams, a British ex-pat living in Botswana, had served three tours in Afghanistan with the Special Air Services (SAS). He stood six feet six inches tall, weighed 265 pounds, and was as solid as a Westinghouse refrigerator. Roger unholstered his Smith & Wesson SD40 pistol, jumped down from the Land Rover, and walked over to Gianfranco. He stopped six feet in front of Gianfranco and slightly to the right.

"Now, what's your problem, sunshine?" Williams asked, holding his pistol down by his side.

"You. You're my problem," Gianfranco answered.

"Oh, really? And why is that?" Williams queried.

Gianfranco slowly lifted his left hand, reached inside his jacket pocket, and pulled out a folded piece of yellow fabric. He took two steps towards Williams and handed it to him.

"What the fuck is this?" Williams quipped sarcastically.

"Open it," Gianfranco said as he took two steps backward.

Williams shook the piece of fabric until it unfolded, revealing the death symbol of the skull and cross monkey wrenches. The big man turned a whiter shade of pale.

Gianfranco asked, "You know who I am?"

"Yeah. But you've got a lot of stones thinking that you can outgun the six of us all alone." Williams said, trying to sound tough while mustering up some courage. He had lost many a hunting friend to Le Gang de la Clé de Singe, and he had seen the bodies all laid out next to one another with the yellow flags draped around their necks. They weren't to be trifled with.

"Who says I'm alone?"

Williams' eyes got big, and he could feel sweat form on the back of his neck.

Rich Verson shouted, "Yo, Roger, what's going on? Let's go while we're young."

Gianfranco, sensing that shit was about to happen, said stoically, "It's your move, cowboy."

Williams squinted his eyes and jerked his arm forward, starting to raise the gun up.

Killing big game from a distance is one thing; killing another human being, especially when the other human being is face-to-face and is a professional killer, is another. Williams had a slight hesitation, which was all Gianfranco needed. The typical reaction would be to raise the gun to shoot the opponent in the torso. Too time-consuming, Gianfranco just raised his rifle ever so slightly and shot Williams in the foot. Then, when he was bent over in pain, Gianfranco fired the kill shot, dropping the big man like a ton of bricks.

PHIFF PHIFF

Within seconds of Gianfranco killing Williams, Cowboy and Sassoon took out the entire hunting party in less than a minute. The boys from W.A.S.P. never got a single shot off.

PHIFF PHIFF

They placed the six of them side-by-side, all wearing the yellow flags around their necks, each with a copy of the manifesto stuffed in their pockets. Once Red Team Two cleaned up and strategically placed the same fingerprint that Red Team One had used at the site of their kill, they headed back to base camp.

When authorities came out to investigate and process both murder scenes, they found only one clean, single, identifiable fingerprint at both sites, that of the American author and world-famous big game hunter Ernest Hemingway.

☠☠☠☠☠☠☠☠☠☠☠

Vermeer said goodbye to Gurragchaa at the Chinggis Khaan International Airport two days after the abduction of Mohammad Khan.

"I want to thank you for all your help," Vermeer said.

"Where are you off to, now? Gurragchaa asked, wishing he could go too.

"Not sure. I'm flying to Kathmandu as a jumping-off point. I'll get further instructions once I land. How about you?"

"I've been asked to return to Khukh Serkhiin Nuruu National Park as a park ranger, but I would prefer to travel with you."

"Hey, the work that you're doing is vital. Besides, I'm sure that there will come a time when you'll be called upon again."

"I am ready."

"Well, thanks again," Vermeer said as he shook Gurragchaa's hand and headed into the Aeroflot terminal. He passed through the security checkpoint and made his way to gate fourteen, where he was one of only a handful of passengers sitting in the waiting area. Over half were Buddhist monks, and Vermeer was the only European-looking one, so he stood out like a sore thumb.

"Good afternoon. First time traveling to Kathmandu?" Asked one of the monks.

"Yes, it is," Vermeer replied.

"Do you mind my asking, business or pleasure?"

"Pleasure," Vermeer said.

"*Qomolangma*?" The monk asked.

"I beg your pardon."

"*Qomolangma.* Mount Everest, as you call it. Are you coming to climb the Holy Mother?"

"No, I'm not a climber."

The monk smiled, held out his hand, and said, "My name is Anurak."

"Tony Sharpe," Vermeer said as he shook the monk's hand.

"I hope you do not mind my asking so many questions. It's just that I don't often get the opportunity to talk to Westerners."

"No, I don't mind at all. And I don't get many opportunities to speak with Buddhist monks. Do you live in Kathmandu?"

"I live in the monastery in Swayambhunath Stupa. It is an ancient temple atop the hill in the Kathmandu Valley. It is one of the oldest religious sites in all of Nepal, built in the beginning of the 5th century AD."

"Sounds beautiful."

"The Tibetans named it 'Sublime Trees' for the many varieties of trees found on the hill."

"Sounds very peaceful."

"It usually is. Although the temple monkeys can sometimes be a bit rambunctious and trying."

"So, what brought you to Ulaanbaatar?" Vermeer asked.

"We were here restoring the Gandantegchinlen Monastery."

"How long were you here for?"

"Three weeks. And you?"

"One week. I met up with an old friend, took in the sights, and caught up on old times."

"Well, Mr. Sharpe, if you have some time while you are in Kathmandu, it would be my pleasure if you would allow me to show you around. Just stop by or call the monastery and ask for me, and we can arrange to get together."

"Why, that's mighty kind of you, Anurak. You know, I just might take you up on your kind offer."

The agent at gate fourteen began to make the boarding announcement: "Good afternoon. This is the pre-boarding announcement for Aeroflot flight 89B to Kathmandu. We are now inviting passengers with small children and any passengers requiring special assistance to begin boarding. Please have your boarding pass and identification ready. Regular boarding will begin in approximately ten minutes. Thank you."

While Vermeer and Anurak, the Buddhist monk, were talking, dozens of passengers had come into the boarding area.

"Wow, I didn't realize Kathmandu was such a hot spot," Vermeer said.

"Most of these people are on a pilgrimage of enlightenment."

"I could probably use some enlightenment," Vermeer said in jest.

The boarding agent called out Anurak's row number to board; he stood up, shook Vermeer's hand, and said, "Please do call me when you get settled. I look forward to hearing from you. Oh, and by the way, Wooch told me to tell you, nice work with Mohammad Khan."

Vermeer sat looking dumbfounded.

Anurak smiled and walked towards the gangway with his fellow Buddhist monks.

Vermeer said to himself as he watched the monks disappear down the gangway, "Fuck me."

☠☠☠☠☠☠☠☠☠☠☠

"Welcome to Camp Letlotse, Minister Mooketsi, Mr. Bentley Hart, and Ms. Kiest." Charles Moby, the owner of Camp Letlotse, said, smiling as he greeted his VIPs.

"Thank you," Bentley Hart the Third said.

"*Ke a leboga.*" (Thank you) Minister Mooketsi replied with a smile.

"It's an honor to have you all. Please follow me," Moby said as he led his guests to the main hospitality building. Four black bellhops dressed in safari jackets and khaki shorts followed close behind, carrying their luggage.

Once inside the reception area, Moby proceeded to go over the itinerary for that night's festivities.

"At five o'clock, we will be hosting a casual open bar get-together. Dinner will be at seven, followed by after-dinner drinks on the veranda.

Before dinner, having the Minister and Mr. Bentley Hart say a few words to the lucky hunters would be nice. If that's all right with you, gentlemen?" Moby asked.

Both Bentley Hart and the Mooketsi smiled and nodded in the affirmative.

Moby grinned as he handed each of them the keys to their rooms and a small packet of information about the camp and its facilities.

"Excellent. Now, these men will show you to your rooms, and please feel free to call upon me if there is anything I can do for you. If not, we will see you all back here at five o'clock for drinks. And again, welcome to Camp Letlotse," Moby said.

As the VIPs left the reception area, neither they nor Moby noticed the two-inch beetle drone perched on the top of the stuffed lion's head above the check-in counter.

Devol had placed the drone there earlier in the day as an eavesdropper. He was able to ascertain the hunter's room numbers and the planned agenda, not only for that day's events but also for the next day's hunting schedule.

He spent the day preparing the mosquito microbots for that evening's swarm attack while the Blue Team of Odin, Lu Wei, Vulcan, Bellator, and Venus were checking and rechecking their gear and weapons, just in case they were to have any encounters with the hunting parties like the Red Team had.

Odin had been in close contact with Fu Hao and Sue B, getting updates on not only the hunting party massacres but also the advancements of the illness of the hunters from the micro drone attacks.

"We just intercepted a message from the camp requesting medical assistance. They are reporting a sudden outbreak of an unknown disease," Fu Hao said.

"Thanks for the update," Odin said.

"We will keep you apprised of any new developments." Sue B added.

"Roger. We are preparing for our swarm launch in about an hour," Odin said.

"Good luck," Fu Hao said.

"Over."

☠☠☠☠☠☠☠☠☠☠☠

At five o'clock, Devol, with the help of Venus, launched the swarm of two thousand mosquito microbots. They flew the throng of drones in from the east, where the sky was getting darker, so as not to alert anyone that winged angels of death were coming their way.

"Ladies and gentlemen, I just want to welcome you all to the first-ever Great Elephant Hunt. I'm Charles Moby, owner of Camp Letlotse, and on behalf of myself and our entire staff, I want to say welcome and good hunting.

Later, we'll hear from the two men who made this special event possible, but for now, drink up, enjoy the evening, and spend some time getting to know one another.

Pholo e ntle!" (Cheers!) Moby said as he held up an oversized mug of beer.

Applause Applause Applause

While the festivities were happening, Devol and Venus distributed the killer microbots to everyone's room. On average, they assigned at least three mosquitoes to each individual, silently waiting in their rooms, ready to strike once they'd fallen asleep.

Just like what happened at Tlou Lodge with the open bar, everyone got way too drunk too early. By the time dinner was served, most people were so inebriated that they were passing out or falling asleep at the dinner table. Even the special guests were all half in the bag.

When they stood up to speak, both Minister Mooketsi and Bentley Hart the Third mispronounced, slurred, and left out words from their speeches, not that anyone was sober enough to notice.

The majority of guests made their way back to their rooms about two in the morning. That's when Devol and Venus went to work, attacking the hunters, guides, and the VIPs. They began to rain Hell from above.

At three o'clock, when they were sure everyone would be asleep, they started infecting the guides and all of the hunters with various fatal diseases. After they had completed that task, they injected Minister Mooketsi and Thurston Bentley Hart the Third. Unlike the guides and hunters, Devol injected them with Botulinum toxin. Botulinum toxin is the most toxic substance known to man. One nanogram (one billionth of a gram) can kill a human instantly.

The Mosquito Microbot that killed Minister Mooketsi found him sleeping peacefully alone in his bed. Devol had an easy time maneuvering the micro-drone to land on his neck and infuse the poison into his body. He was dead before the Mosquito Microbot could fly away.

Thurston Bentley Hart the Third's death was a bit trickier. When Devol took control of the Mosquito Microbots that had been circling overhead, Hart's bed, he found that this would be an unexpected challenge. The cameras on the Mosquito Microbots detected that Hart was in the act of sexual intercourse with Ms. Kiest. She was not on their 'hit' list.

"Mmmmm. Mmmmm. Yeah. Harder!" Ms. Kiest moaned.

"Oh, yeah, baby. Ahhhh, I'm getting close. You?"

"Oh, yeah. Come on. Deeper."

Devol turned to Venus and said, "Go get Odin."

Venus ran off to wake up the team leader while Devol's Mosquito Microbots hovered stationary above.

A bleary-eyed Odin stepped into the drone tent and asked, "What's up?"

"Take a look," Devol said, pointing at the monitor.

"What exactly am I looking at?" Odin said, trying to decipher what he was observing.

"That is Thurston Bentley Hart the Third fucking Ms. Kiest."

"You woke me up to look at this!"

"No. You're here to give me the go-ahead and strike now or wait."

"Is she in any danger?" Odin asked.

"No."

"Then strike now."

Devol's timing couldn't have been better. The Mosquito Microbot landed on Thurston Bentley Hart the Third's left buttock just as both Hart and Kiest were reaching mutual climax.

"Come on. That's it. Deeper. Deeper. Oh, God. Yes!"

"Yes! Oh, Yes! I'm coming," Hart proclaimed.

Just as Hart arched his back as he ejaculated, Devol pressed the injection button. Thurston Bentley Hart the Third died instantaneously. Bentley Hart the Third came and went simultaneously as he collapsed atop Ms. Kiest.

Seconds later, Venus instructed a Mosquito Microbot to land on and inject Ms. Kiest with a minor dose of propofol to knock her out until morning.

The following day, when she woke up, she found Bentley Hart the Third lying on his back, dead as a doornail with a rock-hard erection—commonly referred to as a death erection, angel lust, or terminal erection.

At first, she was mortified, but being the pragmatic person she was, Ms. Kiest decided that letting such an opportunity pass would be impractical and a waste. So, she straddled herself on top of the dear departed and used Bentley Hart the Third as her personal bienfaiteur—not once, but three times—before she alerted the manager, Charles Moby.

She would go to her grave thinking that she killed a man while having sex. That thought always brought a sheepish smile to her face.

☠☠☠☠☠☠☠☠☠☠☠

In a panic, Charles Moby called the Ministry of Health and Wellness in Gaborone, the capital, to alert them that there seemed to be some sort of outbreak occurring at Camp Letlotse.

"What sort of outbreak, Mr. Moby?" The anonymous voice asked.

"There have been two deaths, that of Minister Mooketsi and the American businessman Thurston Bentley Hart the Third," Moby said.

"Suspicious?"

"How would I know."

"Does it look like foul play?"

"No. There doesn't seem to be any signs of wounds or anything. In addition, dozens of our guests appear to have contracted some sort of disease."

"Disease? What do you mean?"

"High fevers, nausea, vomiting, fatigue. You need to send people here as soon as possible!" Moby pleaded.

"We'll be sending people out today."

"Hurry!"

CLICK

Unbeknownst to Charles Moby, a call was made to the Ministry of Health and Wellness in Gaborone from The Tlou Lodge the day before, complaining about a similar outbreak.

A dozen health workers, all wearing hazmat suits, descended on the safari lodge, where they not only found all of the hunters and guides sick with various viruses, but they also discovered two hunting parties that had been apparently massacred by the eco-terrorists Le Gang de la Clé de Singe.

After an examination of Camp Letlotse, the Ministry of Health and Wellness placed both Camp Letlotse and The Tlou Lodge under quarantine until further notice.

Although the Botswana government couldn't prove that the viruses were positively attributed to Le Gang de la Clé de Singe, they did imply that they were somehow involved.

Le Gang de la Clé de Singe sent out a worldwide communiqué denying any involvement, stating that they would never resort to the use of chemical or biological warfare and that these accusations were all just fake news. It was just another political distraction to keep the messaging away from the slaughter of the world's diminishing wildlife populations. They went on to say that they proudly kill poachers and big game hunters the old-fashioned way: open combat.

☠☠☠☠☠☠☠☠☠☠☠

"Good evening. I'm Nigel Williams, and this is BBC World Headline News. Our top story this hour comes from Botswana, Africa, where there is a report of a viral outbreak at two safari camps along the Chobe River: Camp Letlotse and The Tlou Lodge. Both are currently under strict quarantine.

A spokesperson from the Ministry of Health and Wellness told the BBC that at least four different viruses had been found in both camps. Ebola, Marburg Fever, and Hemorrhagic Fever. All deadly and highly contagious.

So far, there have been, all told, over thirty deaths, including the Minister of Environment, Natural Resources Conservation and Tourism, Boipelo Mooketsi, and the American businessman Thurston Bentley Hart the Third, president of Worldwide Affiliates of Safari Partners.

Although the Botswana government cannot conclusively link any of the viral deaths to the eco-terrorist group, Le Gang de la Clé de Singe, the government believes that they are convinced that this terrorist group was behind the attack.

A spokesperson for Le Gang de la Clé de Singe denies the accusations of using biological warfare; they do claim responsibility for the attack and murder of a dozen hunters and guides from both Camp Letlotse and The Tlou Lodge who were out in the field hunting elephants. They were quick to point out that no elephants were killed.

Meanwhile, in other news……"

☠☠☠☠☠☠☠☠☠☠☠

Since Anurak and his fellow monks deplaned well before Vermeer was able to get off, they were nowhere to be seen. He went through customs under the new name of Jake Hanson on a British passport. He walked out of Tribhuvan International Airport and straight to the taxi stand.

"Where to?" The cabbie asked.

"Hotel Shanker Kathmandu," Vermeer said.

"Very good, sir."

The ride was a mere fifteen minutes, although the taxi hardly went more than a couple of hundred feet before turning onto another street with names as long as your arm.

Hotel Shanker is a historic, luxury heritage hotel that opened in 1964 in a building dating back to 1894. It is located in the center of town, next to the historic

Narayananhity Palace Museum. The building's architectural style is neoclassical. The palace was built for General Jit Shumsher Rana (the Southern Commanding General of the Army). The hotel is characterized by exquisite and authentic objects d'art. The hotel sits in the middle of 4.4 acres of gardens in the center of Kathmandu, the modern metropolis.

"Good evening. Welcome to the Hotel Shanker. How may I help you?" The young woman behind the reception counter asked.

"Hello. Reservation for Hanson. Jake Hanson," Vermeer replied.

The young lady's fingers nimbly danced across the computer keyboard and, within seconds, found a match.

"Yes, sir. Mr. Hanson, we have you staying for seven nights. Is that correct?" She asked.

"Correct."

"I see that you have prepaid for one of our deluxe single rooms. Will that be sufficient for you?"

"That will be perfect."

"How many keys will you require?"

"Just onc."

"Now I just need your passport and a credit card for incidentals."

He surrendered his passport, she ran the card and handed him the card key.

"Would you like some assistance with your luggage?"

"I think I can manage. Thank you." He said, holding up his leather bag.

As he started off to his room, the young woman called out after him, "Mr. Hanson."

He turned, "Yes?"

"I see here we have a package for you," She said, holding up a shoebox-sized package.

He took it from her, shook it, smiled, and said, "Mmmm, cookies from Mom."

As it turned out, "Mom" hadn't sent cookies after all; she sent Vermeer his favorite weapon, a Beretta 92FS fitted with an AL-GI-MEC suppressor, seven boxes of ammunition, five M67 hand grenades, one tear gas grenade, goggles, a portable rebreathing device, and a custom-made shoulder holster. At the bottom of the box was a small handwritten card. "Love, Mom." Vermeer recognized the signature to be that of Wooch's.

Since it was getting late, Vermeer decided to grab dinner at the hotel's Kailash Restaurant. The room was brightly lit, as there were no windows. The motif was a pleasant combination of Indian and Chinese with a sprinkling of Nepali.

The room was mostly made up of Chinese businessmen, British tourists, and locals treating themselves to a night out. Being tired and sleepy, Vermeer decided to seek recommendations from his waiter. He started with an appetizer of Gong Bao Chicken, a cup of Cream di Funghi soup, and Pak Choy with Wood Fungus Mushrooms as the main course.

Once back in his room, Vermeer plopped down on the bed, fully clothed, and didn't wake up until the maid knocked on his door at 10 am the following day.

By eleven, he was showered, dressed, and in a cab heading to the monastery at Swayambhunath Stupa to meet up with Anurak. The cab driver took him right to Maitreya Gumba Monastery. There were hundreds of tourists mulling around, gawking, shopping at stalls, taking photographs, and feeding the temple monkeys.

Vermeer found the gated monastery surrounded by parked cars from the visiting tourists. It was a simple white structure with Buddhist decorations in sienna, red, black, white, and golden yellow on the top third of the building.

Outside the iron gate stood two sculptures of the Buddha's lions on either of the gate doors, symbolizing strength, royalty, and bravery. He walked up to the front door, which had a sienna-red background with blue swastikas in each corner and the sacred Zen Buddhism Ensō symbol, often referred to as the "Circle of Enlightenment," painted golden yellow in the center of the door.

Vermeer rang the small bronze bell next to the door to announce his presence. Nothing. He rang it again. Finally, the door opened slightly to reveal a young man with a shaved head, wearing a maroon kasaya. He said nothing. He just looked at Vermeer.

"I'm looking for Anurak," Vermeer said.

The young monk opened the door wider and stepped aside to allow Vermeer to enter. Still, he said not a single word. Once inside, the monk closed the door and started to walk down the hallway. Halfway down, he stopped and saw that Vermeer was not following him. He gave a gesture suggesting that Vermeer should follow him.

They walk all the way through the monastery and out through a back door, where Vermeer sees several monks working in a vegetable garden. The young monk points to the group of men and then goes back into the building.

Vermeer turned and said, "Thank you."

The monk says nothing, nods, and continues back into the monastery.

Vermeer walks into the garden looking for Anurak, which isn't easy since everyone is dressed the same, with shaved heads. He finally spots him. Anurak smiles and nods but says nothing. He takes Vermeer by the arm, and together, they walk to the garden gate door and out into the park that surrounds the monastery.

When they're far from the monastery, Anurak says, "We have taken a vow of silence within the monastery. It's a sign of obedience and devotion."

"Are there others in the order that support the work of Le Gang de la Clé de Singe?" Vermeer asked.

"A few."

"You all know that we kill people. Doesn't that go against everything Buddhism stands for?"

"It is true that we believe in no killing—a respect for all life. We also believe that good deeds outweigh bad deeds and that what happens to a person happens because their actions caused it," Anurak said.

"Karma?"

"That's right, karma. Whatever one puts out into the Universe will come back to them."

"So, what's my assignment?" Vermeer asked.

"There are three brothers who are notorious poachers. They've gone untouched because they bribe all of the local officials, ward captains, the ward chairperson, the deputy mayor, and one or two national officials as well.

Bibek, Manish, and Indragop Neupane are three thugs who strut around Kathmandu like they own the place, and they pretty much do. They are responsible for the capture and deaths of Nepal's most precious and endangered species: the one-horned rhinoceros, the Asian elephant, the snow leopard, and, of course, the pangolin.

"Well, I think it's about time for me to open a can of whoop-ass on the Neupane boys?"

"Whoop-ass?" Anurak asked perplexed

"Karma," Vermeer said with a grin.

The brothers Neupane grew up in one of Nepal's poorest and most inaccessible cities, Jumla. Jumla is located in the Greater Himalayan region and is known for rice cultivation. Jumla is one of the 77 districts in the midwestern hills of Nepal. The highest elevation at which rice is cultivated in Nepal is 3,050 meters. Jumli Marshi, an indigenous rice with a cold-tolerant gene, has probably been cultivated in Jumla on the bank of the Tila River for over 1,300 years.

The Neupane family had been growing rice for over eleven generations. It was a hard existence. Back-breaking work and long hours for pennies a day. Last year, they made 23,600 Nepalese rupees, which is less than 200 US Dollars.

Bibek Neupane grew up dirt poor and was looking for a way to do better. One day, when Bibek was visiting his lady friend, Biswabandita, who works at the Manasarowor Hotel and café, he met an American hunter, Roger Peyser, who was looking to hunt Himalayan musk deer. The killing of musk deer is illegal because they are considered endangered.

Being a typical American game hunter, Roger didn't care about the legality; in fact, he said it just added to the thrill of the hunt. He offered Bibek 500 US Dollars for a successful hunt. Two days into the hunt, Bibek spotted a fourteen-point musk deer. Peyser took aim and fired, killing the prized trophy with one shot.

True to his word, Roger Peyser paid Bibek 500 US dollars in cash. He then offered another $500 if he could smuggle the deer into India. Bibek enlisted the help of his two younger brothers to smuggle the deer carcass into Lakhimpur, India, just across the Nepalese/Indian border, where Roger Peyser was waiting.

From that day on, the brothers Neupane ceased being rice farmers and began their lives of poaching and illegal species trafficking. It was a rags-to-riches story that wouldn't end happily ever after.

“So, where can I find these Neupane boys?” Vermeer asked.

“They have a suite of rooms at the Dearika’s Hotel over on Battisputali Road,” the monk replied.

“Do they have bodyguards?”

“No. They think that they are untouchable because of all the bribes, but they are always heavily armed.”

“Just the way I like it,” Vermeer said with a grin.

“Why?”

“Where’s the challenge in killing an unarmed opponent?”

“So, for you, it’s a game?” Anurak asked.

“Life’s a game. It’s all about how you choose to play the game.”

“Are you just going to kill them quickly?”

“Oh, no. It must be something creative, something that sends a message to others they will remember. A simple death is soon forgotten, but a creative death—well, everyone remembers a creative death,” Vermeer said proudly.

The monk stood silent, rapidly running the string of prayer beads through his fingers, thinking. He turned to Vermeer and said, “As the Master has taught us, ‘There has to be evil so that good can prove its purity above it.”

“Amen to that, *Bhante*.” (How one addresses a Buddhist monk)

“*Bhāgyalē sātha di’ōs*,” Anurak said, holding his hands as if in prayer.

“And good luck to you, *Bhante*,” Vermeer said with a short bow of reverence.

☠☠☠☠☠☠☠☠☠☠☠

"The emergency meeting of the Worldwide Affiliates of Safari Partners. (W.A.S.P.) will now come to order." Mark Philips, acting interim president, announced.

The twelve members of the board of directors sat in anticipation to learn the grisly details from Botswana, where their president, Thurston Bentley Hart the Third, Botswana's Minister of Environment, Natural Resources Conservation and Tourism, Boipelo Mooketsi, and fifty of their top members were either massacred by Le Gang de la Clé de Singe or died of some freak viral outbreak.

"Ladies and gentlemen of the board, before we tackle the business of electing a new president, I think it best that we hear from ex-SEAL Team Commander William T. Brown, better known to us all as Wooch, to report the whole Botswana affair. Commander," Philips said.

applause applause applause

The ex-SEAL Team Commander stepped up to the podium, looking somber. He stood in respectful silence, looking at every member of the board—complete silence for almost a minute.

"Mr. Philips, ladies and gentlemen of the board. It is with a heavy heart that I stand before you today. Once again, I am sad to say that I am here to bear bad news. I have spoken with Botswana's Minister of Justice, Malebogo Kgosietsile, moments ago about the tragic deaths of our members who were slaughtered by those thugs from Le Gang de la Clé de Singe. He has promised me that they are doing everything humanly possible to track these murderers down.

I have also spoken with people at the Ministry of Health and Wellness regarding this freak viral outbreak. They have assured me that they are working with the World

Health Organization and the United Nations to determine how such an outbreak could have occurred. I'm told that they believe it was due to an unusual swarm of mosquitoes that somehow had been infected and carried the disease to that area of the Chobe River.

It goes without saying that this is a major setback for 'The Great Elephant Hunt.' I have spoken with the acting Minister of Environment, Natural Resources Conservation, and Tourism about some form of restitution and possible reimbursement of the $60 million that W.A.S.P. paid for the exclusive elephant-hunting rights. My sense is that he didn't believe it would happen. So, we can either proceed with the hunt or forfeit the money. That's a decision for you all to make. Are there any questions?" Wooch asked.

"Do we know if Le Gang de la Clé de Singe had a hand in the viral attack?" Ms. Hamilton asked.

"To date, there is no evidence to suggest that Le Gang de la Clé de Singe was in any way involved in any chemical warfare," Wooch answered.

"What do you think the chances of any of these murderers will be caught, never mind sentenced for their crimes?" Mr. Duncan Asked.

"Slim. Although a few of their members have been apprehended, only a handful. And even then, it's only been the occasional member, and they rarely turn on one another."

"Why is that? Honor among thieves?"

"I guess there's a bit of that. But mostly, it's because they don't know anyone's real name. They all have pseudonyms that they only go by. So, for example, if someone gets arrested, they can only give the authorities an alias of their accomplice, such as Iceman, Alabama, or Neptune."

"Clever," Ms. Hamilton said.

"Very," Wooch agreed.

"What would you recommend, Commander?" Mr. Williams, the treasurer of W.A.S.P., asked.

"About?"

"Should we send more members over to Botswana in light of the tragedies?"

"That's not for me to say. As you all know, I am ex-military, and my training tells me to analyze and assess all my options before making any tactical decisions.

Now we know Le Gang de la Clé de Singe will continue attacking our hunters. That is their life's mission: the complete annihilation of big game hunting and poaching. So, you have to take that into consideration. I believe the viral attack was most likely a one-off freak occurrence, although we are in a third-world country.

In the end, you all have to decide if the risks are worth the rewards. I leave that to you," Wooch said.

He returned to his seat next to Mark Philips. As Wooch sat down, Philips stood and walked to the lectern.

"Thank you, Commander. That's food for thought, and we will have to, as you say, analyze and assess all our options before making any final decisions.

Now, we have some parliamentary business to discuss. So, Commander, I must ask you to leave us to it. Again, thank you for all you've done for us.

Wooch stood, bowed his head, and left the room. Philips waited until the Commander left the room before addressing the board.

"The first order of business is to elect a new president. The chair will now entertain nominations."

Both the Red and Blue teams made it to their rendezvous point, the village of Toteng, which sits just outside the Chobe National Park on the A3 Highway. Toteng has the distinction of having the oldest directly dated evidence of cattle in southern Africa. The village boasts that it has both a hospital and a school.

The teams met at the Rotwe Accommodations, eight small thatch-roofed stucco guest bungalows. They're not high-end, but they're extremely clean. After three weeks of roughing, it in the bush, a soft mattress, a flushing toilet, and a hot shower do wonders for the spirit.

Odin, Fu Hao, and Sue B were instructed to meet a representative of the Le Gang de la Clé de Singe, Amogelang Tsholofelo, a Chobe Park ranger. The representative would supply them with new passports, Nambia currency, and university credentials. The four of them met in the parking lot of Nani's Tuck Shop on Old Maun Road.

As the team leaders pulled into the parking lot, Odin exited the 1999 blue-and-white Ford Econoline and entered the tuck shop. He purchased four orange Fantas, four bags of Goldfish snacks, and crispy wild salmon skin chips.

While they were noshing on their snacks, a lone man driving a Chobe Park Ford Ranger pickup truck pulled alongside their van. The man, who looked to be in his fifties and was wearing a park ranger uniform, got out of the truck's cab, walked over to the passenger side window where Sue B was sitting, and said, "Greetings. I am Amogelang Tsholofelo."

"Hello, I'm Sue B. This is Fu Hao, and that is Odin. Would you like a Fanta and fish skins?" she asked, holding up a bottle and bag.

"Mmmm, don't mind if I do, thanks."

"Everything okay?" Odin asked.

"As well as can be expected when you have half the Botswana army crawling all over the place. You guys did one Hell of a job. It's shaking the government down to its core."

"Glad we could be of assistance," Fu Hao said with a grin.

"Here are your new identities," Tsholofelo said as he handed over a small canvas zip bag.

"Thanks," Sue B said.

"Well, I best be off. Thanks for the drink and chips. And Godspeed," Tsholofelo said as he got back into the Ranger and drove off, leaving a cloud of dust.

The teams stayed there for two days until a bus arrived to take them to neighboring Namibia, where they would board a ship off the coast of the seaside village of Hentiesbaai.

They would pose as anthropologists and geologists representing the University of Southern California on holiday. Before boarding the bus, they turned over all their weapons and mission-related gear to their local scouts, Dineo Kabelo and Gorata Tsheko. Châtelet and Devol would travel to Namibia with their teams.

Once on board, the teams were given their new identities and background stories.

"These are your new passports and identity briefs. We are supposed to be a group of anthropologists and geologists representing the University of Southern California out here on holiday. I'll be by in a couple of hours to collect the briefs and quiz you. Learn them, we don't want any cock ups," Odin announced.

"Can you tell us where we're going?" Cowboy asked.

"So far, all I know is that we're going to Walvis Bay, a seaport on the coast of Namibia. Once we're on board, I've been told that we'll get our next assignment." Odin said. He gave the budding driver the nod, and off they went.

“How long will it take to get to Walvis Bay?” Venus wondered.

“I was told sixteen to seventeen hours,” Fu Hao answered.

There were multiple groans throughout the bus.

“There’s nothing we can do about it. So, just sit back, relax, and try to get some rest.”

When they crossed the border into Namibia, they all had to disembark to pass through customs. A couple of them were asked some cursory questions about where they were going, where they had been, and whether they had anything to declare. The teams passed through both countries' customs without any problem.

On the way, they made several fuel and rest stops heading due west, Tshootsha, Charles Hill, Gobabis, Ondekaremba, and Windhoek, before turning north towards the coast. Their final stop before arriving in Hentiesbaai was the town of Usakos, which sits on the banks of the river Khan. They stopped for dinner at the Namib Oasis and Deli, a roadside café on top of a hill with outdoor seating that offered a spectacular view of the sunset over the Namibia Desert.

When they reached the Port of Walvis Bay, they could see the ship offshore. The ship was the USS Appaloosa, a dry cargo ship that carried solid goods such as metal ores, coal, steel, forest products, and grains. The Appaloosa was carrying a cargo of wheat and rye.

It took two trips on the ferry to transport everyone from shore to the ship. Once everyone was on board, they were greeted by the captain, Noah Rasmussen, a Danish seamen who had over thirty years of experience piloting cargo ships and sixteen years as a member of Le Gang de la Clé de Singe.

“*Vær hilset*. Greetings to you all. Welcome aboard the USS Appaloosa. I am Captain Noah Rasmussen. I think it would be a good idea for you all to get settled down below, and we'll meet in the mess hall for dinner at nineteen hundred hours. For all you landlubbers, that's seven o'clock. Any questions?"

Vulcan stepped forward and asked, "Yeah, Captain Rasmussen, do you know where we're going?"

"I do, and all shall be revealed at dinner. Now, why don't you follow my first mate, Mr. Pippin, here, who will show you to your cabins where you can stow your gear and relax for a couple of hours."

☠☠☠☠☠☠☠☠☠☠☠

"Good evening, everyone. And again, welcome aboard the USS Appaloosa. I'm Captain Noah Rasmussen. I know you're all interested in where we're headed and your next mission.

I have been in communication with the folks at Le Gang de la Clé de Singe. It appears that gangs in Latin America have been using secret routes to smuggle jaguar parts to China. Criminal organizations headquartered in Bolivia are bribing police and circumventing customs to smuggle jaguar parts to mainland China.

So, we'll be sailing to the Port of Callao, Peru's main commercial seaport. Just 12 kilometers from the country's capital, Lima. You will be met by a local representative, who will accompany you and help you accomplish your mission.

I will be having a more detailed meeting with your team leaders at a later date. Now, are there any questions before we have our dinner?" Rasmussen asked.

"How long of a sea journey are we in for?" Odin inquired.

"Approximately, 24 days. Weather permitting."

"Are we making any stops before we get to Peru?" Wondered Lu Wei.

"None. Unless you count going through the Panama Canal, this is basically nonstop from Walvis Bay to Callao. Anything else?"

"Yeah, what do you have, sea sickness?" Venus said meekly.

"Not to worry, Miss. We have plenty of Sea-Band Anti-Nausea Acupressure Wristbands, Bonine Motion Sickness Tablets, and the newest anti-motion sickness ultra-light Smart Glasses. They're not very stylish, but they do the trick. Anything else?

No? Then let's eat. Tonight, we're having grilled pork chops, baked potatoes, sautéed broccoli, and good old apple pie with ice cream for dessert. Bon Appétit."

☠☠☠☠☠☠☠☠☠☠☠

After a week of surveilling the Neupane brothers from afar, Vermeer decided it was time to make contact. He would check into the Dwarika's Hotel to start spinning his spider's web.

The Dwarika's Hotel, considered one of Nepal's finest hotels, was built by the late Dwarika Das Shrestha, a visionary conservationist. He rescued thousands of ancient carved wooden architectural pieces from around Nepal, then trained Nepali craftsmen to integrate them into his historic hotel.

The Dwarika's Hotel consists of three brick-built buildings, finished with traditional, mostly historic wood window frames salvaged from demolished buildings, many dating back to the 13th Century. The buildings are set around a series of linked paved courtyards lined with trees and shrines. The hotel boasts the world's most extensive private collection of wooden carvings. Vermeer sensed that it would be like sleeping in a museum.

"Good afternoon. Welcome to Dwarika's Hotel. May I help you, sir?" a middle-aged woman reservation agent asked.

She was dressed in the hotel uniform—a white shirt, tie, and grey slacks. Her hair was black, worn down to her shoulders, and her skin was a soft hue of bronze. She wore the mark of the bindi—a small dot on her forehead between her eyebrows. Women traditionally wear bindis for religious purposes or to indicate that they are married. Since she was wearing a wedding ring, Vermeer assumed that she was at least married.

"Yes, reservation for Hanson. Jake Hanson."

After a few quick taps on the computer keyboard, she smiled and replied, "Ah, yes, Mr. Hanson. I see that we have you in one of our Heritage Executive Suites for two weeks. Is that correct?"

"Correct. Would you have anything on the fifth floor?" Vermeer asked, knowing that the Neupane brothers were staying there.

"Oh, I'm sorry, Mr. Hanson. Those suites are completely booked," she said apologetically.

"That's too bad; I was really looking forward to getting a nice view of the city."

She clicked a few keys on the computer, smiled, and said, "Well, I do have one Heritage Junior Suite available. It's quite a bit smaller, but it does have a pleasant view of the Pashupatinath Temple."

"Oh, that would be excellent. Thank you."

"Would you like help with your luggage? Mr. Hanson?"

"Please."

Vermeer had acquired additional gear with the help of Anurak to give the impression that he was a big-game hunter. In addition to another suitcase full of hunting outfits, he had three very expensive-looking rifle cases that drew the attention of several guests and staff, precisely the desired effect that Vermeer was looking for.

☠☠☠☠☠☠☠☠☠☠☠

There came a light knocking at Vermeer's door as he was unpacking. He went to the door and peered out of the 'peephole' to see a burly man who appeared to be in his late twenties, wearing a colorful, patterned *Dhaka topi*. A Dhaka topi is a popular cloth hat that is part of the Nepalese national dress.

"Who is it?" Vermeer asked.

"Mister Hanson, I am a fellow hotel guest. My name is Indragop Neupane. May I come in?"

"Just a minute," Vermeer answered.

He slipped his shoulder holster with a Beretta 92FS on, then put on an Orvis Panama Safari jacket for cover. He then opened the door.

"Come in," He said.

Indragop walked in slowly. As he entered, he gave the room a once-over, looking for anything that might say police or undercover government official. He saw none.

He turned to Vermeer and said, "Mister Hanson, may I ask if you are in Kathmandu looking to do some hunting?"

"As a matter of fact, I am."

"And what are you wanting to hunt, if I may be so bold to ask?"

"Why do you ask?"

"Well, it just so happens that my brothers and I are expert guides. In fact, you will not do better anywhere in all of Nepal."

"I see. And are your brothers as humble as you are…?"

"Oh, I'm so sorry. Please let me introduce myself. I am Indragop Neupane. My brothers and I happen to live at the Dwarika's Hotel, just down the hall from your room," Neupane said with a wolfish grin.

"How cozy," Vermeer quipped.

"Do you have a guide already?"

"No. Not yet."

"Well then, may I suggest that perhaps we could meet later for drinks downstairs in the Fusion Bar. We can talk, and I'll introduce you to my brothers, Bibek and Manish."

"I didn't think Hindus drank."

There are several different Hindu sects. Ours allows us to consume alcohol."

"That's convenient."

"Shall we say six o'clock?"

"Sound good," Vermeer said.

"Excellent. See you at six. Goodbye, sir."

"Good day."

Vermeer found the Fusion Bar to be an eclectic blend of East meets West. The bar itself is made of dark mahogany, running over thirty feet long. Overhead, large dark wooden beams contrast with the brick and stucco walls painted creamy beige. Unlike Western bars that are primarily dark, the Fusion Bar is brightly lit with numerous overhead lights. On the wall opposite the bar are dozens of family photographs of the Dwarika's through the generations. There's a fireplace with an English dartboard and a small stage for live entertainment. That night, the band was a folk-rock group called the Crackles. They weren't Crosby Still

Nash and Young, but Vermeer thought they were decent enough.

Vermeer took a seat at the bar, ordered a Tom Collins, and listened to the Crackle's version of Neil Young's 'Heart of Gold.'

"Mister Hanson. I'd like you to meet my brothers. This is Manish, and this is my oldest brother, Bibek," Indragop said proudly.

Vermeer slowly turned around on his barstool and saw three overweight men wearing ill-fitting Armani suits. They were definitely related. They all had the same round face, as well as similar features: beady eyes, a broad nose, and thin lips. The only marked difference was that each one had different facial hair. Indragop had a mustache, Manish wore a full beard, and Bibek sported a van dyke. They reminded Vermeer of the image from the Smith Brothers cough drops packaging.

He stood up, shook all three brothers' hands, and said, "Shall we grab ourselves a table?"

They took a table out on the patio overlooking the swimming pool. The sun started to drop behind Mount Lamjung Kailas, turning the snow peak a golden yellow in contrast to the cool blue lights of the swimming pool below.

"Can I get you gentlemen something to drink?" Vermeer asked.

"That is very kind of you," Indragop said.

Vermeer called over the waiter, "Gentlemen, what's your poison?"

The brothers were taken aback as they had never heard that phrase before.

"It's just an expression. It means what would you like to drink." Vermeer explained.

A look of relief came over them as they smiled and laughed once they understood.

Bibek looked at his brothers and said, "We'll have three *Tongbas,* and he'll have another Tom Collins."

"*Tongba*?" Vermeer queried.

"It's similar to beer," Manish replied.

"Hmm, I'll have to try it sometime," Vermeer said.

They sat and made small talk about the hotel and the city of Kathmandu until the drinks came.

"Now, gentlemen, Indragop says that you are the best hunting guides in all of Nepal."

"That is true, Mr. Hanson. You will find no one better. We can guarantee you the finest game anywhere in Nepal," Bibek said matter-of-factly.

"Like what?"

Bibek looked around to avoid being overheard before whispering, "Greater one-horned rhinoceros, elephant, even a Be snow leopard."

Vermeer leaned into the brothers and asked, "Aren't those all endangered?"

"And your point?" Bibek said with a large grin.

"How could I get the trophy out of the country?"

"That's why we're the best guides. Not only do we get you your prize, but we also help you get your trophy out of the country."

"What about the authorities?"

Bibek and the others started laughing, "Not to worry. We have connections in all the right places."

"How much is going to cost?" Vermeer asked.

"Well, that depends on what you're looking for."

"Snow leopard."

"Ah, an excellent choice, Mr. Hanson. The cost for the hunt, export, and incidentals would be seventy-five thousand US Dollars."

"$75,000! I might be able to go as high as fifty-five."

"65," Bibek countered.

Vermeer thought for a few minutes before coming back with sixty.

Bibek shook his head, then asked, "What rifles do you have?"

"I have a Mauser M98 .416 Rigby, a Ruger Hawkeye .30-06, and a Weatherby Vanguard .300 Winchester Magnum. Why?"

"We will accept sixty, plus the Ruger Hawkeye .30-06."

"Done," Vermeer agreed.

"We want the cash all up front."

"No. No. No. Mother Hanson didn't raise her son to be that stupid. I will give you one-third tomorrow, one-third after I bag the prize, and one-third when the trophy is shipped."

The brothers huddled and had what seemed to be a heated discussion in their native Nepali about the proposal. Finally, older brother Bibek agreed.

"Shall we drink on it?" Vermeer suggested.

As they raised their glasses, Vermeer said, "*Rāmrō śikāra.*" (good hunting)

☠☠☠☠☠☠☠☠☠☠☠

"Attention, everyone, this is Captain Rasmussen. Sorry to disturb you at such an early hour, but it looks like we're going to be in for stormy weather. I suggest you keep your movements to a minimum. Thank you."

The ship started to roll slightly, surging and swaying with a slight yaw side-to-side. Rasmussen was briefing them on their next assignment in the captain's quarters with Odin, Fu Hao, and Sue B.

"I'll try to keep this brief. As I had mentioned before, it has been reported that gangs in primarily Bolivia are bribing police and getting around customs to smuggle jaguar parts to mainland China."

"How reliable are these reports?" Fu Hao asked.

"Seventy-five intelligence sources across Latin America, including some traffickers, were confirmed in a report commissioned by the International Union for Conservation of Nature in the Netherlands (IUCN NL) that criminals operate established routes and sometimes bribe high-ranking police officers to look the other way.

I'm sure you're aware that the jaguar is a very important species within the ecosystem in which it lives. They are being targeted by traffickers looking to sell their bones, genitals, and teeth to clients in Asia, most of whom are Chinese. The cats are classified as red-listed near-threatened."

"I am so ashamed of my people. They still believe in these old wives' tales, superstitions, and myths about medicinal remedies. We're killing off tens of thousands of endangered animals for nothing!" Fu Hao said.

"What are our assignments?" Sue B asked.

"The Red Team is assigned to make contact with the gang, las Panteras Negras, the Black Panthers, and eliminate them," Rasmussen said.

"And the Blue Team?" Odin inquired.

"The Blue Team will visit the police and government officials who are allowing this illicit trade to happen."

"Visit?" Odin asked, looking for clarification.

"Rub out, annihilate, hit, slay, assassinate, dispatch, obliterate, waste, wipe out, snuff, liquidate, terminate," Rasmussen answered.

"So, you want us to kill them?"

"Ah, yeah. Here are your instructions with the names of your contacts, your new identities, and your team's passports." Rasmussen said as he handed each of them a large manila folder.

The ship was really starting to pitch and roll as the storm was picking up. A voice on the intercom blared, "Would the captain please come to the bridge?"

"I'd better go. You all should go back to your cabins. It looks like it's going to be a rough one, but hopefully, it won't last long."

As Rasmussen started to leave the cabin, Odin asked, "Do you know why we didn't just fly to Bolivia?"

Rasmussen turned and smiled, "It's their way of rewarding you for a job well done by sending you all on a luxurious ocean cruise."

The storm lasted for three days. By the end, just about everyone, even the crew, was a light shade of green. Rasmussen was the only one who seemed unfazed by it all. Because of the numerous storms projected, Rasmussen decided to take a more southern route. It would mean taking longer to reach their destination but considering the toll the storm had taken on everyone, he felt it was worth it. Besides, it would only add two days to the voyage.

They sailed along the coast of Argentina, Brazil, French Guiana, Suriname, Guyana, Venezuela, and Colombia before reaching the Panama Canal. They reached the entrance to the Canal just as the sun was beginning to rise. They could see the city of Colón off to their left, starting to wake up. People begin to arrive at the Panama Canal Admeasurement Office to start their day, loading and unloading cargo ships, and tending to cruise ships as they dock to let the thousands of passengers off to shop and take their pictures standing in front of the entrance to the Panama Canal.

They reached the entrance to the Canal just as the sun was beginning to rise. They could see the city of Colón off to their left, starting to wake up. People were beginning to arrive at the Panama Canal Admeasurement Office to begin their day, loading and unloading cargo ships, tending to the cruise ships docking, and letting the thousands of passengers off to shop and take their pictures standing in front of the entrance to the Panama Canal.

The passage through the Canal took nine hours from Colón to Panama City and the Pacific Ocean. Then, south down to Lima, Peru, to the Port of Callao., where they said goodbye to Captain Rasmussen and the crew of the Appaloosa.

Being from Peru and knowing he had outstanding arrest warrants, Gianfranco was still nervous about entering the country, even with a new identity and wearing a disguise. As he went through customs and immigration, he was pleasantly surprised by how casual and lackadaisical the customs agents were. After passing through customs, both teams made their way to El Mercado (The Market) restaurant in the Residencial Santa Cruz area of town, known for the best ceviche in all of Lima.

☠☠☠☠☠☠☠☠☠☠☠

Following Gianfranco's lead, everyone ordered the ceviche mercado. This dish combines the catch of the day, marinated in tiger's milk, with yellow chili and crispy calamari pork rinds. It is a tribute to the gastronomic traditions of Peru, reflecting its multiple influences, such as Chinese, Spanish, Japanese, and Italian cuisines.

Afterward, two Ford Econoline vans pulled up as the two teams were outside the restaurant saying their goodbyes—one for the Red Team and the other for the Blue

Team. Their destination was to be La Paz to spend the night before the Red team headed north into the Madidi National Park, home to the largest population of jaguars in Bolivia. The Blue Team would be staying at La Paz, home to the largest population of crooked government officials.

Both teams will confront villains and put an end to the illicit trade with extreme prejudice.

Their van drivers were to be their guides. The Red Team guide is Basilio Mamani, a park ranger and tourist guide in Parque Nacional Madidi. He's forty-eight, rugged, extremely fit, speaks six languages, and strongly resembles George Clooney with a beard.

Basilio has had several encounters with *las Panteras Negras*. He was in a three-hour firefight that resulted in four of the Black Panthers being killed, and he and two other rangers were wounded.

After the initial introductions, they began their fourteen-hour road trip towards Madidi. "So, we're off to our first stop, Apolo, located on the outskirts of the park. Apolo is a small rural mountainous village surrounded by farmers, lima, and cattle ranchers. There is a small army post that is still active, but it is mainly used as a supply depot with a handful of troops, so there is nothing to be concerned about. You will be staying at the Hotel Landivar Apolo; it's nice, quiet, and clean. You'll stay there for a couple of days until I can acquire all the gear and supplies that you'll require, and then we'll move into the jungle," Basilio said.

"Is Apolo your home?" Sue B asked.

"Oh, no, I was born and grew up in La Paz. As a student at Universidad Salesiana de Bolivia, I got involved in multiple environmental causes like deforestation throughout the country. From 2001 to 2018, we've lost 7.5 percent of our forests. That's why I joined Le Gang de la Clé de Singe and became a ranger to protect and fight for the environment."

"Well, we're glad you're on our side."

"Gracias. I am very excited that I have something special to show you tomorrow that I think you'll find instrumental in the mission."

☠☠☠☠☠☠☠☠☠☠☠

Eduardo Choque is the Blue Team's guide. He works for the Ministry of Environment and Water as the Assistant to the Deputy Director for Science.

"*Hola y bienvenido a Bolivia.* My name is Eduardo Choque. I suggest we head to the Atix Hotel, where you can drop off all of your luggage, and then we can go somewhere we can discuss the mission."

As Odin introduced the team to Eduardo, Eduardo gave the team a brief introduction to the city of La Paz as they drove to the Atix Hotel.

"La Paz was founded in1548 by the Spanish conquistador Captain Alonso de Mendozza. The city's full name is *Nuestra Señora de La Paz,* which means Our Lady of Peace. La Paz is the highest capital city in the world. With a population of over one point eight million people

See that magnificent mountain off in the distance? That is Mount Illimani; she watches over La Paz. Tonight, after dinner, I will take you all up to Mirador Killi Killi, a well-known destination for a fabulous panoramic view of the city. The city stretches from nonstop from left to right. It is truly a sight to behold.

But first things first. Here we are. I'll wait here while you go and check in." Eduardo said as he pulled up to the hotel entrance.

The Blue Team piled out of the van, and within half an hour, they were all back in it.

"Everything okay?" Eduardo asked.

"Soft as silk. Nice place," Odin said.

"Yeah, it's really cool. Take a look at the façade. It's clad with the native Bolivian wood and Comanche stone used to pave La Paz's streets in the 1920s and 1930s. And if you look at it, it's shaped like a parallelogram. There's nothing like it in all of La Paz," Eduardo boasted.

"Where are we headed?" Lu Wei asked.

"The grounds of the Museum of Natural History. It's a beautiful day, so I thought we could find a nice, quiet area without being disturbed or overheard," Eduardo answered.

☠☠☠☠☠☠☠☠☠☠☠

It being a weekday, the usual hordes of children who inundate the museum and grounds were all in school, so the park was virtually deserted. Eduardo led the Blue Team to a grove of trees far from the museum building.

"I think we shouldn't be disturbed or overheard here," Eduardo said.

"So, what exactly is the mission and the plan?" Odin asked.

"The mission is to eliminate several top-ranking government and police officials who have been taking bribes and allowing the killing and smuggling of Bolivia's endangered jaguars to China."

"How many targets are there?" asked Bellator.

"Nine. Four police and five from the government," Eduardo answered.

"Are they ever in the same place at the same time?" Odin queried.

"There is going to be a gathering of sorts in about three weeks. However, the feeling is that once the Red Team starts their campaign, these folks will catch wind of it and go into hiding. So, we think it's best that we try to take them out individually."

"Where are they? Are they all in La Paz?" Odin asked.

"As a matter of fact, they are all in the wealthy Calacoto suburbs, not far from your hotel," Eduardo said.

"How convenient," Odin said, smirking.

"Yes, isn't it?" Eduardo replied.

"Now, about equipment. I've drawn up a list," Odin said as he handed Eduardo a piece of paper.

Eduardo perused the list, nodded, and asked, "How soon would you like this?"

"By the weekend. If possible."

"It shouldn't be a problem."

"I think we need to see the locations of the targets."

"Would tomorrow be all right? I'd like to get started on acquiring these items," Eduardo said.

"No problem."

"Good. How about I swing by the hotel around six this evening, and we all go out for dinner?"

"That would be great."

"Until then, adios."

Vermeer sat in the Dearika's Hotel lobby waiting, reading a two-week-old copy of the New York Times.

"Mr. Hanson? Are you ready?" Indragop Neupane asked.

"Ready when you are," he said as he tossed the paper down onto the leather couch. His luggage and rifle cases were stacked next to the sofa.

"Shall I give you a hand with your things?" Indragop asked.

"Yes, thank you. That would be nice."

Outside was a Land Rover Defender 110 Camel Trophy Edition loaded to the max, with a heavy-duty roof rack, treaded tires (and two spares) that look ready to bite through the mud. In addition to the spare tires, the Rover is outfitted with some very cool accessories to make it expedition-ready: storage bins, gasoline tanks, cables, and fitted with a snorkel exhaust for traversing deep streams. There was a second SUV, not as tricked out. This was a Toyota Highlander that carried four Sherpas to set up campsites, carry gear, and handle all-around grunt work.

Bibek and Manish were loading foodstuffs when Vermeer and their younger brother emerged from the hotel. Indragop handed Manish Vermeer his luggage and rifle cases, which he stowed on top.

"Ready, Mr. Hanson?" Bibek asked.

"I'm ready," Vermeer said.

Bibek strolled next to Vermeer, glanced around, and softly said so as no one else could hear. "Do you have the first payment, Mr. Hanson?"

Vermeer said nothing; he reached inside the patch pocket of his safari jacket and handed him a white envelope with twenty thousand US Dollars. Bibek twisted towards the vehicle, peered into the envelope, and did a quick count before stuffing it into his back pocket. Then, with a wolfish grin, he shouted, "Okay, let's go! Mr. Hanson, how about you sit up front with me?"

"Actually, if you don't mind, I'd prefer to sit in the back," Vermeer said.

Surprised, Bibek said, "Sure. Whatever you prefer."

Vermeer didn't trust these three as far as he could throw them. He would rather there weren't anyone sitting behind him. It's too easy to get stabbed, shot, or garroted from behind. He got into the passenger seat behind Bibek, the driver, next to Indragop.

They left Kathmandu out on Highway H03, traveling east towards the mountain Village of Dhulikhel, where they switched to Highway H06, which would eventually turn into the Khurkot-Ghurmi Madhya Padadi Highway. Once on the highway, they would head up into the mountainous Makalu Barun National Park and begin the hunt for the elusive snow leopard.

It was rough going. The so-called highways were nothing more than two-lane dirt roads. There never seemed to be more than a couple of hundred yards of straight road before another set of switchbacks appeared. Vermeer was thankful that he never got motion sickness; if he had, this would have been the road trip from Hell.

Traveling the 108 miles to the park entrance took them six hours. Once inside, they parked their vehicles and started the trek towards Makalu, the fifth-highest mountain in the world.

"We're going to have to go up high to get the prize," Bibek announced.

Vermeer zipped up his Montbell Plasma Alpine down parka, slung his Mauser M98 .416 Rigby over his shoulder, put on his Julbo Cham sunglasses, and began to follow Gyalzen, the lead Sherpa up towards the base camp of Makalu, where the climbers go to get acclimated before they attempt to make the climb.

After a few days, they would wander off to the right of the mountain, set up a new camp, and begin searching for a snow leopard. Vermeer hadn't decided on whether he was prepared to kill the Sherpas for helping in the tracking of the endangered species.

He had killed many an African native for their part in the guiding and killing of big game. In an odd way, not killing these men would be an act of racism. No. The code of Le Gang de la Clé de Singe dictated that anybody anywhere in the world who targets, kills, profits, and or supports the killing of any animals that are endangered or any animals that are hunted for sport must pay with their lives. So it was to be the brothers Neupane, and the Sherpas must all pay the price. Death.

☠☠☠☠☠☠☠☠☠☠☠

After two days, they broke camp, hiked five miles east of the climber's base camp, and set up their new camp. Unbeknownst to them, this camp would be their necropolis, a boot hill of sorts.

That night, everyone was in good spirits. There was laughing, drinking, and joking around. Manish brought out several bottles of Raksi. Raksi is a strong drink, clear like vodka or gin, with a slightly Japanese-sake-like taste.

There was a real sense of camaraderie. All eight sat around the campfire, telling stories of past expeditions, adventures, and hunts. As the evening wore on, the tales grew more exaggerated and elaborate. When the fire started to die, and the liquor took its intended effect, people began to wander off to their tents until there were just two: Bibek and Vermeer.

"So, Mr. Hanson, tomorrow you should get your trophy."

"I'm really looking forward to it," Vermeer said, smiling with a stone-cold edge to his answer.

Bibek's eyes narrowed. He felt a wave of uneasiness come over him, but he decided it was just the Raksi.

☠☠☠☠☠☠☠☠☠☠☠

By the time Bibek and his brothers emerged from their tent, Vermeer was standing by the campfire that he restarted drinking a cup of coffee. Shortly after that, Gyalzen and the other Sherpas appeared. The camp slowly came alive as the Sherpas prepared breakfast by heating a large pot of grease. Nepali breakfast is not your typical English or American breakfast with eggs and bacon. Since breakfast is the most important meal of the day, it's meant to wake one up. The chief cook, Nawang, whipped up some sel-roti – fried rice bread shaped like a donut, gwara mari – fried dough balls, and malpuwa – sweet and stodgy fried pancakes. Not exactly the breakfast of champions.

Everyone gathered around the fire, eating breakfast, drinking coffee and chiya tea making small talk.

"So, after breakfast, the four of us gather our gear and head out to start the hunt," Bibek announced.

Vermeer stood up, holding what looked to be a folded piece of yellow canvas in his hands. He slowly unfolded it, revealing the ensign of Le Gang de la Clé de Singe, and asked, "Do any of you know what this is?"

"Where did you find that?" Bibek demanded.

"It's mine."

The brothers jumped to their feet, their plates and cups tumbled to the ground, and their faces acknowledged fear and apprehension. Gyalzen and the other Sherpas sat stoic and did not move.

Vermeer quickly drew his Beretta 92FS 9mm and aimed at the group.

"Bibek, you boys, sit back down," He ordered.

Vermeer took a folded piece of paper, tossed it to Bibek, and said, "Read it out loud so everyone can hear it."

Bibek unfolded the paper and began to mumble to himself.

"Out loud!" Vermeer shouted.

"Let it be known that Le Gang de la Clé de Singe declares a proclamation of war against all Poachers, Big Game Hunters, and all Big Game Safari Outfits as well as anybody anywhere in the world that targets, kills, profits and or supports the killing of any animals that are endangered

or any animals that are hunted for sport. Be forewarned, do so at your peril. You will be hunted down and pay with your lives. Be it man or woman, there will be no exceptions and no mercy; we will show no quarter. You have been warned."

Vermeer could see their minds working overtime, trying to process what was going to happen next and how to stop it.

"What do you want? Money? We can give you money, lots of money. How much do you want?" Bibek begged as he threw the envelope with the twenty thousand dollars at Vermeer.

"I'm not interested in your money," Vermeer said as he attached the silencer to the Beretta 92FS 9mm.

"What *do* you want?" Bibek pleaded.

"I want you to die."

PHIFF

Bibek fell backward, landing on top of the campfire. Manish and Indragop sprung up and started to run in different directions. They didn't get more than five feet.

PHIFF PHIFF

Vermeer quickly turned his pistol back to the Sherpas. They hadn't moved. They sat with their eyes closed, rocking back and forth, chanting prayers. Vermeer stood reverently waiting for them to finish.

When they had finished, Gyalzen opened his eyes, nodded, and said, "We are ready for death and rebirth."

PHIFF PHIFF PHIFF PHIFF

Vermeer positioned the bodies in a row next to each other. Yellow flags were placed around their necks, with a copy of the manifesto inside their pockets. He packed his gear and left. He did leave the Ruger Hawkeye .30-06 rifle that he promised Bibek next to his body. On the body, he left one clear and distinctive fingerprint on the butt of the rifle, that of Sir Edmund Hillary, the first man to reach the summit of Mount Everest.

Vermeer then made the five-mile trek back to where they had parked the five vehicles. He left the Land Rover Defender and took the Toyota Highlander back to Kathmandu. He abandoned the vehicle at the Pashupatinath Temple's parking lot, then phoned the authorities to alert them to where they would find the Neupane brothers and Sherpas.

Before heading to the airport, he stopped at the temple of Swayambhunath Stupa to see Anurak.

"Greetings, my friend," Anurak said.

"Greetings," Vermeer replied.

"I assume it went well."

"Mission accomplished."

"I have something for you," Anurak said as he handed Vermeer a large, padded envelope.

Vermeer opened it. He took out his new passport, credit cards, and background information to become Mr. Bradley Peak. A first-class ticket on the three o'clock Emirates Airline flight to Quito, Ecuador, with a layover in Rome, included.

"Where to now?"

"I shouldn't say. I just wanted to come by and thank you."

"You are quite welcome. Go in peace."

"Before I go, I wanted to tell you a monk joke."

"A monk joke?"

"There was a man who joined a silent order monastery as a monk. He took a vow of silence. He was permitted to say two words every ten years. So, he meditated, prayed, painted, and cleaned for the first ten years. After ten years, he stands before the head monk to speak his two words.

"Room cold."

He returns to his life of meditation, praying, painting, and cleaning for another ten years. Now, twenty years after entering, he once again stands before the head monk to utter his two words:

"Bed hard."

He again returns to his life of meditation, praying, painting, and cleaning for another ten years. Now, thirty years after entering, he once again stands before the head monk and defiantly says his two words:

"I quit."

The head monk looked at him and replied, "Well, you might as well. You've done nothing but complain since you got here!"

☠☠☠☠☠☠☠☠☠☠☠

Basilio was waiting in the van for the Red Team outside the hotel.

"Good morning." He said as the team climbed in.

There was a smattering of good mornings, some enthusiastic, and some mumbles.

"Where are we off to today? Fu Hao asked.

"To a little out-of-the-way spot, where I have what I think is something that you'll find fascinating."

As hard as they quizzed and questioned him, Basilio won't divulge the surprise. They drove west on Highway 16 for over an hour before turning off onto a dirt road that wound deep into the forest. There were two large cargo containers surrounded by several heavily armed guards dressed in camo, carrying AK-47s.

"Here we are," Basilio said as he stepped out of the van.

The team climbed out and followed Basilio to the container, who signed one of the guards to open the metal door.

"Châtelet, I think you'll find this to be right up your alley," Basilio said with a smile as he revealed twelve robotic dogs. Each one was the size of a German Shepherd.

"Oh my God. They're awesome! She squealed.

"What the Hell are those? Robotic dogs?" Sue B asked.

"These are Boston Dynamics robot dogs. They run on rechargeable batteries, with a runtime of 90 minutes. They can run at 3 miles an hour. They navigate over any challenging terrain. There are dual cameras that enable 360-degree obstacle avoidance. If you knock them over, they'll right themselves. No matter the temperature, they will operate between -4 and 113 degrees Fahrenheit and are protected from rain and dirt.

These are equipped with side-mounted machine guns and covered with bulletproof Kevlar. Since they run on batteries, they'll run silently." Châtelet explained.

Basilio laughed at Châtelet's reaction. He walked over to the second container and had one of the guards open it up. Held a hand-operated control and maneuvered another type of quadruped robot out of the container. This one was much larger than the robot dog; it was the size of a male lion.

"Oh, Châtelet."

She was so engrossed with the robotic dogs that she didn't hear him at first.

"Oh, Châtelet," He said louder.

She turned. It took several seconds for what she was looking at to register.

"No way! A Wildcat!" She exclaimed.

She ran over to the beast, examining every inch as she ran her hands over it.

"It's the Wildcat, the fastest quadruped robot on Earth. It can run 20 mph while maneuvering and maintain its balance over rough terrain," she said.

It, too, was covered with bullet-proof Kevlar and equipped with side-mounted machine guns.

"These are game changers," Fu Hao said.

"How many Wildcats do we have?" Sue B asked.

"Twelve," Basilio answered.

"Do we have to have twelve operators? One for each dog?" Cowboy asked.

"Well, you can, or you can program them to follow one, the leader, as it were. If it gets disabled or destroyed, the next one takes over, and the others will follow. They develop a herd mentality." Basilio explained.

"That's true with both the dogs and Wildcats?" Cowboy asked.

"Yes," Basilio replied.

"Can we start working with them, please?" Châtelet beseeched.

"Sure. This is Razor. He has been assigned to your team to instruct and help you learn how to operate these weapons," Basilio said as he handed her the hand controls.

Razor looked to be the pure, outright geek that he was. His camo uniform looked to be two sizes too big. He wore round, thick glasses, and he had a preteen haircut, cowlick and all. But he put a computer or an electronic gizmo in front of him, and he became a master wizard.

No one other than Châtelet knew what the Hell he was talking about. It was decided that the two of them would handle the robotic quadrupeds and drones, while the rest of the Red Team would be old-school warriors, grunts, dogfaces, and GIs.

"How long before you two are proficient enough to go into battle?" Fu Hao asked.

Razor looked at Châtelet, smiled, and said, "No more than two days."

"Good. We'll be back in two days."

Basilio and the rest of the Red Team drove back to Apolo to make final preparations.

☠☠☠☠☠☠☠☠☠☠☠

Arsenio Rojas, the Minister of Environment and Water, was the first to be captured. His limo pulled up to the front of the seven-story cream-and-blue, newly built semi-contemporary building on Av 14 de Septiembre. The building had already been tagged with graffiti and gang signs.

Minister Rojas climbed into the backseat of the silver Mercedes E-Class sedan and began reading La Prensa, the first of three newspapers he reads on his ride home. He was so engrossed in an article about a legislative assembly's probe into a shortage of potable water amid the current drought that he hadn't realized that he was in the wrong part of town or that the person driving the car wasn't Carlos, his regular driver.

"Carlos. Where are we?" He asked.

Bellator turned around and smiled.

"You're not Carlos! Who are you? Where are you taking me?" Rojas demanded.

Bellator raised and fired one shot from a tranquilizer pistol as the minister reached for the door handle.

POP

Rojas was fast asleep within seconds. When he woke up, he found himself bound and gagged, lying on the floor in the back of a cargo van. He could hear voices speaking in English. He heard one man say, "That's one down and eight to go."

Sergio Vargas, the vice minister of Rural Development and Land, and Teo Cruz, the vice minister of Government, were captured together after a meeting with a group of lobbyists from the United States. They were leaving the five-star restaurant Ona, which is located in the Atix Hotel.

Odin and Venus followed the two vice ministers, Vargas and Cruz, into the elevator down to the parking garage. Just as they reached Cruz's blue BMW 750i, a white unmarked Chevy cargo van pulled up. Odin and Venus each pulled their Sig Sauer P226 pistols and forced the two men into the back of the cargo van.

Once inside, Lu Wei placed blindfolds, binds, and gagged them. Placing them on the floor next to Minister Rojas. Odin and Venus get into the van and drive out of the underground parking lot and into traffic.

Still dressed in his chauffeur uniform, Bellator parked the silver Mercedes E-Class sedan at the end of Calle Arezzo. Sitting in the back seat was Vulcan, reading the exact copy of *La Prensa* that Minister Rojas had been reading. They were waiting for Assistant Attorney General Reu Mendoza to return home from the office. Mendoza's new two-million-dollar mansion sat high atop a mountain in the posh La Florida section of town. There were several new homes still under construction on his block. His house was fairly isolated, sitting on a canyon's edge overlooking downtown La Paz.

Bellator noticed that the lights were on in the house. He assumed that Mendoza's wife was home, which could complicate matters. Bellator saw Mendoza's blue bimmer slowly approaching.

"Vulcan. Here he comes," Bellator said as he got out of the car.

Mendoza slowed down as he approached his driveway. As he got closer, he noticed the Mercedes had distinctive government plates of a high official. As he parked his car, Bellator approached, "Excuse me, Señor Mendoza, Minister Rojas would like to have a quick word."

"What about?"

"I'm sure I don't know, sir."

Mendoza looked back at his house and the silver Mercedes. He thought he should go inside and let his wife know he was home, but Bellator could see Mendoza hesitating.

"The Minister said it would only take a minute, señor."

"Oh, all right," Mendoza said as he followed the chauffeur.

"You're not Rojas' regular driver," Mendoza commented.

"No, señor. He called in sick," Bellator said as he opened the door.

Mendoza noticed too late that the man behind the newspaper wasn't Minister Rojas but a black man holding a tranquilizer gun.

POP

The lights went out for Assistant Attorney General Reu Mendoza. When he came to, he found himself bound and gagged, lying next to someone else. He struggles to free himself, but to no avail. The more he struggled, the tighter his zip-ties got. He finally accepted the fact that he had been kidnapped. Hopefully, the government would pay the ransom, and this nightmare would soon end.

The Bolivian Senate has 36 seats. Each of the country's nine departments returns four senators. El Beni is the northeastern department of Bolivia. Within El Beni is Madidi National Park, which Senator Erick Sanchez represents.

Senator Sanchez has been in the Bolivian Senate for three terms and fifteen years. He is married, has four kids, and a dog named *Mancha*. He has also been on the take for fourteen years as a senator. If ever they were under investigation, it would be hard for most Bolivian senators to explain away their wealth, especially Senator Sanchez, whose annual salary is 557,463.09 Bolivian Bolivianos, or about 81,000 US Dollars, while his personal worth is well over 22 million US Dollars. Granted, some of that is from honest investment, but the majority of his wealth comes from kickbacks, bribes, and money from the illegal shipments of endangered jaguars and jaguar parts to China.

The London Club Bolivia is a combination nightclub and karaoke bar. Senator Sanchez has been known to frequent the club in search of young ladies. The keyword is "young." The younger, the better. He has been busted on more than one occasion for being caught with underage girls, but somehow, he has managed to wrangle his way out of trouble. He makes the girl and her family an offer that they can't refuse money, and lots of it.

Venus went to the London Club dressed and made up to look young and sexy in hopes of luring the Senator. Odin, Vulcan, and Devol went in separately as a backup in case the situation got out of hand. Odin observed that Sanchez had a bodyguard big enough to bounce bricks off of. He had to be eliminated from the equation.

Devol took three mosquito drones carrying concentrated doses of Ipecac and attacked the bouncer as he sat drinking a beer while keeping a watchful eye over the senator. It took effect almost immediately; he made his way to the men's room and wasn't seen again.

Venus had her long blonde hair parted in the middle with wispy bangs. She was dressed in a starched white long-sleeve shirt, unbuttoned at the top, with a thin, untied black tie and a short red plaid mini skirt. The skirt was so short that her black lace panties showed when she walked. She wore white mid-thigh opaque stockings and black T-Bar flat shoes.

When she entered, the room became so quiet you could hear the bartender dropping ice into a glass from across the room. All heads turned when she walked through the throngs of people towards the bar where Erick Sanchez sat several stools down from her. She played it cool, never looking in his direction.

"What'll have?" The bartender asked.

"Mmmm, I think I'll have a cosmopolitan, por favor."

As the bartender began to prepare her drink, Sanchez called him over and whispered, "Sergio, her drink is on me." As he handed him a twenty US Dollar tip.

The bartender placed the Cosmo in front of Venus, "Compliments of Señor Sanchez."

Sanchez timed the arrival of her drink to his approaching her. He stood next to her, raised his vodka tonic, smiled, and said with a toothy grin, "*Salud.*"

Venus pursed her Ferrari red lips, smirked, held up her Cosmo, and whispered, "*Salud.*"

"Where are you from?" He asked, leering.

She lied, "America."

"Really? Where in America?"

"L.A."

"Oh, I've always wanted to go to Los Angeles. What's it like?"

"It's just like here."

He perked up as he asked, "Really?"

Venus giggled, "No. It's nothing like here."

Sanchez was intrigued and smitten. She smelled as delicious as she looked. He could feel himself getting hard and whatever game she wanted to play, he'd play it.

"So, what's your name?"

"Tiffany."

"Hi Tiffany, I'm Raúl."

"Hmmm, you don't look like a Raúl. You look like a Juan Pablo."

"Why Juan Pablo?" He asked.

She laughed and said, "Why not."

"Say, how about we go somewhere where it's not so loud?"

Venus finished her Cosmo, licked her lips, smiled, took him by his necktie, and said, "*Vamonos.*" She led him through the dancefloor, out the lobby, and into the parking lot.

He was so entranced that he almost forgot his bodyguard. “Hey, I’ve got to go back and get Fernando, my driver.”

“Let’s take my car.”

“No, I got to go back and get him.”

“Oh, okay. Well, I guess it’s buh bye, Juan Pablo.” She said as she dropped his tie and started walking towards a red Jaguar F-type convertible with the top down. With every step she took, a hint of her black panties would show. This was all too much for Sanchez to pass up. Screw Fernando, let him walk home.

“Tiffany, wait up,” He said as he ran after her.

Erick Sanchez didn’t notice the white cargo van parked next to her Jag because he was too busy drooling when Venus slid into the driver’s seat, flashing her panties as she settled into the seat with her legs spread. And he didn’t see the two men approaching with pistols until it was too late.

Odin placed the 9mm behind Sanchez’s left ear and said in a deadly cold voice, “You try any funny business, and I’ll blow your fucking brains all over Tiffany’s Jaguar. Understand?”

Sanchez nodded and replied with a simple “*Si.*”

Odin walked him to the back of the van, where he was bound, gagged, and blindfolded, then placed into the back of the van along with the other captives.

Once Sanchez was inside the van, Venus switched to the passenger seat, and Odin got into the driver’s seat, cranked up the engine, and drove out of the underground parking lot toward 2568 Av. 20 de Octubre to the Estado Plurinacional de Bolivia Policia Boliviana Comando General to meet Commander Nikolas Justiniano.

Nikolas Justiniano, the brother-in-law of Bolivia’s Ambassador to France, was appointed commander of the

Department of Forest Police and Environment. Justiniano was one of, if not the most corrupt of the lot. He would have sold his own mother if the Chinese thought they could make medicine from her parts. He's shrewd, cunning, and ruthless. His code name is *El Zorro*, the fox. He was so proud of his nickname that he had a vanity license plate of ZORRO on his red Ferrari 488.

Justiniano was superstitious and suffered from obsessive-compulsive disorder. He would turn the key to lock and unlock any door three times, never sit with his back to the door in any restaurant, go through any doorway, always touch the right doorframe with his hand fisted, and always take the same route to and from home.

Commander Justiniano was so focused on driving his route that he didn't notice the red Jaguar F-type convertible and white Chevy cargo van behind him. He felt a light tap from behind when he stopped at a stop sign three blocks from his condo in the upmarket Zona Sur, South Zone. He looked into the rearview mirror and saw a silver Jag with a young man and a beautiful blonde laughing.

He got out of his 488 and walked back to check for damage. Odin and Venus remained in the Jag.

"*Qué pasa,* man?" Odin said lightheartedly.

Justiniano, wearing his police commander's uniform, said nothing as he inspected the Ferrari's bumper. There was indeed a minute dent, which made Justiniano turn as red as his Ferrari. He went nuclear.

"Get out of that fucking car!" He shouted.

Odin and Venus got out of the car and approached Justiniano, who was ranting. Odin looked at the Ferrari's bumper and said, "Hey man, chill out. It's no biggie."

Odin's cavalier attitude enraged Justiniano even more.

"Do you know who I am?"

Odin looked at the license plate and said, "Zorro?"

"That's right. I'm Zorro!"

Odin laughed and replied, "So, where's your mask and cape, Zorro?"

When Justiniano reached for his holstered Beretta 92FS pistol to shoot the contemptuous, impertinent dog down, the white cargo van pulled up alongside Justiniano. Vulcan, who was sitting in the passenger seat, said, "Hey, Zorro! Eat shit and die."

Justiniano spun around to see a young black man pointing a gun at him just before he fired a tranquilizer dart into Justiniano's neck.

POP

Odin and Venus were next to the commander as he started to collapse. They walked him to the back of the van and threw him in, where Vulcan did the honors of binding him, gagging, blindfolding, and placing him next to Señor Sanchez.

Odin got into Zorro's Ferrari and drove south, Venus drove the Jag north, and Devol drove the van west. Devol and Vulcan would meet them at *Los Pinos* Park, which is not far from the Atrix Hotel.

☠☠☠☠☠☠☠☠☠☠☠

"Paging Mr. Bradley Peak. Mr. Paging Bradly Peak. You have a message. Please come to the Emirates Lounge.

Paging Mr. Bradley Peak. Paging Mr. Bradly Peak. You have a message. Please come to the Emirates Lounge."

Vermeer heard the message as he deplaned. He was scheduled to head to his connecting flight LA7042 on Iberia Airlines, which would leave in nine hours, so he had plenty of time to go, relax, have a couple of drinks and snacks, and get his message in the Emirates Lounge at Leonardo da Vinci Airport.

"Hi, I'm Bradley Peak. I believe you have a message for me," Vermeer said.

The beautiful attendant replied, "*Sì, Signore Peak.*" as she handed Vermeer the folded message.

Vermeer unfolded the note, and the message read, "Call 888-634-5789."

He asked the attendant, "Are there any quiet areas available?"

The young woman tapped some keys on her computer, smiled, and said, "*Stanza quattro*. Room four."

"*Grazie*."

Vermeer walked through the crowded waiting room, past the cigar bar and Le Clos Wine Cellar, to the six "quiet rooms." The quiet rooms were small 12 x 12 soundproof rooms with a chez lounge, a small side table, and a floor lamp, where passengers could go to relax and take a short nap between flights.

He placed his carry-on on the side table, took out his phone, and dialed the number.

"Hello, this is Bradley Peak," Vermeer said.

"Ah, Mr. Peak. There's been a slight change of plans. You're now booked on Lufthansa flight LH1871, connecting through Munich. Your final destination is JFK International, where you will be met upon arrival. Do you have any questions?" the anonymous voice asked.

"No."

"Well then, have a safe flight, Mr. Peak."

"Thanks."

"Goodbye."

CLICK

Vermeer checked the flight schedule; flight LH1871 wasn't scheduled to leave for six hours. Vermeer set the alarm clock on his watch and fell asleep.

Razor sent up two AeroVironment RQ-11 Raven UAV drones to surveil the park's areas that have had the most recent jaguar killings in the last week. The Ravens can stay aloft for up to 90 minutes and have a range of six miles. The team had four Ravens, so they always kept two birds in the air.

While Razor was the eyes in the skies, Fu Hao, Sue B, and the rest of the Red Team would be sitting in wait, ready to head off in whatever direction the poachers were. They were outfitted in multi-shades of green jungle ghillie suits, with additional personal enhancements of branches, leaves, and grasses. Châtelet was prepping the dogs of war for an attack.

"Red leader, this is Red One. Bogeys at eleven o'clock of your position," Razor announced.

"How many, Red One?" Fu Hao asked.

"Looks to be close to two dozen heading your way."

"Roger that. How far?" Sue B asked.

"About five clicks."

"Châtelet, get the hounds up and stand by," Fu Hao ordered.

Châtelet powered up the robotic quadrupeds, both the dogs and the Wildcats. She did a quick systems check.

"Standing by. Ready to go on your orders," Châtelet said.

Fu Hao looked at everyone, "Let's move out. Red One, keep us posted."

"Roger, Red leader."

"Red Team, Radio check," Fu Hao said.

Each member answered the call, showing that all radio headsets were working. Once they established that all radio communications were operational, they moved out with Châtelet and the robot dogs bringing up the rear.

From the description that Red One provided, the poachers were unknowingly setting themselves up for a classic pincer attack. The poachers seemed to be trapping themselves by having the Río Hondo on their left, cutting off the west as a way of escape.

Fu Hao would have the Red Team circle off to their right flank, splitting off half of the team led by Sue B to continue past them and get behind them, thereby shutting the back door for a retreat. Meanwhile, Châtelet would unleash her Hell Hounds for a full-frontal attack.

☠☠☠☠☠☠☠☠☠☠☠

Xavier Quispe grew up dirt poor in the small town of San Ignacio de Moxos on the shores of Lake Isirere in the middle of Bolivia. His father was a carpenter—handyman. His mother earned money as a weaver, weaving rugs, ponchos, sweaters, tablecloths, and tapestries, primarily using alpaca, llama, and vicuña wool. She made all her own dyes from boiling down plants and trees.

Xavier was the youngest of seven children—four boys and three girls. Neither he nor any of his siblings received a higher education than fifth grade. All Quispe children were expected to contribute money to the family coffers by either working, begging, or stealing. Xavier chose the latter.

He started by begging for money from the tourists, then tried becoming a pickpocket. He was pretty good at it until he got caught with his hand in an off-duty policeman's pants pocket. That little mistake cost him eighteen months in a juvenile detention center, where he learned the fine art of robbery, burglary, and an assortment of other criminal skills.

By the time Xavier was eighteen, he had been incarcerated for over half of his young age. He developed a rap sheet as long as your arm for primarily nonviolent crimes. There was the occasional assault charge, but nothing involving a weapon. That would come later.

He teamed up with an ex-con, Yerko Cardozo, a notorious bank robber whom Xavier had once been cell mates within a juvenile detention center many years ago. He had recently met by chance outside their parole officers' office. They got together and planned a daring heist of the Banco Nacional de Bolivia in Cochabamba, central Bolivia, in a valley in the Andes mountain range.

"It'll be a piece of cake. It's a small branch with easy access. Ten minutes tops. We walk in, boom, we walk out." Yerko said.

"I don't know," Xavier balked.

"Come on. I guess we'll each walk away with five grand each, easy."

"What about guards?"

"They got two old guys who'll probably piss their pants when we pull out our pieces. I guarantee it. Come on."

"I don't even have a gun," Xavier said.

"Here," Yerko said as he reached behind his back and handed him a .38 Smith & Wesson Model 10 revolver.

Xavier quickly tucked the loaded pistol under his shirt into his pants.

"I'll come by and pick you up tomorrow morning around nine. We'll be back in time for dinner."

It turned out that those two old guys were shotgun-wielding ex-army rangers. And it wasn't them who pissed their pants; after a short exchange of gunfire, Xavier and Yerko surrendered. Yerko sustained a shotgun blast to his left leg, hitting a femoral artery that was so bad that the leg had to be amputated above the kneecap. They were eventually found guilty of armed robbery and each was sentenced to ten years in *El Penal de San Pedro* (Saint Peter's Prison).

San Pedro prison is the largest prison in La Paz, famous for being a city in itself. San Pedro is significantly different from all other correctional facilities in Bolivia. The inmates have jobs inside the community, and they elect their leaders who enforce the community's laws, commonly through stabbing. The prison is home to nearly 3,000 inmates (not including the women and children who live inside the walls with their convicted husbands), with additional guests staying in the prison hotel.

It's not as idealistic as it might sound. There is little tolerance for those who have committed crimes against women and children. Many are killed, and the survivors must pay for the hospital services themselves.

The prison was initially designed to hold 600 inmates. The inmates must either rent or purchase their own cells. On average, most of the prisoners live in cramped conditions, with it being common for a single cell to house five prisoners. But, for those who can afford it, there are cells with private bathrooms, kitchens, and cable television. Unfortunately, Xavier and Yerko could not afford the deluxe accommodations of a private cell. They were housed in the Cancha section, where the drug-addicted inmates are housed and are the most dangerous at nighttime when most of the stabbings occur. Both Xavier and Yerko had, over the course of their ten-year sentence, been stabbed multiple times. Yerko, being that he was considered a gimp, was easy pickings. Whenever Xavier wasn't around to protect him, Yerko was bullied, preyed upon, and eventually stabbed to death over a drug buy gone bad.

When Xavier was released, he left prison with 1,800 Bolivianos, approximately $261 US Dollars, and a one-way bus ticket back to San Ignacio de Moxos, which he cashed in and went to La Paz instead. In La Paz, he met members of las Panteras Negras (the Black Panthers). He fit right in, and after a couple of years, he and his crew were among Bolivia's most successful, ruthless, and deadliest poachers.

☠☠☠☠☠☠☠☠☠☠☠

Lufthansa flight LH1871 landed at JFK airport on time at 11:55 pm. A bleary-eyed Vermeer made his way to customs, where a couple of hundred people from all over the world were forced to stand in long lines waiting to be interviewed by a customs agent.

Vermeer handed the agent his latest passport: Bradley Peak, a US citizen currently living in Manhattan, the Murray Hill area, thirty-eight, and Lexington.

"Where are you coming from?" The agent asked.

"Nepal."

"Business or pleasure?"

"Pleasure."

"What was the purpose of your trip, Mr. Peak?"

"I'm an architect. I was studying the local architecture."

"Do you have anything to declare?"

"Nothing."

The agent gave Vermeer a quick once-over, then smashed the stamp down onto the passport.

THRUMP

"Welcome back," The agent said as he handed Vermeer his passport. "Next!"

Vermeer went to the luggage claim, collected his bags, and made his way out to the passenger waiting area, where friends, family, car service, and limo drivers stood holding signs. He spotted a young woman dressed in a chauffeur's uniform holding a placard with the name "PEAK" on it.

"May I help you with your luggage, Mr. Peak?" She asked, reaching for his leather duffel bag.

"No. I think I'm good. Thank you."

"Very good. Please follow me. We're right outside."

She handed him an 8 x 11 manila envelope as they exited the terminal.

"This is for you," She said.

"Thank you."

Inside the envelope were his new instructions and vital information about his new identity and mission.

The Lincoln Town Car was parked just as she said, right outside. She popped the trunk, and he threw his duffel bag in while keeping the small carry-on with him.

As they settled in, she smiled, "My name is Laura. Welcome back."

"Thanks, Laura. It's good to be back. Do you know where we're headed?" He asked.

"38th and Lex?"

"That's it."

"Well, just sit back and relax. This time of night, it shouldn't take us too long."

"Great."

Within minutes, they were coasting down the Van Wyck Expressway, with hardly any traffic at all.

"Mind if I ask? Where'd ya fly in from?"

"Nepal."

"Nepal! That's awesome. Did you climb Everest?"

"No. Although I could see it."

"Wow."

"Were you there for fun?"

Vermeer smiled and said, "Yeah. I did have fun, actually."

"Cool."

"Have you ever been abroad?" He asked.

"Once. I went to England with my folks when I graduated high school."

"How was that?"

"It was all right. You know, it would have been much better if I had gone with some friends, if you knew what I mean?"

"Yeah. I get it. Ah, you're young. You have plenty of time. Just don't put it off too long."

"What do you do?" She asked.

"Me? I'm a mechanic. I fix things."

"That's neat. Well, here we are, 138 East 38th Street."

"Thanks, Laura. That was a most enjoyable ride. Here's a little something for your excellent service," he said as he handed her a hundred-dollar bill.

"Oh, no, Mr. Peak. The tip was already included in the ride."

"This isn't a tip. Consider it an advance for your travel fund."

"Gee, thank you, Mr. Peak."

"Maybe we'll run into each other somewhere exotic next time. Good night, kiddo," Vermeer said as he entered the apartment building.

☠☠☠☠☠☠☠☠☠☠☠

He unlocked the door on 8C, stepped inside, and switched on the overhead light. The apartment was a small studio. He estimated it to be about 850 square feet. Everything was compact and well organized. There was a loft bed with built-in bookcases on the sides. The TV sat on a small cabinet under the overhead bed. Opposite the loft bed was a love seat with a floor lamp beside it, and between a 48-inch round dining table with four cane chairs. A sealed cardboard box with his name, Bradley Peak, written on the side sat on the table.

Vermeer opened the box to find his weapon of choice, a Beretta 92FS 9mm fitted with an AL-GI-MEC suppressor and two boxes of ammunition. A leather shoulder holster was also included at the bottom of the box.

There was a sliding-door closet with several changes and various clothing, suits, jackets, and footwear for various occasions, all in his size.

He was so tired from twenty-four hours of flight time that Vermeer took off all his clothes, climbed the ladder to the bed, and fell into a deep sleep for over twelve hours, not waking up until one in the afternoon.

Once he was awake, he descended from his elevated berth and went straight into the shower to wash off the traveling dust from his body and the cobwebs from inside his head.

He got dressed, went downstairs, made a left out of the building, and turned right down on Third Avenue. Three blocks south was a deli, Sarge's Deli, where he ordered a salami sandwich on rye with a side of coleslaw. After eating, he returned to the apartment, stopping at a newsstand to pick up a New York Times.

Once he returned to the apartment, he opened his packet and read his mission. It turned out to be one of the most ambitious assignments he had been called upon to do. At the bottom of his orders was an 888 phone number to call once he had finished reading his instructions.

Vermeer dialed the number. The phone rang eight times before an anonymous voice answered.

"Hello?"

"This is Bradley Peak," Vermeer said.

"Please hold."

Seconds later, a recording of Frank Sinatra singing "The Girl from Ipanema" started to play. Old Blue Eyes sang the entire song, the three-minute and fourteen-second version. Then, as Frank began to sing "New York, New York," a familiar voice came on the phone.

"Vermeer. Wooch."

"Yes, sir."

"I have a new assignment."

"All right."

"Don't volunteer so fast. It's extremely dangerous. Possibly a suicide mission. Can you meet me at the main library on Fifth Avenue at four o'clock this afternoon?"

"Yes, sir."

"Good, I'll be in the Rose Main Reading Room on the third floor."

"How will I recognize you since we've never met? Vermeer asked.

"I'll be the one sitting all alone reading the dictionary.

"Four o'clock."

"Four o'clock. See you then."

CLICK

Vermeer looked at his watch. It was three-thirty. The walk to the library would only take about fifteen minutes, so he decided to take it nice and slow. He'd walk over to Park Avenue, turn north to 42nd Street, then over to 5th Avenue and down to the library. He glanced at his watch as he passed by the two lion statues guarding the library, Patience and Fortitude, and climbed the 27 steps to the entrance. One minute passed four.

Vermeer took the stairs to the third floor; he walked west, down the corridor leading to the Genealogy Room, past the Music Room, and into the Rose Main Reading Room. The room was enormous, with two rows of eight twenty-foot tables and four lamps on each table. And eight wooden chairs on either side of the tables. Overhead, there hung twenty massive chandeliers. Every seat at every table seemed to be taken with people reading, doing research, or tapping away on their computers—every table except one.

One table at the very back of the reading room was empty except for a raggedy old man wearing a torn oversized topcoat. His hair was disheveled, his face—what there was to see of it under a large bushy beard—was covered in dirt, and he smelled awful. He reeked of BO and urine. He sat all by himself, reading a large dictionary.

Vermeer found a copy of Roget's Thesaurus, sat across from the old man, and began to read. The old man looked up at the stranger across from him, smiled, and said, "Peak."

Vermeer just nodded as he tried to breathe through his mouth, as the stench of the old man was making his eyes water.

The old man kept his head down as he spoke softly, "There is going to be a W.A.S.P. board meeting in five days. All of the upper echelons will be there to vote on the president, new officers, and board leaders."

"Okay," Vermeer whispered.

"They're going to be heavily protected by several highly trained ex-military bodyguards. I was going to send in a commando raid, but thought better of it. I want something more gentle and less noisy. I thought the Angel of Death (*Der Todesengel*) could come in silently, like the morning fog.

Like I said, it could be a suicide mission, and I'll understand if you say no. There will be no hard feelings."

"Where?" Vermeer asked.

"Twenty-three Park Avenue. Apartment 5C. The apartment belongs to Margaret Hamilton, an uberwealthy widow who was and is an avid hunter, along with her dead husband and two sons. She was among the first women to be credited with killing the Big Five: lion, leopard, rhinoceros, elephant, and Cape buffalo. She's seventy-two years old, sharp as a whip, and an eagle-eyed crack shot. Rumors are that she always has at least two pistols on her at all times."

"Charming," Vermeer smirked.

"There are to be twelve members attending. I have all the information, dossiers of everyone scheduled to attend, as well as several diagrams and architectural drawings of the building. Everything is in an envelope in the back of this dictionary."

"Okay."

"If you need to get hold of me, call that 888 number. Questions?"

"Yeah. Everyone?"

"Everyone!"

Wooch stood up and walked out of the room, leaving the dictionary in front of Vermeer. He slid the massive book over to him and began leafing through it until he found a small-sealed envelope. He folded it and placed it into his back pocket, then stood up and carried the two books back to their proper resting place.

Vermeer walked back to his apartment on 38th Street, passing Twenty-three Park Avenue on the way. The Italian Renaissance revival-style building was initially constructed as a mansion in 1890 for James Hampden Robb, a retired businessman and former state assemblyman and senator, and his wife, Cornelia Van Rensselaer Robb. Since then, it has been used as the clubhouse of the Advertising Club of New York and the Sphinx Club and now houses seventeen multimillion-dollar condos. Soon, it will be the scene of a horrific massacre.

Captain Rodrigo Soliz and Lieutenant Adalberto Camacho of the National Police Corps were in charge of dealing directly with *las Panteras Negras*. They were responsible for negotiating with the butchers, shippers, and Chinese. They would receive the payments from the Chinese cartels and distribute payments to the poachers and government officials.

When the phone rang, Lieutenant Camacho and his secretary, Ms. Eva Gutierrez, had just returned to his office after having lunch and a quickie. She ran over to her desk and picked up the receiver.

"Lieutenant Camacho's office," Gutierrez answered.

It was a young woman's voice; she had an Asian accent and sounded frantic.

"This is Zhou Ling. I must speak to Lieutenant Camacho. It is very urgent," Fu Hao said.

Gutierrez asked, "What is in reference to?"

"L*as Panteras Negras*."

"One moment, please. I'll see if he's available."

Gutierrez hit the hold button and said, "It's a Zhou Ling. She says it's urgent. It has to do with *las Panteras Negras*."

Camacho looked perplexed, trying to recall the name Zhou Ling. He knew of a Zhou Wei but couldn't recall a Zhou Ling.

"Find out what she wants."

"He can't come to the phone at the moment. Is there something that I might be able to help you with?"

"You tell Lieutenant Camacho and Captain Soliz that they are to come to Bosquecillo de Pura Pura in one hour."

"Why?"

"If no one comes. They are in big trouble."

"Who are you?"

"Zhou Ling. Me with *Fujian Hēishǒu dǎng*."

"Hold on, please."

"She says she's with the Fujian Mafia and that you and Captain Soliz must meet her at Bosquecillo de Pura Pura in one hour, or there will be big trouble," Gutierrez said.

"Here, let me speak to her!" Camacho said as he grabbed the receiver from his lover.

"Hello, this is Lieutenant Camacho."

"You and Soliz, come to Bosquecillo de Pura Pura in one hour."

"Why?"

"We found a traitor in *Las Panteras Negras*, who is planning to go to the newspaper. You come."

"Why does Captain Soliz have to come?"

"I don't know. I'm telling you that it's urgent. You come. One hour."

"Now, you listen to me!"

CLICK

"Hello? Hello!" Camacho held the receiver in his hand, pissed off. It would take almost an hour to get to the park. There wasn't any time to consider alternative options. He handed the phone back to Gutierrez, grabbed his hat, and said as he was leaving, "Eva, call Soliz. Tell him I'll be downstairs waiting in front. Tell him I'm explaining in the car."

Fu Hao called Odin to let him know that Soliz and Camacho were on their way. She hung up and continued with the Red Team towards the gang of poachers.

When Captain Soliz and Lieutenant Camacho pulled into Bosquecillo de Pura Pura's parking lot, they saw what looked to be an Asian woman with long black hair and two men. They were all wearing sunglasses and standing alongside a red Jaguar F-type. They were so fixated on the woman and her two companions that they did not notice the white Chevy cargo van parked alongside the Jag.

Camacho parked the black BMW 750i next to the red Jag.

"Are you Zhou Ling?" Camacho asked.

The woman nodded and smiled.

"What's this all about?" Soliz barked.

Lu Wei, the only Asian, stepped forward and said, "We've discovered an informer in *las Panteras Negras*. We have him here in the trunk."

He led the two police officers towards the back of the Jag. He opened the trunk to reveal Vulcan, who appeared to be bound and gagged. Soliz and Camacho looked at each other in disbelief.

"Who the fuck is this guy?" Camacho asked.

"This is the creep who was going to rat you out," Lu Wei said.

Camacho and Soliz started to reach for their pistols as Odin and Bellator snuck up from behind and stuck their Sig Sauer P226 revolvers in the small of their backs.

"Not so fast, *muchacho,"* Odin said. He and Bellator led them to the back of the cargo van. Devol was waiting to bind, blindfold, and gag them. With the help of Odin and Bellator, he placed them in the back of the van with the others.

All the targets had been collected with the exception of Captain Juan Carlos Flores, the head of La Paz's *Grupo Especial de Seguridad* (the Special Security Group). He was the most elusive, but he was easily captured just outside of his house. Devol had placed a mosquito microbot in his Mercedes while he got into his car after work. They followed him as he drove home. About two blocks from his house, Devol had a robot insect sting him in the back of his neck with a massive dose of propofol. By the time he parked his car in the driveway, he was totally unconscious. It was easy enough for Bellator and Lu Wei to extricate him from his car and into the back of the waiting van. Once everyone was inside the van, Eduardo drove off.

"Blue Four to Blue One. Over," Lu Wei said.

"Blue One, over," Odin replied.

"The falcon has landed and is heading home."

"Roger," Odin answered.

Odin turned to Vulcan and Venus and smiled, "That's the lot of them. Let's go."

Vulcan dropped the cargo van into gear and headed toward Vesty Pakos Zoo, twenty minutes south of downtown La Paz. By the time they arrived, Eduardo and the rest of the team were waiting for them in the zoo's abandoned main parking lot. The time was two-thirty in the morning.

A third car pulled up shortly after Vulcan arrived. It was Angel Vasquez, the head zookeeper and loyal Le Gang de la Clé de Singe member. He rolled down his window and shouted, "Follow me to the second entrance."

Entrance number two couldn't be seen from any roads or highways. They all parked their vehicles next to each other and began unloading their cargo: nine men who were blindfolded, gagged, and had their hands zip-tied behind their backs. As Odin and the others started to unload the men, Vasquez went to get a motorized utility cart.

"Here. Let's use this," Vasquez suggested.

"Okay, let's load them up," Odin said.

They piled one body on top of another until all nine were stacked up in the back of the cart.

"Follow me," Vasquez said.

"Basilio, you, Venus, and Devol stay with the vehicles and keep an eye out. We'll be back soon," Odin ordered.

The cart, loaded with its human cargo, headed past the condors, badgers, spectacled bears, and lion display to the jaguars. The jaguar exhibit was three times the size of any other exhibit. The captives became agitated as they began to become aware of their surroundings.

Odin, Lu Wei, Vulcan, and Bellator dragged each prisoner from the cart, stood them upright, and removed their blindfolds. They looked around, trying to figure out what the Hell was going on. Why were they standing in front of the jaguar exhibit?

"Gentlemen, you're all wondering what's going on. Do you recognize this?" Odin said as he held up the yellow ensign with the black skull and crossed monkey wrenches.

Everyone's eyes bulged out of their sockets, and they all started to talk in unison, but since their mouths were gagged, they came out as muffled screams.

"*Mmmppphhhhmmmm!!!Mmmppphhhhmm!!!Mmmppphhhhmm!!!*"

"Gentlemen. Gentlemen. Let me put your concerns to rest. We've brought you all here to die. You've all been involved in the illegal trade of jaguars and jaguar parts.

And as you know, Le Gang de la Clé de Singe believes that anyone who targets, kills, profits, and or supports the killing of any animals that are endangered or any animals that are hunted for sport will be hunted down and pay with their lives. There will be no exceptions and no mercy; we will show no quarter," Odin said as he gave the nod for Lu Wei and Bellator to place the flags around their necks and the manifestos in their pockets.

While shackles were attached to each captive's leg, Vasquez had gone to the equipment lot and driven a small boom lift with a ten-foot platform back to the jaguar exhibit. Dangling from the platform were nine six-foot lengths of heavy-duty chains, which were subsequently attached to each prisoner's shackles.

Once all of their shackles were attached, the boom lift's arm was raised, causing the captives to hang upside down. Many of the men wriggled, trying to free themselves, but to no avail. When all efforts proved useless, the boom arm raised the nine inverted men up and over the twelve-foot protective fence into the yard of the jaguar's exhibit.

Vasquez lowered the men, so their heads were a foot above the ground. He then reached into his pocket and, held what looked like a garage opener, pressed the red button that electronically opened the door that would release a dozen jaguars into the yard.

☠☠☠☠☠☠☠☠☠☠☠

Vermeer sat in the apartment studying floor plans of 23 Park Avenue, as well as recent photographs of the building. As it turned out, the apartment building on E 35th Street that butts up to the building's rear was vacant because it underwent a total renovation. There is scaffolding, mesh netting, and cables covering the entire construction site. He would be able to make his way up through the vacant building to the roof, then, with a grappling hook and rope, scale the twelve-foot wall of 23 Park Avenue and make his way over the two-foot parapet to the roof.

From the satellite photographs, he could see that besides the industrial air conditioning and heating unit, which took up a third of the roof's real estate, there was a small patio table with chairs, a few plants, and a couple of chez lounges. It appeared that there were also two utility sheds. Knowing there would be several ex-military armed guards, some would undoubtedly search the rooftop. He would need to do a preliminary reconnaissance before the event, which was to take place in three days.

Murray Hill is primarily a residential area, especially in late evenings; things are pretty quiet, and there is not a lot of traffic or people on the streets. At 2:30 am, Vermeer packed his gear into a backpack and walked the five blocks from his apartment to 104 E 35th Street, the building under renovation. He checked to make sure there wasn't anyone observing him as he picked the lock to 104. Once inside, he slipped on a pair of Coast XPH34R personal headlamps to maneuver around all the materials, equipment, loose boards, and other construction hazards. He worked his way up to the fourth floor and onto the roof. He saw that the way the building was situated, the entire roof area was in complete shadow. Vermeer turned off his headlamp, opened his backpack, and removed the rope with a grappling hook.

It took two tries before successfully hooking onto the parapet two stories above. He removed his windbreaker and Nike sneakers and wore a pair of La Sportive TC Rock

Climbing Shoes. By 3 o'clock, Vermeer was up and onto 23 Park Avenue's roof. He spent an hour investigating all the possibilities of a secure hiding places. He decided on the inside of the air conditioning shaft. The intake duct had several curves at the entrance before forming a vertical tunnel. There was plenty of room for him to crouch down and not be seen by anyone passing by. He attached two heavy-duty O Hooks on the inside, so if he needed to, he could attach two carabiner clips onto a safety belt that he would wear, hanging inside the air shaft and conserving his strength.

Vermeer returned to the apartment by 4:30. He turned off his phone, shut the blinds and blackout curtains, and didn't wake up until two p.m. When he turned on his phone, he had six calls from the same 888 phone number but no messages. He took a hot shower, shaved, and dressed before calling in.

"Hello. Moe's Delicatessen," The anonymous voice answered.

"Hello, I'd like to place an order."

"Pick up or delivery?"

Vermeer began to place his order, which was in code in case someone might be listening.

"Delivery, please. I want to order two kosher salamis (two Beretta 92FS 9mm's), a loaf of Jewish rye with seeds (an AL-GI-MEC suppressor), six jars of new pickles (six boxes of 9mm ammunition), and a dozen black and white cookies (12 M69 Hough-Explosive Fragmentation hand grenades)."

"I can have that delivered to you within the hour."

"Very good."

"I just need the name and address."

"Bradley Peak. 138 East 38th Street. Apartment 8C."

"Thank you."

"Thank you. Goodbye."

CLICK

Moe's Delicatessen panel van pulled up to the curb an hour later. A short man in his fifties, wearing a white cook uniform, jumped out of the van. He walked to the back of the van, opened the back door, and pulled out a large cardboard box filled to the top with two long salami sticks sticking out. He carried the box into the lobby, where Vermeer was waiting for him. He handed the deliveryman a hundred-dollar bill, took the box, and rode the elevator back to his apartment.

He unpacked the box, placing the weapons to the left and the deli treats to the right. After he checked all his equipment, he made a hefty salami-on-rye sandwich with a couple of kosher new pickles and popped open an ice-cold bottle of Coney Island Lager. Vermeer sat at the small dining room table and looked out the window, watching people walk up and down Lexington Avenue while repeatedly going over the details of the upcoming mission in his head.

☠☠☠☠☠☠☠☠☠☠☠

At eight o'clock in the morning, Xavier Quispe, along with his band of mercenaries, were returning from a successful night of poaching jaguars. A total of eight adult *Panthera oncas* were shot and slaughtered.

The jungle was hot and humid, and the air was thick, making breathing difficult. With all the moisture in the air, shafts of sunlight streaming through the dense overhead canopy made visibility only a few meters in any direction.

Because of the thick canopy, Razor had to readjust the AeroVironment RQ-11 Raven UAV drones to include heat-seeking capabilities to detect any life forms below. He decided to use the traditional parallel track search pattern used in air search and rescue missions. The PTS pattern is a rectangular pattern that traverses a defined path over the ground in a systematic manner.

Razor and Châtelet were each in control of one of the drones. Each drone would stay aloft for ninety minutes before having to return to base to switch out batteries. With a total of four AeroVironment RQ-11 Raven UAV drones, they could keep two "birds" in the air at all times.

It was ten-twenty when Razor spotted the poachers. They looked to be resting by the Río Hondo, which would have trapped them, at least from the west. They radioed Fu Hao and Sue B.

"Red One, calling Red Team. Over," Razor said.

"Red Team. Go," Fu Hao answered.

"Bogies now, one click due north."

"Send in the hounds. By the time they arrive, we'll be in position," Fu Hao ordered.

"Roger that," Châtelet said.

Fu Hao and her team, Hazael, Basilio, and Gianfranco, would position themselves to the poacher's right, while Sue B and her squad, Cowboy and Sassoon, would go past the resting poachers if they tried to retreat. When Sue B got into position, she radioed Fu Hao.

"Red Leader, we are in position. Over," Sue B said.

"Roger, so are we," Fu Hao replied.

"Red Team. This is Red One. Hounds are minutes away," Châtelet radioed.

"Attack! Attack! Attack!" Fu Hao ordered.

Châtelet decided to hold back half of the robot dogs and the Wildcats in reserve. The first attack would be with six of the quadruped robot dogs, coming into the poacher's camp fast, with guns blazing.

Xavier Quispe and his crew were lounging by the riverbed, enjoying the cool breeze from the flowing river. Xavier had posted three sentries to be on the lookout for intruders: one to the north, one to the east, and one to the south.

The southern sentry shouted out, “Xavier, I hear something coming, fast.”

Those were his last words before one of the hounds opened fire, killing him instantly. The six robot dogs were on them in seconds, firing their side-mounted machine guns.

RATATATATAAT RATATATATAT RATATATTTAT RATATATATATAT RATATATATAT RATATATATATATAT RATATATTATAT RATATATATAT RATTATATTTATATAT RATATATAT RATATATATATATTTT

Several of the men started to run in different directions. Xavier and his most loyal men gathered their weapons and began to return fire. Confounded by these robotic weapons, the Hell Hounds didn’t seem disabled when hit.

Châtelet sent in the rest of the robot dogs and six Wildcats from their right flank. The wildcats carried more firepower and were considerably faster. Still, the dogs were more challenging to hit because they were lower to the ground and could better hide amongst the jungle vegetation.

Sue B and her squad encountered four men heading north.

“*¡Detener! Suelta tus armas*,” (Halt! Drop your weapons) Sue B shouted.

They stopped dead in their tracks. They heard a voice but could not see anyone since Sue B and her squad wore ghillie suits that blended seamlessly into the jungle.

“*Suelta tus armas*,” Sue B yelled.

They instinctively raised their weapons and began to fire indiscriminately in all directions.

KA-POW KA-POW KA-POW KA-POW KA-POW KA-POW KA-POW KA-POW KA-POW KA-POW KA-POW KA-POW

They fired aimlessly until they ran out of ammunition and had to reload.

Sue B called to her team, “Fire!”

PHIFF PHIFF PHIFF. PHIFF PHIFF PHIFF PHIFF PHIFF PHIFF PHIFF PHIFF PHIFF PHIFF PHIFF PHIFF PHIFF PHIFF PHIFF

Within a matter of seconds, all four men were lying on the ground dead.

The six men who ran off to the east ran into Fu Hao and her team.

Fu Hao wasn't as generous to these men; she didn't give them the option to surrender.

"Fire!" She shouted to her team.

PHIFF PHIFF PHIFF. PHIFF PHIFF PHIFF PHIFF PHIFF PHIFF PHIFF PHIFF PHIFF. PHIFF PHIFF PHIFF PHIFF PHIFF PHIFF PHIFF PHIFF PHIFF

When the smoke cleared, no survivors were standing. Xavier Quispe and three of his men were the only ones still alive. They surrendered to the quadruped robots. All the robots were equipped with electronic voice simulation, so when Châtelet spoke into a microphone, Xavier would hear a synthesized voice, neither male nor female.

"Surrender. Put. Your. Weapons. Down. Escape. Is. Futile," A Wildcat declared.

"Fuck you!" Xavier shouted as he pointed his AK-47 at the beast and began to fire. Bullets bounced off the Kevlar covering, ricocheting all over the place. A bullet deflected off of a nearby tree, hitting one of his friends in the head, killing him. Xavier dropped his weapon and ordered his men to do the same.

"Surrender. Put. Your. Weapons. Down. Escape. Is. Futile. This. Is. Your. Last. Warning!" The Wildcat announced.

The last remaining poachers looked at each other and dropped their weapons.

"Put. Your. Hands. Up. Do. Not. Move," The Wildcat commanded.

They did as they were told. They gazed at the river, pondering whether they could survive the fast-moving current. None of them were good swimmers; besides, they knew there was a deadly waterfall not 500 meters downstream.

Xavier and the two last remaining poachers stood with their hands up, surrounded by two dozen killer quadruped robot dogs. They soon saw what looked like waking bushes carrying rifles approaching them from the east. The leader grabbed the hood and pulled it off, revealing a thirty-something Asian woman.

Xavier and the others noticed that these bushes were carrying their dead friends and laying them down next to each other.

Minutes later, Sue B and her team arrived carrying their four dead poachers. They lay their bodies down next to the other six lying by the campfire.

"Have you ever heard of Le Gang de la Clé de Singe ?" Fu Hao said as she held up the yellow ensign.

"Yes. But what do you want with us? We did not do anything wrong," Xavier said defiantly.

"No? What's in those bags?" Fu Hao asked, pointing to four blood-stained canvas bags.

"In there? Nothing. Just some rations and supplies," Xavier lied.

"*Ábrelos*," (Open them) She snapped at one of the other men standing next to Xavier.

He ambled to the bags. He knelt down, unbuckled the clasp, reached inside, felt around, and pulled out a Walther PP .22lr semi-automatic pistol. He spun around only to find Fu Hao's Sig Sauer AS50 sniper rifle pointing at his face.

"*Déjalo caer*," (Drop it) She said.

The man hesitated, then began to raise the pistol. Fu Hao shot him in the head, blowing half his face off, and a large portion of his brains splattered all over the four canvas bags.

She aimed her rifle at Xavier and ordered, "You. Open the bag."

He ambled over to the bag, stepping over the body of his dead comrade, knelt down, reached in, and pulled out the severed head of a jaguar. Its cold, lifeless eyes were open. They reminded Fu Hao of those portraits that seemed to be staring at and following her no matter where she stood.

"Put it down. And stand up," She said.

Xavier did as he was told. He stood up. Sweat was beginning to cover his face, but it wasn't because of the jungle's heat.

"Now go back to your amigo."

The two remaining poachers stood next to each other, trying not to show fear. Fu Hao reached into her ghillie suit and produced a piece of paper, which she handed to Xavier.

"Read it." She said.

He looked at it and answered, "I cannot read."

She took it back and began to read aloud, "*Let it be known that Le Gang de la Clé de Singe declares a proclamation of war against all poachers, big game hunters, and all big game safari outfits, as well as anyone anywhere in the world who targets, kills, profits from, or supports the killing of any animals that are endangered or hunted for sport. Be warned, do so at your own risk. You will be hunted down and pay with your lives. Whether man or woman, there will be no exceptions and no mercy; we will show no quarter. You have been warned.*"

"Please, Señora. We are poor peasants trying to make a living for our families. You should be going after the ones who truly profit. Please show mercy," Xavier begged.

Fu Hao read again from the paper she held, "*You will be hunted down and pay with your lives. Be it man or woman, there will be no exceptions and no mercy; we will show no quarter.*"

POW POW

Gianfranco and Hazael each fired one fatal shot, killing Xavier and his cohort. The team then neatly placed them next to their accomplices, placing the yellow ensign around each of their necks and a copy of Le Gang de la Clé de Singe's manifesto in their pockets. The four canvas bags were laid next to Xavier's body. On one of the bag's plastic name tags, Cowboy affixed a single pristine fingerprint of Juan José Torres González, the 50th President of Bolivia. He was popularly known as "J.J." (Jota-Jota).

J.J. was installed as president in a coup d'état in 1970. In 1971, he was ousted.

"Red One. This is Red Leader. Over," Sue B radioed.

Châtelet answered, "This is Red One."

"Recall the pack. Over."

"Roger. Bringing the pack home. Over."

ed in a U.S.-backed coup. He was eventually murdered in 1976 in Buenos Aires in the U.S.-supported campaign Operation Condor.

Suddenly, all of the robotic dogs came back to life. Their "eyes" lit up, and they turned around and began to trot back to the home base silently. Some were limping from having sustained damage in the skirmish, but overall, they performed admirably. Best of all, there were no Red Team deaths or wounded.

As the combined Red Team marched back to base, Sue B told Fu Hao, "These robotic dogs are going to be a real asset."

"Yeah, these puppies are a real game changer," Fu Hao replied.

☠☠☠☠☠☠☠☠☠☠☠

When the metal door on the jaguar house opened, sixteen South American jaguars wandered into the exhibit's open spaces. It didn't take them too long to discover nine government and police officials hanging upside down inside their perimeter, suspended from a boom lift. At first, they were leery of these strange creatures invading their territory until the alpha male began to investigate.

When the big cat approached, the nine captives began to squirm and muffle their screams. Being territorial, the big cat became emboldened and attacked Arsenio Rojas. They were scratching and mauling him about the face and torso. Once the others smelled the blood and saw that there was no resistance to the attack, the slaughter, carnage, and butchery grew into a frenzy. A couple of the cats jumped onto the wriggling bodies, their claws digging deep into the men's flesh, scratching, clawing, and ripping large chunks of meat and muscle out of their prey. One male jaguar was able to dislodge Nikolas Justiniano from his tether, forcing him to fall to the ground, where four females ascended upon him and proceeded to tear him limb from limb, literally.

Once the attack started, the massacre was over in a matter of minutes. All nine men, or what was left of them, were strewn all over the exhibit grounds. Adalberto Camacho was the only one who seemed to be still alive. The gaffer's tape had been ripped off in the mauling. He was sobbing and moaning, "Please help me. Please."

His pleading attracted the attention of several cats, who went to investigate; seeing that he was still alive, a large male clamped onto his throat, suffocating him to death.

After his demise, there was silence, with an occasional growl or snarl from the jaguars.

The members of the Blue Team hung nine Le Gang de la Clé de Singe yellow flags on the chain-link fence, one for each captive, along with one copy of the manifesto with a perfectly readable fingerprint of Domitila Barrios de Chungara. She was one of one of Bolivia's famous labor leaders and feminists, who sadly passed away in 2012.

☠☠☠☠☠☠☠☠☠☠☠

"Good evening. I'm Nigel Williams, and this is the BBC World Headline News. Our top story this hour comes from La Paz, Bolivia, where there is a report that nine members of the Bolivian police and government officials were brutally murdered by the international eco-terrorist group known as Le Gang de la Clé de Singe. It appears that the nine officials have been linked to an international jaguar smuggling ring that has been known to be trafficking animal parts to China.

A spokesperson from the La Paz Police Service told the BBC that nine men were bound and gagged and hung upside down in the jaguar exhibit at the Vesty Pakos Zoo, where the big cats attacked, killed, mutilated, and ate them. Many of the remains were beyond recognition.

The Bolivian government has launched a full-scale investigation into the trafficking allegations and the murder of these individuals. A two-hundred-thousand-dollar reward has been posted for any information leading to the arrest and conviction of the perpetrators.

In a related story, two dozen known jaguar poachers have been found murdered in Parque Nacional Madidi. Among the dead, it has been reported that the notorious Xavier Quispe-poacher, aka El Buitre (the Vulture), was among the dead. Claiming responsibility for their deaths is the eco-terrorist group, Le Gang de la Clé de Singe.

While the government of Bolivia does not condone the actions of Le Gang de la Clé de Singe, it is conducting a full investigation into the allegations of members of the Bolivian government's involvement in illegal animal trafficking. Two Chinese nationals have been arrested and are expected to be expelled in connection with the trafficking.

Meanwhile, in other news……"

☠☠☠☠☠☠☠☠☠☠☠

Vermeer made a point of scouting 23 Park Avenue every night. He knew it so well that he could maneuver the entire space blindfolded. Two nights before the scheduled assassination, he managed to enter apartment 5C while Mrs. Hamilton was fast asleep. He bypassed all of the alarms and security systems to study the layout, the flow, and where there might be anything that might prove to be an obstacle. The night before the meeting, he planted a couple of "trinkets" scattered on the roof, just in case. On the climb down, he placed a series of rock climbing pitons into the crevasses of the two buildings where they met. He was able to secure the black climbing rope so as not to be visible from the rooftop.

Friday night, Vermeer, wearing a long black duster and carrying a backpack, walked into the vacant renovation building after hours. He took off his coat to reveal a black ninja-style uniform. Opening his backpack, he donned his special shoulder holster that carried his two Beretta 92FS 9mm fitted with AL-GI-MEC suppressors, eight extra ammo clips, five M67 hand grenades, and one tear gas grenade. The M67 fragmentation hand grenade looks unlike the traditional hand grenade; it's round and looks like a green apple with a thick stem. Its fuse delays detonation between 4 and 5 seconds after the pin is released.

At eight o'clock, he began his accent to the rooftop. As he neared the parapet, he could hear men's voices. They were laughing and joking around. Their first mistake was not paying attention and not taking their job seriously. One should never become complacent while on sentry duty.

When Vermeer reached the top, he peered over the three men standing in a group towards the front of the building. He climbed over the top ledge and headed for the air conditioning duct where he had installed the O Hooks. He climbed inside, attached the two carabiner clips to his safety belt, and waited to see if the three guards were to be the only ones stationed on the roof. Did they have a routine for patrolling the area, or was it random? Random is more dangerous; a set routine is more predictable and more accessible to take advantage of.

Mistake number two was that they had a set routine for surveilling the rooftop. Every fifteen minutes, one of the sentries would walk the roof's perimeter in a counterclockwise path. It appeared that they would each take a turn walking around the edge of the building. The total time to complete two turns around the building was precisely twelve minutes.

Once Vermeer had established the timing of their rooftop surveillance, he waited for the next sentinel to pass by. As he heard someone approaching, he raised himself in the air duct, aimed at the man, who had stopped with his back to Vermeer to look out towards the East River. Vermeer fired one shot, striking the man between the shoulder blades.

PHIFF

The force of the bullet forced the man over the edge and sent him tumbling down onto the roof of the renovated building below.

It took fifteen minutes for the other two to realize their associate was late. Vermeer heard one of the men say, "Where the fuck is Ricardo?"

The other replied, "Ah, he's probably having a smoke."

"Go and see."

"Why me?"

"Just go."

Vermeer listened for the second man to appear. He looked over the edge and spotted his comrade lying spread eagle on the roof below.

"Hey, Louis, come quick!" The man shouted.

Vermeer heard Louis's running footsteps moving closer. He couldn't have planned it better. Right before him stood the two guards peering over the building's ledge—mistake number three.

PHIFF PHIFF

Over the ledge, they both plummeted. They were both dead before they hit the rooftop. When Vermeer peeked below, it looked like they all landed one on top of the other. Since they were all wearing black suits with white shirts, they appeared to be one big hodgepodge mélange of black and white.

Vermeer slowly advanced towards the front of the building, to the door leading down into the apartments below. He cracked the door open and listened. There was silence in the hall, although he could hear music and chatter coming from apartment 5C.

As he descended the staircase, no one appeared to be guarding the front door. He waited for several minutes to see if anyone would come. No one did. He then carefully walked down the stairs to 5C, placing his ear against the front door to listen.

"Welcome, ladies and gentlemen. It's so nice to see so many familiar faces here tonight," Ms. Hamilton said.

There was a short round of cheers and applause.

"As you all know, we are gathered here to elect the new president and board members of W.A.S.P. After the devastating loss of dear Thurston Bentley Hart the Third, who died while on safari in Africa during that terrible massacre at the hands of those deplorable terrorists Le Gang de la Clé de Singe.

Those thugs will never deter us from our God-given right to bear arms and kill anything walking, crawling, or flying on this earth! Our country has had enough. We will not take it anymore, and that's what this is all about. And to use a favorite term you all created, We will kill them all.

Cheers, applause, and chants of "Kill them all! Kill them all! Kill them all!"

"And we'll fight. We'll fight like hell. And if you don't fight like hell, you're not going to have a country anymore.

Our exciting adventures and boldest endeavors have not yet begun—my fellow W.A.S.P.'s, for our movement, our children, and our beloved country.

And I say this despite all that's happened. The best is yet to come."

An eruption of cheers, applause, and chants of "Kill them all! Kill them all! Kill them all!"

Vermeer put his air-tight goggles on and placed the portable rebreather in his mouth. Holding both Beretta 92FS 9mm locked and loaded, he rang the door buzzer with the muzzle of the pistol.

Placing both barrels on the door, he began firing through it as soon as he saw the light from the peephole shine through.

PHIFF PHIFF PHIFF PHIFF PHIFF PHIFF PHIFF PHIFF PHIFF PHIFF PHIFF PHIFF PHIFF PHIFF PHIFF PHIFF PHIFF PHIFF

There was a distinctive thud that came from the person who was killed peering through the peephole. Vermeer raised his right leg and kicked the door in with all his might. He heard the panic and screams coming from inside. He pulled the pin on the tear gas grenade and lobbed it into the foyer as he entered.

MMFFFTTTT

People began to cough and gag. He felt the whizz of a bullet going by his head. He ducked low, spun around, and fired two shots, striking the assailant in the torso.

PHIFF PHIFF

Stunned and disoriented, the people in the apartment were easy targets.

PHIFF PHIFF PHIFF PHIFF PHIFF PHIFF PHIFF PHIFF

Before going to look for other people, Vermeer set a trip wire with an M67 grenade at the front door in case someone was able to slip by him.

He went throughout the house looking for, finding, and eliminating all the W.A.S.P. board members and their so-called bodyguards.

PHIFF PHIFF PHIFF PHIFF PHIFF PHIFF PHIFF PHIFF PHIFF PHIFF PHIFF PHIFF PHIFF PHIFF PHIFF PHIFF

One of the last people he encountered was the hostess herself, Ms. Margaret Hamilton. She stood in her bedroom holding two M1911 .45 caliber pistols, one in each hand and pointed at Vermeer as he entered the room.

"Eat lead, dirtbag!" She screamed as she pulled the trigger on both weapons.

CLICK CLICK

Vermeer smiled, "I emptied them two nights ago while you were sleeping."

"You bastard!" She said as she tried to fire again.

CLICK CLICK

She threw them at his head but missed.

He raised his Beretta slowly and fired once, hitting Ms. Hamilton squarely between the eyes. This sent her cartwheeling backward, head over heels, until she landed on top of her prized elephant leg footstool, her eye gazing up at the stuffed lion's head mounted on her bedroom wall hanging over her bed.

Before leaving Ms. Hamilton, Vermeer placed the yellow flag of Le Gang de la Clé de Singe around her neck, just below her Tiffany Victoria pearl necklace. He stuck the manifesto in the lion's mouth. As he was leaving, he went about the apartment, placing yellow ensigns around the necks of all the corpses.

In the distance, he could hear police sirens approaching 23 Park Avenue. As he was making his way out the door, a large, powerful man grabbed him from behind in a bear hug.

"Gotcha!" The man snarled. It felt like a boa constrictor trying to squeeze all the air out of him. Vermeer's ribs felt like they were about to crack, and his arms were restricted by his sides, but as he squirmed from side to side, he was able to reach his Ridge Runner belt with a hidden belt buckle dagger. Once the dagger was in his hand, Vermeer began stabbing his assailant in the leg, forcing him to loosen his grip. Vermeer was able to jab the blade deep into the man's right thigh. The attacker let out a bellowing howl, allowing Vermeer to spin around and jam a M67 grenade into the man's gaping mouth. He pulled the pin and spun around, kicking the man in the stomach. He knocked him down with a karate Gedan Mawashi Geri kick and a low roundhouse punt. Four seconds later.

BARRROOOOMM

On his way out of the front door, Vermeer intentionally tripped the trip wire attached to the grenade, all the while chanting, "Kill them all. Kill them all. Kill them all."

By the time he reached the roof, the trip-wired explosive device went off.

BARRROOOOMM

He peered over the roof's ledge and saw a dozen police cars and three fire trucks pulling up to 23 Park Avenue. He was over the back of the roof, past the three dead bodyguards, and back in his apartment two blocks away by the time the police made their way up to and entered 5C.

☠☠☠☠☠☠☠☠☠☠☠

The Red and Blue team was extricated from the village of Apolo, Bolivia, and quickly bused back across the border into Peru. Once they were safely back in Lima, they were separated, broken down into two-person teams, and sent in different directions for a bit of R&R until they received their new assignments.

Odin and Lu Wei went to Quinto, Ecuador. Vulcan and Bellator flew to Bogota, Colombia. Venus traveled with Fu Hao and Sue B to Rio de Janeiro. Cowboy and Sassoon headed to Buenos Aires. Gianfranco and Hazael were sent up to Caracas, Venezuela. The three techno heads, Châtelet, Devol, and Razor, stayed in Lima to tweak and refurbish the robotic dogs of war.

☠☠☠☠☠☠☠☠☠☠☠

"Good evening. I'm Nigel Williams, and this is the BBC World Headline News. Our top story this hour comes from New York City, where there is a report that over sixteen people associated with the Worldwide Affiliates of Safari Partners, better known as W.A.S.P., have been murdered in the exclusive Park Avenue apartment of New York's socialite, Ms. Margaret Hamilton.

Apparently, Ms. Hamilton was hosting a party for the leading members of the Worldwide Affiliates of Safari Partners when it's believed that a lone gunman broke into the home and killed all sixteen people in attendance. There were at least five security guards killed among the dead.

Police haven't released the names of the killed until all family's next of kin have been notified. However, some of the deceased are believed to be among New York City's society's elite.

The massacre has been attributed to the international eco-terrorist group known as Le Gang de la Clé de Singe. It appears that the lone assassin left the terrorist group's calling card. A yellow flag, blazoned with a black skull with crossed monkey wrenches, gave the appearance of a pirate flag draped around the victim's neck.

An unconfirmed police source has told this reporter that only a single fingerprint not belonging to any of the guests was found. As bizarre as it seems, that print belongs to 20th-century American novelist Edith Wharton. Wharton drew upon her insider knowledge of New York's aristocracy to portray the lives and morals of the Gilded Age. She is most famous for her Pulitzer Prize-winning novel, The Age of Innocence.

Why and how her fingerprint was left at the crime scene remains a mystery.

Meanwhile, in other news……"

☠☠☠☠☠☠☠☠☠☠☠

"Zimbabwe!" Sue B said.

"Yup. Zimbabwe. I just got the word from the old man," Fu Hao answered as she hung up the phone.

"When do we go?"

"The teams will start going over in dribs and drabs starting tomorrow."

"Red and Blue?" Sue B asked.

"No. It's just us against a large, organized poaching syndicate working in the Savé Valley Conservancy. It looks like we'll be working unofficially with their rangers, the Special Species Protection Unit (SSPU)."

"So, when do we leave?"

"The Day after tomorrow. We'll get our passports, IDs, and tickets this afternoon. We'll fly into the main airport, Joshua Mqabuko Nkomo International, outside Bulawayo. And we'll meet the rest of the team at the Motsamai Guest House. As usual, we'll be greeted by someone called Ruko Ncube when we arrive."

Moments later, Odin hung up on his call for the Blue Team's assignment.

"So? Where are we off to?" Lu Wei asked.

"New York City."

"You're kidding, New York?"

"We're on a rescue mission. Vermeer just got arrested on suspicion of killing over a dozen of W.A.S.P. members last night," Odin said.

☠☠☠☠☠☠☠☠☠☠☠

As Vermeer returned to his apartment, he passed a Moe's Delicatessen truck parked at the corner of 36th and Lexington. He went to the driver's side window and handed the driver a large paper bag filled with the weapons he had used in the Park Avenue attack. The driver handed Vermeer a duplicate-looking bag filled with delicatessen food: potato latkes, a pint of matzo ball soup, chopped chicken livers, and a dozen assorted bagels.

As he headed to his apartment on 38th Street, he passed by the police lookout box, where the NYPD had stationed a police officer across the street from the Cuban

Mission ever since there were two bombings of the Mission in the mid-1980s.

Once the call went out after the Park Avenue massacre, Office O'Malley alerted HQ that he had spotted a male suspect carrying a large bag entering the apartment building located at 38th and Lexington.

At six o'clock a.m., a light rapped at Vermeer's door. He climbed from the loft bed, peeked out the peephole, and saw two men holding police ID cards with badges.

Vermeer opened the door. The men standing in the doorway looked like they had come out of Hollywood's central casting. They were both crew-cut, square-jaw, nondescript, deadpanned coppers who had grown up watching too many episodes of Dragnet.

"Mr. Peak. I'm Detective Kelly, and this is my partner Detective McCarthy. May we come in?" They were in the apartment before he finished his sentence.

"Um, sure. Come in."

"Do you live alone, Mr. Peak?" Kelly asked.

"Yes. What is this about, detective?"

"Murder. Where were you last night between the hours of eight and midnight last night?"

"Murder! Who was murdered?" Vermeer exclaimed.

"Where were you, Mr. Peak, between eight and midnight?" Kelly pressed.

"I was at the movies. I went to the Kips Bay 15. They had a retrospective of Bogart films: The Maltese Falcon, Key Largo, and To Have and Have Not. Great films. Have you ever seen them?"

Neither of the detectives answered. Kelly ignored the question and asked, "Did you go with anyone? Can anyone vouch for your being there?"

"No. I went alone. I did buy some popcorn and a soda. I don't know if anyone noticed me or not."

"Can I ask what you were wearing?"

"You can ask," Vermeer said, then nothing.

Kelly wasn't amused. "So! What were you wearing, wise guy?" He demanded.

Vermeer, getting annoyed, answered, "Why? You looking for some fashion tips, detective?"

"Listen, smartass; you want us to ask these questions downtown at the station?"

"Not particularly."

"Then answer me. What were you wearing last night?"

"A black shirt and black pants. What's this all about?"

The other copper, Detective McCarthy, playing the good cop, answered, "There was a multiple murder over on Park Avenue last night. Not far from here. We've had several witnesses say that they saw a man wearing all black carrying a black backpack in the vicinity. Do you own a black backpack, Mr. Peak?"

"Yeah. Me and seven million other New Yorkers. Do you?"

"Where is it?" McCarthy asked.

"You got a warrant?" Vermeer countered.

Vermeer could see that both Detective McCarthy and Kelly were getting pissed. He ran a scenario through his mind of how easy it would be to kill these two and dump their dead bodies down the garbage chute, then blow town.

"So, you want to play hardball!" Kelly barked.

"We'll be back with a warrant and tear this place apart, asshole," Detective McCarthy sneered—no more nice guy.

Vermeer looked around the one-room studio and said, smiling, "That'll take all of three minutes."

"Very funny. You think you're some kind of comedian?"

"You think you're some kind of detective?" Vermeer sniped.

Kelly slapped Vermeer across the face hard, cutting his bottom lip. He stood there, hands on his hips, daring Vermeer to retaliate, smirking.

Vermeer stared coldly directly into Kelly's eyes. He touched his lip with his right hand and saw that he was bleeding.

Kelly said to his partner, "You saw it, McCarthy; this little punk tried to assault me."

Vermeer's reprisal was lighting fast. Detective Kelly never saw the punch coming. A closed knuckle jab to Kelly's throat, crushing his windpipe and forcing the big Irish policeman to crumble to the ground like a sack of Irish spuds. As the startled Detective McCarthy started to fumble for his pistol, Vermeer gave a side snap kick to McCarthy's midsection, forcing him to tumble backward, knocking his head against the wall, rendering him unconscious.

Vermeer looked around the small one-room apartment and saw that he really and truly fucked up. He got his phone and made a call.

"Wooch. I fucked up," Vermeer said.

He explained what happened and asked for his advice.

"I suggest you call the police, explain what happened, and give yourself up after you get rid of this phone and all incriminating evidence, which shouldn't be too much. I'll call Moe's and have them send a cleaner. Sit tight and try not to do anything stupid. We'll get you out."

"Got it. Sorry, sir."

"Just stick to your story and stay calm."

"Roger."

CLICK

Vermeer did as he was instructed. It was just minutes when someone from Moe's Delicatessen came by with a delivery. He exchanged Vermeer's black backpack, black shirt, and pair of black pants for new ones with the ones he had the night before and took his burner cell phone.

As the driver from Moe's left, several police cars and an ambulance pulled up to Vermeer's apartment building. As the driver was pulling away, he saw Vermeer being placed into the back of a squad car in handcuffs and two men being carried out on stretchers.

☠☠☠☠☠☠☠☠☠☠☠

Vermeer was taken to the NYPD's 17th Precinct for questioning and booking.

"Okay, have a seat over there," Detective Muldoon ordered.

Vermeer did as he was told. He sat on one side of an old, beat-up wooden table covered with scuffs, stains, pen and pencil incoherent scrawls, and a few carved initials. A uniformed officer released him from his handcuffs.

Muldoon sat opposite the prisoner. He dropped a leather-bound notebook onto the table before he plopped down into his chair. Vermeer guested that the detective was in his fifties. He had short, almost shaved grey hair, a pencil mustache, and looked to be thirty pounds overweight.

"You have the right to remain silent. Anything you say can and will be used against you in a court of law. You have the right to an attorney. If you cannot afford an attorney, one will be provided for you. Do you understand these rights as I have read them to you?" The portly constable asked.

"I do."

"Do you want a lawyer?"

"Nay."

Muldoon slowly opened the notebook and flipped through several pages before he came to a blank page. He clicked his ballpoint pen open and asked, "Name?"

"Brad Peak," Vermeer answered.

"Brad or Bradley?"

"Bradley, but my friends call me Brad."

"We ain't friends, Bradley," Muldoon said as he scribbled Vermeer's alias.

"And you are?" Vermeer asked.

"Detective Sergeant Muldoon," Muldoon grudgingly offered up.

"Thank you."

"Is one thirty-eight, East 38th Street, your address?"

"Yes."

"What do you do for a living, Mr. Peak?"

Vermeer thought momentarily before answering, "I'm in commodities."

"What, like trading in corn, soybeans, and things like that?"

"Lead."

"Lead?"

"Yeah, I deal in lead," Vermeer smirked.

The detective dropped his pen onto the notebook, sat back in his chair, and asked, "So, Mr. Peak, what the Hell happened? Why did you assault my two detectives? This better be good."

"Well, Detective Muldoon, I was sleeping when I heard the doorbell. I got out of bed, opened the door, and found two policemen standing in my doorway.

They identified themselves. I asked for their identifications, which they showed me as they entered my apartment without asking permission.

Detective Kelly asked about my whereabouts from last night. I told him I had gone to the movies at Kips Bay 15. He asked several other questions before asking me for permission to search my apartment, which I denied. He got angry and slapped my face, cutting my lip, as you can see.

I felt my life was in danger, so I defended myself. Once he was down, the other detective started to reach for his gun. Since I didn't want to be shot dead in my own apartment, I knocked him out as well. I then called the police, and as they say, the rest is history."

"Why didn't you want them to search your apartment if you had nothing to hide."

"I should allow any cop in the city to come in and search my apartment without cause. I think not," Vermeer said.

"Well, we're searching it now," Muldoon sniggered.

"Yeah, well, now you have cause," Vermeer countered, grinning.

"You don't seem to understand that you're in a world of shit, Mr. Peak."

"Why is that?"

"You've assaulted two police officers. You're going to be charged and arrested."

"What about my assault? Is Kelly going to be charged and arrested for assaulting a civilian?"

"No. He and Detective McCarthy will be put on administrative duty, and an internal review will look into the matter."

"Yeah, and meanwhile, my ass goes to jail. I sit in a cell behind bars, and they go and sit behind a desk. Doesn't seem all that equitable, does it?"

"You should have thought about that before striking an officer."

"While I was bleeding on the floor from those two goons. I could have stood there and had them beat me to death or shoot me in the back because they felt scared. What a couple of pussys"

"We'll see how tough you are after a few days in Rikers."

"Don't worry about me, flatfoot. I'll be just fine."

"Sure you will," Muldoon said, chuckling.

The rotund copper stood up, grabbed his notebook, and started to walk out of the room, mumbling, "Sit tight. I'll be right back."

Half an hour later, two uniformed police walked in, signaled for Vermeer to stand, to turn around, and then proceeded to handcuff him. They led him out of the room and down the hall to be processed. Mugshots, fingerprinted, his clothes taken and replaced with an orange jumpsuit. He was then placed in a holding cell until there were enough prisoners to justify a trip to Rikers Island.

The van ride was uneventful. He rode with seven others: three African Americans, three Hispanics, and two Caucasians. When they arrived, he was singled out and brought to the warden's office.

"Mr. Peak, we have a problem," Warden Johnson said sternly.

"We do?"

"It seems that your fingerprints belong to someone who is wanted by Interpol."

"Really. That's odd."

"Yes. It is odd. Care to explain?" Johnson asked.

"Well, obviously, it's some kind of mistake."

"Possibly. We've been asked to keep you in a special detention facility until this matter can be explained."

"Cool, something special. I am expecting my attorney to come sometime tomorrow."

"Mr. Peak, you will, of course, be able to confer with your legal counsel as soon as they arrive. In the meantime, Officer Karr will show you to your cell. That's all."

Vermeer was taken to the Otis Bantum Correctional Center, where he was confined to an isolation ward for high-profile inmates.

As Officer Karr pushed Vermeer into the cell, he quipped, "You're too late for dinner. You'll have to wait for breakfast."

Vermeer asked, "Shall I give you my order now or wait until I see the menu?"

"Very funny, asshole," Karr sneered as he slammed the cell door shut.

CLANG

"Geeze. Doesn't anybody have a sense of humor?"

☠☠☠☠☠☠☠☠☠☠☠

Odin and the rest of the Blue Team arrived at JFK within an hour of each other. Odin and Lu Wei arrived first from Ecuador at eight-fifteen PM. Vulcan and Bellator flew in from Bogota, Colombia. Venus left Fu Hao and Sue B in Rio de Janeiro, where she first flew back to Lima to meet Devol, and then onto New York.

The members of the Blue Team were met in the visitors' greeting arrival area by Terry Bell, aka Neptune, one of the senior associates of Le Gang de la Clé de Singe. He stood off to one side, holding a large sign that read, "Singe Bleus" (Blue Monkeys).

Terry got involved in dozens of anti-war, peace groups, and environmental causes in the 60's and 70's. He was one of the first to answer the call from John F. Kennedy and join the Peace Corps. He was sent to the small village of Lwabiyata, Uganda, to help villages build schools, enhance primary health care, and provide agricultural assistance. Usually, you sign up for a two-year hitch, but Terry did three tours. During that time, he saw the devastation that poaching and trophy hunting were doing to the wildlife.

He was approached one day while drinking in the City Bar in Uganda's capital, Kampala. The City Bar is the oldest in Kampala. Terry had finished filling out his discharge papers from the Peace Corps and was having a bit of a celebration with a group of coworkers when he was approached by a friend of a friend who worked at the Canadian Embassy. Her name was Juliette Williams; she worked in the Foreign Agriculture Services department and was a Le Gang de la Clé de Singe member. Juliette had heard about Terry's agitation, distress, and anger about the senseless annihilation of the wildlife population in the country as well as the world. He had attended and spoken at several official governmental and private conferences against big game trophy hunting, especially the need for more armed rangers to combat illegal poaching in Uganda's national parks. The results were always the same; they formed more task forces to study the problem. So, when Juliette approached him about becoming an eco-warrior, he was more than ready.

The first thing he did when he was released from the Peace Corps was to lead a raid against a local band of known poachers in the Bakora Game Reserve. They captured six men who were caught in the act of butchering a mother rhinoceros while its baby stood by crying in terror. They turned them in to the local authorities along with photographic evidence, as well as the actual rhino horn. The six men spent thirty days in jail and were released with a small fine.

Four months later, he and his team captured the same six men out on a poaching patrol setting snare traps. This time, Terry, who had since taken the code name Neptune, placed the yellow flags around each of their necks, read them the manifesto, and proceeded to shoot each man in the head. He arranged their bodies all in a row with a copy of the photograph of them slaughtering the mother rhinoceros four months earlier.

Once their bodies were discovered, the police found a single fingerprint on the photograph belonging to Uganda's ex-president, Idi Amin Dada Oumee. Better known as the "Butcher of Uganda," he is considered to be one of the most brutal despots in world history.

Neptune and his raiding party were feared throughout Uganda's national parks and game reserves. Within the next two years, poaching declined by over 50%. Although the Ugandan government denounced the actions of

Neptune and Le Gang de la Clé de Singe, they did turn a blind eye. It wasn't until they started killing white, wealthy trophy hunters that the government began to take action.

Le Gang de la Clé de Singe continually moves its people around the world to protect them. Neptune had missions in seven African nations, nine in Asia, three in South America, and eight in the United States. He was eventually located in New York, where he held more of an administrative position and eased into out-of-field action work.

Once the Blue Team was all in the van and the introductions were completed, he drove them into Manhattan to the Beekman Tower on 3 Mitchell Place.

"Your rooms have all been reserved and paid for. I'm sure you're tired of flying all day. Get some rest, and I'll meet you downstairs in the lobby at nine AM. We'll grab some breakfast. Good night," Neptune said.

☠☠☠☠☠☠☠☠☠☠☠

There are plenty of countries across the world that have notable poaching problems. Most of them are found in central and southern Africa and Southeast Asia. However, out of all the countries in the world, most experts agree that Zimbabwe has the biggest poaching problem. In the past three years, over three hundred and twenty elephants were killed by poachers, primarily for their tusks, estimated to be worth over one hundred million dollars on the black market. Last year, close to 150 elephants were killed by poachers using cyanide to poison salt licks at watering holes, inducing a slow and agonizing death.

At the current rate of poaching, it is estimated that by 2050, there will no longer be a single wild elephant in all of Africa. Of all the gangs of poachers in Zimbabwe, the

Camdeboo Boys were the most notorious, prolific, and evil of them all. Some gangs specialize in rhinos, lions, elephants, and pangolins, but not the Camdeboo Boys. They were equal-opportunity poachers. If it walked, crawled, slithered, or flew, the Camdeboo Boys would hunt, kill, and poach any of God's creatures to extinction, and that included any man or woman who tried to stop them.

The Red Team was tasked with a little extinction of their own: the complete annihilation of the Camdeboo Boys and the sending a message to all wannabes to cease and desist all poaching activities, or this fate will befall you, too.

☠☠☠☠☠☠☠☠☠☠☠

Ruko Ncube stood in the guest arrival area holding a sign for Sharon Dansby and Jessica Chou. Fu Hao and Sue B spotted the sign amongst the crowd waiting for arriving passengers. Ruko Ncube was an alias whose code name was *Shumba ine Moyo*, translated from Zimbabwe's native Shona language, Lionhearted.

Of the 200 game scouts, Ruko Ncube is one of the elite fifty specially trained and armed anti-poaching park rangers at the Savé Valley Conservancy. They also work closely with the Lowveld Rhino Trust, which maintains a highly trained, well-armed, and equipped army of over 30 rangers. Together, they patrol over 3,200 square kilometers, but they're still not enough.

"Good evening, ladies. I am Ruko Ncube. I hope that your flight was pleasant."

"Nice to meet you, Ruko," Sue B said.

"How was your trip?" He asked.

"It was Long. But we got here in one piece. That's what counts," Fu Hao added.

"Is the rest of the team here?" Sue B asked.

"Yes. You are the last. Come, let me show you the way. Do you need any assistance with your luggage?"

"No. We're good," Fu Hao and Sue B answered in unison.

Sue B quickly added, "Jinx on you. You owe me a Coke."

Fu Hao smiled and said, "Yeah, I never understood that. But, okay."

After stowing everyone's gear on top of the Ford Transit 12- 12-passenger van, Ruko and the Red Team high-tailed it out of Joshua Mqabuko Nkomo International Airport. He jumped onto the Robert Mugabe Way heading south, which is a straight shot through downtown Bulawayo to the Malindela suburbs, where the Motsamai Guest Lodge sat nestled behind a thick grove of Baobab trees, keeping it hidden from the street. An eight-foot wooden fence surrounded the half-acre estate with lush evergreen gardens, several fountains, and a swimming pool.

The lodge is an all-white stucco, two-story colonial-style hotel adorned with Doric-style columns and two European-style villa symmetrically curved staircases that greet guests upon arrival.

Ruko had arranged for the entire Red Team to stay on the second floor. Fu Hao and Sue B had always felt safer not being on the ground floor. If trouble came, they wanted to be holding the high ground. They knew that the second floor might be more challenging to escape from, but if it ever came to a shootout, they weren't going to be taken alive anyway. So, they might as well take out as many of the bastards before cashing their chips in as possible.

Once everyone checked in, they all went for dinner at Nando's Jason Moyo for flame-grilled spicy peri-peri chicken legs. Then, for some relaxation, they went to the Shisha Lounge for some beers. Hazael got adventurous and tried hookah smoking. Not a good idea.

"Hazael, man, I've never seen anyone that shade of green before. How do you feel?" Cowboy asked.

"Oh, man. I don't feel so good," He said as he ran off to find the bathroom.

Twenty minutes later, he looked and felt better when he came back.

"Feeling better?" Sue B asked.

"A little better. But I must say that peri-peri chicken tasted much better going down than it did coming up."

☠☠☠☠☠☠☠☠☠☠☠

Standing in the lobby of the Beekman Hotel, waiting for the Blue Team, was Neptune (Terry Bell) and a distinguished-looking gentleman wearing a three-piece blue pin-striped suit and holding a leather briefcase. As the elevator opened, Odin and the remaining Blue Team emerged as one giant glob of humanity. Once they all spread out in a semicircle gathered around Neptune and the stranger, Neptune made the introductions.

"Good morning, all. I'd like to introduce you to Mr. Malcom Meriweather, Esquire. He will be representing Bradley Peak."

Now, using the name James Warner, Odin shook the advocate's hand, "It's a pleasure to meet you. Let me introduce you to everyone. I'm James Warner. This is Veronica Teller (Venus), Billie Chan (Lu Wei), Roger Washington (Vulcan), Bobby Sanchez (Bellator), and Michael Thompson (Devol.)"

"It's very nice to meet you all. Might I suggest we all walk down to the UN Plaza Grill for breakfast? I've reserved a private room so we can discuss Mr. Peak's case undisturbed."

"Excellent suggestion," Odin said.

They strolled down 1st Avenue towards the United Nations building to 47th Street, a short two-block walk. As one might expect, the UN Plaza Grill was quite elegant. Their private room overlooked the UN building and the East River.

Once all the orders were taken, Mr. Meriweather, sitting at the head of the table, opened a notepad from his briefcase, clicked his pen, and began, "Now, just to clarify who and what my role is here. I have been hired to legally represent Mr. Peak. I have been requested to have two of you accompany me, as part of my legal team, when I go to visit him to discuss his case.

I do not know, nor do I want to know, your alternative motives or plans. That is between you and Mr. Peak. So, that being understood, which two of you will accompany me to visit our client?

Odin raised his hand and said, "That would be Veronica and me."

"Very good, Mr. Warner and Ms. Teller. After breakfast, the three of us will take my town car to the NYC Courthouse on Centre Street for the arraignment. The two of you shall be registered as paralegals in my employ. If someone asks you any questions, try not to speak other than to use the time-honored attorney-client privilege. Got it?"

"Got it," Odin acknowledged.

"Great. And I understand that Mr. Thompson will be serving as our driver," Meriweather said.

"That's correct. If that's okay with you, Mr. Meriweather?" Odin asked.

"What the Hell. The more the merrier."

"I'm Mr. Meriweather, and these are my associates. We're here to see our client Bradley Peak," the barrister announced to the guard stationed at the entrance to the courthouse.

The guard lackadaisically thumbed through several pages on his clipboard until he announced, "Peak, Bradley is being held on the fifth floor. I will need you all to sign in, please." He said as he handed the sign-in sheet to Meriweather, who proceeded to sign his name as well as Odin and Venus.

"Here you go," Meriweather said as he returned the clipboard to the guard.

When they reached the fifth floor, Meriweather, Odin, and Venus entered the detention area where the prisoners were being held before entering the courtrooms. Devol went up the public elevators to see which courtroom Vermeer would be appearing in.

As they approached the detention area, Meriweather laid his leather briefcase on the metal detector conveyor belt to be x-rayed. Odin and Venus had specially made metal Halliburton lead-lined cases, which they had to open for examination. Unbeknownst to the screening guards, hidden within the cases were hundreds of robot mosquito drones, each equipped with cameras and carrying a potent dose of propofol.

Once they had safely passed the inspection area, Odin and Venus released the insect drones, which Devol controlled inside the courtroom using his cell phone. Devol separated and placed the drones in strategic areas of the courthouse, having them land on the ten-foot-high ceilings and spread out so they would not be noticed. Once in place, Devol deactivated them until needed.

As Odin and Venus walked from the visitors' entrance to the room where Vermeer was waiting, they released several dozen mosquito drones undetected, even as they were passed by both inmates and guards.

Inside the attorney/client meeting room sat Vermeer, staring out the window. He dressed in a cheap Moe Ginsburg suit. He was looking out on the East River, watching several commercial ships sailing up and down to and from the New York Harbor.

A uniformed officer stood inside the room. Once Meriweather entered, he said, “Thank you, officer. We’ll call you when we’re done.”

“I’ll be just outside,” The guard said as he left the room.

“Mr. Peak, my name is Malcolm Meriweather. I will be representing you. These are my associates, Mr. Warner and Ms. Teller.” He said as he shook Vermeer’s hand from across the interview table.

As Meriweather was getting settled, opening his briefcase, and taking out his pad and pens, Odin asked, "How are you doing, man?”

“Mmmm, okay.”

“You sure? You look like you’ve been roughed up a bit?” Venus asked as she saw the bruising on his face.

“Yeah, well, Rikers isn’t for the weak or faint of heart. But I’ve given as good as I’ve got.”

“Well, if all goes well, you won’t be here much longer,” Odin said.

“Mr. Meriweather, you may not want to hear this,” Venus said.

The dapper attorney took a pair of earbuds, placed them in his ears, and started listening to Dean Martin croon about how everybody needs somebody to love.

Odin opened his hand, revealing one of the mosquito drones to Vermeer.

“Once you’re in the courtroom, we will begin to quietly attack everyone with one of these little buggers. Each mosquito will inject the person with a non-lethal dose of propofol that, within minutes, knocks them out for at least fifteen minutes.

Once everyone is asleep, you'll get up and walk out of the building. A white Ford Focus will be waiting downstairs in front of the building, and Vulcan will be waiting for you. You remember Vulcan?"

"Big African American from Alabama?"

"That's him. He'll drive you to a safe house where you'll be secure until we get you out of the country."

"Will you be coming with me?"

"Oh no. We're also going to be knocked out. But don't worry—we have people throughout the building if things get tricky."

"Thank you."

"No worries," Venus said, smiling.

"All right, we'll see you in court," Odin said as he tapped Meriweather on the arm.

"So, everything good? Are you ready, Mr. Peak?" Meriweather asked.

"Yep, let's rock and roll," Vermeer answered.

☠☠☠☠☠☠☠☠☠☠☠

"All rise. This Court, with the Honorable Judge Harold B. Stone presiding, is now in session. Please be seated and come to order." The bailiff announced.

Judge Stone was a hard-nosed, no-nonsense, cold-hearted adjudicator. Known for believing that the defendant was more than likely to be guilty and, therefore, was incumbent upon him to prove his innocence. The burden of proof was on the defendant rather than the prosecutor.

"You may be seated," Stone said as he sat down behind his large oak bench, which he had raised two feet higher than all the other judges in the courthouse. He liked the idea that everyone, especially the defendants, had to look up to him, and he had the extreme pleasure of looking down upon them.

"Good morning, ladies and gentlemen. Calling the case of the People of New York versus Bradley Peak. Are both sides ready?"

District Attorney William Valley stood and stated, "Ready for the People, Your Honor."

Malcolm Meriweather stood and said, "Ready for the defense, Your Honor."

Judge Stone turned to the bailiff and said, "Please bring in the first potential juror."

As the bailiff left the courtroom to herd in the group of unwilling citizens who weren't smart enough to wiggle their way out of jury duty, Odin and Venus released several dozen mosquitoes into the courtroom.

While the bailiff was out of the room, Meriweather stood to address the bench, "Your Honor."

"Yes, Mr. Meriweather, what is it."

"Your Honor, I would ask the Court to remove my client's handcuffs while the court is in session. I feel that seeing him in handcuffs might prejudice the jury. Besides, there are four armed bailiffs in the courtroom."

"Your client killed a dozen people and attacked two New York detectives!" Stone said snidely while giving Vermeer the stink-eye.

"Accused, Your Honor. He is yet to be convicted."

"Mr. Valley, does the prosecution object to the defendant not being shackled in court?" Stone asked.

The Prosecutor rose, glanced over to Meriweather, who had a pleading look, and said, "No objection, Your Honor."

"Bailiff, remove the defendant's handcuffs," Stone barked.

"Thank you, Your Honor," Meriweather humbly said.

Stone looked down on Meriweather and gave a disdained, “Harumph!”

Devol sat in the gallery's back row, secretly manipulating the micro air vehicles. He initially had all of them positioned above him on the ceiling. He carefully began to attack everyone seated in the courtroom, starting with the people sitting in the gallery, the onlookers, victims’ family members, witnesses, and several reporters. No one noticed as people began to nod off, sitting upright in the gallery benches.

Devol began with the pool of potential jurors and, finally, the bailiffs, court clerks, and the prosecution team. Judge Stone suddenly became aware and alarmed when his four burly bailiffs collapsed. He stood up from his seat just as a mosquito drone injected a dose of propofol directly into his carotid artery. He slid back down into his chair, slumped over, and bumped his head on his specially engraved gavel lying on the bench, leaving a knot the size of a walnut on his forehead.

After all, forty-seven occupants, including Meriweather, Odin, and Venus, were sleeping soundly. Vermeer got out and waltzed out the door. Devol had given himself a smaller dose, just so he’d have some propofol in his system as well, just in case he got tested.

Vermeer had no trouble walking out of the courtroom and easing out of the courthouse. He found Vulcan sitting out front of the courthouse in the white Ford Focus with the engine running.

“Vulcan?” Vermeer asked.

“Yep, get in, man,” Vulcan said with a great big toothy grin as he pulled out into traffic heading uptown.

“How’d it go?” Vulcan queried.

“Great! Technology is a beautiful thing.”

“You look a little worse for wear, man,” Vulcan said, giving his passenger the once-over.

“I had a little dispute with a couple of my cellmates.”

"What happened?"

"Two of them wanted me to go steady, and the third one thought that I was involved in controlling Jewish lasers floating in outer space, causing fires in California. So, I decided to smash my face against their fists until I wore them out."

"You okay?"

"Oh, yeah. As they say, you should see the other guys. Two of them will be peeing sitting down from now on, and the Jew hatter is seeing never-before-discovered stars."

"Man, I like your style," Vulcan said with admiration.

"Thanks. Say, where are we headed?"

"West Harlem. A friend of mine has an apartment uptown on Broadway, between West 136th and 135th Street. It sits atop this dynamite Caribbean restaurant, Mofongo del Valle."

"What pray tell is mofongo?" Vermeer asked.

"Mofongo is a Puerto Rican delight made with fried mashed green plantains, mashed garlic, and small pieces of crunchy chicharrón. It is served with goat, pork chunks, chicken, ham, shrimp, crab, squid, octopus, and my favorite conch," Vulcan exclaimed.

"Sounds delicious."

"Well, that's good, my friend. Because that's what you'll be having tonight."

"*Good Evening. Tony Treadwell, here, and this is WPIX Action News. Tonight, we have breaking news! Police are investigating the escape of this man, Bradley Peak, who was standing trial for the multiple murders of the Worldwide*

Affiliates of Safari Partners, also known as W.A.S.P. board members and their bodyguards.

While Peak's trial was in session today, it seems that all forty-seven occupants of courtroom seven in the New York Municipal Court House were incapacitated and knocked out cold, except for the defendant, Bradley Peak.

Peak is seen here in the video exiting the building and getting into a white Ford Focus, which turned out to be stolen and was found abandoned several hours later in the Bowery.

New York City Police Chief Joe O'Reilly told WPIX reporter Julie Chan that forensics are currently combing over the vehicle for any fingerprints and DNA. O'Reilly said that the police believe that the people in the courtroom were somehow drugged or gassed. The investigation is ongoing.

Mayor Davis Epson has made a statement calling for help from the FBI shortly after the eco-terrorist group Le Gang de la Clé de Singe has recently claimed responsibility for the massacre of the members of W.A.S.P. and masterminding the daring escape of Bradley Peak.

The police and FBI ask that if anyone sees this man, do not approach him; he is considered armed and dangerous. Contact the FBI or your local police. There is a one-million-dollar reward for information resulting in the capture and conviction of Bradley Peak.

Now, in other news...."

The Ford Transit 12 van was loaded and heading east towards Savé Valley Conservancy by 8 AM. Ruko decided to take the A9; even though it was a toll road, it was the fastest route. A little over six hours straight through, but they were going to stop in the town of Masvingo to pick up some gear, foodstuffs, and arms.

Just off the A9, as they were entering Masvingo, the campus of Julius Nyerere School Of Social Sciences Great Zimbabwe University, where parked in the parking lot sat an old beat-up faded red 2000 Toyota Land Cruiser with a camper. Standing beside the pickup with a ten-foot python wrapped around her neck was an ancient-looking woman, a voodoo priestess called Mami Wata, selling secret potions, voodoo dolls, and good and evil charms. She was not the original Mami Wata from the 1880s but the fourth-generation Mami Wata. She was famous for causing the infamous "*Kwekwe Drought*" that lasted seven years until finally, the villagers paid 400 trillion Zimbabwean dollars ransom for her to call the curse off. 400 trillion Zimbabwean dollars is the equivalent of USD 160.

Mami Wata also deals in the black market. For anything one wants or needs, especially weapons, Mami Wata is your one-stop shopping center.

It was close to one in the afternoon when Ruko and the Red Team pulled into the University's parking lot. Mami Wata was coming out of her camper with a woman client, whom she had just read her fortune. The woman was crying uncontrollably. She had just found out that her man was cheating on her with another man. As the distraught woman was walking away, Mami Wata stood in the parking lot, counting the money the woman had paid to find out the bad news.

"Mami Wata!" Ruko shouted out as the Ford van pulled up alongside her truck.

"Ah, Mester Ruko. How be you, child?" She said with a toothless grin.

As the entire Red Team disembarked from the van, the old voodoo sorceress greeted each one, staring deep into their eyes.

"Aw, Lordy, Lordy. Ya'll are the *Memitim's*."

"The what?" Fu Hao asked

"You is all the executioners. The slayers of the evil ones," She said with saucer-sized eyes.

"Mami Wata, do you have something for us?" Ruko asked.

"Over yonder in that shed," She said, pointing to a dilapidated wooden shack across the street from the University. She handed Ruko a key to the padlock. The shed was filled with various camping gear, boxes of food, freeze-dried packets, canned goods, bottled water, and canvas duffle bags containing their weapons of choice.

After the Red Team quickly surveyed the shed's contents and began loading the gear into the Ford van, Ruko handed Mami Wata an envelope filled with US Dollars. As she peeked inside, she let out a squeal of joy.

"Ohhh, Mester Ruko. I tink I loves you. Now, you all be careful."

"I love you, too Mami Wata. You take care."

Mami Wata walked to the van and stopped Gianfranco before he got in. She pulled him aside and whispered, "You stay here, boy."

"What?"

"I see death nearby. You stay here."

"I can't. I must go."

"If you must go, here, take this," she said as she placed a leather necklace with a severed chicken foot attached.

"It will keep you safe. Now go."

Gianfranco looked down on the talisman, kissed the venerable old voodoo queen on the cheek, and said, "Thank you, Mami."

☠☠☠☠☠☠☠☠☠☠☠

Vermeer looked back on New York harbor from the tiny porthole in the crew's quarters aboard the 86-foot wing sail catamaran christened Seas the Day. She was hoped to be a real contender for last year's America's Cup, but foul weather, a cracked mast, and a shredded mainsail dashed any hopes of her returning the Cup from New Zealand. Damn Kiwi's.

After spending two months hiding in the apartment above the Caribbean restaurant, Mofongo del Valle on Broadway in West Harlem, the top brass at Le Gang de la Clé de Singe devised a plan to smuggle Vermeer out of New York on the Seas the Day, which was leaving New York after a two-week public exhibition and fundraising venture before setting sail to Italy. While waiting, he colored and cut his hair, grew a mustache, wore colored contact lenses, and lost twenty-two pounds. He received his new identity; his new identity is to be Enzo Berlusconi from the seaport of Genoa on the Italian Riviera. His credentials have him as a wealthy yacht broker.

Vermeer was brought on board an hour after the FBI and completed a thorough bow-to-stern search of the vessel minutes before weighing anchor. As they were prepared to set sail, a Coast Guard cutter pulled alongside, boarded the Seas the Day for one last inspection, and compared the crew's list with the actual personnel.

A young lieutenant, Lee Cherry, was smartly dressed in all white. He was multilingual and spoke to the international crew in their native language.

The lieutenant first asked if Vermeer spoke English. Vermeer smiled and held up his thumb and forefinger, indicating that he spoke very little English by saying, "*Un po.*"

"*Signore Berlusconi, qual è la tua posizione nell'equipaggio?*" The Lieutenant Cherry asked Vermeer, wanting to know what his job was on the crew.

"*Lo sono l'uomo dell'albero.*" Vermeer answered in flawless Italian. Vermeer's position was to be the mast man.

The mastman's main job is to assist with the fast hoist of sails during maneuvers. The mastman and bowman work hand in hand and assist each other on hoists and drops. The main communication is with the bowman, pitman, and boat captain.

"*Di dove sei?*" Cherry asked.

"*Genoa. Sei mai satao?*" Vermeer replied.

"No, I've never been," Cherry said, almost to himself.

"*È bellissimo!*" Vermeer beamed.

"*Posso vedere il tuo passaporto?*" Lieutenant Cherry asked, holding out his hand.

Vermeer reached inside his small locker and handed the Lieutenant his passport. Cherry examined it and handed the passport back.

"*Grazie,*" Cherry said as he moved on to the next crew member, the starboard trimmer from Madrid, Spain.

"Hola."

☠☠☠☠☠☠☠☠☠☠☠

Two days out from New York Harbor, the Seas the Day was met by a reefer ship named the Yokushi Empress.

A reefer ship is a refrigerated cargo ship typically used to transport perishable commodities that require temperature-controlled transportation, such as fruit, meat, fish, vegetables, dairy products, and other items. On average, there would be a crew of twenty-one to twenty-two men working on a reefer vessel.

The Empress set sail from Wilmington, North Carolina, loaded with frozen poultry, pork, and beef, heading for Porto Alegre, Brazil. They rendezvoused approximately eighty nautical miles east southeast of Savannah, Georgia.

Vermeer thanked the Captain and crew of the Seas the Day for their hospitality and support not only for him but for the cause.

"Mister Berlusconi, welcome aboard. I'm First Mate Robert Yung. Captain Ernesto sends his regrets. He is currently occupied and cannot receive you at this moment. He would, however, like for you to join him for dinner tonight in his cabin."

"That would be very nice. Please thank Captain Ernesto for the kind offer," Vermeer said.

"Very good, sir. I shall come by your cabin at seven this evening to collect you. Steward Hardy, here, will show you to your cabin. Afterward, feel free to explore the ship, or if you'd like, you can lounge on the fantail. Enjoy."

The steward Hardy said, "Your cabin is right this way."

Vermeer followed his guide down the passageway to what would have been an officer's cabin. It had a single bunk, a small desk, a tiny closet, two portholes, and no private bathroom. His cabin was located right below the main deck. He cracked the porthole to get some fresh sea air. That's when he overheard two deckhands speaking in Portuguese.

"*Você o viu?*" (Have you seen him?)

"*Não. Você tem?*" (No. Have you?)

"*Sim, ele nâo parece tão duro.*" (Yeah. He doesn't look so tough.)

"*Quanto é a recompense*?" (How much is the reward?)

"*Um milhão de dólares Americanios*." One million US Dollars.)

"*Quando é que a polícia vem buscá-lo*."(When are the men from Interpol coming to get him?)

"*Amanhã à tarde*." (Tomorrow afternoon.)

Vermeer was surprised at first, but a million dollars is a mighty temptation. He opened his satchel and checked his arsenal of weapons: two Berettas fitted with AL-GI-MEC suppressors, six boxes of ammunition, and three M67 grenades—more than enough firepower to accomplish what needed to be done.

He closed his cabin's portholes, checked the passageway to ensure no one was around, and dialed the emergency number on his satellite phone.

"Hello," An anonymous voice on the other end answered.

"Hello, this is Vermeer. I am in need of assistance."

"Code."

"Yankee. Alfa. Lima. Whiskey. Foxtrot."

"One moment."

Two minutes of silence passed before he heard.

"What is your situation?" The voice asked.

"I am aboard the Yokushi Empress heading towards Brazil off the coast of Savannah, Georgia. I am going to be betrayed by the captain and crew. It seems that this time tomorrow, I could be in the hands of Interpol." Vermeer said.

"Do you have a plan?"

"I do. When can you have a rescue vessel in the area?"

"One moment."

Another couple of minutes of silence.

"A vessel can be in the area by 4 am this morning."

"Excellent. I will contact you when I am available for recovery."

"Is there anything else that you need?"

"Just luck. Over."

CLICK

☠☠☠☠☠☠☠☠☠☠☠

Vermeer wandered throughout the ship as if he were a tourist. He went from stem to stern, from the starboard side to the port side, from the bridge down to the keel. As he roamed about, he made no secret that he was looking at and investigating the intricacies, complexities, and workings of the vessel.

He carried on conversations with two deckhands, one deck officer, the ship's chief engineer, and even the chief cook. When his tour of the ship was completed, he had managed to place three time bombs aboard the ship. Two in the engine room and a third bomb in the very front of the ship that would destroy the ship's bow thrusters.

First Mate Robert Yung came by at seven to bring him to the captain's mess for dinner. Captain Ernesto and three other officers were seated at the table when the two men entered.

"Captain Ernesto, may I introduce you to Mister Berlusconi," First Mate Robert Yung said as he sat to the captain's right.

Captain Ernesto stood, shook Vermeer's hand, and said, "It is a pleasure to meet you, *Signore Berlusconi*. Won't you please have a seat?"

"*Grazie*," Vermeer replied.

Captain Ernesto introduced the other officers seated at the table: the second engineer, the chief officer, and the navigation officer. The conversation stayed light-hearted. They shared several bottles of wine and appetizers before the main course.

"I hope you like fish, *Signore Berlusconi*. Our chief has prepared one of his specialties: Sicilian-style baked Cod," First Mate Yung asked Vermeer.

"Oh, yes. It's one of my favorite fish dishes." Vermeer said smiling.

Ernesto held up a bottle of Sauvignon Blanc and asked, "Would you care for some more wine?"

"*Sì grazie*," Vermeer said as he held up his wine glass.

The cook brought out the meal when the radio operator came in with a weather report.

"Captain, sorry to interrupt. But we just received this advisory from the NWS National Hurricane Center." The man said as he handed the captain the report and left.

Captain Ernesto read the communique aloud, *"At 500 PM EDT (2100 UTC), the center of Post-Tropical Cyclone Beto was located near latitude 31.566 North, longitude -78.581 West. Beto is moving toward the west-northwest near 55 mph (89 km/h), and this general motion is expected to continue through tonight. On the forecast track, the center of Beto will emerge over the western Atlantic this evening.*

Maximum sustained winds are near 50 mph (85 km/h) with higher gusts.

Some strengthening is forecast tonight, but the cyclone should become absorbed by a frontal system by tomorrow.

Tropical-storm-force winds extend outward up to 310 miles (500 km), mainly to the southeast of the center. A sustained wind of 39 mph (63 km/h) and a gust of 46 mph (74 km/h) were recently reported at St. Augustine.

Gentlemen, we seem to be in for a nasty bit of weather. Please advise all hands, secure all cargo, and prepare for a rough ride. *Signore Berlusconi*, it would be best if you stay in your cabin until we ride out this storm."

"When can we expect rough seas, Captain?" Vermeer asked.

"I would say in the next hour or so," Ernesto replied.

Suddenly, the dinner table seemed to erupt—the sound of suppressed rapid gunfire from underneath the dinner table.

PHIFF PHIFF PHIFF PHIFF PHIFF PHIFF PHIFF PHIFF PHIFF PHIFF PHIFF PHIFF

Plates of food exploded, and the table began to splinter from underneath, shattering wine glasses and bottles. The officers sitting at the table began to tumble backward, somersaulting over each other as their blood splattered against the bulkheads of the captain's mess, eventually collapsing in a heap.

The only two left alive were Captain Ernesto and Vermeer, who pointed his Beretta 9mm at the man seated at the head of the table.

"So, you and your men were planning on turning me in for the reward to Interpol?"

"No. I swear, Signore Berlusconi, I would never betray you or Le Gang de la Clé de Singe."

"Do you know who I am, Captain?"

"You are *Signore Berlusconi.*"

"Well, that is my current pseudonym. But I am called *Der Todesengel, L'angelo della morte, L'ange de la mort,* even, *O anjo da morte.*"

"The Angel of Death!" Ernesto said, shaking with fear.

"You've heard of me?"

"Sí. You're the stuff of nightmares."

"You swore allegiance to Le Gang de la Clé de Singe. You know we do not tolerate traitors, Captain Ernesto. Were you not paid handsomely for this mission?"

"Yes, but I swear on my mother's grave. Please, my wife died last year. I have two sons, please."

"No, Captain, you have two orphans."

PHIFF

The captain and all the senior officers lay dead in a row. Vermeer placed the traditional yellow flags around their necks before leaving the captain's mess and heading down to the radio room. The radio man who brought up the weather communique sat alone, listening intently to the radio with a Bose headset. He was unaware that the Angel of Death was standing behind him.

PHIFF

Vermeer disabled the radio and any ability to send a distress signal. He also disarmed the GPS tracking device to let other ships know their whereabouts. Afterward, he headed to the main deck, where the free-fall lifeboats were stowed. There was one on each side of the ship. Vermeer incapacitated the lifeboat so it would eventually sink before releasing the unmanned lifeboat on the port side. He then made his way to the starboard-side lifeboat.

Once inside, he strapped himself into the helmsmen's seat. He tested the engine, set the propeller in neutral, made sure that the wheel amidship was in the "O" position, closed the automatic drain plug, and disconnected the ship-to-boat electric plug. Then he closed the hatches and ventilators and closed the secure door, locking it behind him, and pulled the hydraulic pin, which released the boat from the davit. The boat slid through the tilted ramp and fell three stories into the six-foot swells. He restarted the engine, opened the ventilation system, and drove the small lifeboat away from the Yokushi Empress.

Vermeer glanced at the time. His TAG Heuer chronograph showed that it was 8:55 pm. Two minutes till the bombs he planted on board the ship were set to go off. He steered the lifeboat around so that it was facing the mothership. There was a series of muffled detonations from inside the ship, then minutes later, a flash of light and an enormous explosion.

BARROOOMM!

The Yokushi Empress sat quietly, rocking back and forth on the six-foot swells when it started to list to the port side and trim towards the bow. As she began to take on more water, the ship began to sink faster. Vermeer could see from the fire on board that the crew was frantically looking for the lifeboats. He saw several men jump overboard, some with life jackets, most without. He turned the lifeboat around and sailed away from the Yokushi Empress as she went under.

The seas began to get rough, and the 24-foot lifeboat began to bob up and down in the Atlantic like an orange cork. The small craft can travel at 6 knots an hour for at least 24 hours, giving it a range of approximately 144 nautical miles.

Vermeer activated the GPS rescue signal on the channel being monitored by his recovery team. It was now ten o'clock, and his rescue party wouldn't be there for another six hours. The storm was intensifying; the waves were over twenty feet high. The little orange skiff was being thrown around like a fishing bobber that a great white shark was hitting. One minute, the craft was riding on the crest of a twenty-footer, then thrown down into the trough and smashed upon by the full force of the wave smashing down on it. There were many minutes that the boat would be upside down before righting itself for the next onslaught of battering and pummeling.

Vermeer knew that the rescue mission would be dangerous, and there was every possibility that it could fail. It all depended on what Beto would do. If it stalled, the rescue would be called off. He did have enough provisions and water to last three to four weeks. Once the Yokushi Empress had been classified as missing, a thorough search would begin for survivors. If he were to be picked up by another vessel, the chances of his not being recognized and recaptured would be slim to nil.

☠ ☠ ☠ ☠ ☠ ☠ ☠ ☠ ☠ ☠ ☠

Fu Hao and the rest of the Red Team had been dispatched ten miles north of the tiny village of Chichindwe and the Turwi River in the Savé Valley Conservancy. Razor had spotted three men butchering a poached rhino from the Raytheon Killer Bee recon drone he had been monitoring.

The team was driving by using their three modified Can-Am Maverick X3 X RC Turbo RRs guided by Razor and the drone's GPS. They were coming in hot and heavy from three sides, cutting off all escape routes.

The Red Team was all dressed in ghillie suits that blended in with the scrubby landscape. Once they were within three hundred feet, they went on foot. Wearing headsets and Apple watches equipped with military GPS, they kept in constant contact with Razor and the other teams. Fu Hao and Sue B were Red Leader, Cowboy, and Sassoon were Red One, and Gianfranco, Hazael, and Ruko were Red Two.

Red One spotted the poachers first, they were in the process of using a chainsaw to cut off the rhino's massive horn. The rhino wasn't dead, only wounded. The fact that the poor creature wasn't dead meant nothing to the poachers.

"Red Leader. Red One. We have visual contact of the bogeys," Cowboy whispered.

"Red One. Red Leader. Fire when ready," Fu Hao ordered.

"Roger."

Both Cowboy and Sassoon raised their sniper rifles and fired one shot each.

PHIFF PHIFF

Two men were killed with headshots, spraying the man holding the chainsaw with a fine red mist of blood and brains. Cowboy and Sassoon could have also killed the third poacher, but they needed a prisoner.

The surviving poacher screamed, dropped the chainsaw, and started to run. Unfortunately, he ran right into the arms of Fu Hao and Sue B. The man immediately dropped to his knees and begged for forgiveness.

"Lie down on the ground. On your stomach!" Sue B commanded.

Gianfranco, Hazael, and Ruko were the first to arrive; by the time Cowboy and Sassoon appeared, the poacher had been zip-tied and was lying on his stomach, begging for his life.

Fu Hao nodded to Ruko to start with the interrogation. She wanted Ruko to speak because of his native dialect.

"What is your name?" Ruko asked.

"Masimba Muyambo."

"Where is your village?"

"Chiredzi."

"Camdeboo Boys. Where are they?"

"I do not know."

"You do know. And you will tell me."

"I do not know. I swear!"

Cowboy had picked up the Muyambo's chainsaw and started it up. Masimba jerked around and began sobbing.

"Camdeboo Boys. Where are they?" Ruko asked.

"I do not know."

"Masimba. First, we will cut your right foot, then your left. Next, your right hand, then the left, and then we'll just leave you here for the hyenas."

"I do not know. I swear!" Masimba howled.

Ruko gave Cowboy a nod. Cowboy revved up the chainsaw.

VVVGGRRRRRRR VVGGGRRRRRRR

Ruko knelt down to Masimba on the ground and asked, "The Camdeboo Boys. Where are they?"

Cowboy started to move towards Masimba, holding the chainsaw so he could see it coming at him.

"Chisumbanje! No, please do not kill me." Masimba cried.

"Chrisumbanje? Where is that?" Fu Hao asked Ruko.

"It is a village in the Dowoyo communal land on the eastern bank of the Savé River. It is about a six-hour drive from here," Ruko said.

"Where in Chrisumbanje are they?" Ruko asked, still kneeling.

"They will kill me if I tell."

"I will kill you if you don't," Cowboy said as he revved up the chainsaw again, inches away from Masimba's face.

VVVGGRRRRRRR VVGGGRRRRRRR

"The building behind Zineku Night Club, closest to Kujokochera Service Station."

"Are they there now?" Ruko inquired.

"No. They meet there only on Saturdays."

"That's tomorrow. Get him up and take him to the others. We'll meet you back at base camp." Fu Hao said to Cowboy and Sassoon.

Sassoon helped the captive up off the ground and walked him back to where his confederates lay dead. He held onto Masimba's arm while Cowboy laid the two bodies next to each other, placed the yellow ensigns around their necks, and stuffed the manifesto into each of their pant's pockets. He then walked over to Masimba and tied the golden flag about his neck.

"You know who we are," Cowboy asked.

"Yes." Masimba wept.

"Who are we?"

"You are the Monkey Gang."

"That's right. The Monkey Wrench Gang"

Masimba turned his back to Cowboy, looked at Sassoon, and pleaded, "Please, kind sir, do not…"

PHIFF

Cowboy fired one shot. Masimba slowly collapsed to the ground next to the other two poachers. Cowboy took the chainsaw and removed the rhino's horn from the dead creature. Later that night, they cast the horn into the campfire until it burned completely so no one would profit.

When they were well away from the dead rhino and poachers, Ruko called the Savé Valley Conservancy rangers station to report the killings and gave them the GPS coordinates. The park rangers called in the Zimbabwe Republic Police to assist in the investigation of the massacre of the three poachers.

When they arrived at the scene, the rangers and police found the three men had their noses chain sawed off as they had with the rhinoceros. As usual, there were no signs of any evidence left at the scene. They only found the trademark of Le Gang de la Clé de Singe, a single fingerprint of someone completely unrelated to the crime. In this instance, the famous Zimbabwean journalist Onesimo Makani Kabweza. They found it on the chainsaw. Kabweza has been dead for over twenty years.

☠☠☠☠☠☠☠☠☠☠☠

BLEUURGFF BLEUUURGFF BLARGHHH

Vermeer retched into one of the seasick bags that the lifeboat provided. It was the seventh one he had filled in the last four hours. Usually, he never got motion sick, but this wasn't normal. Being tossed around like a rodeo clown, knocked about continuously by a rambunctious Brahma bull for hours on end. He was battered, beaten, and bruised. As David Byrne sang, "*This ain't no party, this ain't no disco, this ain't no fooling around. This ain't no Mud Club, or CBGB's, I ain't got time for that now.*"

He didn't hear the ring of his satellite phone due to the roar of the storm and all the noise inside the lifeboat, as things were spinning and crashing all around, but he felt the vibration.

"Hello," He answered in a raspy voice. His throat was sore from all the vomiting he had done.

"Yankee, Alfa, Lima, Whiskey, Foxtrot. What is your situation?" the voice asked.

"As well as can be expected flopping around in the Atlantic like a corn kernel in a Jiffy bag."

"The rescue chopper has just taken off from Dufuskie Island, Georgia. It should rendezvous with your position in two hours. Can you copy?"

"Roger. Copy."

"How is your craft holding up?"

"Surprisingly well. No leaks, so far."

"The storm should be subsiding by the time the chopper arrives."

"Roger."

"God's speed, Yankee. Alfa. Lima. Whiskey. Foxtrot. Over."

"Over."

CLICK

☠☠☠☠☠☠☠☠☠☠☠

At 6:30 pm, Ruko pulled his 1988 blue Oldsmobile Cutlass Supreme into the Kujokochera Service Station. Steam gushing from underneath the hood.

A pair of mechanics stood staring at the Oldsmobile as it swung wide, making a giant U-turn, and ended up facing the street next to the gas pump. They were standing under the hydraulic car lift with a Jeep Cherokee hovering above their heads. They were draining oil into the drip pan as the blue whale slammed to an abrupt halt, kicking up a plume of red dust.

Ruko got out of the car, approached the elder of the two, and said, "Hey, old timer, check under the hood, add some fluids, fill up the tank, and keep the motor running."

The oldest of the two, a crusty looking bald man with a wooly grey moustache walked over to Ruko, "Say what?"

Ruko flashed a fifty-dollar bill, handed it to the old grease monkey, and said, "There's another one just like it when I get back."

The old man grabbed a worn-out red rag from out of his back pocket and lifted the hood amidst a cloud of scalding hot steam.

"You got it. The old man said.

Ruko opened the trunk, took out an all-black Remington 870 Tac-14 pump 12-gauge shotgun, and grabbed a handful of shells.

"You boys, stay put and keep your heads down," Ruko ordered.

He looked around; there was a small diner, the M&M Foods next to Svikai Nepano Barber Shop, or he was away, wandering the Big 5 Supermarket. He decided on M&M Foods; it gave him the best vantage of the Camdeboo Boy's clubhouse.

He ordered a bag of fried Mopane worms and a bottle of ice-cold Whawha beer. He sat outside on the veranda and watched the back of the building for activity. There was none.

Meanwhile, a white Ford Transit van parked just outside the compound where the Camdeboo Boy's haunt was located. Moments later, what looked to be a UPS truck pulled into the compound—inside, dressed as delivery personnel were Châtelet and Razor. As Razor opened the back door, Châtelet activated the robotic quadrupeds, robot dogs. One by one, they walked down the ramp Razor had placed at the back of the truck. First came the 24 robot dogs; Châtelet arranged them to encircle the building. Next, she released the twelve wildcats, six stationed at the front and six covering the back.

It wasn't long before Razor noticed a large crowd of onlookers standing with cell phones documenting the what-have-you, laughing and thinking this was some kind of stunt. That was until one of the wild cats shot a tear gas canister into the building's window.

SHWOOOM-KRAKKK

Fu Hao and the Red Team bailed out of the Ford van when that happened. Everyone was dressed in S.W.A.T team black combat uniforms, each carrying an AK-47 style assault rifle. At that point, the onlookers began to scatter and panic.

Châtelet switched on the mobile device jamming system so one could call the police. She then took control of the robotic quadrupeds and announced to the occupants inside that they should surrender their weapons and come out with their hands raised above their heads. Since her voice was transmitted through the robotic dogs' speakers, it sounded very synthesized.

The Camdeboo Boys' response was that of return gunfire. Thus began what would forever be known as the "Camdeboo Massacre."

Châtelet and Razor, maneuvering the wildcats, as well as the robot dogs, began to attack the building. First, one of the wildcats fired a rifle grenade, blowing the front door to smithereens.

BAWHOOOOOOOOOOM

Razor sent in the dogs, firing their automatic weapons. A firefight ensued; the gun battle was fierce, lasting over thirty minutes. Eventually, the robo-dogs secured the first floor.

BRACKA BRACK BRACKA BRACKA BRACK BRACKA BRACKA BRACK BRACKA BRACKA BRACK BRACKA BRRRRAAKKAKKAKAKKAKKAKKAKKAKKAA

BUDDA BUDDA BUDDA BUDDA RATATATATATATATA BRACK BRACKA BRACKA BRACK BRACKA BRACKA BRACKA BRACKA BRACKA BRACKA THUKKA THUKKA

When the smoke cleared, eleven Camdeboo Boys lay dead.

Next, they sent in the wildcats, who, because of their agility, were able to climb the stairs. As the wildcats ascended the stairs, Châtelet fired another tear gas canister in advance of the wildcats reaching the top of the stairs.

SHWOOOM-KRAKKK

As the building filled with gas, the nefarious gang of poachers started breaking the windows to let the gas escape and make their getaway. As they did, the Red Team began firing their assault rifles, trapping the villains to fight it out with the robotic quadruped wildcats.

Ruko saw some of the Camdeboo Boys trying to climb out of the back windows. He fired several rounds up at them, killing two and discouraging others from trying to slip away out of the back windows.

CLICK BABOOOOM CLICK BABOOOOM CLICK BABOOOOM CLICK BABOOOOM CLICK BABOOOOM

The assault continued for another forty-five minutes.

BRACKA BRACK BRACKA BRACKA BRACK BRACKA BRACKA BRACK BRACKA BRACKA BRACK BRACKA BRRRRAAKKAKKAKAKKAKKAKKAKKAKKAA BUDDA BUDDA BUDDA BUDDA RATATATATATATATA

SHWOOOM-KRAKKK

BRACK BRACKA BRACKA BRACK BRACKA BRACKA BRACKA BRACK BRACKA BRACKA BRACK BRACKA BRACKA BRACK BRACKA BRACKA BRACK BRACKA BRRRRAAKKAKKAKAKKAKKAKKAKKAKKAA BUDDA BUDDA BUDDA BUDDA RATATATATATATATA BRACK BRAAACKA BRACCCKA BRACKKK BRACKA BRACKA BRRRRAAKKAKKAKAKKAKKAKKAKKAKKAA

A fire broke out on the second floor, members of the Camdeboo Boys tried jumping out of the windows, they were shot and killed by the robot dogs once they had landed on the ground.

BRACKA BRRRRAAKKAKKAKAKKAKKAKKAKKAKKAA BUDDA BUDDA BUDDA BUDDA RATATATATATATATA

The fire soon began to consume the building, and the skirmish was finally over. Off in the distance, the sound of fire and police sirens could be heard. Châtelet and Razor recalled the robotic quadrupeds. Those that were disabled and could not return were set to self-destruct. They were manufactured, so there would be no serial numbers and no way of tracing them back to anyone with Le Gang de la Clé de Singe.

The Red Team planted a large Yellow flag in flag in front of the burning structure and nailed a copy of the manifesto on what was left of the front door.

"Let it be known that Le Gang de la Clé de Singe declares a proclamation of war against all Poachers, Big Game Hunters, and all Big Game Safari Outfits as well as anybody anywhere in the world that targets, kills, profits and or supports the killing of any animals that are endangered or any animals that are hunted for sport. Be forewarned, do so at your peril. You will be hunted down and pay with your lives. Be it man or woman, there will be no exceptions and no mercy; we will show no quarter. You have been warned."

The Red Team got back into the Ford van, followed the UPS truck loaded with the remaining robot dogs, and drove north on the A10.

Ruko casually walked back to his Oldsmobile, where the old mechanic stood, looking gob-smacked. He handed him the other fifty-dollar bill and said, "Thanks, pops."

He dropped the car into gear and peeled out, leaving the old man standing in a cloud of red dust.

☠☠☠☠☠☠☠☠☠☠☠

The all-black Sikorsky MH-60 Jayhawk helicopter lifted off from a secret Heliport on the windward side of the tiny island right on time. The estimated rendezvous with their target would be twenty-two hundred hours.

Tommy "The Badger" Stofac became a member of Le Gang de la Clé de Singe two days after his discharge from the army. He served four tours of duty flying with the 54th Medical Detachment (Helicopter Ambulance). Tommy flew over seventy missions in either a Bell UH-1H Huey or a Sikorsky UH-60 Black Hawk in Afghanistan. He was wounded twice in combat, earning him two Purple Hearts, a Bronze Star, and the Distinguished Flying Cross.

While Tommy was fighting overseas, his wife, Darlene, worked on board Sea Shepherd's flagship, the MY Steve Irwin—the 194-foot cruiser used in their direct action campaigns against whaling and illegal fisheries activities.

They were in the Southern Ocean, just north of Australia's Casey Research Station in Antarctica, when the Japanese whaling ship Nisshan Maru rammed the Steve Irwin.

Eight Zodiacs were deployed to disrupt the Japanese whaling season. Two zodiacs were tasked with fouling the whaling ships' propellers. While the six other zodiacs attacked the ship from all sides, some fired canisters of butyric acid (stink bombs), and others threw bottles of methyl cellulose powder onto the vessel's deck. Both would contaminate the whale meat, making it unusable.

The crew of the Nisshan Maru resorted to using water cannons, throwing grappling hooks to try to snare the Sea Shephard warriors, and firing shotgun pellets full of rock salt to try to discourage the anti-whalers from attacking them.

During this latest attack, Darlene was in the process of firing a stink bomb canister when she got hooked by a grappling hook in her shoulder, causing her to be pulled out of the zodiac into the frigid waters of the Southern Ocean and sucked under the whaling ship. By the time the zodiac was able to reach her body, she had drowned. The Japanese denied any responsibility for her death, claiming that it was her actions that caused her death. The International Whaling Commission, like the United Nations Commission on the Law on the Sea, has opened an investigation.

Shortly after his discharge from the Army, Tommy was approached by a Le Gang de la Clé de Singe representative, who contacted him about joining. Four weeks later, the Badger was flying missions for the Monkey Wrench Gang.

The all-black Sikorsky MH-60 Jayhawk helicopter was encountering severe weather as it headed out to try and rendezvous with the lifeboat containing one lone assassin, Vermeer.

On board, the Sikorsky was his co-pilot, Greyhound, and two PJs (pararescuemen) who would jump into the icy Atlantic waters to extract Vermeer and help haul him up into the helio. Flounder was the rescue swimmer, and SkeeBall was the backup swimmer and hoist operator.

Tracking the lifeboat's GPS beacon signal, the flight took fifty-five minutes to reach Vermeer.

"Yankee. Alfa. Lima. Whiskey. Foxtrot. This is Monkey medEvac. Do you read?" Badger radioed.

"Monkey medEvac. This is Yankee. Alfa. Lima. Whiskey. Foxtrot. I read you loud and clear. Over," Vermeer answered.

"I am preparing to drop a swimmer into the water. I need you to have your life vest on and open the hatch when I say. Do you copy?"

"Copy."

Flounder jumped into the 12-foot swells with surface winds of 60 miles an hour. He landed four feet from the bright orange lifeboat, turned to SkeeBall, and gave the thumbs up.

"Yankee. Alfa. Lima. Whiskey. Foxtrot. Open the hatch."

Vermeer did as he was told. Immediately, water poured into the lifeboat, pushing him back into the vessel. He eventually made his way out and into the waiting arms of Flounders, who hooked him into the harness. Both he and Vermeer were hoisted up to the safety of the helicopter. The operation took only minutes before they returned to the base from Dufuskie Island.

"How you doing?" Flounder asked.

"Much better now that I'm out of that carnival ride," Vermeer replied.

"Well, we'll be on solid land in less than an hour," Skeeball said with a toothy grin.

"I owe you guys big time," Vermeer said.

☠ ☠ ☠ ☠ ☠ ☠ ☠ ☠ ☠ ☠ ☠

"Wooch, here."

"Commander, this is Anchor at Command Central."

"What is it?" Wooch asked.

"We've lost contact with Monkey medEvac. The last radio contact was right after they extracted Vermeer. Badger radioed to the base that the flying conditions were horrific. We can only assume that they were flying at low altitudes and probably got hit by a rogue wave that took them down."

"Have we sent out a rescue mission?"

"Yes, sir. Although, because of the weather, our expectations are low."

"Keep me posted."
"Of course."
CLICK

☠☠☠☠☠☠☠☠☠☠☠

By the time police and the fire department reached the Camdeboo Boys' hideout, the building was a blazing inferno. The police had difficulty deciphering all the crazy stories witnesses told them. The best they could figure out was that these four-legged mechanical monsters attacked the building and that a group of ninjas, all dressed in black, shot at the people inside the building.

Once the fire department had put out the fire and police were allowed in, not only did they find all of the Camdeboo Boy's burnt bodies, but they also found the remnants of melted robot dogs.

Because the Yellow ensign bears the sign of the skull with crossed monkey wrenches hanging outside of the building and the manifesto, it is clear that this is the work of Le Gang de la Clé de Singe.

As the police were combing through the burnt wreckage of the Camdeboo Boy's clubhouse, Ruko and the Red Team were sitting down to dinner in Chimoio, Mozambique's fifth-largest city, less than a hundred miles from the Kujokochera Service Station.

The Red Team stayed in Chimoio for six days before saying goodbye to Ruko, who had to return to his Ranger unit. Once he had left, they got a message that they were being reassigned to Uganda to infiltrate a criminal organization that trafficked pangolins to Asia.

Fu Hao brought the team together to inform them of their next assignment.

"We're off to Uganda," Fu Hao announced.

"What's our target?" Hazael asked.

"A criminal outfit called the CD4's. They specialize in the trafficking of thousands of pangolins to Asia."

"Jesus Christ! What the fuck is wrong with people?" Cowboy said.

"Greed," Fu Hao answered.

"These people won't stop until every living thing is killed or poached, and then what?" Sue B asked.

"Then, we'll be out of a job. Grab your gear, and let's move out," Fu Hao sighed.

☠☠☠☠☠☠☠☠☠☠☠

"Good evening. I'm Nigel Williams, and this is the BBC World Headline News. Our top story at this hour is from New York City. Sources tell BBC that the suspected killer of Worldwide Affiliates of Safari Partners socialite Ms. Margaret Hamilton and sixteen others, who escaped from police custody, is still missing. The killer was believed to have been using the alias Bradley Peak, although authorities think that he has probably changed his identity. A worldwide search is underway; police say they will not stop searching until the suspect is captured.

Meanwhile, in other news……"

☠☠☠☠☠☠☠☠☠☠☠

Inspector Morse and Volker from Interpol landed at Ronald Reagan Washington National Airport early in the morning from England's Heathrow Airport, bleary-eyed and suffering from a bad case of jet lag. They had come to see the world's most preeminent dactylographer, eighty-one-year-old Doctor Thaddeus Nussbaum, PhD, who teaches at the FBI Headquarters in Quantico.

Thaddeus Nussbaum, a little over five feet three, has thinning grey hair, sports medium-length beards, thick wire-rim bifocals, and a black Yakama with an embroidered Star of David in the center. On his left forearm is a faded, crudely applied six-figure tattoo given to him when he entered Auschwitz as a young boy. *990358*.

Dactylography is the scientific study of fingerprints. Morse and Volker have come to find out how Le Gang de la Clé de Singe has been able to access famous deceased people's fingerprints, which they leave behind at all of their crime scenes.

"Doctor Nussbaum. How are you? I'm Inspector Morse, and this is my associate, Inspector Volker."

"Hello. I'm fine. How's by you? What can I do for you, gentlemen?" He asked.

"We're trying to understand how is it possible that a rouge eco-terrorist organization such as Le Gang de la Clé de Singe can get a hold of such an array of famous people's fingerprints?" Inspector Morse asked.

"What's not to understand? They most likely troll the shadowy corridors of the Dark Web." Nussbaum answered.

"How would they know if the prints are authentic?" Morse queried.

"They would have to have access to someone knowledgeable in the science of dactylography, who would be able to compare the fingermark to an authenticated and verified print that had been deemed to be legitimate."

"Someone like you," Morse said.

"*Zikher* (Of course), although there are hundreds of expert dactylographers worldwide."

"Is there anyone in particular that comes to mind that we should be looking at, Doctor Nussbaum?"

The good doctor thought briefly before saying, "There are two that you might want to look at. Dimitri

Yahontov, the lead dactylographer in the Soviet Foreign Intelligence Service."

"The SVR?" Morse asked.

"Correct. And the other is Gilgamesh Hosseinzadeh of the Iranian MOIS."

"Why those two?"

"Well, who better to want to support a terrorist organization that disrupts and harasses the West and especially Americans' rights to hunt than the Russians and the Iranians?" Nussbaum said.

"Would you know of any websites dealing with these illegal fingerprints?"

"I'm sorry, I don't. I don't go onto the Dark Web. And I must tell you that I don't believe that purchasing images of fingerprints is illegal. Like just about anything, there are people who are interested in collecting the strangest things: shrunken heads, Victorian-style medical displays, death masks, and even human tattooed skin displays."

"Makes my Topps baseball card collection sound tame," Morse said.

"Is there anything else that I can do for you, gentlemen?" Nussbaum asked.

"No, Doctor Nussbaum. I think that's it. Thank you for your time. Here is my card, in case you think of anything else that might be useful," Morse said as he handed the doctor his card.

Nussbaum took the card, placed it in his shirt pocket, and said, "I hope I was of some help."

"You were indeed. Thank you again. Goodbye."

"*Zay gezunt* (Goodbye), gentlemen."

Doctor Nussbaum waited fifteen minutes before grabbing his sports coat and walking out of the main FBI Academy building on Bureau Parkway, across Administration Drive to the parking lot to his blue Ford Taurus sedan. He proceeded to drive to the FBI Laboratory's parking lot, park the car, and made a call with an encrypted burner phone.

"Hello," A familiar voice answered.

"Hello. This is *Voron* (Raven)."

"Yes?"

"I wanted to let you know that I had two Interpol inspectors come to see just now."

"What did they want?"

"They wanted to know who I thought were the most likely dactylographers supplying Le Gang de la Clé de Singe with fingerprints."

"Who did you suggest?"

"I told them I thought it was either Gilgamesh Hosseinzadeh or Dimitri Yahontov."

"Excellent. Is that all?"

"No. I have obtained several new prints that I'm quite proud of." Nussbaum said gleefully.

"Who?"

"Well, I have acquired prints for Al Capone, John Dillinger, the Son of Sam, David Berkowitz, and I even got J. Edgar Hoover."

"Hoover? That's great."

"Yeah, and I just got Mother Teresa and Pope John Paul the Second. I should be getting others equally as good next week."

"Very good, Raven. I'll have someone pick them up at the usual place tomorrow."

"Yes, sir."

"We'll talk soon."

"Goodbye, Wooch."

CLICK

☠☠☠☠☠☠☠☠☠☠☠

THE END

But the revolution continues...

M. Ward Leon – the Author

M Ward Leon is a former advertising creative director who started his career at Doyle Dane Bernbach, New York, during the Mad Men era. While at DDB, his writing on the Volkswagen Rabbit campaign included him in the Smithsonian Institution Advertising Archives. His writing recently earned him two Emmy Awards for Public Service advertising.

He is a graduate of California State University, Los Angeles and an alumnus of Art Center College of Design.

He is the author of *Blood of the Beast* • *Revenge of the Beast* • *Wounding of the Beast* • *Fury of the Beast* • *The Strange and Curious Cases of Roscoe Brown, Detective NYPD* • *City of Angels Trilogy* • *Ambush at Fig Tree Gulch* • *Ishmael My Life After Moby Dick* • *The Fine Art of Murder* • *Black Rain in Little Tokyo* •

www.ingramcontent.com/pod-product-compliance
Lightning Source LLC
LaVergne TN
LVHW040041080526
838202LV00045B/3442
9781961504264